Also by Lucy Score

THE
BLAST
FROM THE
PAST

LUCY SCORE

Bloom *books*

Published by Bloom Books, an imprint of Sourcebooks
P.O. Box 4410, Naperville, Illinois 60567-4410
(630) 961-3900
sourcebooks.com

Originally published as Riley Thorn and the Blast from the
Past in 2022 by That's What She Said Publishing, Inc.

Cataloging-in-Publication data is on file with the Library of Congress.

Printed and bound in the United States of America.
LSC 10 9 8 7 6 5 4 3 2 1

To Casara for always being awesome.

1

Riley was dumped unceremoniously onto the floor and immediately began fighting her way free. They'd taken her upstairs. The music and giggling were much fainter.

Someone whipped the material off her head, and she fought to get a full breath into her lungs.

It was dark, so it was the smell that hit her first, and she knew exactly where they'd taken her. The creepy, smelly closet.

She had to keep her wits about her, Riley reminded herself. Any second now, the cops would arrive and the drugs would wear off. Nick would break out of his office and find her in no time. And if she kept the bad guys occupied up here with her, everyone would be safe.

The overhead light snapped on.

"You *idiot*."

Riley blinked, trying to bring the woman into focus. She had a faint southern accent. Not the *bless-your-heart* genteel kind but the *wrestle-gators-in-the-swamp* kind.

"Here we go again," said the man who'd carried her upstairs. "You told me to bring you Dolly. I brought you Dolly. Nothing I ever do is good enough for you."

The woman gestured angrily at Riley with the gun she

held. "Does she look like the right Dolly Parton to you? I swear, I should have divorced your dumb ass years ago."

The man sneered. "Well, good news for you because my cousin Otis never got ordained, so we ain't never been married." It was Zorro. The guest who had been handing out cups of punch.

And the woman peeled off her Guy Fawkes mask and glared at Zorro.

"Lurlene and Royce, I presume?" Riley scooched up against the back wall of the closet. She could have sworn she heard a hissing noise come from the grate.

"Great." Lurlene threw up her hands. "Second Dolly knows our names. That means that tramp already opened her big mouth."

"What's the big deal?" Royce asked, dragging off his Zorro hat.

"The *big deal* is now we have to kill them all."

"Uh, can I interject here?" Riley raised a hand. "I'm sure we can work something out so no one needs to die."

Lurlene beaned her with a roll of painter's tape. "Shut her up, and then tape her hands and feet together," she ordered Royce.

"She ain't goin' nowhere," he argued.

"Well, I don't want her screaming or trying to run away when we kill her."

"Have you always been this bloodthirsty?" he wondered.

"Yes! You just haven't paid any attention to me for thirty years!"

"It sounds like you two are under a lot of stress," Riley said, frantically searching for a way to connect with her captors. That was what her favorite show, *Made It Out Alive*, always said. Well, that and *don't ever let yourself be taken to a second location*, which she'd already screwed up. "Running your own business isn't easy."

"Oh, for Pete's sake. Shut your damn trap, whoever the hell you are," Lurlene snarled, pointing the gun in Riley's face. "Tape her up good, Royce."

"Don't get your panties in a twist."

"If you think for *one second* I'm going back to scrubbing country club toilets or worse, you got a rock in your head where God shoulda put a brain. We have a billion dollars on the line here. I'm not walkin' away from yacht money."

"All right. All right. No need to lose your dang mind again. If you want Dolly dead, she's dead," Royce muttered. He grabbed Riley's hands roughly and wrapped the tape around her wrists several times.

"Wait," she said. But the next piece of tape covered her mouth. Which was a stupid, amateur mistake to make seeing as how she could just reach up with her bound hands and remove the tape. But she decided to keep that information to herself until she could use it to her advantage.

There was a very distinct hiss behind the grate.

Royce made quick work of taping her ankles together. "Happy now?" he demanded and tossed the tape. It bounced off the floor and hit the grate, knocking it askew.

"Not yet," Lurlene said, crossing her arms and tapping her foot.

Royce made a big show of being annoyed when he pulled a knife out of his belt and opened the blade in Riley's face. She flinched and flattened herself against the wall.

She was *not* going to die in a stinky closet during Nick's birthday party.

2

Riley Thorn was finding being psychic while chipping away at her to-do list to be more complicated than she'd thought.

She swiped the roller through the pan of primer and sneaked a peek at the man in the closet next to her. Gabe was tall and broad and muscled in ways that suggested an inhuman metabolism. He had his back to her, his own roller working methodically. His dark skin and black workout gear were still pristine despite the fact that they were slathering primer onto the walls of the creepy, smelly closet, which was attached to one of the seven questionably livable guest rooms in her new house.

Riley, by contrast, looked as if she'd wrestled with Casper the Friendly Ghost just before he exploded.

"You are pausing to focus," Gabe observed without turning around.

Busted.

"Sorry. This multitasking-psychic thing is tougher than I thought," she said, getting back to work.

Technically everything about being a psychic was tough.

The intrusive thoughts that weren't hers, the confusing ethics of mind reading, the constant decision-making. Did the guy in the cereal aisle need to know that he was going to get fired Friday? Did the mechanic at the tire store really need Riley to tell her that Aunt Marmella had wanted her to inherit the mantel clock but Cousin Bruno had stolen it during the wake?

"Try again. Paint the wall, and open your mind," Gabe told her.

She took a deep breath and immediately regretted it as the scent of something "earthy" and rotten hit her nose. Something had definitely been living in here at one time. Riley hoped the paint job would take care of the smell and envisioned her psychic garage doors opening wide.

They were practicing reading minds while distracted by physical tasks. Usually, in order to read someone's mind, she had to mentally drop into what she called Cotton Candy World, a place that existed inside her head, filled with puffy clouds and friendly, invisible spirit guides who communicated with her in code.

Sure, the occasional stray thought from a passing stranger presented itself to her. But recent events, including a murderous city mayor and a vigilante serial killer with a bomb, had highlighted the need for mind reading on the fly.

Yeah. It was as weird as it sounded.

She wondered what Nick was doing, then guessed she already knew. It was the same thing he'd been doing since August.

He hadn't come to bed again last night. Since they'd moved out of one crumbling mansion on Front Street into another, her private investigator boyfriend had spent more nights in his new home office than he had in their bed. Now they were only having sex two or three times a week, down from the baker's dozen of the summer.

She blamed her grandmother.

When the great medium Elanora Basil told a man that the woman who'd disappeared on him six years ago—the woman whose presumed death had still weighed on him—wasn't actually dead, it was bound to stir things up.

Since that fateful summer day, Nick had redoubled his efforts to find Beth Weber. Retracing his steps through the investigation files. Calling old witnesses. Revisiting old anonymous tips. Scouring cold case forums online for rumors.

While Nick obsessed about the past, Riley quietly kept her eye on the future. In the mornings, she trained with Gabe. The afternoons were reserved for work. But as Santiago Investigations' office manager, her workload had lightened considerably since Nick hadn't taken a new case in a while. Instead, she'd been using the time to chip away at the never-ending to-do list of a homeowner with a dilapidated eight-bedroom Tudor mansion.

"Being present in the moment is a gift," Gabe said behind her.

Damn it. Her brain was full of chatter this morning, and for once, it was all her own.

She dipped the roller into the pan again. She needed to buy more primer. Oh, and pumpkins for the front porch. Some decorations might make the place look less "haunted house" and more—

Gabe cleared his throat pointedly.

She let out a growl of frustration. She was a psychic, gosh darn it. A powerful one. Sort of. The latest in a long line of gifted women. She could paint a damn wall and read a damn mind at the same time.

Mental pep talk complete, Riley stared hard at the wall and forced her hand to move the roller in the V-shaped coverage she'd seen on YouTube. She breathed—through her mouth—and covered decades' worth of stains with a thick coat of eggshell-white stain blocker.

"What did the skeleton say to the bartender?"

"Ha! I got it," she announced triumphantly as Gabe's message finally floated into her brain.

"You have stopped painting again."

"Damn it!"

"You are capable of great things, Riley," her friend said. "You can do this."

"I can do this," she said through clenched teeth.

She focused on the white. The clean, fresh start that erased the past. A blank slate.

"I'll have a beer and a mop." The punch line was out of her mouth before she even realized it was in her head. She turned to find Gabe's wide, proud smile.

"You have done well."

"So have you," she noted. Gabe's wall was finished and perfect. And still not a dot of paint on him. Something rustled in the vent at the back of the closet. "Let's get out of here and celebrate with breakfast."

They cleaned up the paint supplies and headed downstairs. Riley wondered if they had any sesame bagels left. She'd worked her way through two bags of them in the past week alone, and for some reason, the craving was even stronger this morning.

She frowned halfway down the stairs. "Do you smell bacon?"

Gabe sniffed the air. "It does indeed smell more like breakfast meat than decomposing body," he agreed.

She grimaced. They'd gotten the mess of a riverfront Tudor on half an acre for a steal. Mostly because of the guy who'd gotten murdered in the secret passageway and stunk up the place that summer. Her sister, Wander, still had to wear nose plugs when she visited to protect her psychic snoot.

Hoping that Nick had taken a break from his investigation to fry up some bacon, Riley hurried into the kitchen.

It was a large room with orange flowered wallpaper and a hodgepodge of cabinetry and countertops that didn't exactly match but also didn't totally clash. The stove top was new, the oven was older than Riley, and the massive Kelvinator refrigerator was a throwback to the Jurassic age.

In the midst of old and new, the purple-haired Mrs. Penny had her orthopedic shoes propped up on the hideous yellow table in the middle of the room. Perky at eighty-one, Lily Bogdanovich waved a pair of tongs at them from the ancient stove where a pan of bacon sizzled. A fleck of glitter sparkled on the handle of the frying pan. Riley's oversize dog, Burt, tore his hopeful eyes away from the bacon to wag his tail at them.

She sighed. "That explains where the dog went. What are you two doing here?"

"When I saw you mowing the yard between our houses yesterday, I just knew it was an invitation for breakfast," Lily announced happily. "Your kitchen has better light for making breakfast."

"But you forgot to leave a door unlocked for us, so I broke a window in the mudroom," Mrs. Penny said.

Riley did not have the energy to waste today arguing with her neighbors about yard maintenance and visitation etiquette. Instead, she helped herself to a cup of coffee and headed over to the corner of the room, where three neatly labeled clipboards hung in a row. She plucked the one labeled *Riley's To-Do List* off the wall and crossed off *Prime smelly closet* and *Train with Gabe* with a flourish. Then she added *Clean up glass in mudroom*. In a futile effort, she took Nick's to-do list off the wall, flipped back several pages, and added *Replace broken mudroom window* right under *Mow lawn* and *Fix office door latch*.

She wanted to cross *Mow lawn* off his list, but since she'd already added it and crossed it off her own list, she decided it could stay on his for next week in hopes that he would actually at least look at the list.

"Your hair is looking exceptionally purple today, Mrs. Penny," Gabe said to his elderly roommate. To help Riley become a better psychic, he'd moved in next door while Riley had been staying with the pack of geriatric troublemakers. Even after she'd moved out, he'd stayed as a babysitter, light-bulb changer, and fire-extinguisher operator.

"Thanks," she said. "Your head's looking pretty damn shiny today."

"It is kind of you to notice. What are you making for breakfast, Lily?" Gabe asked.

Lily and her twin brother, Fred, were co-owners of the Bogdanovich mansion next door. Not only were they roommates; they also shared a hobby of recreating recipes.

Some turned out okay, and some were natural disasters. The bacon looked safe, but Riley had concerns about whatever was smoking in the oven.

"Eggs, bacon, and Cracker Barrel hash brown casserole," Lily announced before glancing at Riley over steamed-up glasses. "You really need to look into getting more than one pan, you know."

"Pots and pans are on the buy-it list." Which was just as long as the fix-it list. Riley turned her attention to the woman with the makings of a chocolate goatee on her face. "Mrs. Penny, what are you eating?"

"Nothing," Mrs. Penny lied despite the small mound of candy wrappers on the table in front of her.

"That's for trick-or-treat night!"

Mrs. Penny shrugged. "If you didn't want anyone eating it, you should hide it. Not leave it sitting out for anyone to find."

"I *did* hide it." Riley had squirreled away the new candy stash in one of the empty kitchen cabinets after she and Nick had accidentally eaten the first stash. It turned out buying Halloween candy that you liked was a terrible idea.

"Yeah, but you hid it behind the gluten-free kale chips along with your stash of Jelly Krimpets. Those kale chips only camouflage junk food from your mom, not an expert PI like me."

"Being a partner in Nick's business does not automatically make you a private investigator," Riley reminded her.

"Says you."

"Says Pennsylvania state law. Look, I'm studying up on investigations and licensing." Riley held up a textbook she'd bought off eBay. She paused to blow a speck of glitter off the cover. "We could study together."

"Studying's for nerds," Mrs. Penny said dismissively as she unwrapped another mini Butterfinger with chocolaty fingers. "I'm gonna get me some real-life experience."

On a sigh, Riley crossed the kitchen and rummaged through the bread drawer. No sesame bagels. Damn it.

Gabe dropped a canvas tote onto the counter in front of her. "I brought sesame bagels and vegan cream cheese."

She pounced, snatching the bag out of his hands. "Gimme!"
She nearly tore a hole in the bag freeing a bagel.

"Someone's hangry," Mrs. Penny observed.

"I'm not hangry," Riley snapped. For the past week, she'd craved sesame bagels like she had some sort of vitamin deficiency. This was her third bag this week. And every night, she dreamed about fancy shoes and costume parties on merry-go-rounds until she woke up dizzy.

A loud thud followed by a series of bangs caught their attention.

Burt's ears perked up, and he trotted out of the kitchen.

Riley put down the bagel and followed the dog.

The banging wasn't coming from the outside. It was coming from Nick's closed office door.

"You okay in there?" she asked, leaning against the wall.

There was another thud and then a violent rattling followed by silence. "No," came the mopey response.

Riley reached up above the doorframe and found the flat key. "Sometimes the latch sticks when you close it. Remember?"

"Now I do," Nick growled.

"It's on your to-do list," she said, inserting the key into the latch and wiggling it.

"I said I'll get to it when I get to it, Thorn. Now get me *out of here*."

The latch sprang open, and Riley rolled the pocket door into the wall. "Oh my."

Nick Santiago was naked from the top of his sexy, dimpled face all the way down to his bare feet. There was quite a lot to appreciate. Lean, hard muscle. Dark ink over strong arms. Just the right amount of chest hair. Meaty thighs. And a spectacular penis that seemed to always be ready for action.

And when he turned to the side, she spotted a few flakes of glitter on his ass. "Sleep stripping again?" she asked.

He looked down, then shrugged. "I fell asleep rewatching WNEP's special on Beth when she went missing." The morning grumpiness seemed to burn off for a moment, and his gaze softened on her. "How'd you sleep?"

"Fine," she said. He didn't need to know that she'd had the dream again.

"You get into a fight with the Stay Puft Marshmallow Man?" he asked, observing her paint-splattered arms.

She shook her head. "Gabe and I doubled up on training and housekeeping. We primed the smelly closet."

Naked Nick reached for her, hooking his fingers into the waistband of her sweatpants. "I told you I'd help you with that."

"I know." She peeked over his shoulder at the war zone of his office. "But you've been busy, and Gabe didn't mind."

"As soon as I find Beth, I promise I'll help out around the house more."

She gave him a small smile rather than opening up a can of worms. "Sure. No problem," she said instead.

"Good morning." He slid those fingers from her waistband around to her back.

"Morning," she said, melting against him. Nick's touch was an automatic aphrodisiac to her.

"How's my girl?" he asked.

"I could go for a little naked quality time today if you're available." She slipped a hand down his chest and across his abs. "It's been a while."

"Yo! Riley! Where do you keep the chocolate syrup?" Mrs. Penny, still wearing her chocolate goatee, bellowed as she hustled into the foyer. Her eyes lit up behind her bifocals when she spotted them. "We got a code man fanny out here, Lily!"

"Fuck," Nick muttered as a girlish shriek echoed off the kitchen walls.

Lily sprinted through the swinging door into the foyer at top speed. She caught sight of Nick and skidded to a stop. "Now that is some prime man fanny."

She wasn't wrong, Riley thought as Nick used her body as a shield. Even with his heart-shaped scar, it was a prime fanny.

"Why are they in our house?" he growled.

"Our kitchen has better light," she explained.

"And better Halloween candy," Mrs. Penny added.

"And firmer man fanny," Lily interjected.

"Everybody back to the kitchen," Riley ordered. "Nick, go find your pants."

"Party pooper," Lily pouted.

"What's with you and all the sesame cravings this week?" fully clothed Nick asked her when he joined them in the kitchen. He helped himself to a KitKat that Mrs. Penny hadn't yet devoured.

Lily gasped and dropped the tongs. Bacon grease splattered everywhere. "Riley, are you *pregnant*?"

Nick choked on his KitKat. Riley couldn't tell if the panic on his face was related to lack of oxygen or to the idea that she could be knocked up.

"I knew you looked a little fluffy around the middle," Mrs. Penny said, pointing at Riley's abdominal region with a Hershey bar wrapper.

Riley peered down at her stomach and frowned.

"Would you like me to perform the Heimlich maneuver?" Gabe offered solicitously.

"What? No!" Riley sputtered. "I mean, no, I'm not pregnant. You'll have to ask Nick about the Heimlich." She'd already triple-checked her birth control pill pack this week. Plus, with the dramatic dip in her sex life, the odds were definitely not in favor of an oops-baby.

Nick waved Gabe away and washed the KitKat down with a hit of coffee. "You're sure," he rasped.

"I'm positive," she said dryly before turning her back on him and slicing her bagel.

Gabe joined Mrs. Penny at the table and produced a tall cup of what looked like liquefied spinach.

Nick's eyes narrowed. "Hang on a second. You people travel as a pack. Where's Fred and Willicott?"

As if on cue, a power tool roared to life somewhere in the house.

Nick took off out of the room at a run.

"Look, as much as I love you guys, you really need to not just show up and cook a meal—" Riley paused for a moment and listened to the raised voices coming from the hallway. "Or start renovations without asking." She dropped both slices into the toaster and hit the lever.

"Hey, I work here. I'm *supposed* to be here," Mrs. Penny said, holding up both chocolate-covered hands. The eighty-year-old was now a not-so-silent partner in Nick's private investigation firm, Santiago Investigations, a decision Riley was certain Nick was bound to regret.

"I'm just saying it would be nice if you called before you came over—or at least didn't break in."

"And I'm saying if you gave us all a key, we could come and go as we please without breaking more windows," Mrs. Penny said, crossing her arms over her chest. She had a tiny piece of glitter on the end of her nose.

"I would never wish to invade your privacy," Gabe said earnestly. His brown-eyed puppy-dog gaze slid to the bowl of Halloween candy.

Riley rolled her eyes. "Help yourself. I'll buy more candy."

Gabe's biceps bulged cheerfully as he dove for the candy bowl.

Nick returned to the kitchen and shoved a circular saw onto the top shelf next to the refrigerator. "For the last time, if I want your help with renovations, I'll ask you," he said to the men who followed him.

"Look at all these sexy ladies," Fred said, patting the frosted tips of his boy-band toupee. He wore a pair of harem pants and a T-shirt that said YOGA DOES A BODY GOOD. The Bogdanovich twins had the market cornered on lusting after the opposite sex.

Mr. Willicott shuffled in behind Fred. The man could pass for an elderly Denzel Washington…if Denzel was grumpy and confused most of the time.

The toaster spit forth her bagel and, with a glance over her shoulder at Gabe, Riley snagged the nonvegan cream cheese from the fridge.

Nick came up behind her and settled his hands on her

hips. "I need you to babysit today, Thorn," he said, rubbing his stubble against her neck.

Riley dropped her knife. "Again? I was going to ask you to take me shooting again. I feel rusty."

"As soon as I find Beth, everything will go back to normal. I promise. I just need you to hang in there for a little longer." His lips tickled their way down her neck. "Please, Thorn?"

She was helpless against that.

"Fine. But you owe me. And the first order of business when you find Beth is to figure out what's rotting in the smelly closet upstairs."

His grin was lethal. And the flash of dimples had her knees going weak.

"Anything for you, Thorn."

"Breakfast is served," Lily trilled.

3

After breakfast, Nick gave the boot to as many elderly neighbors as possible before heading into his office. He'd taken the second room on the left off the foyer because it connected to Riley's office at the front, though unfortunately it was through a door that had been paneled over. *Remove paneling from office door* was buried somewhere on page four or five of his to-do list.

He'd get to it eventually. There were a lot of things he'd get to. Including organizing his office and getting some real furniture. His temporary desk consisted of a paint-splattered folding table he'd borrowed from Riley's dad. There was a large whiteboard on wheels in the middle of the room with dozens of photos and notes scrawled in marker pinned to its surface.

But for the time being, the place looked like a police station file room had vomited up decades of paperwork. It was a whiteout inside, with enough paper on the floor and every flat surface to look like Liberty Mountain Ski Resort in February.

It was fine. It was functional for the time being.

Every detail of Beth Weber's disappearance was in this room, including the answers. He just needed to find the key.

He took a sip of coffee and studied the photo stuck to the

center of the board. Dark hair, a perpetually flirtatious smile. Mischievous brown eyes. In high school, Beth had been a peppy cheerleader. In college, a peppier sorority sister. She'd loved attention and pretty things…as well as annoying her mother and driving her big brother crazy.

Detective Kellen Weber, Nick's brother from another mother and former partner in the Harrisburg Police Department, had taken the disappearance of his little sister hard. They both had. And in the long-standing tradition of testosterone, neither of them had handled it well. They'd blamed each other and, until Riley, had allowed that blame to ruin their friendship.

It had been six long years since Beth had disappeared. Six years with no clues, no hope. Six years of grief that had slowly turned to a grim acceptance that what was lost could never be found. Until Riley's grandmother, famous psychic medium and all-around snooty pain in his ass, Elanora Basil, had announced that she couldn't contact Beth's spirit because she wasn't dead.

Just like that, he and Weber were partners again, trying to uncover a trail gone cold.

Only this time, they had hope.

"Hey."

Nick turned away from Beth's smiling face to find Riley standing in the doorway.

Four months into this relationship thing, and she still made him feel weird glowing shit in his chest whenever she walked into a room. She'd dressed for the day in jeans and a red tank top under a fuzzy cardigan. Her thick wavy hair was pulled up in one of those messy knots that all women seemed to favor and all men wanted to deconstruct.

"I promise I'm not going to keep dumping her on you. I just really need to focus on this." He gestured behind him at the mess.

His girlfriend's warm brown eyes swept the room to take in all "this" before returning to him. "I miss you," she confessed.

"How can you miss me? We live together. We work together. We have sex together," he teased.

"You've been…busy."

He closed the distance between them.

Riley Thorn was everything he hadn't known he wanted. Everything he hadn't thought he deserved. And as soon as he found Beth and brought her home, he would make sure Riley knew exactly how he felt.

He hooked a finger into the neck of her tank top to see the color of her bra. Red to match.

"I'm not too busy to appreciate you," he said.

"Are you talking to my boobs?"

"Step away from the rack, Nicky." Nick's cousin Brian and his wife, Josie, rolled into sight. Brian was flashing his wife a lecherous look as he wheeled his chair toward them. His hair was standing up all over, and his shirt was missing a button. Josie looked like a self-satisfied bird of prey. She was dressed in head-to-toe black. Her fingernails were painted a morbid purple that matched her thick smudged eyeliner.

Brian was Santiago Investigations's secret weapon when it came to technology and light hacking. He was a computer genius and incurable gossip. Josie was the muscle of the company. If Nick ever needed someone scared shitless, he sent Josie in to do her thing.

On the outside, they were the odd couple, but beneath those exteriors, Nick knew Brian and Josie shared a deep bond of what really mattered in life. Like a shared interest in collecting antique weapons.

"Hey, guys," Riley greeted them. "How's the baby making going?"

The couple shared another look, this one downright filthy.

"Practice makes perfect," Josie said, stepping past them to enter his office.

"What is this?" Nick asked, stopping Brian before he followed.

"Impromptu staff meeting," his cousin said innocently.

"I didn't call a staff meeting," he said.

"Hence the impromptu part, *boss*," Josie said.

Nick shot Riley a look. "Thorn?" he began.

She raised her palms. "Don't look at me. I had nothing to do with whatever this is."

"You're my psychic girlfriend. You're supposed to tell me what's going down before it goes down."

"I'll try to remember that," she said before ducking past him and entering the office.

Nick's temper stirred. He didn't have time for this. He had leads to follow, threads to unravel. Beth Weber was out there somewhere, and he was going to find her.

"Brian," he said, warning in his tone.

His cousin gave him a slap on the shoulder. "Relax, Nicky. You had to know it was coming."

That was the problem. He had no idea what was coming. And if there was one thing Nick Santiago hated, it was surprises.

"Don't start without me," Mrs. Penny bellowed as she hustled across the marble foyer with her cane. Burt trotted after her, snarfing up the steady sprinkle of crumbs shed from her generous bosom. "I've got some cases we can work!"

"Can't wait," Brian said under his breath. He wheeled himself into the office with Nick's surprisingly loud silent partner in his wake.

Nick blew out a breath and debated making a run for it.

"You'd never make it. My mile time is almost a full minute faster than yours," Josie called from inside.

"Fuck," he muttered and turned to face his office, remembering to leave the door open so as not to get locked in with these pains in his ass. "Let's get this shit show over with."

Riley was leaning against his desk. Her nose was twitching, and if she hadn't known what this bullshit meeting was about, he bet she did now.

Mrs. Penny flopped down onto the cheap couch he'd dug out of Lily and Fred's basement. She ignored the waterfall of papers that spilled out of folders onto the floor.

Nick leaned against the bookcase closest to the door, keeping his options for escape open.

Brian cleared his throat and looked pleadingly at Josie, who stood like a tiny deadly sentry behind Nick's desk.

She rolled her eyes. "Fine. I'll do it." She locked in on Nick. "You need to start working paying cases again."

Possibly sensing the uprising, Burt tiptoed over and sat at Nick's feet.

"And why is that, exactly?" Nick crossed his arms over his chest and dared his insolent employee to keep going.

Josie wasn't the least bit intimidated. "You're spending all your time and resources on a case that isn't bringing in any cash. We're twiddling our thumbs while you're turning down paying work."

His jaw went rigid. "I don't see how that's anyone's business but my own."

Riley shifted uncomfortably against the corner of his desk.

"How are you gonna keep this big-ass roof over your head if you're not bringing in any cashola?" Mrs. Penny demanded.

"At least I *have* a roof over my head," he shot back.

"Look, Nicky," Brian interjected. "We get why finding Beth is your priority. None of us are asking you to give up on that. We just think you need to find some balance, or we could be heading into some seriously lean times."

"I didn't invest in this business just to watch it go belly-up like some whale carcass in Ocean City," Mrs. Penny piped up.

Nick's hands clenched into fists. No one told Nick Santiago what to do. Especially not when it was about his business in his own house.

"Thorn?" he asked, zeroing in on Riley, who looked as if she'd rather be anywhere but there.

She winced. "Uh, yeah?"

"Do you agree?"

"I guess I can see both sides?"

That wasn't the answer he wanted. "Way to have my back."

"Oh, quit the wounded macho bullshit," Josie groused. "Riley's too nice to give it to you straight. But I'm not. You're fucking up. This place doesn't look like a place of business. It looks like the lair of a deranged psychopath with an obsession."

No one had ever accused Josie Chan of pulling punches.

"I think what Josie and Brian are trying to say is that we're all happy to pick up the slack on other jobs so you can focus on finding Beth," Riley cut in.

"In order for slack to be picked up, there has to be some," Brian said. "We're all waiting around, watching you turn down paying gigs while you comb through every detail of a cold case."

So he'd turned down a couple of paying gigs over the past few weeks. So what?

Okay. Fine. *All* of them. It wasn't a big deal. He wasn't going to divide his time between serving divorce papers, working some boring disability fraud case, *and* finding Beth. Every single one of them knew how important this case was to him. They were the ones who should have been cutting him the slack.

"So I should just give up on finding her then. That's what you're all saying," he said, ignoring what they were actually saying. "I should just settle for the fact that she's probably alive and focus on cutting you paychecks."

Burt leaned heavily against Nick's leg, probably as a warning to shut the hell up before he said something even stupider.

"Oh, goodie. Here comes Selective Hearing Nicky," Josie quipped as she studied her fingernails.

"You want slack? You want balance?" he railed.

"Well, yeah," Brian admitted.

"Fine." Nick turned to Mrs. Penny. "Penny, what did you bring us?"

"I brought a couple of real primo cases," she announced, perking up and shifting on the couch.

Nick couldn't tell if the ensuing sound was a fart or just the frame creaking under her.

"I'm all ears," he said. The rest of his team looked like they wanted to escape.

It turned out that his new partner was eager for a post-retirement career. Unfortunately, she still hadn't quite grasped exactly what they did at Santiago Investigations. The cases she'd proposed so far had included finding a set of missing car keys, investigating a kid she thought was cheating in one of her online video games, and solving Jimmy Hoffa's disappearance.

She produced a digital tablet from the back of her elastic-waist slacks. "All righty. My pal Esther thinks her dirtbag grandson is stealing her Big Top figurines and selling them on eBay."

Brian scrubbed his hands over his face and groaned. "Next."

Mrs. Penny shifted again, and this time Nick was ninety percent sure it was a fart. "Fine. No biggie. There's this guy at the gym who alters his selfies so he looks like he's way hotter than he is on his online dating profile."

"How would you know what his dating profile looks like?" Riley asked.

"Lily found him. They're both on the Hook Up," Mrs. Penny explained.

Great. Now they had an octogenarian begging to get catfished on a dating app.

"I thought you put parental controls on her phone," Riley said to Nick.

"It's on my list," he said defensively. There were a lot of things on his list.

"We can't let him get away with that shit. A five needs to look like a five online. It's illegal to pretend he's a nine," Mrs. Penny insisted.

"Uh-huh. What else?" Nick asked.

She adjusted her glasses and peered down at the screen. "My daughter-in-law's niece's cousin is being bullied at school by some overgrown jackwagon named Lance."

Nick waited, knowing there had to be an even worse one.

"Then there's the Dog Doody Bandit."

Bingo.

"The what?" he asked mildly as his team's eyeballs collectively rolled toward the ceiling.

"The Dog Doody Bandit," she repeated. "You know how some weirdos leave snacks out for delivery drivers?"

"It's nice, not weird," Riley interjected.

"It's weird," Mrs. Penny insisted. "Anyway, someone's been stealing the snacks and then leaving dog crap behind. All over the neighborhood! This punk has ruined a lot of shoes. No one knows when the bandit will strike next. I say we catch him in the act and make him eat the doody!" She punched a fist into her palm for emphasis.

The room was uncomfortably quiet.

"Who thinks we shouldn't take on any of these *primo* cases?" Nick asked.

Everyone but Mrs. Penny raised their hands.

"And who owns this business?" he continued.

Everyone's hands went down. He and Mrs. Penny raised theirs.

"Congratulations. We officially have a full caseload. Josie, you're on the knickknacks."

"But I hate the elderly and knickknacks," she complained.

"Bri, you get to make sure the gym rat looks like a rat."

His cousin bared his teeth at him. "You're kidding me, right?"

Nick ignored him. "Penny, you're on the doody."

"Yes!" She gave a celebratory fist pump.

"Thorn." Nick's gaze landed on his pretty psychic girlfriend, who should have warned him that he was facing a mutiny. "You've been wanting to get more involved in investigations. Congratulations. It's your lucky day. You get Lance the bully."

Riley raised an eyebrow at him, and he was eighty-seven percent sure he was in trouble.

"*I* wanted the bully," Josie grumbled.

"And I wanted a team that wasn't a bunch of whiny pains in my ass," Nick countered. "I guess none of us are getting what we want."

"Hang on," Brian said, holding up his hands. "How are we going to make any money off these cases?"

"It's part of the seven touches. Duh," Mrs. Penny announced.

"Who are we touching, and can we use weapons?" Josie asked.

"It's marketing law, dummies. Nobody buys anything unless they've tried it seven times for free," Mrs. Penny said.

Nick was ninety-nine percent sure that was bullshit.

"So you're suggesting in order to make money, we don't charge *anyone* for our services," Riley reiterated carefully.

"Exactly. Every potential client gets seven free cases, and then we charge them for the eighth," Mrs. Penny said proudly. "Think of us like a drug dealer with a new supply of disco biscuit. You wanna get your clientele hooked so you give 'em seven freebies."

"Disco biscuit?" Riley repeated. "I'm so old."

"And you're okay with this, Nicky?" Brian clarified.

"Why wouldn't I be?" Nick challenged.

Josie stepped out from behind his desk and glared him down. "You're going to regret this, Santiago," she said, jamming her index finger into a pressure point on his chest.

It instantly took him to his knees. "Ow!"

"Leave him alone, babe. You know what he's like when he gets in this mood," Brian said and drew his wife back.

Nick rubbed his chest and slowly climbed back to his feet. "What mood?"

"The stubborn head-up-your-own-ass, no-one-can-tell-you-anything-because-you're-gonna-do-what-you-want mood," his cousin said.

Oh. That mood.

"My condolences," Josie said to Riley as she and Brian headed for the door.

4

I don't have time for a field trip," Mrs. Penny groused in the passenger seat of Riley's Jeep. "I've got a Dog Doody Bandit to catch."

"This won't take long," Riley promised, changing lanes as a white limo rode up on her bumper.

"*Bet I could bag some walleye today,*" the spirit of Riley's uncle Jimmy announced in her head as she took the Harvey Taylor Bridge over the Susquehanna River toward the West Shore. The Jeep had belonged to him until his untimely death by hoagie in his fishing boat. Riley had inherited the vehicle along with the spirit of her fish-loving uncle.

The limo pulled even with her and stayed there. Its tinted windows prevented her from seeing the driver.

"That is an elongated vehicle," Gabe observed from the back seat. Burt the dog shoved his head between the front seats to get a look.

"You've never seen a limousine before?" Riley asked Gabe.

"I have not. Who could require such a long car? Very tall people?"

"Rich people or rich people's kids," Mrs. Penny said. "Probably a couple of punk-ass teenagers joyriding through

Taco Bell's drive-thru before the homecoming dance. Hey, who wants tacos?"

The limo backed off and slid in behind the Jeep, this time keeping a safer distance.

"We can get lunch later. I need your help first."

"Help with what? I'm pretty gassy today, so manual labor isn't in the cards."

Riley scrambled for a reason and then picked the first one that popped into her head. "I need your help picking out a costume for Nick's surprise birthday party. His birthday is on Halloween." She'd already suggested to Nick they throw a housewarming birthday party for friends and family.

Nick had said he'd rather throw himself into a tank of sharks.

"Well, you came to the right person. I'm great at Halloween," Mrs. Penny announced. "What are we thinking? Slutty? Sexy? Borderline pornographic?"

"*You could dress up as a fisherman for the party,*" Uncle Jimmy suggested.

"I am very enthusiastic about this surprise social gathering," Gabe piped up. "I have always wanted to be invited to a surprise party."

Riley glanced at him in the mirror. "You've never been to one before?"

"Never. We do not celebrate birthdays where I am from," he said wistfully.

"Where *are* you from?" Riley asked. Gabe's history was shrouded in mystery, and no one had managed to dig very deep beneath his cuddly surface.

"I am from many places," he said with a peaceful smile.

"Care to narrow it down? Manhattan? Miami? Montreal?"

"How many strippers are you thinking?" Mrs. Penny cut in.

"What is a stripper, and how many are usually required for a surprise party?" Gabe asked.

Riley tightened her grip on the steering wheel and fought

the beginnings of a headache as Mrs. Penny explained exotic dancing to Gabe. This whole babysitting-Nick's-business-partner thing was getting old fast.

She'd known Nick was too distracted by his investigation. She'd noticed the rest of the team was starting to worry. And it hadn't escaped her that the one thing he hadn't done was ask his psychically gifted girlfriend to help him. So she hadn't volunteered.

Now they were all paying the price, and it was up to her to fix it.

All she had to do was find Beth, keep Mrs. Penny from alienating the population of Harrisburg, and snap Nick out of his obsession. All before the business went bankrupt and they lost the house.

By the time she pulled up in front of the brick two-story at 69 Dogwood Street in Camp Hill, Mrs. Penny was explaining a strip club's champagne room to poor Gabe, and Riley's headache was full-blown.

The limo eased past and then continued on down the block.

Riley unbuckled her seat belt. She spared a glance next door at Chelsea Strump's property. The damage caused by a stampeding cow, a flattened fence, and a madman seeking vengeance had been completely erased from the emerald-green lawn. The destroyed shrubbery had been replaced, the glitter had been power washed away, and the Strump side of the new fence was a glossy white.

Her parents' side of the fence looked more like an ode to the 1960s with its kaleidoscope of color.

"Heh. Remember that time you got abducted over there?" Mrs. Penny asked, jabbing Riley in the ribs.

"It rings a bell," she said dryly.

"What's wrong?" Blossom Basil-Thorn demanded from the open front door. She clutched a cup of tea in a PEACE, LOVE & GODDESS mug.

The neon PSYCHIC READINGS sign was not lit in the window this morning.

On Mondays, Wednesdays, and Saturdays, Riley's mother performed tarot readings out of the house. Blossom was an above-average tarot reader, but her motherly instincts were even more impressive.

"Hi, Mom," Riley called as she and her entourage climbed out of the Jeep. "We need your help with some *party planning*."

Blossom's eyes narrowed as she sniffed out the lie.

Riley nodded subtly in Mrs. Penny's direction.

Blossom's eyebrows winged up toward her frizzy hair. "Ohhhh, okay, sweetie," she said in exaggerated casualness. "Come inside. Hello, Burty boy."

Burt trotted up to his grandmother and enjoyed a vigorous rubdown.

Daisy, her father's spite cow, mooed from the backyard.

"I can't believe Chelsea next door didn't make you get rid of Daisy," Riley said as they entered her childhood home. It smelled like homemade soap and fennel tea.

"Since that whole abduction and explosion, she's been too scared to say a word to us. Every time we go out in the backyard, she runs inside and locks the door. It's been wonderful!"

"Where's Dad?" Riley asked.

"Your father's at the farm store looking for cow shampoo." *Of course he was.*

"Let's get this show on the road. I've got dog doody to track," Mrs. Penny said, shoving her hands into the pockets of her boob-height pants.

"Mrs. Penny, I need your expertise on a Halloween costume." Riley pushed her toward the stairs. "Something appropriate for Nick's party."

The elderly woman perked up. "Right! I'm on it."

"You can start in the closets and then work your way up to the attic," Blossom suggested.

"Consider it done."

"Stay out of my dad's underwear drawer," Riley called after her. She waited until Mrs. Penny had disappeared from sight before turning back to Gabe and her mother. "I need your help."

Blossom rolled her eyes. "I know, sweetie. My cards and crystals are ready, and this tea is for your headache."

———————

"So you want to find this Beth person?" Blossom frowned as she shuffled her favorite tarot deck.

The sunroom was warm with the autumn sun slanting through the windows. Burt barked cheerfully in the backyard as his favorite cow friend, Daisy, chased him around and through the vegetable garden.

A series of thumps and thuds came from the second floor where Mrs. Penny was riffling through her parents' possessions.

Riley nodded. "Yes."

Gabe was already seated in lotus position on a meditation cushion. He rolled out his neck and shoulders as if preparing for a workout.

"Are you sure?" Blossom pressed, her forehead lined with concern.

"Why wouldn't I be?"

"Beth was someone important to not just Detective Weber but also Nick. We don't know what the consequences of finding her could mean for your relationship."

"Mom, I'm more concerned with the consequences for Beth if we don't find her. What if she's been tortured every day of her life since she disappeared?"

Blossom waved a dismissive hand. "That only happens on *The Vampire Diaries.*"

"Then what if some sicko took her and has her locked up in a moldy basement where she became one of his eight wives—"

"Okay. Fine. Real life is terrifying too. I just wanted to make sure you were considering the consequences. I once gave a reading to a woman whose husband emptied their retirement savings and bought his twenty-two-year-old stripper girlfriend a condo. The wife ran him over and then smashed her car into the condo's lobby. She went to jail."

"Did they meet in the champagne room?" Gabe asked.

"You know, I never thought to ask," Blossom told him.

Riley waved her hands to get everyone's attention. "Every day that Nick doesn't find Beth, he spirals deeper into this obsession. He's hardly sleeping. When he eats, it's using six-year-old case files as paper plates and napkins. Seriously, there's mayonnaise and bread crumbs all over his office. He's putting all paying work aside so he can focus on finding Beth. The sooner we locate her and bring her back, the sooner things can get back to normal."

If normal was a possibility.

When Riley was being honest with herself, late at night when Nick hadn't come to bed yet while she was eating a bowl of ice cream under the covers and binge-watching her favorite survival show, she could admit that she was maybe the slightest bit nervous about finding Beth.

Nick had never dated the woman—one of the very few in the Harrisburg region apparently. He'd claimed that his flirtation with Kellen Weber's little sister had been just to annoy his friend. But his life had been so tangled up with her disappearance that there were a million ways saving Beth could change things. Including Nick rescuing the long-lost woman and falling madly in love with her on the spot, kicking Riley to the curb, and forcing her back to the Bogdanovich mansion where she would have to share a room with Lily…or worse, Mrs. Penny.

Riley looked at Gabe, who was twisting his arms together in pretzel-like fashion. "If I ever need to move back to the mansion, can Burt and I share your room?"

Her muscular spiritual guide beamed. "It would be my greatest honor. We would have ice cream Wednesdays until you recover from your broken heart."

Riley patted her friend on his beefy forearm. "You're the best, Gabe."

"It is kind of you to notice."

The front door opened and closed softly. Riley's sister, Wander, floated into the room looking ethereal and glowing in yoga clothes. "I'm here to help," she said. "Hello, Gabriel."

A saccharine-sweet moment of mooniness passed between Wander and Gabe. Riley was fairly certain that they were in love but that neither one of them had made a move beyond hand-holding. Something she would have to poke her nose into later.

"I called in your sister in hopes that Wander's powers might give us an extra boost," Blossom explained.

"Good idea, Mom."

All Basil women had psychic abilities. Riley's grandmother, Elanora, was a terrifying person and a powerful medium. Blossom was a gifted tarot card reader. Riley saw visions of the future, talked to the dead, and could sometimes read the minds of the living.

And Wander had a psychic snoot.

She could sniff out echoes of scents long since passed, like a dearly departed grandfather's aftershave…or the dead guy in Riley's secret passage…or the cooler of fish Uncle Jimmy had accidentally left in the Jeep one humid August.

"Hey Wander," Riley said.

Her sister greeted her with an aloe-scented hug before delving into her vegan leather messenger bag. "My Wiccan friend Mertha let me borrow his locator-spell pendant. I thought it couldn't hurt to try."

She produced a large ugly amulet that looked as though it had been commissioned by someone's fussy great-aunt Eugenia. Riley winced and realized that wasn't an assumption, it was a reading.

"*I'll have you know that amulet was designed by none other than Sir Theobold Vincent,*" someone's great-aunt Eugenia huffed in her head.

"*Sorry, Great-Aunt Eugenia. Your amulet thing is really nice,*" Riley told her. She turned her attention back to the living. "So exactly what should we do? I know I can just pop in and talk to my spirit guides, but I was hoping we could do something more structured. Something that would get us more specific answers." Her spirit guides talked in a strange kind of visual code that she didn't yet fully understand.

Blossom rubbed her palms together. "I think we should start in a circle to link our power. Gabe, you'll help Riley and Wander as they communicate with their spirit guides. I'll use the necklace thingy, and if all that fails, I'll consult my cards."

"It is a wonderful plan," Gabe announced.

Blossom beamed at the man's praise.

A toilet flushed upstairs.

"Great. We just need to find Beth before Mrs. Penny gets bored going through Mom and Dad's closets," Riley added.

"Then let's circle up. Time's a-wasting," Blossom said.

A meditation cushion hit Riley in the face. Wander caught the one their mother threw in her direction.

They joined Gabe on the floor; then in the center of their circle, they dumped the amulet, a pile of crystals, the deck of tarot cards, and a printout of a map of the United States.

"Okay, folks. Let's get this show on the road," Riley said, pulling a photo of Beth that she'd snagged from Nick's case file and adding it to the pile. "We're looking for this woman. Elizabeth Weber. Are you guys ready?"

Team Psychic Shenanigans nodded, joined hands, and closed their eyes.

Riley dropped into what she called her spirit guide realm.

"Oh my. Someone wanted to have sex this morning but didn't," Blossom teased.

"Mom!" Riley hissed.

"Sex is a very natural thing. There's no need to be embarrassed by it."

Riley thought she heard a wistful sigh coming from Wander. "Can we please focus on Beth and not anyone's sex life?"

"Of course, dear."

The clouds pulsed brighter, and Riley wondered briefly what her spirit guides looked like. Were they the clouds themselves, or were they something else hidden beyond the ether? Were they human? Did they look like supermodels or regular people? Little pastel squirrels scampering around the universe and collecting energetic nuts?

A subtle river of energy poured forth from Gabe through her left hand, recentering her. On her right, Wander's energy danced between their clasped hands, light and delicate like the bubbles in a glass of champagne.

From somewhere farther away, she could hear her mother quietly chanting as she shuffled cards.

"Okay, spirit guides. Come out and play. I need some help finding Beth Weber." Bringing the image from the photo to mind, Riley concentrated hard.

She braced as the clouds began to part. Anticipation rose in her blood, making her heart thump faster. Then her body was flying through the mists like Peter freaking Pan.

It seemed dark, and there was music. A Christina Aguilera club mix thumped inside her head. Shoes. Magenta platform wedges moved against some kind of rough gray carpet.

"This might be a little too specific," Riley said. "How about a more general location?"

She forgot to brace, and her stomach dipped violently as she rocketed out of the shoe vision and into another. Scenes flashed before her eyes at high speed. A fast-food restaurant. Houses. A blur of commercial buildings. Circling around and around until the vision became a circle. And then finally, one perfect sesame bagel floated in the spotlight of her consciousness.

"Seriously?"

Riley's stomach growled, and she fell back into her body with what would have been a splat if not for Gabe's energy steadying her.

"Damn it," she muttered.

"I'm getting hints of sesame chicken and Miss Dior," Wander whisper-sang next to her, her nose wrinkled as she tried to sniff out the exact scents.

"Sesame chicken?" Riley repeated. *What was with the sesame everything? Did she have a nutritional deficiency, or was it an actual clue?*

"Your gift is a true marvel," Gabe told Wander.

"Thank you, Gabe." She gave the man a genuine eyelash flutter.

"Riley, what did you see?" her mother asked, holding the amulet stock-still over Pennsylvania. Or maybe it was Maryland? It wasn't a very good map.

"Isn't that supposed to be moving?" Riley asked.

Her mom shrugged. "Maybe she's not in the country. I should have brought down the old globe."

Riley filled them in on her confusing vision, beginning with the shoes and ending with the bagels.

"Sesame-flavored food products? An interesting theme," Gabe noted.

"Any idea what it could mean?" Riley asked.

"Are you pregnant?" Blossom asked.

"No! Jeez, Mom."

"When I was pregnant with River, I craved cashew-butter smoothies. I had two a day for six months," Wander reminisced.

"I remember that. But no, I'm not pregnant. Between me eating a dozen sesame bagels this week and Wander smelling sesame chicken, I think we can safely assume it's a clue, not a pregnancy," Riley concluded.

"It's probably for the best," Blossom mused. "After all, if Beth comes back and ruins everything between you and Nick—"

"Thank you, Mom," Riley said dryly.

"Maybe the tarot reading will tell us more," Wander offered hopefully.

"Good thinking, sweetie."

They sat in silence even though Riley's hip flexors were starting to complain as Blossom shuffled and dealt the chosen card.

"The eight of cups," Blossom said, triumphantly holding up the tarot card.

Riley blew out a breath in relief. The eight of cups didn't predict violence or death or impending doom. It was a happy card.

"I'm sensing a new adventure. Walking away from everything and starting over fresh," Blossom continued.

Riley's shoulders tensed. "Is it a card for Beth?"

Her mother shrugged. "That's who I was trying to read, but it could be for anyone associated with her."

Anyone associated with Beth. Including Nick Santiago.

Riley had an uneasy feeling...and a craving for sesame chicken.

Mrs. Penny clomped into the room, her arms full of clothes and what looked like at least one of Blossom's good bath towels. "All set. Who's hungry?"

5

Christian Blight wasn't someone you'd want to run into in a dark alley. It wasn't just the neck tattoos. Or the shaved head, with the exception of the blond rattail at the base of his skull. Or the twenty pounds of muscle he'd put on under his orange Camp Hill prison jumpsuit.

It was the calculation in those cold blue eyes.

Those eyes bored into Nick as a guard removed the cuffs.

"Nicky Santiago. Back again so soon?" Blight asked, taking the seat across the rickety table from him.

Prison visitation rooms created a creepy Venn diagram that brought both the prisoner and the visitor uncomfortably close to the other's world.

"Maybe I missed you," Nick said flippantly as the guard left the room.

"Or maybe you and your cop buddy don't have anything better to do than harass an innocent man."

"You had a dozen baggies of X in your cargo pants when you were arrested, smart-ass," Nick pointed out.

Blight opened his palms, the picture of calm. "I told you they weren't my pants," he said.

It was a familiar tune that Nick had been listening to for the last six years. "I'm not here to talk about your pants."

Blight met Nick's gaze. "Let me guess," he said with a smirk. "You and your cop boyfriend think today's the day I'm going to confess to setting the fire and tell you I had something to do with your girl disappearing."

"Something like that," Nick said.

Blight gave him a humorless smile. "Unfortunately for you, today is not your lucky day."

Nick wasn't about to tell a prisoner that his psychic girlfriend's psychic grandma had told them Beth wasn't dead. "That missing girl has a name, and you know it. You knew her. But for some reason, you're still too chickenshit to tell the truth."

"Going with the provoke-a-defensive-male-reaction technique again today?" Blight asked.

Nick crossed his arms and stared at the man.

Blight had landed on Nick and Weber's radar a few days after Beth's disappearance, thanks to a video from the scene of the fire that had surfaced. The footage not only showed the warehouse explosion but also revealed Christian Blight having a heated conversation with a glow-stick-wielding Beth Weber.

The fire had started during an illegal rave attended by Beth and some of her giggly girlfriends. She and her posse had given their initial witness statements to officers on scene before being sent home. Beth had disappeared the very next day.

The fire had been ruled an arson and never solved.

What was supposed to have been a polite conversation with a potential witness had turned into an arrest for a parole violation when Blight had pulled a gun on them and tried to jump out of a second-story window.

From day one, the man had infuriatingly maintained his innocence in both Beth's disappearance and the arson. What further infuriated Nick was the fact that if he hadn't been sure Blight knew something about Beth, he might have actually liked the man.

"Santiago, you have got to be the most optimistic, tenacious motherfucker in the world," Blight said with a rare smile.

"I see that word-of-the-day toilet paper is working out for you," Nick observed.

Blight flipped him the middle finger. "Fuck off. I got degrees in English, philosophy, and business in here."

"Congratulations, Jane Austen. Did you murder Schrödinger's cat and then set up an online swag store to launder money?"

Blight dipped his chin. "A layered insult that shows active listening. Maybe you're not the same idiot bacon you were six years ago."

"Look, pal." Nick crossed his arms. "I'm smart *ex*-bacon. Which is bad news for you because that means I don't have to play nice."

Blight shook his head, still managing to look amused. "Are you aware of the definition of *insanity*?"

"I'm more interested in the definition of *kicking your ass*."

His quarry tut-tutted. "There are only two emotions in this world: love and fear. And you, my friend, are operating out of fear."

That philosophy degree had taken Blight's reactivity down to that of a Buddhist monk. Nick missed the old Blight, who'd had his sentence increased twice, once for punching a guard in the balls and once for trying to drown a fellow inmate in a washing machine. Granted, both victims had deserved it. But Nick wasn't interested in thinking of Blight as a tragic hero.

He was tired and frustrated, and he knew for certain that Blight knew something about Beth.

Nick slammed his palm down on the table. "Listen, you rattailed wannabe cult leader. I know you knew Beth, and I know you had something to do with her disappearance."

"Where's your proof?" Blight smirked, flashing his teeth and making Nick want to punch every single one of them out of his face. "You know you've only got a few more weeks to harass me like this. I get out soon. No more showing up and dragging me out for yet another interrogation. I'm rehabilitated, motherfucker."

Rehabilitated his ass.

Christian Blight would walk out of prison and right back into his life of crime.

Only now he was armed with a business degree, so he'd probably be even better at selling drugs or whatever crime he decided to pursue.

Nick leaned in. "Maybe Weber can't show up on your doorstep once you're out, but I'm a private citizen. I'll show up at your mom's dinner table. I'll be on the barstool next to yours at Arooga's when the Steelers are playing. I'll follow your sister down the goddamn produce aisle. I'll take your grandma to church on Sundays. And I won't stop until you tell me what you know about Beth Weber's whereabouts."

Something stirred in Blight's cool eyes. Something dark and unsettling.

"Love and fear," Blight repeated. "You start messing with the people I love, I won't hesitate to give you a reason to fear."

"That sounds like a threat."

He opened his hands. "Just stating facts. You bring your obsession anywhere near my family, I'll pay a visit to yours. Maybe I'll start with one of your dad's restaurants, give the people a few new reasons to give him shitty reviews online. Or maybe I'll swing by Dr. Santiago's office and talk prescription drug sales."

It took a Herculean effort, but Nick kept his expression impassive.

Blight leaned forward, intertwining his fingers. "Of course, I'd love to have a nice long chat with that pretty psychic girlfriend of yours. She seems to be quite the magnet for trouble."

Nick's blood went cold for the span of a heartbeat before the Santiago rage turned it to boiling. "You go anywhere near Riley or my family and you can fucking forget prison. You'll be headed to the graveyard in a shitty pine box that gives your dead ass splinters."

Blight's smile was humorless. "Then we have an understanding."

"Know what I understand from all my visits here?" Nick asked through clenched teeth.

"What's that?"

"That it takes a guard thirty-five seconds to open that door." With that, he lunged across the table and landed a satisfying right hook. Blight's head snapped back, and Nick's knuckles sang.

"Did you have to go for the nose? Now I won't be able to breathe right," his opponent complained, holding his nose.

"Yeah. I did." Nick was so busy enjoying the blood dripping from Blight's nose that he missed the windup. The man's fist connected with his eye, ringing Nick's bell.

"Ow! Why are your knuckles so pointy? You shave 'em down with a shiv?"

"I punch block walls for fun, dumbass."

The door flew open, and an annoyed-looking guard holding half a sandwich entered. "What the hell is going on in here?" he demanded.

"He tripped over his shoelaces and fell into the wall," Nick insisted, pointing at Blight.

"Then he slipped on my nose blood and hit his face on the table," Blight added.

"That's exactly what happened," Nick concurred.

"You're both assholes," the guard said.

———

Nick was in the prison parking lot holding a cold Pepsi to his eye when his phone rang.

Detective Dick.

"What?" Nick answered testily.

"Did you seriously just break Christian Blight's nose?"

"The law enforcement gossips are fast today," Nick said. "Clarence didn't even put down his sandwich before he came in to break it up."

"You know Blight can press charges against you," Weber said in his snooty I-have-a-stick-up-my-law-abiding-ass voice.

"He started it," Nick said defensively.

"He *made* you show up at prison and interrogate him?" Weber didn't sound like he believed him.

"It wasn't an interrogation. It was more of a conversation."

"Great. So you're in one of *those* moods," Weber said.

"You know, if this is how women feel when someone insinuates they have their period, I'm surprised more dumbasses don't get hit in the face with chairs," Nick mused.

"What were you doing talking to Blight?" Weber refused to be distracted.

Nick ran a hand through his hair. "Just going over old leads. Nothing new."

"He stick with the story?"

"Same old, same old."

Weber swore.

"Look, man. We're gonna find her and bring her home," Nick insisted.

"It's been weeks, Nicky. We haven't turned up any new leads, and without more manpower, we're just spinning our wheels."

"Don't you fucking start the whole let's-give-up whiny baby chorus." He'd heard enough of that refrain today.

"Who's saying we should give up?"

"My entire goddamn team, including Mrs. Penny, cornered me for an intervention today. They think I'm spending too much time looking for Beth and not enough time doing my actual job."

"Are you?"

"Oh, fuck off. You of all people know how important this is. We're closer than we've ever been to bringing her home. I'm not gonna waste my time on cases that don't matter right now."

Weber was quiet for a beat, and then he sighed. "I think we need to talk to Riley."

Nick hedged. "We're making progress on our own."

"Your psychic girlfriend's psychic grandmother told us Beth was alive. I can't exactly use that as a reason to reopen the case, but I still think our best bet is to use Riley to find her."

Use Riley. Weber's words echoed in Nick's head.

"We don't need to bring her into this," Nick said.

"You keep saying that."

"Yeah, well, I keep meaning it."

"I don't need your permission to talk to her, you know," Weber pointed out.

"We're not asking Riley to get involved. Every time one of us needs her help, she ends up in the line of fire." Nick wasn't willing to endanger her again.

"Isn't that why you're teaching her how to protect herself? Teaching her to shoot, showing her self-defense, practicing situational awareness."

The muscle under his bruised eye was starting to twitch. He *had* been doing those things…until Beth's case had taken precedence.

"Look, whoever the hell is responsible for Beth's disappearance is obviously dangerous. I'm not making my girlfriend a target, and neither are you."

Not even if it meant finding Beth faster.

He needed Riley to keep her distance from Beth. And he needed to make this one right on his own.

6

11:33 a.m. Friday, October 25

Well, that was a waste," Riley muttered to herself as they piled back in the Jeep.

"Are you kidding? Look at the outfit I picked for the Halloween party." Mrs. Penny produced a lacy white negligee from the pile of textiles she'd "borrowed" from the Thorns.

Riley fumbled her phone in her lap. "I'm not wearing *that* to Nick's party. It's my mother's! What if I invite his parents?"

"I didn't pick it for you. That's *my* costume. I'm going as a sexy femme fatale. Think I can order one of those thigh holster thingies on the internet?"

"You will make a lovely body-positive femme fatale," Gabe said supportively from the back seat.

"Damn skippy I will."

Trying to erase the image of her elderly neighbor in borrowed lingerie, Riley pulled away from the curb. She was tired and hungry and still had no idea where Beth was.

"Gimme your phone. I need some fresh tracks to get into investigator mode," Mrs. Penny demanded.

Riley handed over her phone and headed in the direction of Route 15.

"What is our next destination?" Gabe asked.

"Lunch." Thanks to her sister, she had a craving for sesame chicken.

"Well, I suppose my investigation can wait until after lunch," her elderly passenger decided.

"*I wouldn't say no to an egg roll*," Uncle Jimmy yelled in Riley's head.

They were rocking out to Drake halfway to the only restaurant in the city that didn't care if a very large dog sat at the table when Riley spotted a flash of white in the mirror.

Her pulse quickened when a familiar-looking stretch limo changed lanes three cars back.

As a psychic, she had grown to distrust coincidences.

With determination, she tried her best to focus on driving while she cast her mind back to the limo and its occupants.

"Is everything all right?" Gabe asked over the music.

"Yep. Totally great," Riley lied as her palms started to sweat against the wheel. Multitasking was hard enough on its own without being depleted after her psychically intensive morning.

"You know, life doesn't suck," Mrs. Penny mused, drumming her hands on the dashboard. "I've got a sexy new outfit for the party. I'm gonna plow my way through a beef-and-broccoli platter. And I got a hot case to work."

Riley was too busy breaking into a sweat over concentrating on staying in her lane and being psychic to respond. There didn't seem to be any nefarious vibes coming from the limo, but she wasn't about to take any chances with her dog, one of her best friends, and a farty old lady in the car.

Instead, she stomped on the accelerator, throwing her passengers back into their seats.

Mrs. Penny hooted as she clung to the Jeep's oh-shit handle. "Yeehaw! Where's the fire?"

"No fire. Just hungry," Riley said, crossing the bridge toward Harrisburg at twenty miles over the legal speed limit.

The traffic-device-timing gods were on her side as the Jeep eked through a yellow light and headed into the heart of the city.

She kept her eyes glued on the limo stopped at the red light in the rearview mirror until she made the left onto North Third Street.

Eggrolls and Stuff was located in an old Pizza Hut that had gone out of business a decade ago. The parking lot was cracked, leaving patrons to park wherever the hell they felt like since the lines had long since eroded.

Riley pulled right up to the front door. "You guys go on in and order for me. I just remembered an errand I have to run."

She didn't have to tell Mrs. Penny twice to get out of the car and go eat. The woman scooted her way off the seat and was inside the restaurant in less than thirty seconds.

"Do you sense trouble?" Gabe asked through her open window.

Burt gave Riley's shoulder, neck, and chin a lick before he climbed out.

"Everything's fine. I just saw that limo again. I want to make sure they're not actually following us. Can you keep Burt and Mrs. Penny safe until I get back?" she said.

"I will do so. Be very careful, my friend," Gabe said.

"I'll be fine," she promised.

She left him and her dog staring after her with matching concerned expressions as she burned rubber out of the parking lot.

"Come out and play, suspicious limo," she sang under her breath as she headed back the way she came.

She didn't have long to wait. She found the limo idling at the curb, taking up three parking spaces one block down. She cruised by, keeping her eyes on the road and playing it cool.

"Does this mean I'm not getting an egg roll?" Uncle Jimmy wondered.

"I'll get you an egg roll. I just have to make sure we're not about to be kidnapped or murdered first. It's called priorities."

"No need to get your hip waders in a twist."

She ignored her dead uncle and watched in the rearview mirror as the limo made a U-turn and followed her.

Bait taken.

The relief at luring the occupants of the limo away from her friends was short-lived when she realized she had no idea what to do next.

She still wasn't picking up any murderous vibes. Only a strange mix of anxiety, excitement, and Christina Aguilera music.

Riley felt around on the passenger seat for her phone. Even if Nick was still in a snit over the team meeting this morning, she knew he wouldn't hesitate to swoop in and save her.

It was too bad her phone wasn't there.

"Damn it, Mrs. Penny," she groaned.

No phone. No help. No idea who was following her. Her day was going from bad to worse in a hurry.

She needed to find out who they were, preferably with witnesses present.

"Crap." There was only one way she could think of to bring the situation to an immediate and probably safe end.

"*Is this a good idea?*" Uncle Jimmy wondered as Riley slammed on her brakes in the middle of the road.

"Does it really matter at this point, Uncle Jimmy?" she asked, opening her door and jumping out.

She marched down the double yellow lines toward the limo as it screeched to a halt. A woman wearing enormous sunglasses and clutching an extra-large iced coffee laid on the horn from the minivan behind the limo.

"Stay there in case I get murdered," Riley called, pointing at her.

"I don't have time to witness a murder. My kid just puked all over his art teacher," she yelled back before whipping the minivan into the other lane and speeding away.

Riley sensed nervous energy rising as she approached the limo. It mixed with her own adrenaline, carrying her forward. "Hey! You behind the tint! Wanna tell me why you're following me like a creep?" she demanded, rapping her knuckles against the driver's window.

It didn't lower.

But the back door opened, and a pair of magenta platform wedges hit the asphalt.

"Exactly what good is a psychic vision if it doesn't make sense until after it happens?" Riley muttered to her spirit guides.

They pulsed out what she assumed was an apology.

Riley wasn't sure who she'd expected to pop out of the back seat, but it sure wasn't a curvy blond in a leopard-print minidress.

The woman's hair was huge, but it evened out the proportions of her more than well-endowed chest. She wore oversize sunglasses and a gigantic necklace made out of what looked like miniature gold bars, all pointing south toward her impressive cleavage. She looked like a trophy wife on her way to some brunch fundraiser.

The stranger reminded her vaguely of Bella Goodshine, the blond and busty local weatherwoman and female-face-blind fiancée of Riley's idiot ex-husband. It was a mark against the stranger.

Riley felt the way she always did when faced with a woman who took pride in and invested in her appearance: frumpy AF. Yet another point against her fabulous stalker.

"Why are you following me?" Riley demanded.

The woman beamed at her as if she'd been waiting for that very question. "Well, it's kind of a long story," she said apologetically. "How about we go for a drive, and I'll explain everything? I have a bag of *amazing* dark chocolate with antioxidants we could share."

"Are you seriously trying to lure me into your vehicle with candy?"

The leopard-print stalker pursed her glossy pink lips as if she hadn't considered the fact that she was committing a felony. Then she let out a bubbly giggle. "Well, now that you mention it, I guess I am. Oops!"

Riley decided to get straight to the truth. She inhaled deeply and zeroed in on the woman's thoughts. The cotton candy clouds appeared in her mind's eye. They looked a little dimmer than they had earlier that morning. Dimmer and less puffy.

"Hey, spirit guides."

It was as far as she got before the clouds began to spin. Slowly at first and then faster and faster. Like a carousel picking up speed. It was making her dizzy.

"Want to slow down the Skittles barf merry-go-round before I…?"

The clouds tangled with images spit out too rapidly for her to hold on to them. There was a plane on a tarmac. But before she could focus in on it, it was gone.

She caught a glimpse of a dark room, thick velvet curtains, silk wallpaper, and a huge four-poster bed. She thought there might have been someone else in the bed, but then the wallpaper disappeared, replaced with cheap paneling. The luxurious bed morphed into a mattress and box spring on the floor.

Riley's stomach lurched as she was sucked back into the darkening cloud tornado.

"Are you okay? You don't look so good." The voice sounded like it was very far away, and she couldn't tell if it was her leopard-print stalker or someone else on the edge of her consciousness.

Riley felt her legs buckle, and then there was pain in her hands and knees. Was it her pain or someone else's? The nausea cramping her stomach was definitely her own, but everything else was too fuzzy as vertigo tilted the world until she didn't know which end was up.

"Oh God. I don't like this," she groaned to her spirit guides, who didn't seem inclined to make it stop.

The bed disappeared, and in its place, she saw a car. A cheap sedan. She couldn't see the driver, but Riley read a giddy wave of excitement. Happy anticipation.

Only now the car wasn't a car. It was a windowless van. And the excitement had turned dark.

Danger.

Someone—a blond, no, wait, a brunette—was walking

47

past it, oblivious. The door slid open silently. The image disappeared in a disorienting flash.

Heat.

She felt it blasting her. Dangerously hot. She felt like screaming, then realized other people around her were already screaming. Panic. Confusion. She felt something. A rush of satisfaction that definitely wasn't hers as the heat got exponentially hotter.

Lessons needed to be taught.

"What lessons? Who needs to be taught a lesson?" she asked weakly.

"I think she's going to toss her cookies," someone said.

Then the heat was gone. Sucked away by an invisible cosmic vacuum cleaner. Riley felt herself lurch again and had no idea if it was her physical body or her psychic motion sickness.

All she could see was thick black darkness.

Wait.

There was something pink glowing in the distance.

No, not pink.

Yellow.

Green.

Orange.

Happy.

Mad.

Oops.

Oh crap. She was going to throw up. Or pass out. Maybe both.

Sesame chicken.

She was so hungry.

Nick was going to be so pissed.

It was her last thought before the colors disappeared and she was left alone in the dark.

7

R iley came to on buttery-soft leather with the scent of one of those expensive perfume samples she and Wander used to get at department stores tickling her nostrils. Her mouth was dry. Her head hurt. And she felt like her brain was on the spin cycle.

Slowly, she forced one eye open.

A pair of unnaturally blue eyes peered back at her. "Oh good! You're alive," the person attached to the blue eyes said.

"Are you wearing contacts?" Riley asked on a rasp.

"I am," the eyeballs chirped with enthusiasm. "Do you like them? They're European. They change color in different light. I can give you the number for Dr. Picard."

"I don't want a contact lens reference from a kidnapper," Riley croaked. She let her head flop to the side and tried to take in her environment.

In addition to the leopard-print minidress woman, she saw cream-colored leather seats, gray carpet, and a faux wood built-in bar stocked with a bottle of champagne and the afore-mentioned chocolate. Christina Aguilera's *Back to Basics* album played softly in the background.

Yep. She was definitely in the limo. *Freaking great.* The

first rule of getting abducted was *Don't let yourself be taken to a second location.*

Depending on how long she'd been unconscious, they could've been anywhere. They could've been halfway to New Jersey or Perry County or wherever blond bombshells took bodies to dispose of them.

Ugh. Nick was *definitely* going to be pissed. Although, maybe his obsession with Beth's disappearance could work in her favor. Maybe he wouldn't notice.

"I didn't kidnap you, silly. I just had my driver carry your unconscious body to the back seat and then drive away."

Riley eased herself into a seated position. She wanted to look out the window to gauge their location, but the postural change sent her head spinning again. She was exhausted, dizzy, and still strongly considering throwing up.

At least it didn't feel like the car was moving. Sitting still was good.

She slumped against the door. "No offense, but that sounds exactly like kidnapping. Where's my Jeep?"

"It's in the parking lot at Savannah's on Hanna. You know. The gentlemen's club? I didn't want to leave it running and unlocked in the middle of Harrisburg. You never can be too careful. There are criminals everywhere."

"You should know, kidnapper." Riley scrubbed her hands over her face, willing the vertigo to abate.

In the beginning of her reluctant journey to embrace her psychic powers, every vision had left her dizzy and nauseated. But this was so much worse. She was tired and shaky. Her mouth was dry, and her stomach was rolling. Had she been drugged?

Gabe would know.

Wait. Gabe.

Burt.

Mrs. Penny.

Crap. They'd probably already eaten her sesame chicken.

"You passed out before I could introduce myself," the stranger said. "My name is Sesame."

Riley dropped her hands and blinked at the woman. "Seriously?"

Sesame the Stalker nodded perkily.

"Well, that explains that," Riley muttered, pinching the bridge of her nose. "Okay, Sesame, where are we? What time zone are we in? Did you drug me? Where did you get those shoes?"

Her captor took an enthusiastic slurp of a dark purple smoothie and admired her own shoes. "Thanks! They're Chelsea Paris. She's an *amazing* designer."

"Way to focus in on the important question. What are the odds that you'll let me go so I can get back to my boyfriend before he calls out the National Guard to look for me?"

"Boyfriend?" Sesame said the word like it was a liquor-soaked cherry in her mouth—delectable. "I'm so glad you brought it up because that's definitely an item on our agenda to girl talk about!"

"I'd rather girl talk about why you abducted me, followed by a heart-to-heart about where we are and which side of the *murder-me* or *let-me-go* fence you're leaning toward."

"Oh my God. You're hilarious. My research said nothing about you being so funny," Sesame said. She shimmied in her seat as if the excitement were too much for her. "I'm *so* glad I started with you. I think we're going to be great friends."

"Great. Are you some kind of serial kidnapper who locks women in her basement and forces them to pretend to be her best friend?" Riley was definitely going to fall out the door and attempt to crawl away if someone started talking about skin suits and lotion.

Sesame waved a hand at her and laughed. "Stop! You're too much."

The door opposite the one Riley had wedged herself against opened, and a man in a suit appeared.

In a panic, she lifted a foot and both hands to ward him off.

But rather than grabbing her and dragging her from the vehicle, the man thrust a large cup filled with some kind of green liquid at her.

"Thank you, Wilhelm," Sesame said.

"Do not spill this on the upholstery or the carpet," he said in a vaguely German accent. The look he gave Riley suggested that he expected her to do just that.

"We'll be extra super careful," Sesame promised earnestly.

When Riley didn't accept the frowny man's offering, Wilhelm shoved the concoction into a cupholder, pointed his fingers at his eyeballs and then at her, and disappeared.

"Wilhelm is *very* particular about his upholstery," Sesame explained.

Riley looked down at the liquid. "You can't poison me again," she told Sesame. She wanted a drink so badly. Her mouth felt like the damn desert.

"It's not poison, you goof. It's an energy smoothie from Fresh Pressed. I thought it might perk you up when you came out of your faint. By the way, it's *so* nice to see Harrisburg finally embracing the health-conscious consumer."

"Fresh Pressed? Harrisburg?" Riley repeated. "We're still in Harrisburg?"

Hope was a rabid chipmunk in her stomach.

"Of course we are. You didn't hit your head when you fainted, did you? Or maybe you did earlier today? You were talking about merry-go-rounds a lot. Is that what happens when you have a psychic vision? I've never met a real psychic before, but I did a lot of reading up on you and your grandmother."

Riley's head was spinning, only now it was less about the vertigo and more about confusion. But her mouth remained a dusty, cracked canyon floor. The smoothie was looking better and better.

"How do you know I'm psychic?" she rasped, willing her mouth to produce the tiniest bit of saliva.

Sesame looked bemused. "Do I look like the kind of businesswoman who makes a pitch to my target audience without doing any research?"

Having no idea if her kidnapper looked like a researcher or not, Riley assumed the question was rhetorical and grabbed the smoothie. Throwing caution to the wind, she took a big gulp. It wasn't terrible. In fact, she couldn't even taste whatever made it green.

She kept on slurping until a blinding pain hit her behind the eyes. "Ergh! Brain freeze! Or poison! I'm not sure which!"

"It's definitely not poison. I mean, I guess it *could* be. But I promise you if it's poisoned, Wilhelm and I didn't do it. Maybe the smoothie barista was having a bad day. Or the kale farmer could have used some kind of illegal insecticide," Sesame said, considering all the possibilities.

The pain lessened, then finally disappeared, and Riley slumped back in her seat in relief. "Thank God. Just brain freeze," she said.

But brain freeze made her think of Gabe. And thinking about Gabe made her think about how worried he must be.

"Oh good!" Sesame cheered. "Now that you're feeling better, I can tell you my story."

"And then I can go?" Riley pressed.

"I'm hoping you won't want to go, but if you absolutely want to leave after you hear what I have to say, I won't stop you," her kidnapper said with an amicable shrug.

There was nothing this woman could say that would make her choose to stay.

"Great, then let's get started," Riley said. The faster Leopard Boobs Sesame spilled her story, the sooner she could escape.

Sesame put her own smoothie back in the cupholder and smoothed her hands over her dress like a speaker preparing to address a crowd. Riley sensed a vague wave of excitement, but after her last psychic spelunking experience, she chose not to focus on it.

"Like I said, my name is Sesame," the woman said.

"Uh-huh. Yeah. Got that. Let's skip ahead to the part where you decided to follow me and my friends this morning."

"Oh, I don't like skipping to the end like that. That's like reading the last chapter of a book before you even start it. No spoilers here," Sesame said with a dismissive wave of her hand.

"Fine." Riley sighed. "Start at the beginning." She picked up her smoothie and took a careful sip. Pleased when her head didn't explode, she took another one.

Sesame folded her hands in her lap. "Well, it all started when I was born."

"Nope. No way. I'm not here for your prequel. Fast-forward to the second act or the relevant part," Riley insisted.

Her captor's pink lower lip protruded in a pout. "You know, I put a lot of effort into getting here and finding you. You'd think you'd be the tiniest bit interested in why."

"I'm sorry. You're right. Please continue," Riley said. The smoothie really was making her feel better. She really should drink more fresh juice. Maybe then her skin would be more glowing and dewy like Sesame's.

"Sesame isn't my real name."

Riley slapped a hand to her own chest in mock surprise. "No, really?"

"I know, right? I *look* like a Sesame now." The woman waved a hand over her face and chest regions. "But the lovely lady you see before you didn't exist a few years ago."

"You look pretty mature for someone who didn't exist until recently," Riley observed, staring pointedly at Sesame's excellent rack.

"Oh, you." Sesame giggled. "Anyway, as I was saying, my real name is Beth."

Riley choked and sent a fine mist of green smoothie in a 180-degree arc all over Wilhelm's precious upholstery.

8

Is your phone-answering arm broken?"

Nick glanced up at the door to his office and spied Mrs. Penny and Gabe trying to wedge themselves through it at the same time.

"I'll call you back," he said into the desk phone before hanging it up.

He only just managed to dodge the burrito Mrs. Penny hurled in his direction. It bounced off the bookcase behind him and landed on the floor with a splat.

Burt bounded into the room, pounced on the floor burrito, and swallowed it whole.

The dog's burrito radar never failed.

"Damn it, Penny," Nick complained. "You know how he gets when he eats people food."

"One burrito isn't gonna kill him after what he ate at lunch," the old lady insisted with a wave of her pale, wrinkly hand.

Nick did not have time to deal with a dog with digestive distress today. "What did Burt eat at lunch?"

"Burt consumed an entire platter of sesame chicken, including the egg roll," Gabe announced.

"Riley is going to kill you two," Nick told them.

"That's why I threw the burrito," Mrs. Penny said in exasperation.

"You threw a burrito at me because Riley is going to kill you?" Nick clarified. Conversations with his elderly business partner often ended in him experiencing a persistent eye twitch. He probably should have listened to Riley's warning about his partnership with the old woman. But in his defense, he'd been drunk at the time.

Mrs. Penny threw up her arms, sending her triceps flapping. "It's like talking to a damn toaster."

"Mrs. Penny and I are concerned about Riley," Gabe said, picking up the loose end of the conversation out of the knotted ball of twine.

Nick started to massage his eye, then winced.

After getting punched in the face at the prison, he'd come home and added several items to his buy-this-shit-for-home-security list. Then he'd picked up where he left off annoying the witnesses listed in Beth's case file.

He'd made it through three annoyed contacts, all of whom had expressed the strong desire that he give up on the case and leave them the hell alone. That alone was enough to give him a headache. These two were going to push him into a full-blown aneurysm.

He shoved his thumbs into the corners of his eyeballs to ward off the distant throb. "Okay. Why are we concerned about Riley?"

"You'd know if you'd answer your stupid phone. We got ourselves a code cabbage casserole!"

He sifted through his memory banks for his neighbors' ridiculous call codes. "Someone broke into the house?" he asked. "Yours or mine?"

"Did you eat a bowl of Big Dummy Wheat Flakes for breakfast?" Mrs. Penny demanded, stomping an orthopedic shoe on the floor.

"Not to my knowledge," he answered as Burt shoved

his head into Nick's lap, happily licking refried beans off his muzzle. He gave the dog a pat and wondered if refried-bean farts would peel some of the hideous wallpaper in the guest room upstairs. "That's what a cabbage casserole is. A sparkle poo is when someone is being targeted by a known serial killer."

It sounded ridiculous even as the words came out of his mouth.

Mrs. Penny threw up her hands again. Burt watched hopefully for another burrito to be thrown. "Fine. What's the code for *Your girlfriend dropped us off at Eggrolls and Stuff and never came back*? Do you know how hard it is to find an Uber that will pick up Marmaduke here?"

"I'm sure if Riley didn't come back for you, she had a good reason."

He could think of a million reasons why anyone wouldn't want the pair in their vehicle. Hell, he didn't particularly want them in his office.

If he could get Tweedledee and Tweedlebiceps out of his office, Nick could call Harrisburg's retired fire chief and grill him about the warehouse arson again before the guy headed into his cycling class.

Gabe politely raised a gigantic hand. "If I may interject. I believe Mrs. Penny may have inadvertently left out an important piece of information."

Nick gestured at the man, then flipped open the folder containing the arson inspector's report. "Interject away, Dwayne Johnson."

"Riley dropped us off because a suspicious elongated vehicle was following us."

Mrs. Penny slapped herself in the forehead, knocking her glasses askew. "Oh yeah. The limo. Forgot about that."

On the verge of banning the Two Musketeers from his office *and* his house, Nick paused. "What. Limo."

"The one that followed us to Riley's parents' house while we were planning your sur—"

Moving swiftly for a large man, Gabe grabbed one of the couch cushions and held it over Mrs. Penny's face.

"Mmmph!" The elderly woman waved her arms in an attempt to dislodge the upholstery.

"Do not listen to her. She is full of deep-fried foods and is speaking gibberish," Gabe insisted.

"What. Limo." Nick demanded, harnessing the last iota of his self-control.

Mrs. Penny finally succeeded in batting the cushion away. "Smells like farts! Disgusting!"

"A limousine followed us to the home of Riley's parents. It appeared again when we left for lunch. Riley, fearing for our safety, dropped us off at the restaurant and led them away."

Nick felt his heart stop and then restart in overdrive. He shot out of his chair, a familiar sense of panic clutching at him.

"That's the last we saw of her," Mrs. Penny said. "We had to eat her sesame chicken so it wouldn't get cold. Well, we ate the second platter after Burt ate the first one."

"Riley promised to return when it was safe. However, she did not come back," Gabe continued ominously.

"Where's my phone?" Nick barked, frantically clearing paperwork off the shitty table he used as a desk like he was the star of a porno.

Why was his office such a fucking mess?

And why the fuck did his girlfriend constantly feel the need to insert herself into dangerous situations? Didn't she know what happened to nice girls who got too close to bad people?

He should have been more vigilant. Had he learned nothing?

Burt galloped around the desk and nosed through the mess like he wanted to be part of the search party.

Mrs. Penny shrugged. "How the hell should we know? We tried to call you when we realized Riley probably got herself abducted and murdered, but you were too busy to answer. Really, this is all your fault."

"Not helping, Penny," Nick snarled as he pounced on the coffee table and started sorting through the debris. Old newspaper clippings. Photocopies of police reports. The remains of last night's cold pizza snack. Or was that last week's cold pizza snack?

Finally he found his phone under a coffee mug that had mold growing in the bottom.

He'd been too distracted. Once again, he'd shoved his head up his own ass and someone else had paid the price.

With shaking hands, Nick dialed Riley's number.

"Gee, if only we'd thought to call her," Mrs. Penny said.

Half a second later, Riley's phone rang. In the room.

His geriatric partner pulled his girlfriend's phone out of her pants pocket and wiggled it at him.

"We were unaware that Mrs. Penny was still in possession of Riley's phone," Gabe said, looking at his canoe-sized feet in chagrin.

"Not my fault I wanted to rock out in the Jeep."

The Jeep.

Nick turned his back on them and scrolled through his apps. "She drove off in her Jeep, right?"

"Weren't you listening?" Mrs. Penny squawked.

He ignored her and opened his tracker app. The Jeep was parked on Hanna Street.

"What the hell is she doing at Savannah's?"

"The nudie club? Hoo, boy! Now we get to show Gabe here a real-life champagne room. Stick with me, big guy, and I'll educate you on all the fun stuff," Mrs. Penny promised.

"Where are my fucking keys?" Nick snarled, staring at the red dot on his screen as he patted his pockets.

He didn't have a good feeling about this. And the second he found Riley, he was going to give her one of those weeklong loud lectures about personal safety. Then he was going to take her away for the weekend. Somewhere without elderly neighbors and missing persons and suspicious limos.

"I'll borrow Willicott's car," Mrs. Penny volunteered. "Gabe 'n' me will follow you over, and if she's not there, we'll stay put in case she shows up again. We'll need a lot of singles so we don't look suspicious."

Panic clawed at him as Nick scoured his office for his keys. "Why is it such a goddamn mess in here?"

Goddammit. He hated when other people were right. He kicked the easel leg in frustration and sent the whiteboard crashing to the floor.

"Told you he was gonna lose his shit," Mrs. Penny stage-whispered.

"Burt the Good Boy has discovered your car keys," Gabe said, holding up a slobber-covered set of keys. The dog sat with his tail swishing back and forth over a missing person report from Kansas.

Nick snatched the keys out of the man's hand, gave Burt a quick pat on the head, and started for the door. "You two go home and stay by your phones. If you hear from her, you call me immediately."

Mrs. Penny snorted. "He says that like he's gonna answer the phone this time."

With clenched teeth, Nick glared at her. "I *will* answer. Finding Riley is our priority. Nothing else matters."

"The victims of the Dog Doody Bandit would beg to differ," the old lady claimed.

Nick growled at her.

She held up another burrito in a threatening manner. "Come at me, bro."

"Where do you keep getting these burritos?" he asked as he shoved his keys into his pocket and called up Weber's contact on his phone.

"I was upset. And when I get upset, my blood sugar drops, so we made the driver swing through the Taco Bell drive-thru," Mrs. Penny explained.

"I enjoyed something called a gordita. Mrs. Penny called it 'eating my feelings,'" Gabe added.

This was what Nick got for working with amateurs…and accepting money from old ladies.

He was going to find Riley, handcuff her to his side, and turn this house into a fortress with a state-of-the-art security system so no one could ever take her away again.

"Is your face well?" Gabe asked with concern. "It appears to be bruised."

"I walked into a None-of-Your-Damn-Business sign," Nick snapped.

Burt's ears perked up, and he scrambled out of the room.

"I'm calling Weber. You call Brian and Josie. Explain what happened, and have them meet me at Savannah's," he told Gabe.

The man gave a noble bow. "It would be my great honor."

"Can't believe you expect us to not go to the nudie club," Mrs. Penny grumbled.

"Why are you going to a strip club?"

Nick whirled around and found Riley, his beautiful, alive, very-much-in-trouble girlfriend, leaning against the doorway. She looked pale and shaken, but a quick count assured him she still had all her limbs attached.

Burt danced around her as if he'd been as worried as Nick.

"Oh good. She's not dead," Mrs. Penny observed helpfully as she bit into the burrito.

"Does anyone want to explain why my dog has sesame-chicken and burrito breath?" Riley asked weakly.

"Where the hell have you been?" Nick demanded. His legs ate up the distance that separated them, and then he was crushing her to his chest.

"Mmmph mmmm," she said. He loosened his hold incrementally, and she peered up at him. "Guess this means you noticed I was missing," she said softly.

"I swear to God, Thorn. If you decide to lure one more stalker away, I'm going to lock you in the smelly closet."

It wasn't exactly the *I love you and I'm so relieved you're safe* that he was feeling inside. But he was confident his girlfriend knew him well enough to see past the bluster.

"I love you too. And I was never in any real danger. What happened to your face?"

"He was attacked by a rude sign," Gabe explained.

"I'm not letting you go for at least another hour," Nick

decided. "After that, the lecture begins, and for the next week, you can't be more than ten feet from me at all times."

"What the hell happened in here, Santiago? Was there some kind of struggle?" Detective Kellen Weber strolled into the room, his hands in his suit pants pockets.

"That's Nick's housekeeping style," Mrs. Penny said through a mouthful of beef and refried beans.

"What are you doing here?" Nick snapped.

"I called him," Riley explained. "This involves both of you."

"What involves both of us?" Weber asked.

"I am very happy to see you, Riley," Gabe said, his eyes misty.

"I'm sorry I scared you," she said.

Nick refused to let her go, so she awkwardly turned in his arms to hug Gabe.

"I saw a porno that started like this once," Mrs. Penny said.

Riley sighed and released Gabe. "Thanks for ruining the mood, Mrs. Penny."

She lifted the burrito in toast. "Anytime."

Burt's back end rumbled, and the dog jumped as if he could escape his own stench.

Riley groaned. "Why does everyone keep feeding him people food?"

"We are very sorry," Gabe said solemnly. "Burt ate your lunch while Mrs. Penny was attempting to put buffet shrimp rolls in her pants."

"Shrimp rolls make a great midnight snack," Mrs. Penny piped up.

"Will someone explain what the hell is going on?" Weber demanded.

"Riley got kidnapped by a limo and taken to Savannah's," Mrs. Penny said. "Did they make you dance before you escaped?"

"Are you feeling well?" Gabe asked her.

"You do kinda look like you might toss your cookies," Mrs. Penny observed. "Unrelated, do you guys have any cookies?"

"I'm fine," Riley insisted. But there was definitely something wrong with her pallor.

"You should sit," Nick decided. "Sit and tell me who I need to hunt down."

Riley firmly put her hands on his chest, then looked between him and Weber. "I think after Mrs. Penny and Gabe take Burt out, we should all sit down."

Nick didn't like the sound of that at all.

9

R iley loved the mansion's living room. Well, now that it was no longer inhabited by a colony of bats. It was a large airy space at the front of the house, sparsely decorated with mismatched, cast-off furniture she'd found online and at yard sales. The black marble fireplace was flanked by twin window seats. Through the front windows, the Susquehanna River lazily flowed south across Front Street.

But none of the room's occupants were taking in the views. They were all watching her expectantly.

Still dizzy from her bizarre psychic encounter with Beth… er, Sesame, Riley felt exhausted, woozy, and totally unprepared for the fallout of the bombshell she was about to drop.

She squirmed in Nick's lap. "Nick, I know you're glad to see me alive, but you're going to have to let me go so I can do this."

"Nope," he said. "Oh, we're going to dinner tonight. Then I'm taking you to the beach for the weekend."

Reassured by the overprotective-boyfriend routine, she cupped his cheek. "I appreciate that, and I would love to. But I have a feeling you'll have something more important to do in a minute."

"Nothing is more important than you," he insisted vehemently.

She wasn't sure if it was the aftereffects of her psychic flu or whether it was Nick being romantic that made her weak in the knees.

"Barf!" Mrs. Penny complained from the floral fainting couch in the corner. She had her hand in a bag of pork rinds.

Gabe smiled encouragingly from the rattan rocking chair near the doorway. It creaked every time he rocked forward.

"I don't mean to be rude, Riley, but I've got a medical examiner waiting for me at the morgue," Weber said, looking at his watch.

She had a feeling that corpse was about to be bumped down the homicide detective's priority list.

Riley extricated herself from Nick's embrace and got to her feet. She felt like she was standing on the deck of a cruise ship during hurricane season. "Okay, I'm just going to get this over with. I met someone today."

"Speak up. I can't hear you over the crunching," Mrs. Penny hollered.

Nick shot to his feet. "Are you breaking up with me? Because I'm not going to let you. I know I've been distracted, but that's all over—"

Riley pushed him back down into the chair. "I'm not breaking up with you," she assured him. Movement in the doorway caught her eye.

It was Mr. Willicott, lugging a soup pot and wearing Riley's green cardigan that had gone missing from the laundry room a few months earlier. "Who the hell are you?" he demanded to someone just out of sight.

"Shoo. Go away, elderly person," came the whispered reply.

"Crap," Riley muttered. She'd been given strict instructions on how this was to go down.

Burt abandoned his pork rind watch and pranced into the foyer to sniff the visitors.

"Who is Willicott talking to?" Nick demanded.

"That's what I want to tell you," Riley said, pulling out the Fresh Pressed napkin with the notes she was supposed to follow. Clearing her throat, she began to read. "Into every life there comes a special person whose presence is missed…uhhh…" She paused and squinted at the smeared ink. "Something about absence."

"Are you reading a speech?" Weber asked from his stance against the fireplace.

"I'm trying to, but there's a lot of green smoothie on it. There was a spitting incident."

The ear from one of the golden cherubs under the mantel landed with a thunk on the floor behind Weber.

Ignoring it, Riley found her spot on the napkin and pressed on. "When that person returns to your life, bringing with her joy and…something I can't read…uh… 'those who missed her will become whole again.'"

Reading was giving her a headache to go along with her full-body ache.

"Thorn, what the hell is this?" Nick demanded, rising from his chair again. "Did you join a cult today?"

Riley put her hand on his chest to hold him in place. "I don't think so. Um, without further ado, I give you your missing piece."

There was a pop, and a shower of pink confetti filled the doorway. Burt joyfully jumped in the air, biting at the confetti.

"That better not be glitter," Mrs. Penny muttered.

"Ta-da!" Sesame stepped into the doorway, hip-checking Burt out of the way and thrusting her arms into the air like a large-breasted ringleader.

Mr. Willicott sidled up next to her. "Wanna see my lobster?" he asked, still holding the pot.

Sesame grabbed the lid off the pot and threw it into the foyer. "Go fetch," she said before resuming her grand-entrance position. Mr. Willicott shuffled off after the lid.

Riley wished she could crawl into bed and sleep for the next eighteen or so hours.

"You didn't make friends with another serial killer, did you?" Nick asked, no longer trying to get past her.

Riley turned to look at him, then instantly regretted it as the room began to spin. She leaned against the wingback chair she'd bought at Wander's neighborhood yard sale. "Do you recognize her?"

"Do I recognize Miss Confetti? No. Who is she? Is she the one who took you to Savannah's?"

Oh boy. This wasn't going well.

Riley carefully spared a glance at Weber, who looked just as annoyed and confused.

"Hi, Kelly. Hi, Nicky. It's me, Beth," Sesame said, lowering her arms.

Nick went rigid against Riley. She could feel the hammering of his heart under her hand.

Weber was frozen to the spot, staring at the woman in the door.

"Looks like the po-po is about to poo-poo his pants," Mrs. Penny whispered loudly.

"Is this the Beth whose disappearance caused a rift that involved headbutting between Nick and Detective Weber and who was presumed dead until Elanora informed you that she is indeed alive?" Gabe asked as he ceased his rocking.

"That's me," Sesame said, raising her arms again. When no one reacted, she dropped them to her sides. "Why aren't they jumping up and down and hugging me, Riley?"

"I told you it might be a little bit of a shock," Riley said.

That was putting it mildly.

Nick made a low wheezy sound like a stepped-on accordion.

Weber's mouth was hanging open. Mrs. Penny aimed a piece of pork rind at him. It bounced off his chin, and Burt happily scarfed it off the floor.

"Damn it. Missed," she muttered, standing up on the couch to get a better angle.

Riley was at a loss. The entire room felt like it was pulsating with shock and confusion, and she was too exhausted and barfy to do anything about it. "Are you okay?" she asked Nick.

He shook his head from side to side and said, "I think so."

Suddenly Weber made a gasping noise. His hands flew to his throat.

"Ha! Got one," Mrs. Penny said with a celebratory fist pump.

"Okay. I think he's choking," Riley said, feeling just a tiny bit hysterical. She tried to go to him, but her knees buckled, and she had to settle for collapsing in the chair.

"This really was not the welcome I was expecting," Sesame said and pouted.

"I am trained in the Heimlich maneuver." Gabe jumped out of the rocker. The arms of the chair gave complementary cracks and fell to the floor.

"Be gentle!" Riley cautioned Gabe.

"It is best if you go limp," Gabe suggested as he put his enormous arms around Weber, who was turning a terrifying shade of blue.

"Which way to the kitchen before this lobster wakes up?" Mr. Willicott bellowed from the foyer.

Gabe thrust his closed fists back and up into Weber's abdomen.

There was another audible crack, and then the pork rind launched from his throat. They all watched in slow motion as it sailed in a high graceful arc.

"Nooooo," Riley moaned as Burt launched himself into the air off a tufted ottoman.

But it was too late.

The dog caught the soggy pork rind in his mouth and swallowed it in triumph before his paws hit the rug.

"What the hell is going on in here?" Josie demanded from the doorway, where she and Brian stared on in a mix of fascination and horror.

10

N ick poured himself six fingers of bourbon into a Solo cup and drank half of it down.

The burn chased away the fog of shock, bringing the living room back into sharp focus. He stared hard at the single electrical outlet. It was a twenty-foot-by-thirty-foot room with one fucking outlet. It, along with the rest of the damn house, was on the fix-it list he'd been ignoring. The list he'd planned to tackle as soon as he found Beth.

But instead of breaking a witness or tracking down the missing piece of the puzzle and going in guns blazing, a woman claiming to be Beth Weber had waltzed into his house after scaring the shit out of him by abducting his girlfriend.

It had been a fucking day, and it was barely after noon.

The woman bore zero resemblance to the girl who'd vanished six years ago. No amount of Nicky-and-Kelly-ing was going to convince him that the busty, leopard-print-wearing woman sitting on his couch was Beth fucking Weber.

A scam, he decided, the cup making an ominous cracking noise in his hand. It had to be a scam.

Brian wheeled back into the room with a bag of ice and an ACE bandage.

"Here," he said, offering them to Weber, who was sitting on the couch clutching his abused ribs and staring at Beth—or whatever her real name was—next to him.

Gabe had left to escort Willicott and Mrs. Penny home before any more damage could be done.

Josie, ever alert for threats, had taken a sentry position behind the couch in case "Beth" required a choke hold.

His gaze traveled to Riley, who looked like she was taking slow deep breaths.

He wanted to go to her. Wanted to brush her hair back from her face and force her to tell him what was wrong since he wasn't the mind reader in the relationship. But his feet were rooted to the spot.

His hand and wrist were wet. Looking down, he realized he'd cracked the cup the whole way down. Hurriedly he chugged the contents; then, because it was a thirty-dollar bottle of booze, he licked his forearm.

He slammed the cup carcass down on the mantel and leaned into the cool marble, his gaze on his boots.

Sensing her, he glanced up as Riley approached, listing to the side as if the gravitational pull of the earth was crooked today.

"You okay?" they asked in unison.

"You first," he insisted.

She slid her hands into the back pockets of her jeans. "Sure. Yeah. Totally fine. You?"

"Great. Awesome."

"Good. Good." She nodded, then tipped backward and caught herself against the bookcase.

Nick frowned. "Are you drunk?"

"No! You're the one winning the one-man bourbon-chugging contest."

"I was thirsty. You're the one stumbling around like my uncle Martin after he's hit the eggnog on Christmas Eve."

"I'm fine," she said, looking anything but fine.

Nick scrubbed his hand over the back of his neck. "So she's

a fraud, right? A scammer?" Beth Weber had not just wandered into his house after an unexplained six-year absence.

Riley blew out a breath, then bit her lip. "I'm not sure."

"You're not sure? Can't your spirit guides tell you?"

Her gaze flicked to the couch. "I...I'm having trouble getting a read on her."

"What the hell does that mean?" He knew he sounded like an impatient asshole, but the circumstances and the bourbon called for it.

She shook her head, then immediately stopped, squeezing her eyes shut.

"That's it. You're sitting the hell down, Thorn," he ordered.

"I'm fine," she repeated with belligerence.

"Oh really?" He poked his index finger into her shoulder and smirked when she swayed backward. He caught her by the arms and backed her into the chair. "Sit the hell down and stay away from Busty Barbie until I know who she is and what she wants."

"Bossy," she muttered but didn't try to get back up.

She looked like she'd seen a ghost... Scratch that. The woman talked to ghosts on the regular. She looked like she *was* a ghost. Frowning, he slapped a hand to her forehead. "You don't have a fever."

"I'm *fine*. Go talk to her."

Nick wrapped both hands around the back of his neck and ignored the twitching under his swollen eye.

"So, *Beth*, where the hell have you been for the last six years?" Josie asked, leaning over the back of the couch, playing with a switchblade. Brian sat in front of Weber and "Beth" with his fingers poised over his laptop keyboard, ready to investigate anything that came out of this woman's mouth.

Nick felt a swift rush of gratitude for his team. Even if they were assholes most of the time and had tried to commit a mutiny that morning. They still had his back when it counted.

"You know those are illegal, don't you?" Weber said, eying Josie's knife.

"You know you have bigger things to worry about, don't you?" she shot back.

"I go by Sesame now," the woman on the couch piped up, bringing the attention back to her.

Nick shot a look over his shoulder at Riley, who held up both palms.

That explained the recent weird cravings.

"Okay, Sesame," Josie said, "you show up here and expect us to believe that you're Beth Weber, yet you look nothing like her."

Sesame giggled. The sound of it rang something deep in Nick's memory banks. "I didn't expect you to take me at face value when my face is so much better looking now. So I brought proof."

She reached into a tiny leopard-print purse and produced a piece of paper folded into a small rectangle. She handed it to Josie, who shook it violently to unfurl it.

"DNA results," she muttered, scanning the paper before handing it over to Brian.

"Well, let's get this part over with so we can pop some champagne and celebrate." Sesame scooted to the edge of the couch.

"We don't have any champagne," Nick announced, crossing his arms over his chest.

"Of *course* you don't, Nicky," Sesame said. Her smile wrinkled her nose in almost exactly the same way Beth's used to. "I sent my driver to pick up a few bottles."

"You have a driver?" Josie asked. "What's his name, date of birth, and Social Security number?"

"You are a delight," Sesame said. "We'll get to Wilhelm later. In the meantime, have you ever heard of amnesia?" When no one said anything, she continued. "It's a medical condition that results in the loss of memories."

"We know what amnesia is," Josie said. "Anyone who's ever watched a soap opera knows what amnesia is."

"Great!" Sesame clasped her hands in her lap. "So I had

amnesia. I woke up with no memory of Harrisburg or Beth Weber or, well, anything. The people I was with insisted that they were my family and that I'd suffered a head injury."

Josie turned to look at Nick. "Boss? You wanna take this?"

Nick glanced at Weber. He still didn't look like he was capable of, well, anything. "Fine," he said, stepping forward. "Who were the people you were with? Were they the ones who abducted you?"

Sesame beamed at him. "I'm so glad you asked, Nicky. The people I was with were the Hemsworths. I thought they were my in-laws."

"Why would you think that?"

"Because their son told me we were married."

"And you just believed him?" Josie asked incredulously.

Sesame shrugged. "He took me home and introduced me to three boys who called me Mom. There were pictures of us on the walls. I never suspected he was lying."

"Where were you?" Nick asked.

"A small town in Arizona."

"So some random guy, what? Hit you on the head, drove you across the country, and convinced you you were Sesame Hemsworth of Bumfuck, Arizona?"

"Well, Nicky, I know how unbelievable it must sound—"

"Do you, 'Beth'?" he said, putting air quotes around her name.

"Same old grumpy Nicky," she said, unfazed by him, much like the real Beth had been. "I prefer Sesame now, but if it makes you more comfortable, you can call me Beth."

"How about I call you—"

A movement out of the corner of his eye caught his attention and cut off his insult. Riley slumped even lower in the chair with her eyes closed, her head lolling to the side.

"Thorn? You good?" he snapped, hurrying to her side.

She groaned, then whispered. "I don't feel so good."

"You want some water? Some food? Burt ate your lunch. You're probably starving since your dog ate your lunch."

"I just need to stop the spinning," she whispered hoarsely.

Nick felt helpless. If there was one thing he fucking hated, it was lying schemers in his living room and also feeling helpless, so two things. "Here." Dragging her and the chair over to the wall, he braced one of her hands against the wall, then adjusted her legs so one foot pressed into the floor. "Better?"

She opened one eye, managing to look both nauseated and amused. "What are you doing?"

"One hand on the wall. One foot on the floor. It worked for the drunk spins in college."

"Riley, are you dizzy again? Do you want another smoothie? I can text Wilhelm," Sesame offered.

"No, thank you," Riley told her. "Just go on with your story."

Nick was torn. On one hand, he wanted to lecture Riley on getting kidnapped and making herself sick while he carried her up to bed and force-fed her ginger ale and soup. On the other, he wanted to expose this busty fraud, then make Weber arrest her.

"Why did this guy abduct you in the first place?" Josie asked, getting back to the topic at hand.

"Well, it's all a little fuzzy. But I *think* it had something to do with me hiring a carpenter here in Harrisburg to do something and then not paying him right away. I must have bumped my head when we were arguing about his invoice. The next thing I knew, I was Sesame Hemsworth and the carpenter was my husband. I worked in his family's corner drugstore and felt like a fish out of water, but I blamed it on the amnesia. Soon I was bonding with his three children like they were mine," Sesame explained. Her lower lip quivered. "I thought they were mine," she said. Then she began to wail. "But they weren't. It was all a lie, and when I finally remembered who I really was, they all packed up and fled to Colombiaaaaaaaaa."

"Like, South Carolina?" Josie pressed, ignoring the woman's distress.

"Nooooo! Like South Americaaaaaaaaa."

Nick studied Sesame closely as something tickled at his gut.

Sesame was crying without actual tears. Beth Weber had been a gifted actress who went all in when it came to trying to get out of trouble, but she had never mastered manufacturing real tears.

Lots of people couldn't cry on command, he reminded himself. Lots of people giggled and wrinkled their noses in the same way.

It wasn't her. It couldn't be. Not when she'd just shown up of her own free will and announced herself with a confetti cannon. Not when he hadn't figured out where he'd gone wrong. Not when he hadn't made it right.

"So your disappearance had nothing to do with the warehouse fire?" Nick asked.

"What warehouse fire?" she asked in a tiny voice. "I still don't remember everything leading up to the amnesia. Did I witness a crime?"

Brian cleared his throat and jerked his head at Nick.

Reluctantly, Nick left Riley and crossed to his cousin.

"Results confirmed. Legit lab. Legit staff. Legit results," Brian said quietly, showing him his screen. "Sesame Hemsworth is Beth Weber."

"Told you so," Sesame chirped.

Weber let out a sound like a creaky door.

"Holy shit." Nick blew out a breath that was straight bourbon and stared hard at the new and maybe-not-so-improved Beth. "I think I need to sit down."

11

Y ou buying that dog and pony show?" Josie asked, nudging Riley's foot with her combat boot.

Riley opened her eyes and was relieved when her head didn't try to somersault off her shoulders. They were alone in the living room. Nick was making her a snack to tide her over until the pizza he ordered arrived. Sesame was stocking the refrigerator with champagne and introducing her brother to her limo driver. Brian had hustled out of the room at top speed, presumably to start confirming Sesame's story.

"Not a word," Riley admitted.

Josie released a sigh. "Thank God I'm not the only tit-immune person in this house."

Riley grimaced. "Gross. I really don't think Kellen was checking out his sister's rack."

"He didn't know she was his sister right away, did he?" Josie pointed out, leaning against the fireplace surround. She was the kind of person who preferred to be on her feet facing the exits, ready for any threat. "I know Nicky's happy she's alive, but that woman just paraphrased the plot of *Overboard* as an explanation for why she's been missing for six years."

"Great movie," Riley said, rubbing her head. "I thought

it was just me **who** kept picturing Kurt Russell while she was talking."

"She **might be** the real Beth, but she's really lying about what she's **been up** to for the last six years. I mean, are they seriously **buying the** whole my-fake-husband-forced-me-to-get-a-bunch-of-**plastic**-surgery and I-can-afford-a-limo-driver-on-a-small-town-**drugstore**-sales-associate-salary song and dance?"

"They're **happy**," Riley said. "They're not thinking straight."

Josie **thumped** the back of her head against the marble. "You need **to tell Nick.**"

"Me? **You saw** how he reacted to the whole your-obses-sion-is-going-**to-put-us**-out-of-business conversation. Now you **want me to say, what?** 'Gee, Nick, it's great to have Beth back and all, but I **think** she's lying about everything, and you and Kellen just **aren't seeing** it.'"

"I mean, **I would** throw in a few mentions of him being a gullible idiot, **but** your way is fine too."

Riley groaned. "Why don't *you* tell him?"

"Because **he's** not going to listen to me. He probably won't even listen **to you.** But you're his girlfriend. You don't get to chicken out **on this.** It's your duty as his partner to call out his dumbassery."

"Have **you ever** considered writing greeting cards?" Riley asked, wearily **rubbing** her hands over her face. She felt a little steadier but **a lot more** tired. If she and Josie were right and Beth…er…**Sesame** was lying, the shit hadn't even begun to hit the fan.

"I hate **greeting** cards," Josie said.

"I'll add **them** to the list right under the elderly and knick-knacks," Riley **promised.**

"What **do those** spirit guides of yours say about Ms. Pants on Fire?"

Riley **looked at** the doorway to make sure no one was eaves-dropping **in the foyer.** "I don't know. Every time I try to get in her head, the **world** starts spinning like some possessed carnival ride. I can't **see anything** for longer than a split second. And by the time I focus on it, it's changing into something else. I passed out in the middle of the street when I met her."

Josie's dark purple lips pursed tightly. "You don't think she's a witch or some kind of evil psychic, do you?"

"How should I know? Are there evil psychics?"

Josie scoffed. "There's evil everything."

Riley tried to sit up straighter. "There has to be an explanation. And hopefully a remedy. I don't want to spend the rest of my life with a case of psychic motion sickness."

"Maybe Gabe will know what the hell is wrong with you?" Josie offered.

Riley perked up. If anyone would understand, it was Gabe. Well, Gabe or her grandmother, but she was only crossing that bridge if absolutely necessary. "Is he still here?"

Josie shook her head. "Mrs. Penny took him to return Willicott's lobster to the neighbor's saltwater aquarium."

"Sentences you only hear within a hundred-foot radius of the Bogdanovich mansion."

"Hey," Nick said, appearing with a plate of peanut butter toast and a ginger ale. "Eat this."

His mood was impossible to gauge by normal human means, and Riley wasn't feeling up to another visit to drunken Cotton Candy World yet.

He was glaring at her. *Bad sign.*

But he'd cut her toast diagonally. *Good sign.*

"Thanks," she said as she took the plate from him.

"I'm still going to yell at you later," he said, stuffing the corner of a paper towel into the neck of her shirt like a bib.

Riley sighed and took a bite of toast. "Yeah, I figured."

"So I guess with Sesame back, we should start looking into these mysterious Hemsworths, right, boss?" Josie said hopefully.

"*I* can start looking into the bastards who took Beth."

"Sesame," Josie and Riley corrected him.

"Whatever," he said. "But my team is already occupied with their *primo* cases. So I'll have to handle this investigation on my own."

Josie's eyes narrowed to dangerous slits. "You spiteful, grudge-holding—"

"Finish that sentence, and I'll give you every case Penny suggests for the next month."

"You wouldn't."

"Oh, I would because I'm a spiteful, grudge-holding Neanderthal."

"That's a lot nicer than what I was actually going to say," Josie shot back.

"Message received. Now go away, Jos," Nick ordered.

"I don't have to take this abuse. I'm going to go find my husband," she announced. She threw double middle fingers over her shoulders and stormed out of the room on her tiny elfin feet.

"That wasn't very nice," Riley observed. She took a gulp of ginger ale.

"She's not a very nice person," Nick agreed.

"I meant *you*."

"I'm the boss," he insisted. "When the team falls out of line, it's up to me to kick their asses back into line."

"Yeah, but what if they weren't really *that* out of line?"

He leveled her with a look. "Et tu, Thorn-ay?"

She started to roll her eyes, then decided against it. "Come on. Even you aren't that stubborn."

"Try me," he challenged.

"I don't think I'm feeling good enough to spar with you," she decided.

"Bottom line is I was right. I looked for Beth, and I found her." He snagged a piece of her toast and bit off the corner.

"You looked for Beth, and *I* found her," Riley argued.

She'd had a rough day. Not only was she feeling like she'd spent an entire day on a vomit comet, but she also couldn't tell how her boyfriend felt about the unexpected return of the woman he'd spent years searching for. Now everything felt off-kilter.

Nick shrugged. "The way I see it is it doesn't really matter.

I set out to accomplish something. It's been accomplished. The business didn't go under. Everyone's concerns were unfounded. I was right. Everyone else was wrong. Now everyone else has to suffer the consequences."

She didn't care for his logic or how he lumped her in with the rest of the team.

"That is *not* a helpful approach to leadership." It was like she was trying to teach a throw pillow how to make hollandaise.

"Look, Thorn. Santiago Investigations is no democracy. Get used to it."

"But why are you punishing *me*? I didn't lead any insurrection. I never said a word about how much time you were spending on the case."

He clapped a hand on her knee. "You didn't lead it, but you didn't put a stop to it or give me a heads-up. We're supposed to have each other's backs."

"Even when one of us is being a stubborn jerk?" she shot back.

He tweaked her nose. "At least you're being a cute stubborn jerk."

She was going to smash peanut butter toast in his stubborn jerk face if one of them didn't change the subject in a hurry. She took a cleansing breath. Then another one.

"Are you gonna hurl?" he asked with concern.

"No," she said primly. "I was going to ask you how you feel about Beth…er…Sesame coming back."

Was he happy?

Did he know Sesame was lying?

Was he too blinded by happiness to realize she was lying?

Was he coming to the realization that he'd always been in love with Beth and that he couldn't continue this farce of a relationship with her, but he didn't know how to politely ask Riley to move out?

"Good," he said with a brisk nod.

"Good?" she repeated. Good? That was all the man had to say about Beth's reappearance after years of grief and worry?

"Yeah. Good," he said.

"Great," Riley said, her tone uncharacteristically snippy.

"Now all I have to do is track down the assholes who took her, ruin their lives, and make sure they never come near her again."

"Awesome. Hey, unrelated. Have you ever seen the movie *Overboard*?" she asked.

"No. Why?"

"No reason."

12

R iley was mid-snore when a polite throat clearing woke her. She jolted awake and found Gabe looking down at her. "Where am I? Where is everyone? Where is Bethame? I mean Sesame."

Laughter erupted from somewhere in the house.

"The others are dining on pizza in the room of no purpose." The room of no purpose was the sunroom between the dining room and the kitchen at the back of the house. It had a weird layout and no real furniture yet because Riley couldn't figure out what the space was for.

She felt better, she realized. Still tired. Still a little woozy but steadier—like the day after the stomach flu. She yawned. "Why not the dining room?"

"The chandelier fell from the ceiling and broke on the table," Gabe explained. "Nick's small scary cousin-in-law Josie informed me that you wished to see me."

Riley sat up and noticed that Gabe's hands and forearms were covered in taco-themed bandages. "What happened to you?"

"I was injured repeatedly by a crustacean."

"Wow. Save a guy with the Heimlich and suffer a lobster attack in the same day."

"I will be sharing many colorful experiences in my diary tonight."

A loud snore erupted nearby. Riley looked around and found Burt on a pile of throw pillows that the dog must have pulled off the couch and stacked at her feet.

"Burty boy, you had a rough day too, didn't you?"

Burt lifted his head off a tufted tangerine cushion, looking adorably dazed with his tongue poking out the side of his mouth.

"Sometimes it's really creepy how he seems to understand exactly what we're saying," she observed.

"I concur. Did you wish to discuss Burt's linguistic comprehension with me?" Gabe asked, looking as if he'd enjoy nothing more than philosophizing about just how much English the dog understood.

"Actually, it's a psychic thing. Let's walk and talk if I'm capable of it," she said.

Burt wasn't about to let them leave without him after hearing the word *walk*, so they got his leash, and together they slipped out the front door and headed south on Front Street. The afternoon was warm, but the trees along the river were a showy riot of reds and golds. The fresh air made her feel even better as nature recharged her batteries.

Riley quickly explained her reaction to Sesame as they walked, stopping every few feet for the dog to sniff and pee.

Gabe frowned thoughtfully.

"What do you think? Did I somehow fry my powers?" she asked. For as long as she'd wanted to just be "normal," the idea of suddenly losing her psychic powers was disorienting.

"Rest is our most valuable resource. A well-rested psychic is a good psychic. Are you sleeping well?"

Riley hedged. "I've been sleeping okay." It wasn't exactly the truth. She hadn't been sleeping well since Nick had stopped coming to bed at night. "Maybe it's some kind of psychic defense?" she asked as Burt bit the head off a dandelion and spit it out onto the sidewalk.

"In order to have a psychic defense, one must be psychic," Gabe explained.

"So it's possible she has some kind of ability. But neither Nick or Kellen ever mentioned it, and you'd think it would have come up given their proximity to my…uh…gifts." She was still uncomfortable referring to her powers as gifts when they mostly served to get her in trouble.

"Not everyone who is gifted realizes they are gifted," her friend professed.

"Are you being all philosophical right now, or do you mean that literally?"

"Perhaps both…or neither."

Riley blew out a breath. "If psychic defenses exist, does that mean psychic attacks do too?"

He continued his slow, measured steps like a monk mindfully wandering his garden. "There are some who abuse their gifts for personal gain."

Two lady joggers hustled past them on the sidewalk.

"Hello, gorgeous hunka man bear. I'd like to jump on those shoulders and ride him into the sunset."

"Gah! Did that dog just fart, or did all the fish in the river die?"

Riley celebrated internally. Clearly her psychic faculties were coming back online.

"Okay. What's the best way to figure out if Sesame is some kind of psychic? Wait around and see if she starts picking winning lottery numbers and talking to dead people?" she asked.

"The best way to learn something about anyone is to spend time in their shoes."

"I don't suppose you mean that literally?" she asked. Sesame had great shoes.

"I am afraid not. I believe that for us to assess the reasons for your psychic flu, we must spend time with the trigger."

"Crap. I knew you were going to say that," Riley lamented.

"Of course you did. You are psychic," Gabe pointed out.

They stopped walking when Burt began to execute his pre-poop ritual, circling a spot on the grass in earnest. Riley hoped she'd brought a bag big enough to handle sesame chicken, burrito, and pork rinds.

"Fine. We'll spend time with Beth. I mean Sesame. What do I do if it happens again? I know the ol' close-the-spiritual-garage-door thing would probably help stop it, but I can't get a read on someone if my defenses are up."

Burt was circling faster now.

"After you rest and recover for a few days, I will teach you a new technique for defense. It is much the same as our practice this morning."

Riley bit her lip. Some rest and recovery sounded luxurious. But time was a luxury she couldn't afford. "I'm worried we might not have a few days. If Sesame is up to something, it's important that we know what it is sooner rather than later." She peeked at him out of the corner of her eye. "I promise I'll rest up after we find out what's going on."

Gabe nodded slowly. "If you are sure your powers are not depleted."

"They're not," she assured him quickly.

"That is good. Because if they *were* depleted and you insisted on pushing yourself, you could be spiritually injured."

"No spiritual-injury potential here," she insisted.

"Then I suppose there is no time like the present. And to ensure your success, I will join you in your reading of Sesame. We are stronger together."

Great. They could be stronger *and* dizzier together.

"You're a good friend, Gabe."

Burt stopped his frantic circling abruptly and squatted. Both humans politely turned their backs to give him privacy.

"Sooooo. How are things with you and Wander?" she asked, rolling to the balls of her feet as she stared out across the Susquehanna River.

Gabe had recently professed his affection for her sister by standing up to their grandmother and escorting Wander on an ice cream date. But to her knowledge, the couple hadn't gotten naked yet.

His smile went soft and dreamy. "Wander is a lotus blossom of great wisdom and beauty."

Riley wouldn't have been surprised if the big guy had hugged himself in joy.

"So…good then?" she guessed.

"Wonderful. She is wonderful. And I am wonderful when I am around her." Gabe heaved a sigh that she swore tickled the leaves on the shrub ten feet ahead of them.

Another jogger, this one in a hot-pink sports bra and matching leggings, approached.

"My, my. Look at the buns oh on dear lord! Is that soft serve coming out of that dog?"

On their way back home, Gabe chivalrously insisted on carrying both doody bags—because one definitely hadn't been enough—and walked Riley through a simple technique for warding off psychic attacks by both projecting a defense and producing an offense.

"I think I've got it. It's like putting up a screen over my open psychic garage door," she said as they followed the cracked walkway from the driveway to the front porch. The concrete would need to be repoured and the landscaping ripped out. At this point, she couldn't tell what was weeds and what was on purpose. It was all on the list.

"That sounds like an adequate analogy," Gabe agreed amicably.

The door burst open, revealing Mrs. Penny on the threshold, holding a piece of pizza in one hand. "Where'd that doody come from?" she demanded, pointing with the pizza.

"From Burt. Don't you remember feeding him an entire platter of Chinese food and then a burrito?" Riley said.

Mrs. Penny either couldn't hear her over the chewing or wasn't interested in what Riley was saying. "I better take it down to the lab and have it analyzed. This could be the break in the case I've been waiting for."

"This literally just came out of him five minutes ago," Riley argued as she let the dog in question off his leash.

"A good investigator never takes a suspect's word at face value."

"*I'm* a suspect?"

"Everyone's a suspect until proven innocent," Mrs. Penny said. "Hell, *I* could be the Dog Doody Bandit. I won't know for sure until I complete my investigation."

"I'm starting to worry about you," Riley confessed.

The elderly woman tossed the pizza crust over her shoulder and reached for the doody bags. "Gimme those."

Burt took a flying leap across the threshold after the crust.

Riley heaved a defeated sigh as Gabe handed over the bags.

"How do you even have access to a lab anyway?" Riley asked.

"That's need-to-know," Mrs. Penny said, slipping a gigantic pair of tinted wraparound shades over her glasses. "I'll let you know if you're the Dog Doody Bandit."

"Gee, thanks," Riley said as the woman left with her "evidence."

Inside, it sounded as if the pizza party reunion was still underway. They followed the laughter to the room of no purpose and found Weber, Nick, Brian, and Sesame sitting around the battered poker table Riley had brought up from the basement. Nick, though distracted by his search for Beth, had seemed briefly excited about it. At the time, Riley had thought it sweetly optimistic of him to assume he would have more than one friend to play poker with. His track record with male acquaintances trended toward combative.

Josie was in the opposite corner, stress eating a slice of pepperoni pizza and glaring at the happy crew.

Wilhelm the limo driver was doing standing lunges in the corner.

"That's not weird or anything," Riley observed.

"Do you remember the time I auditioned for *America's Next Pop Star?*" Sesame asked.

"You mean the first time Mom disowned you?" Weber teased. "You climbed out of your bedroom window while you were grounded and talked a high school senior into driving you to Manhattan."

"That was pretty ballsy of you to audition for a singing show when you sound like a cat in a washing machine when you sing 'Happy Birthday,'" Nick remarked.

Sesame tossed a cherry tomato from her kale salad at him. "Very funny, Nicky. It wasn't about being a talented singer. It was about being interesting enough to get discovered."

Weber rolled his eyes. "I forgot. You were born to be famous."

"You need to do something," Josie hissed as she approached them. "This chick just recounted the plot of *Dumb and Dumber* to explain how she got here from Arizona, and those idiots—including my idiot husband—ate it up like she was spoon-feeding them chocolate syrup."

Riley blew out a breath and rolled her shoulders. "Fine. Let's get this over with. Gabe?"

Her friend nodded stoically. "I am ready."

Riley took a seat at the poker table next to Nick. Gabe stood behind her.

"You look like you're feeling better," Nick observed.

She couldn't help but notice he didn't try to drag her into his lap or feel her forehead or kiss the hell out of her. The overly affectionate Nick who was glad she hadn't been kidnapped ceased to exist the second Sesame had walked into the house.

If her mother hadn't planted that seed of doubt that morning, Riley guessed she wouldn't be reading into his every move. But Blossom had planted the seed, and now Riley was analyzing Nick's every word and deed for confirmation.

It made her feel a whole different kind of crappy.

"I am feeling better. I think it was just a weird virus," she fibbed.

"Want some pizza?" Brian offered, pushing the greasy box in her direction.

She held up a hand. "I think I'll hold off on that for now," she decided. Riley turned to Sesame. "Sesame, this is my friend Gabe. I don't think you two officially met in the chaos."

"It's so nice to meet you, Gabe. What kind of workouts do you do?" Sesame asked. "Your muscle tone is phenomenal. I know personal trainers who would kill for those quads. Have you ever thought about modeling or acting? You'd be rich and famous in a heartbeat."

"I have not considered either."

· "So, uh, what other fun memories of Nick and Kellen do you have?" Riley asked, changing the subject.

"Only a million," Sesame chirped.

As she began to recount some story about Weber's rehearsal dinner and a garter snake, Riley slid carefully into her spirit guide world. The clouds were back to their normal pastel shades instead of the messy spin-art version she'd suffered through earlier that day. Maybe they weren't quite as puffy or bright, but they still passed for normal.

She sensed Gabe's presence join her and felt an instant calm wash over her.

"Okay. Here's the plan. I'm going to open up these garage doors, protect myself from the carousel of crazy, and you spirit guides are going to give me whatever you can on Bethame. Got it?" Spirit Riley said to her spirit guides.

The clouds pulsed a little brighter. A muted response, but it still counted.

"I'll take that as a yes. Let's do this thing."

"I too am ready to do this thing," Spirit Gabe said.

Please don't let me barf, she chanted to herself as she envisioned her spiritual garage doors slowly rising.

"Deploy the protective filter," Gabe's voice instructed gently.

With great effort, Riley imagined a colorful screen stretching across the opening. The individual strands glowed with a protective purple sheen.

"Just like a screen door," she said under her breath.

"What was that?" Sesame asked, looking at Real World Riley expectantly.

Oops. She'd said it out loud.

Nick was staring at her too, with an unreadable yet still sexy expression.

"Uhhh." Riley's mind went blank.

What rhymed with door that she could turn into a believable sentence?

Lure?

Swore?

Whore?

"She said she'd like a pour," Josie said, coming to her rescue.

"Uh, yes. That's exactly what I said." Riley reached for the two-liter bottle of soda and dumped some into one of the empty plastic cups next to the pizza. "So, Sesame, what was it like remembering your life before your amnesia?"

Sesame blinked rapidly. Her thick lashes looked as if they were capable of creating an actual breeze. "Well, it was overwhelming for one. I thought I was never going to remember, and then there I was, standing in a store, when it all came rushing back."

Riley's nose twitched, and the clouds in her head parted. She found herself standing next to a mannequin in an unnatural pose in an upscale department store. There was a man next to her with his back to Spirit World Riley. He had thick dark hair that curled at the ends and virtually no butt at all.

Sesame was admiring a suede minidress the color of violets. She turned to Mr. No Butt and held it up with a smile. A happy rush of warmth that didn't belong to Riley spilled through her. She peeked at the price tag and flinched. "Twenty-five hundred dollars? Seriously?"

"It is a very pretty dress," Spirit Gabe said.

Then suddenly the dress and the man were gone, and the luxury apparel was morphing.

"Oh crap. It's happening again." Riley felt sweat break out

on her forehead. Her nose twitched again as the department store melted out of existence and reappeared as the deli section of a grocery store.

Her stomach swooped, and her head started a violent spin.

Sesame was there. But instead of admiring a $2,500 minidress, she was pushing a cart full of nutritious snacks and staring at a pack of organic hot dogs.

Everything was blurry, and somehow gravity was pulling at Riley from the wrong direction.

"Strengthen your filter." Spirit Gabe sounded like he too was on the verge of vomiting.

She tried to shift her attention away from the dizzying spiral of her brain, but it was to no avail.

"Six years of amnesia, and it was the hot dogs that made me remember," Sesame said with a giggle.

"Dad always loved grilling hot dogs," Weber recalled.

"Help me out, spirit guides," Riley begged through clenched teeth as she fought to stay in the vision. She was sweating from the effort to push out a defense and pull in access to Sesame's thoughts. But the clouds in her head were whirling together like a tornado. The pinks and blues turned murky again, and she felt herself being spit out of the spirit world.

She came back into her body with a jarring thud. "Oh God. Dislike," she groaned. The room was spinning so fast she didn't even care that Nick, Brian, Weber, and Sesame were looking at her like she'd lost her mind. Wilhelm didn't seem to notice because he'd moved on to squats.

"Are you okay?" Sesame asked, looking concerned.

Riley tried to read something, anything from the woman. Sinister intent. Guilt for wrecking her brain. Triumph. But all she felt was genuine concern.

"Totally fine," she lied.

"I am feeling rather unwell," Gabe said.

Riley carefully turned her entire body to look at him in case her head was about to detach itself. Her friend lay prone on the floor while Burt licked his face.

"You and me both, buddy," she said.

"What the hell is wrong with you two?" Nick demanded.

Weber was looking at them with suspicion.

"It must be flu poisoning," Riley slurred.

"Did you mean the flu or food poisoning?" Sesame asked.

"Yes. I should go to bed so I can die," Riley croaked.

"I believe I will stay here for several hours," Gabe announced.

"On that note, I should probably get Beth…er…Sesame to my place so she can settle in before either one of us catches whatever the hell that is," Weber said.

"It was nice knowing you," Riley said as Weber and his sister left the room.

"I'll meet you guys out front and tag along," Nick said.

Great. He was already choosing Sesame over her. This sucked.

She heard Nick push his chair back from the table, then felt strong arms picking her up.

"I saw your nose twitching," Nick said as he headed for the doorway.

She closed her eyes and pressed her face into his chest. "Must be allergies."

"Allergies and flu poisoning. Not you trying to poke around in a traumatized woman's head?"

"I'm too dizzy to make up a plausible excuse. I just wanted to make sure she was telling the truth. I don't want you to get hurt."

"Leave Sesame alone, Thorn. I don't want you digging around in her brain without her permission."

"But she's lying," Riley said weakly. "I'm just trying to protect you."

Nick jostled her higher as he started up the stairs. "I repeat. Leave her alone. You worry about protecting yourself, and I'll handle her."

"What about Gabe?" she asked pitifully.

"I'll rent a forklift and dump him on the couch," he said,

kicking their bedroom door open. He deposited her onto the bed and leaned over her. "Now, you're going to stay in this house until I say it's okay for you to leave."

The entire room was spinning.

"You can't ground me. I'm a grown-up."

"We'll fight about this later."

Riley was too miserable to argue.

13

Constance Weber's house hadn't changed since Nick had last been there several years prior. Neither had the woman herself.

She answered the door of the white ranch house in a charcoal sweater set, sensible loafers, and a frown that showcased the lines on her face. Her silvery hair was scraped back in its customary bun. Nick liked to think her grumpy demeanor could be blamed on the number of hairpins stuck in her scalp.

By his calculations, Constance—never Connie—was in her early sixties. But she'd always seemed as though she was trying to pass for older. As if she felt it was her duty as a "good Christian," the highest compliment she was known to give to others, to view life on earth as purgatory.

She eschewed makeup, explaining that it was for "whores and liars." The only jewelry she wore was her plain gold wedding band and a cross on a chain. Her wardrobe was made up entirely of grays and beiges because she felt that black was too dramatic and colors were for women desperate for attention.

In other words, the woman was not exactly a bucket o' fun.

"Hello, Kellen," Constance said before fixing Nick with her piercing stare. "Nicholas."

"Mrs. Weber. You're looking lovely as always," he said.

She sniffed. "Only the cheapest of sinners put stock in their appearance."

"Mom, we've got some news," Weber said. "Can we come in?"

Her eyes narrowed and flicked back and forth between the men on her doorstep. "If it's the same kind of news as Gladys Walsh's grandson and his 'roommate' Darius shared, I'd rather you didn't."

Near as Nick could tell, the woman had spent her lifetime defining her own version of faith, which involved being as judgmental as possible toward everyone who wasn't exactly the same as her. She'd changed churches every time she felt the congregation or leadership became "too accepting" until she'd finally stopped going altogether.

Now she spent her Sundays attending a virtual megachurch that tolerated no one.

He was almost sorry Riley hadn't come along. Getting her take on Mommie Dearest would have been fun, though he supposed there were some heads no one should peek into.

Weber cleared his throat in annoyance. "Nick and I aren't dating, if that's what you're concerned about."

"He could do worse than me, don't you think?" Nick asked with his most charming grin.

Constance gave them another hard look as if trying to decide if they were worth opening the door for before relenting. "Fine. But I just washed the coffeepot, and I'm not making you a fresh batch."

"Always a pleasure, Connie," Nick said as he strolled across the threshold.

"Pleasure." She scoffed as if it were a dirty word.

Really, with a mother like Constance, it was a miracle Weber wasn't more fucked up. Not that Nick would tell his friend that. Weber would probably take it as a compliment.

They stepped into the small tile foyer that smelled like potpourri and arthritis cream. Next to the coat closet was a four-foot-tall velvet painting of the crucifixion. Even the lambs were frowning.

"Beth is alive," Weber said, cutting to the chase.

If it had been his own mother that he was breaking monumental news to, Nick would have gotten her liquored up beforehand. But Weber's relationship with Constance had always felt like less mother-son and more stranger-stranger.

There was a flicker of something in Constance's flat green eyes, but no hint of surprise registered on her face. Instead, the woman crossed her arms over her chest. "What makes you so sure?"

"Surprise!"

Constance looked past Nick and Weber to Sesame, who appeared on the front stoop with her arms stretched overhead like a game show host.

Constance's nostrils flared ever so slightly, and her lips pressed together even tighter until they disappeared completely.

"Elizabeth," she said finally. No one had ever accused the woman of being too affectionate. Or even just affectionate. Nick was fairly certain she had ice water running in her veins instead of blood.

"Actually, it's Sesame now," her long-lost daughter announced, waltzing into the foyer. "But don't worry, Mom. I figured you wouldn't be comfortable calling me that."

"I will most certainly *not* call you that. Your name is Elizabeth."

Undeterred by the lackluster welcome, Sesame grabbed her mother by the shoulders and pressed an exuberant kiss to her cheek. "It's good to see you too, Mom. I missed you!"

Constance sniffed. "I suppose you think you'll be staying here without considering what an inconvenience unexpected guests are to their hosts."

"Hang on a second," Nick said.

Weber elbowed him, then grunted when the elbowing hurt him more than it did Nick. "You promised to stay out of this," Weber wheezed.

Nick had promised just such a thing. But his curiosity and his appreciation for button pushing voided that agreement.

"I just want to clarify something," Nick said. He turned back to Constance. "Your daughter has been missing for six years. You were so sure she was dead you put an empty urn in a cemetery crypt. Yet the first thing you say to her when you find out she's alive and well is what an inconvenience it is to have her home?"

"Leave it alone, Santiago," Weber ordered through gritted teeth.

"That reminds me. You owe me money for your interment," Constance said to her daughter.

"I'm sure we could work something out," Sesame said, undeterred by the iceberg of all mothers. "And not to worry. I'm staying with Kellen. Wow! This place is like a time capsule," she said, approaching a small side table and picking up a framed family photo that was at least twenty years old. Beth was the only one smiling in it.

Constance took the frame from her daughter and put it back in its spot. "So you're home now."

"I am, and I can't wait to catch up with you."

"I'm sure there is very little of your life that I will approve of," Constance guessed.

"Mom, she was abducted and only just escaped," Weber said.

Constance fingered the cross at her neck. "I told you dressing like a Jezebel would cost you. It seems as though you've learned nothing since you left."

"Okay, you know what, lady?" Nick began.

But Weber stepped in front of him and slapped a hand to his chest. "Don't."

Nick knew all he had to do was tickle his friend in the ribs and he could get around him to give Constance the Cactus a piece of his mind. But it wasn't worth it.

"Always a treat to see you, Connie. Let me know if you need any help zipping up your Satan suit for trick or treat."

"Get out of my house," Constance said, pointing toward the door.

He grinned. "My pleasure."

Back on the sidewalk, he pulled out his phone.

Nick: Remind me to introduce you to Weber's mom someday. She's a peach.

Riley: Really?

Nick: No! She's a horrible person. It's a miracle her kids didn't turn into mass murderers.

Riley: There's still time.

Nick: How are you and the Not-So-Woolly Mammoth feeling?

Riley: Less like death. More like garbage.

He started to ask if she wanted him to pick up dinner, but Weber and Sesame exited the house and joined him on the sidewalk.

"Well, *that* was warm and fuzzy," Nick said. "I can see where Weber gets the stick up his ass, but I can't figure out how you turned out the way you turned out."

Sesame gave a hair toss. "She can't help being her any more than I can help being me. I just learned the easiest ways to get around her."

It was true. The Beth he'd known had been a gifted liar, deploying her skills to stretch and change the truth for her own benefit. She was charmingly manipulative. He'd often thought that she would have made a good undercover cop.

Weber's phone rang, and he answered it with a brisk "Weber."

"That's his work voice," Sesame whispered, eyes twinkling.

"How can you tell?" Nick asked as they stood shoulder to shoulder.

"His voice dropped half an octave, and that line between his eyes got deeper," she said, pointing at her brother's face. "Remind me to recommend a plastic surgeon. A little Botox would smooth that tell right out."

Beth, on the other hand, didn't have any tells. She could lie straight to your face, and you'd never know it. She'd always had a gift for rewriting reality to suit her.

"Very observant. How come you never became a cop?" Nick asked.

She laughed. "Have you ever met a rich cop?"

"Only the crooked ones."

"Exactly. Besides, I prefer to have more fun making money."

"You must be doing okay if you could escape in a limo," he observed.

"Turns out I have a head for business. With my help, I took my in-laws' outdated storefront and turned it into a thriving multistate enterprise," Sesame said proudly.

"So you're rich?"

"Not rich enough," she said.

"Why didn't your mom ask you where you've been?" Nick asked.

"She didn't?" Sesame asked, her blue eyes wide and innocent.

"No. She didn't. Seems a little cold even for her," he mused.

She gave a perky shrug. "Who can tell with my mother? She was probably in shock. People react to unexpected news in all kinds of ways."

Weber ended his call and rejoined them. "I need to go into the station to take care of a few things. Why don't you come with me, and you can make your statement, Sesame?"

"Statement?" she repeated.

"Your case is still open. Once you give your statement, we can revive the investigation."

She was wringing her hands now. "I—I was really hoping we could keep this just between us for a little bit."

"Beth…I mean, Sesame, you're never going to be able to put this behind you while that family is still out there. What if they do this to someone else?" Weber said gently.

Nick wouldn't be able to put it behind him either.

"I'm just not ready to make a statement," she said, her eyes going glassy with unshed tears. "It's too traumatizing."

"Are you in danger?" Weber pressed.

Sesame stomped her foot. "Of course not!"

"How can you know for sure?" Nick asked her.

"I–I just do. I can't talk about it right now. It's too overwhelming."

"Look, Weber. It's already been six years. What's a few more days?" Nick argued.

"I'm a cop. We don't just sit back and let criminals get away with things like abduction. The trail gets colder every day. You know this."

"I also know that treating your sister like a witness is callous even for a Weber."

Weber turned back to his sister. "They kept you for six years and let your family think you were dead."

"I know. But it's just so...so upsetting." Her lower lip quivered courageously. "I just don't think I'm ready to talk about it, and it's not like there's anything you can do about it since they left the country." On that, she buried her face in her hands and let out a wail.

"Nice going," Nick said, slapping Weber in the gut.

The man doubled over on a pained breath. "I hate you," Weber wheezed.

Nick gestured toward the audibly sobbing Sesame. "If you stop being a dick, I'll stop hitting you in the broken ribs."

Weber glared at him, then relented. "Fine. Sesame? I'm sorry for pushing you. I just need to know that you're safe, and the way I can do that is by doing my job."

"They're not criminal masterminds, Kelly. It's not like they're going to fly back into the country and bonk me on the head to make me forget again."

Weber looked like he'd just been asked to sell his soul to the devil...or his mother. "Fine," he said, shoving a hand through his hair and making it stand up on end. "But you have to tell me what happened sooner rather than later."

She nodded. "I will. I promise. When I'm ready."

"Should someone go back in there and tell the dragon lady

not to tell anyone that her long-lost daughter is back from the dead?" Nick asked, hooking his thumb at the Weber house.

Sesame shook her head. "She won't tell anyone."

———

Nick was headed home with takeout, turning things over in his head, trying to fit puzzle pieces together, when his phone rang.

"What's up, Jos?"

"Clowns."

"What about them?"

"Old lady Esther's treasured figurines are all clowns," she snarled.

"I don't see a problem."

"I *hate* clowns. I hate clowns more than I hate old people. I saw Stephen King's *It* at a sleepover in second grade and never recovered. Now you want me to save an old lady's hideous clown collection from her stupid grandson's eBay account?"

"You said you wanted to work," Nick reminded her smugly. "We all have to pay the consequences for our choices."

"I'll make you pay for yours, Nicky Santiago."

"I doubt that."

He disconnected the call and pulled into his driveway. But instead of getting out, he thought about his own choices and the consequences they could bring.

Reluctantly, he opened his text messages.

Nick: If a stranger with neck tattoos and a shaved head shows up at your office in a couple of weeks, don't talk to him. Call me. Then call the cops. Same goes for Dad.

Mom: Now what have you done?

Nick: Why do you always think I did something?

Mom: Because you always do something.

14

Sesame waved as she strutted out of her brother's condo building in skintight leggings the color of rhubarb and a matching sweatshirt that looked like it was made out of a real sheep. Her blond hair was pulled back in a high ponytail.

"I feel underdressed," Blossom said from the rear bench seat.

Riley did too. She also felt exhausted, achy, and still a little bit woozy. But she sensed there was some kind of ticking clock on the whole Sesame situation, and she didn't have time to waste on recuperating.

"Okay, everyone. Remember the plan," she said to the rest of the occupants of Wander's hybrid minivan.

"We are taking Sesame to yoga and not telling Nick," Gabe recited from the passenger seat.

Riley was relieved that Gabe was going along with the plan. He'd warned her that she was cruising close to psychic burnout and that if she pushed herself too hard, she could do serious damage. Of course he'd said it in Gabe-ier language, so it had sounded more philosophical.

But she'd been tired and run-down before, and that hadn't stopped her from solving a murder and saving lives. She could afford to tough this out too. And as long as Nick didn't find out she'd snuck out of the house shortly after he had gone on "errands," she figured there would be no harm.

"Good," Riley said. "Wander?"

Behind the wheel, Wander rivaled Sesame in the style department. She wore a pair of turquoise yoga pants and a matching crop top that made it impossible to believe that the woman had birthed three children. "I'm doing an extra-long meditation at the end of class to help open up her defenses," she said.

Riley nodded her approval. "And that's when we'll try to sync up our powers and break through."

Blossom raised her hand from the rear bench seat.

"Yes, Mom?"

"I just want to state for the record that I am against psychic bullying. I can't morally support that."

Riley groaned. "Mom, are you suggesting that I'm trying to get rid of the competition by assaulting her psyche?"

"No, of course not, sweetie. I'm only saying sometimes Basil women get a little nuts when we think someone is after our life partners."

"It's true," Riley's dad, Roger, said, leaning forward next to Blossom. "One time, your mother thought I was dirty dancing with her second cousin Karen, and she threw an entire cheesecake at me."

"Turns out your father was giving her the Heimlich after she choked on a tofu ball. Boy, did I feel silly," Blossom said.

"Gabe gave Detective Weber the Heimlich yesterday," Riley said.

"You did?" Wander asked, sounding impressed.

"It was nothing," Gabe said humbly.

"It was very heroic," Riley insisted.

"We would never use our powers for ill intent," Gabe assured Blossom.

"I'm just saying, just because you can't read her mind doesn't mean she's up to no good."

"Look, she's not being truthful about what happened to her. Which means she could still be in danger," Riley pointed out. "Anything we can learn about where she's been could be helpful in keeping her safe. And I can't learn anything if I end up violently carsick every time I try to get a read on her."

"All right. All right," Blossom relented. "But if this poor girl develops a mini stroke or a rash all over her face during class, you are grounded, Riley Thorn."

"What is with everyone grounding me?" she muttered just before Sesame climbed into the minivan and took the empty seat next to her.

"Thank you so much for inviting me to yoga," she said perkily. "It's been ages since I've unrolled my mat."

"No problem," Riley said. She made the introductions to the rest of the vehicle occupants.

"What kind of yoga have you practiced?" Wander asked Sesame as she steered them in the direction of the studio.

"My favorite is hot yoga. I just love working up a good sweat."

"Is it true what they say about Arizona being a dry heat?" Riley asked.

"It's totally true. When I first got there, I was like, 'This is way more comfortable than Pennsylvania's humidity.'"

Sesame prattled on about the effects of dry heat on hair volume as Riley met her mother's gaze in the mirror.

See, I told you, she telegraphed smugly with her eyebrows. *She admits to knowing she'd left Pennsylvania.*

Blossom rolled her eyes. *Yeah, yeah. Fine. But still no face rashes.*

Wander's yoga studio was located on the second floor of a two-story brick building on Twenty-First Street in Camp Hill. Beneath it was an antique store that did a brisk business moving musty treasures from the past.

Wander pulled the minivan into the last spot at the back of the lot along the alley, and they all piled out of the vehicle.

Riley spotted her best friend, Jasmine, climbing out of her

snazzy Lexus SUV. Jasmine Patel was the kind of beautiful that made men—and some women—lose their train of thought midsentence. She made a mental note not to unroll her mat between Jasmine and Sesame.

"Wow. The Thorns are traveling in a pack now?" Jasmine called, glancing up from her phone.

"Just doing our part for the environment," Blossom insisted.

"What are you doing?" Riley asked as her friend fell into step with her.

"Trying to decide if I should order creepy lifelike spiders or fake snakes for overnight delivery," Jasmine said.

"Breakup gone bad?" Riley asked. A successful elder law attorney, Jasmine had shockingly bad taste in men. If she wasn't falling head over heels for an inappropriate date, she was seeking revenge on one.

"Yep. Now Greg has to pay the price for not telling me he was engaged."

"Why not order both? Then you'll have something ready for next time," Riley suggested.

"Good thinking. Add to cart. So who's the new girl?" Jasmine asked.

"For the purpose of today, she's my new friend Sesame."

"Got it. Give me the dirt after class?"

"Definitely."

They made their way toward the side door of the building. Riley was holding the door for her entourage when she spotted a lone man with dark curly hair admiring the display of raffia fans in front of the antique shop. Between his sunglasses and the fan, most of his face was hidden from her.

She sensed something. A vague feeling of…what?

Longing?

Frustration?

Sadness?

Riley tried to dial in her focus to get a clearer read, but it sputtered, then died, and the man disappeared around the front of the building.

"You coming, Rye Bread?" Roger asked.

Riley snapped out of her trance. "Uh. Yeah, Dad. Let's go."

"Hey, that pink girl starts making you wanna barf again, you let me know. I'll take care of it."

She grinned at her father. "How are you going to take care of her?"

"I'll just do what I did when you got carsick as a kid."

"Roll down all the windows, chant 'Don't puke,' and then buy me a ginger ale?" Riley asked.

"Yeah, but this time when I open the window, I'll toss her out of it."

"Thanks, Dad. Let's hope hurling a woman out of a second-story window isn't necessary."

"But if it *is*, you just say, 'Window,' and I'll make it happen," Roger promised.

They trooped up the stairs and entered the studio.

"Crap," Riley whispered under her breath. Marie Santiago was limbering up in the front row in head-to-toe Lululemon.

"What's wrong?" Sesame asked, appearing at Riley's side.

"Nick's mom," she said, nodding at Marie, who was giving Gabe the *come-hither* look and patting the empty spot next to her.

"Oh my God, is she still super snobby and judgmental but also classy, which makes you want to not care what she thinks while still wanting her to approve of you?" Sesame asked.

Riley looked at the woman in head-to-toe pink. Her eyes were lavender today. "Yes. That's *exactly* it. But she's never going to approve of me. I didn't make a very good first impression."

"How bad could it have been?"

"She thought I was a homeless person."

"Why would she have thought that?" Then those lavender eyes traveled over Riley from head to bare feet. "Never mind. I'm sure she'll come around."

Riley glanced down at her outfit.

Her black leggings had a hole in one knee from Burt discovering a taco sauce stain and eating through the material.

And groggy from yesterday's bout with her mysterious malady, she'd grabbed the first clean shirt she could find, not realizing until it was too late that it was Nick's, not hers.

"How would you feel about going shopping after class?" Sesame asked.

Riley decided to not be insulted by the well-meaning offer since it would give her more time with her quarry. "I'd love to," she said.

The woman let out a high-pitched squeal and clasped her hands under her chin. "Shopping is my favorite!"

"I had a feeling."

"Welcome, everyone. If you'll all find your places, we'll begin," Wander announced, sinking gracefully into a seated position on her organic vegan yoga mat that had been handwoven by artisans in Costa Rica.

Riley unrolled her mat between her father and Sesame. Jasmine was in the row ahead of her, sandwiched between two hot shirtless guys who were already vying for her attention. Gabe glanced over his shoulder from the front row and nodded at Riley. She gave him a nervous thumbs-up. Someone tapped her on the shoulder, and Riley found her elderly neighbor Fred behind her. He was wearing a new toupee that stood up in the middle like a faux-hawk.

"Is it my new prescription, or does everyone keep getting better looking in this class?" he whispered.

"I guess Wander attracts beauty," Riley whispered back. "I like your hair."

He patted it like a cat. "Thanks. It's from the David Beckham collection. I also ordered the goatee, but it's on backorder."

Marie delivered a sharp "Shhh!" and a hard stare from the front row.

"Sorry," Riley muttered back.

"Let's begin," Wander said as the sound of chanting monks filled the room.

15

S esame's yoga flow appeared to be unhindered by her large
breasts. She flowed through sun salutations with ease, never
wobbled once in tree pose, and somehow even managed to
equally distribute the weight of her impressive rack to balance
on her hands in crow pose.

Riley noticed this a second before she tipped too far forward
and nearly smashed her nose into the floor.

"Good try," Sesame whispered encouragingly.

"Don't give up, sweetie," Blossom called from the other
side of Roger. They were both in a modified crow pose that
didn't endanger their noses.

A drop of sweat dripped off Riley's chin and hit the mat.
Wander's yoga classes were never exactly a walk in the park, but
with Sesame to her right, judgmental Marie in the front row,
and not nearly enough sleep after a bout of psychic vertigo, she
felt ready to collapse on the floor.

Sesame suddenly contracted her freakishly strong core and
shot her legs backward, landing lightly in a high plank. The
back row offered up scattered applause.

Damn it.

Desperately, Riley gave a little hop, tipping forward until

her weight was entirely on her hands and her toes came off the ground. It was an ugly, deformed crow, the kind of bird that, if you saw it in nature, you'd assume it had recently flown into a plate-glass window, but it still counted.

"Great work, everyone. Let's work our way down to the floor," Wander called from where she was adjusting Marie's respectable-looking crow.

She shot Riley a nod.

They moved through the final poses of class before finally flopping onto their backs into corpse pose. Well, Riley flopped. Everyone else activated their abs and rolled down with control. She would master that next time, she decided.

"You got this, Rye Bread," her dad whispered next to her.

She gave his hand a squeeze and took a shaky breath. She did got this...er, have this. Probably. She wasn't *that* distracted by Nick's distance or exhausted from yet another night of poor sleep. She was fine. Totally, almost one hundred percent fine.

"Allow your eyes to drift closed," Wander said softly.

Riley followed the rest of the class and shut her eyes.

"Now imagine your heart chakra opening, shining an emerald green like a beacon," she told the rest of the class.

Riley ignored the prompts and instead sat up and dropped into her spirit guide world.

The cotton candy clouds were there. They definitely didn't seem nearly as bright or as puffy, but she didn't have time to worry about what that meant.

"Now move your attention to your third-eye chakra. Visualize it opening and glowing a deep purple," Wander said from far away. "You are safe here. It's okay to open yourself up."

Riley took a breath and blew it out. "Okay, spirit guides. We're going to give this another try with backup. Show me what you can about Sesame without making me feel like my head is on a revolving microwave plate."

Instead of a swoopy full-color vision like they usually delivered, Riley felt something.

Loneliness.

It nudged at her gently but insistently, like Burt did when he wanted a treat.

Was Sesame sad? On the surface, she seemed so happy and bubbly. Where were her visions? Why couldn't she see anything?

A warm steadiness stole over Riley, and she realized Gabe and her family were with her.

There were shadowy flickers coming through now. Nothing Riley could make out clearly. But there was a man, a kiss, a dazzling swoop of love. Memories, perhaps? Or was this something Sesame wanted and didn't have?

Another feeling elbowed its way in. It felt...solidifying. Harder, sharper than hope. Determination.

Sesame was sad and willing it away with some sense of purpose.

Wow. Was this what motivation felt like? Riley had only experienced a focus and a drive this intense when her life or someone else's was at stake.

Was this how other people got things done, like training for marathons or keeping noses to the grindstone through medical school?

The determination had completely eclipsed the loneliness now. Whatever Sesame's purpose was, it was more important to her than wallowing in sadness. And Riley could see why. The sadness had no energy to it. It was pasty and lethargic. But this determination felt like a rainbow infused with a triple shot of espresso.

Through the shadows, she began to catch more glimpses. Red velvet. Flashes of light. A floor-length gown. A man's hand on a woman's waist. Success. The kind that other people saw.

"Remember where you came from," Wander instructed the class. "Think about what brought you here."

Everything was rewinding into a blur of color and sensation. Riley's head started to spin slowly like a merry-go-round warming up. Immediately, she felt a reinforcement of energy coming at her from her mother, sister, and Gabe.

Then out of the shadows, she saw him.

A man, practically a boy. Cute. He was in a car, and someone was running toward him. Riley felt a giddy rush of joy. And a trickle of sweat. The sweat was definitely hers. But the joy belonged to someone else. Then it was gone like someone had snapped a finger. The man-boy was replaced with what looked like a sinister evil twin. He had a comical goatee and villain-like eyebrows. There was someone in his arms. Someone he was dragging backward. Someone who struggled against him.

Riley's heart thundered in her chest, and the world spun faster and faster.

"Oh no. Here we go again," she groaned.

"Hold on, sweetie," Spirit Blossom called to her.

"Strengthen your screen door," Spirit Gabe encouraged from somewhere beyond the clouds.

Riley gripped the mat under her body with her fingers until they ached, and focused on reinforcing the psychic netting around her. It took everything she had, and it still wasn't enough.

Something popped. It was one of the clouds. Then another and another. They were disappearing like balloons stuck with a pin, one after another. It was dark and cold without the glow of the clouds. It was a void.

She felt panic and recognized it as her own.

"Slowly coming back into your body." Wander's voice floated to Riley on an empty echo. The dizzying shadows slipped away. Her empty spirit world tilted suddenly, and Riley dropped back into her body and opened her eyes.

Gabe, her mother, and Wander were all watching her as the rest of the class stretched and smiled their post-yoga smiles at each other.

"Do I need to throw anyone out a window?" Roger asked in a loud whisper.

She shook her head. "I think we're good, Dad."

She felt shaky and out of sorts. Not really dizzy but somehow floaty, as if she'd lost her tether. Looking around the studio, she realized something was wrong. Very wrong. She couldn't hear anyone's thoughts. Not even a whisper of them.

"Is that going to be a problem?" her mother asked.

"What?" Had her psychic cohorts witnessed the big bang ending to Cotton Candy World?

"That." Blossom pointed to the front row where Sesame and Nick's mother were in conversation.

"Crap."

Riley tried to get to her feet and jump over a yoga mat, but her knees buckled, and she fell into one of the shirtless guys.

"Sorry," she apologized and stumbled her way to the front of the room.

"There you are," Sesame said, beaming at her. "I was just telling Mrs. Santiago—"

"*Dr.* Santiago," Marie interjected imperiously.

"Anyway, as I was saying. I was *so* disappointed Riley swept your son off his feet before I could put my accidental pregnancy plan into play."

Riley blinked rapidly. "Uhhh."

Sesame heaved a dramatic sigh. "I really thought I'd be Mrs. Nick Santiago. Can you imagine me at your dining room table every holiday, Mrs. Santiago? Well, I guess you would have had to come to our place since it was before my house arrest ankle bracelet came off."

"Who is this woman?" Marie demanded, looking at Riley.

"This is Sesame."

"Nick's ex-girlfriend," Sesame supplied and wrapped an arm around Riley's shoulders. "Don't even get me started on how long I stalked this one after I realized she and Nick were together after he broke up with me. I couldn't decide if I should stage an elaborate ruse that made it look like Nick was cheating on her or if I should just save a bunch of time and run her down with a car. But Riley turned out to be such a bighearted, smart, charming, loyal woman, I decided to make her my friend instead and find someone else to trap into marriage."

Marie looked at Sesame as if she were a piece of gum that dared stick to the bottom of her shoe.

"Oooh!" Sesame squealed. "I'm going to see if I can steal

sweaty hot guy's wallet so I can see if he's rich. If he is, I'll meet-cute him in the parking lot. Lovely meeting you, Mrs. Santiago."

"That's Doctor—oh, screw it. Is that ridiculous story true?" a shell-shocked Marie asked as Sesame flitted across the studio.

Riley shrugged. "As true as anything else she says."

Marie shivered. "Well then. Have a…nice day."

Mouth open, Riley watched Nick's mother leave the studio.

Sesame waited until she was gone, then danced back over to Riley.

"What was that?" Riley demanded.

"That was a glimpse at what could have happened if Riley Thorn hadn't snagged her son's heart," Sesame said with a shoulder shimmy.

"She told me to have a *nice* day without even choking *or* rolling her eyes," Riley said. "That's the nicest thing she's ever said to me. You're a diabolical genius."

Sesame tossed her long ponytail over her shoulder. "I'm very gifted in knowing my audience. Anyway, I called Wilhelm to pick us up. The limo has amazing trunk space for shopping."

Riley blinked. "Sounds…er…good." She spotted her mother and Wander waving at her from outside the restroom door. "I just have to…uh…go to the bathroom with my entire family. We're very close."

"That must be nice," Sesame said indulgently.

———

Riley slipped into the restroom and found it occupied by nearly everyone in the class. It was a small room with one stall, a sink mounted to the wall, and a trash can. Blossom was perched on the sink while Roger straddled the trash can. Gabe was sitting on the toilet lid with Wander at his side. Fred, who didn't like to be left out, was standing on the toilet tank.

"Well, this isn't suspicious at all," Jasmine observed from the diaper changing station as Riley flipped the lock.

"Okay, here's the abridged version for Jas," Riley began.

"Sesame is Beth Weber, who went missing six years ago after witnessing a warehouse firebombing. The case went cold. She was presumed dead until she showed up yesterday claiming she's had amnesia this whole time, but I'm not buying it."

"Okaaaaaay," Jasmine said. "So why don't you just read her mind?"

"Every time she tries to, she gets all passy-outy," Blossom volunteered. "We came along for moral psychic support."

Riley hooked her thumb in her mother's direction. "What she said. We just tried to sneak past her defenses while everyone was relaxed in corpse pose."

"As one does," Jasmine said.

Nothing threw her friend. Riley knew she could call Jasmine in the middle of the night and tell her she'd accidentally murdered someone, and Jasmine would show up with shovels, a tarp, and an alibi.

"I think I got a look at the man who abducted Sesame," she told them.

The restroom erupted around her.

"This is why I always told you and your sister not to go anywhere near strangers with candy in vans," Blossom said.

"I kept smelling beef jerky and potato chips," Wander mused.

"It's hot in here. Imma open a window," Roger announced.

"Was he hot? What kind of car does he drive?"

"What are we doing in here?"

The last two were from Jasmine and Fred respectively.

Gabe remained silent, an uncharacteristic frown on his handsome face.

Riley raised her hands in the international symbol for *calm the hell down*. "Guys, relax. The point is it worked. I was able to get in with your help without passing out or vomiting, and no one had to be thrown out any windows."

"Huh?" Jasmine said.

Blossom elbowed Roger.

"Forget it," Riley said. "I'm going shopping with Sesame and seeing if some normal girl talk can tell me anything."

"Oh, I'm so in on this," Jasmine decided. "I can smell a lie over text. Besides, I need a new pair of shoes. I threw my favorite stilettos at an idiot last night."

"Your father and I are gonna get out of here. We have to go pick up some beet juice at the wellness center. If we don't pick it up today, it'll go rancid."

"Like you could taste the difference," Roger muttered.

"He's just grumpy because he feels like pink stools aren't manly," Blossom explained. "I'm proud of you for not giving Sesame facc boils even though you're threatened by her, sweetie."

"Gee, thanks, Mom."

"Oh! I'm making my special kombucha party punch for Nick's birthday party," Blossom said.

"Party?" Riley repeated.

"Gabe told us about the surprise party you're throwing Nick," Wander explained.

"Yes. I am very excited to attend my first surprise party," Gabe admitted.

"Right. Nick's surprise birthday party," Riley said, kicking herself for the throwaway fib that had come back to haunt her.

Jasmine put her hands on her hips. "You're throwing a Halloween surprise party and you didn't tell me?"

"Well—"

"I already got my costume picked out," her dad announced proudly as he helped her mom out of the sink.

"What's the theme?" Jasmine asked Riley.

"I haven't really gotten that far," she admitted.

"I'm going as a Scottish laird," Fred said from the toilet tank.

Everyone started discussing costumes as Riley's internal panic rose another notch.

Gabe approached. "Are you all right?"

It wasn't the time or place for a private conversation, so she looked him straight in the sternum and fibbed. "I'm fine. Just a little tired."

To be fair, she didn't know what had actually happened.

She just knew that she'd messed up. Big time. She felt exactly the way Diana Hendricks had looked in high school when she'd crumpled to the soccer field after the audible pop of her ACL tearing.

"I sensed something amiss. I felt your powers—"

"Hey! You know what?" Riley interrupted him with a pat on the muscly chest. "Why don't you and Wander grab some lunch? You guys were a huge help today, and you deserve a break. Maybe you could decide on a party theme for me?"

Gabe stood a little taller. "You would entrust me with this important duty?" he asked, forgetting all about the something amiss.

"I would trust you with anything," Riley said truthfully.

Wander's shy smile lit up the bathroom. "I'd love to have lunch with you. Have you been to the Vegetable Hunter yet, Gabe?"

"Nothing would give me more pleasure," the man mountain said to her sister. Gabe turned back to Riley. "Use caution, and please don't give away your phone to an elderly person."

"I promise," she said, giving his arm a squeeze. Well, it was more of a pinch since her fingers didn't quite span the top of his forearm. "Oh, wait! Before everyone disbands, remember the most important thing…"

"Don't tell Nick," they all said.

16

Y ou're out of your jurisdiction," Nick called out as he approached the man playing a one-sided game of chess on a cardboard box. His friend Perry was wearing a cast-off rugby sweater two sizes too big and a snazzy fedora with a feather in it.

Perry combed a hand over his white beard without looking up from the chessboard. "Nicky Santiago. Looking for your friend?"

Nick handed over the second coffee he was carrying and took the vacant seat across the board. "Now, how'd you know that?"

Perry was what the cool kids referred to as *housing challenged.* He spent his days acting as a one-man neighborhood watch for a three-block stretch of Third Street. At night, he slept in a dilapidated shack near the railroad tracks. He didn't so much rely on as enjoy the generosity of business owners and residents. He also knew everything that happened in the city. Given the number of times the community had attempted to get him into an apartment, Nick suspected Perry's nomadic lifestyle was mostly by choice.

"Just had a feeling. He's busy fishing a body out of a dumpster down there," Perry said, nodding toward the end of the block where the cops had cordoned off the street.

"Anybody we know?" Nick asked. That morning, he'd left Riley, who'd still looked pale and a little shaky, in bed with strict instructions not to move until he was back. Then he'd hit the gym, where he found a rotten banana in the gym bag he hadn't used since that summer. After a satisfying workout, he'd headed to his cousin's house to see if Brian had managed to dig up anything on the Hemsworth bastards.

And just like he'd suspected, the only Hemsworths of note Brian had found were of the Hollywood-movie variety.

Sesame was lying, and Nick wanted to know who she was protecting: herself, her brother, or her abductors.

Perry shrugged and moved one of the tall pointy pieces to a different square. Nick was not a chess aficionado.

"Nah. Just an idiot who smacked his head and fell into a dumpster."

"So not a homicide?"

"Not unless you can accidentally murder yourself."

"I'll let Weber know," Nick promised and got to his feet.

"Be careful out there," Perry cautioned.

"I always am."

His friend snorted. "You're rarely careful. But at least it hasn't caught up to you yet."

Perry wielded sarcasm with the deft touch of a master.

Sure, Nick had made a few rash decisions in his day. Including the time he'd let his temper get the better of him and confronted a murderer at a swanky shindig. The psychopath had retaliated by burning down Nick's office and apartment. But everything had worked out in the end. He'd moved in with Riley, gotten a new TV, and never had to file all the paperwork that burned up in the fire.

"As much as I love our vague philosophical discussions, I've got work to do." Nick said.

"You know what they say about men who spend all their time working and not enough time enjoying time with their pretty girlfriends," Perry mused, nudging one of the horse-head pieces into position.

"What do they say?"

"They're idiots."

It was Nick's turn to snort. "I'll see you around, Per."

"Thanks for the coffee, Nicky. If you're in the mood for a meatball sub next week, I wouldn't say no to half,"

Nick waved over his shoulder and headed in the direction of the emergency lights.

On scene, he ducked under the tape, nodded at a few of the uniforms, and walked right on up to the dumpster. It was a rusted-out contractor version shoved up against the side of the skeleton of a row home.

Every once in a while, an investor with more money than brains decided he was going to rehab a shit house on a shit block in the city. One out of ten succeeded. The rest either ran out of cash and patience or gave up when someone shot out their brand-new replacement windows or showed up dead in their dumpster.

He wrapped his knuckles on the metal. "Knock knock."

Weber's head popped out of the top. When he spotted Nick, his eyes narrowed. "You can't just walk onto the scene of an unattended death."

Only Detective Kellen Weber would choose to spend the morning after his sister rose from the dead knee-deep in trash and dead bodies.

"Funny. Thought that's what I just did."

The medical examiner's van rolled up to the curb, and Weber gingerly climbed out of the dumpster. While the man's pants and white button-down were still pristine, the set of his jaw told Nick that Weber was still in pain from yesterday's pork rind debacle.

"Wait here," Weber ordered, then shucked off the latex gloves on his way to talk to the ME.

Nick peered into the dumpster and spotted Sergeant Mabel Jones next to the body of a white guy in his midthirties with a large dent in his forehead. His FREE THE WEED shirt was stained with dried blood and other juices usually found in trash receptacles.

"Another day in paradise, Jonesy?"

She grinned up at him. Even knee-deep in garbage and corpses, Jones's black hair didn't dare escape the strict bun. "Nicky Santiago. What brings you to my dumpster?"

"Gotta talk to the boss," he said.

"Picked a good day for it. Haven't seen him in this good of a mood since the Men's Wearhouse had their two-for-one sale."

"That so?" he said neutrally.

Mabel held out a hand, and he hauled her up. She landed lightly and brushed construction dust and insulation off her uniform pants.

"Gimme," she said, reaching for his coffee.

He handed it over.

She took a hit of hot caffeine and studied his face. "You know something," she guessed.

"I know lots of somethings," Nick hedged.

Mabel was a smart cookie with good instincts, and she was terrifying in the interrogation room. Things he'd enjoyed during their brief, four-date relationship several years ago. Things that didn't serve him in this situation.

Until he got to the bottom of it, the less the rest of the world knew about Beth Weber's whereabouts, the better.

"You know why the boss is looking like he just doubled his tie wardrobe. What's up?"

He shrugged. "Maybe he finally got laid."

Mabel snorted and handed his coffee back.

"Sergeant Jones, I hope you're not sharing information with a civilian," Weber said, appearing behind her out of nowhere.

"Spooky," Mabel whispered.

"Like a vampire on his way to church," Nick agreed. He turned his attention to Weber. "Don't be a dick just because you got your ribs crushed by Black Hulk Hogan."

"I wouldn't have to be a dick if you'd stay out of my crime scenes. Besides, I can't have you puking all over another corpse."

"One time," Nick snapped. "I did that one time."

"Clearly nobody got laid last night," Mabel said to herself.

"For your interest in my private life, you can help the ME pull the body out of the dumpster, Sergeant," Weber told her.

"Looking forward to it, Detective," Mabel said with a fake smile before pulling on a fresh pair of gloves and heading back to the dumpster.

"What are you doing here, Nicky?" Weber asked.

"Brian's been digging through shit in Arizona and can't find any family named Hemsworth that fits the description."

"He better not be doing anything illegal."

"Let's skip your TED Talk on how important the justice system is while you refuse to acknowledge how broken it is and skip to the part where we both have a vested interest in finding these assholes."

Weber looked like he was chewing on his own teeth in an effort to swallow his lecture. "One person has all the answers we need," he said finally.

"Yeah, and how do you make a woman talk when she doesn't want to?"

"You lock her in interrogation and start chipping away at her story until she breaks."

"No wonder you're divorced."

"Fuck off, Nick. I'm busy. I've got a body to deal with. My ribs feel like they turned to chalk dust. And all I want to do is get answers out of my sister, but she's not talking."

"Accidental death. Dumb shit got high, cracked his head on that exposed rafter up there, and swan dived into a dumpster. Case closed."

"We have procedures for a reason," Weber said, absently rubbing his ribs.

It was an old argument between them. Nick had left the force in a fit of temper when the metaphorical headbutting had escalated into actual headbutting. "Look, let's focus on how we're going to get you-know-who to talk. It's not like we can just take her down to the station and throw her into a room with Jonesy."

Weber looked over his shoulder, then steered Nick to the sidewalk away from all the ears. "We need her statement sooner rather than later. But she says she's not ready."

"So how do we get her ready? At least ready enough to tell us what happened, even if it's off the record."

"She *cried* in my kitchen when I pushed for information."

"Did you hit her with a phone book? Threaten to put your mom in prison?"

"No! I asked nicely. And then she got all sniffly and started hiccupping and said it was too traumatic to deal with yet. So I felt like shit and stopped asking questions."

"Were there real tears?" Nick pushed.

"How the hell should I know? I was busy making her tea and giving her my bedroom because it has a bigger closet and a private bathroom."

"We need her to tell us enough that we can get a lead on these assholes," Nick insisted.

"And bring them to justice," Weber added pointedly.

"Or road-trip to Arizona, have a little chat with everyone, and then bury the bodies in the desert on the way home."

"You maybe wanna not plan a murder on an active crime scene within earshot of half the homicide squad?" Weber suggested.

"Are you really going to be satisfied with just putting the asshole responsible for Beth's disappearance behind bars?"

Weber slid on his aviators. "That's justice."

Nick rolled his eyes. "Your parents should have watched less *Columbo* and more *Punisher* when you were a kid."

"Vigilantism isn't justice. It's anarchy."

"You're telling me that there isn't the smallest part of you that wants to go beat this family into a coma?"

Weber ripped off his sunglasses. "What do you want from me, Nicky? You want me to tell you that for the last six years, I couldn't sleep because I didn't know where my sister was? Or that last night was the first night I couldn't sleep because I'm afraid that what she went through was worse than death? I want whoever's responsible to feel what I felt for the rest of his worthless fucking life."

Nick clapped him on the shoulder. "That's better. Doesn't it feel good to come play on the dark side? What do you say you quit this whole law-and-order thing, join Santiago Investigations, and we go vigilante on every asshole who slipped through the court system's fingers? They'll make a TV movie out of us."

Weber put his hands on his hips and studied the ground.

"Come on. It sounds kinda good, doesn't it?" Nick teased.

"You're such a pain in my ass," Weber complained.

Nick grinned. "Thorn says the same thing."

"You don't deserve her."

"No shit. I'd appreciate it if you didn't remind her."

"Is she feeling better?"

"She and Machu Picchu were down for the count last night. I forced her to stay home and rest today. She said it was just the flu."

"Good. So how do we make my sister talk?" Weber asked. "Neither one of us is exactly equipped to cajole answers out of a woman who doesn't want to give them."

"I've got an idea on that front. We need a woman to school us on open communication."

Weber snorted. "I'm guessing neither of our mothers are on that list."

The idea of Marie Santiago and Constance Weber offering anyone a safe space to be honest had both men laughing. At least until the gurney wheeled past them.

17

I totally get why you're attracted to the gray one, but this red screams *fierce*," Sesame said, shoving a red sweater at Riley and pushing her toward the dressing room.

"She's right, Riley," Jasmine agreed over the rim of her champagne glass.

Apparently when women arrived at a boutique store in a limo, champagne was an automatic part of the shopping experience.

Riley reluctantly closed the curtain and stared at the clothes they'd forced on her. She'd stayed under control in the athleisure store and bought a pair of unholey, slightly ugly high-end leggings from the sale rack for twenty-two dollars. While both Sesame and Jasmine seemed determined to make her open her wallet, she was distracted by all the thoughts swirling in her head, including the fact that she now had only a few days to pull together a surprise Halloween party for her boyfriend, who wasn't going to be speaking to her if he found out she'd not only left the house but decided to meddle with Sesame.

To top it off, she hadn't had a single stray thought from a stranger or shimmer of a vision since Cotton Candy World had disintegrated. For once, the only voice in her head was her own.

"Who put this corset in here? I just want to be comfortable," she complained over the top of the curtain. *And not go bankrupt.*

"And I just want you to show off your assets while being comfortable," Sesame insisted. "One does not have to be exclusive of the other. Your brand doesn't have to be First Thing I Found on the Floor."

"I like this girl," Jasmine called from somewhere in the store. "Is it the champagne talking, or are these distressed mom-jean shorts made for me?"

"Made. For. You," Sesame insisted. "Add a pair of tights, and you can wear them all fall too."

So far, they'd accomplished a lot of shopping and very little girl talking. Riley yanked the sweater over her head. "Where'd the rest of it go?" she demanded, looking in the mirror.

Behind her, the curtain whipped open, and Sesame and Jasmine peered over her shoulder at her reflection.

"It's a crop top," Sesame explained.

"A hot crop, Ry. Look at your boobs."

Her boobs did look decent framed in the square neckline. But there was no hem to tuck into jeans, no extra fabric in the back to hide her butt.

"The boobs are fine. But look at my butt."

"Oh, I am," Jasmine said. She made a growly noise and playfully swiped at Riley with invisible claws.

"You can *see* my butt."

"You say that like it's a bad thing," Sesame said.

"There's cellulite there. And it's bigger than it should be."

"Everyone has cellulite, and why are you letting someone else tell you your butt is too big?" Sesame demanded.

"Griffin used to leave liposuction brochures in my underwear drawer," Riley said.

Sesame frowned. "Who the hell is this Griffin, and how long would it take before someone noticed he was missing?"

"Griffin is her four-foot-tall man-baby ex-husband with a dick the size of a Q-tip," Jasmine said.

"Nick punched him in the face and threw him into a dumpster," Riley said as she tried to tug the hem over her belly button.

"That's the Nicky Santiago I know and love!" Sesame sang.

Riley sucked in a breath and accidentally choked on her own spit.

"Hold up," Jasmine said, putting her champagne down with a hard clink. "When you say you love my girl's guy, I'm going to need you to clarify that before I fill your bed with fake insects or reptiles."

Jasmine could change gears from friendship to stab-your-eyes-out-with-a-stiletto in a heartbeat.

"I want to be you when I grow up," Riley wheezed.

"At the risk of finding a lizard in my bed, I confess that I love Nicky," Sesame said. "I always have."

Riley's world was tilting again as she coughed. Only this time, it had nothing to do with psychic visions.

"As a brother," Sesame added.

Jasmine crossed her arms and stared hard at Sesame. "You're saying you never made out with him, 'accidentally' walked in on him in the shower when he slept over at your house, or got him drunk and had sex with him in the nurse's office after he lost the homecoming game?"

"Those are some very specific examples that we should probably talk about later. But no. I've always loved Nicky as a big brother. Beneath that stubborn I-know-everything exterior is a teddy bear of a guy who just wants to do right by everyone he loves. But…"

"But what?" Riley croaked.

Sesame picked up a denim jumpsuit and held it up to her chest. "But that stubborn exterior is about a mile thick. Nick and I could never have been together in that way. What entertains me about him would be exactly what would make me hate him in a relationship." Sesame gave a dramatic shiver.

"Sure, he's stubborn, but he's not that bad," Riley said defensively.

Sesame shook her head, and her heavy tumble of golden curls shimmered around her shoulders like someone had turned on a fan and a camera.

"Yes. He is," Sesame countered. "That's why you two are a perfect match. You are the only person I know in the whole world who could put up with 'I'm Nick Santiago and what I say goes,'" she growled.

It was an admittedly decent impression of the man in question. Jasmine applauded.

"But you also bring him balance," Sesame continued to Riley. "You challenge him, and that's probably one of the things he loves best about you. You're strong enough to live your own life, to disobey Nick law when necessary. You're not afraid to call him out on his own bullshit. You recognize that he's strong enough to take the criticism *and* that your relationship is healthy enough to handle the bumps."

"Well, I wouldn't go *that* far," Riley said, guiltily considering all the things she hadn't opened her mouth about recently.

"It works for you two. You get to forge a life together. One where you figure out what you both want and go from there. But I already know what I want. I was born knowing. I didn't need to be challenged by my partner. I needed a guy who had no problem automatically agreeing with me. It streamlines so many issues if he would just trust me and focus on my goals."

"I can't decide if that's just bravely narcissistic or actually smart," Jasmine mused.

Riley couldn't decide if it was suspicious or not that Sesame had switched into the past tense, as if she'd already found her partner.

Sesame returned the jumpsuit to its rack and picked up a lacy bra top. "I know what I want out of life. I'm not going to apologize for it or wait around on someone else to support me. I'm going to work for it. And someday, when it pays off, it'll all be worth it."

"So what do you want?" Riley asked.

"Simple. I want to be rich and famous and loved by everyone."

"Well, you're rolling in your own limo with your own driver. I'd say that's a good start," Jasmine observed.

"Speaking of, why is Wilhelm doing calisthenics in the corner?" Riley asked.

The limo driver—who definitely had not forgiven Riley for her accidental smoothie spray—was pumping his way through a set of push-ups next to a headless mannequin that looked like it was part of a football huddle.

"Oh, his physique is very important to him. It's one of my favorite things about him."

"How long have you known him?" Riley asked. Maybe Wilhelm held the key to the Sesame-Beth mystery.

"Four days. Isn't he just the best?"

Riley blinked. "You've known him less than a week, and you trust him? After everything you've been through?"

"When purposes are aligned, what's not to trust?" Sesame asked. "Wilhelm and I both understand that how we look on the outside is the first impression we make on the world. You're telling your audience who you are before you even open your mouth. So when you show up to yoga class with your boyfriend's mother in a gigantic T-shirt and holey leggings, what do you think you're saying?"

Riley winced. "Uh, that I'm low maintenance and need to do laundry?"

Sesame held up her hands. "If that's how you want to be defined by the world, then by all means, be proud of it."

"It's not that simple," Riley argued.

"Why isn't it that simple?" Jasmine asked. She held up her empty flute, and the stylish sales associate scampered into the back room.

Riley took another look at her reflection. "It's not that I don't care. It's that there are extenuating circumstances to looking good."

"Like what?" Sesame prodded.

"Like circumstances that a woman who travels in a limo and one whose leather briefcase cost more than my mortgage payment will never understand," Riley said.

"I think she might be talking about us," Sesame whispered.

Jasmine rolled her eyes. "You think? Seriously, Riley. Talk to us. What's this about?"

Riley flopped down into a wicker chair outside the dressing room. "I was broke. Okay? When Griffin and I got divorced, I had to pay him money for breaking his stupid nose. I lost my job, my home, my car. All because I bet on the wrong guy. So maybe buying a fifty-dollar sweater is nothing to an attorney with a hella-sweet condo and an entrepreneur with great shoes. But it's all still fresh to me."

"Oh, sweetie," Jasmine said, shaking her head. "You're an idiot."

Riley blinked. "Excuse me?"

In a show of impressive muscle, Jasmine spun her and the chair around so Riley was facing the mirror. "You forgot one thing."

"What's that?" Sesame asked, popping up over Riley's other shoulder.

"That you are Riley Fucking Thorn—sidebar: if that's your real middle name, I'm going to be so happy—and Riley Fucking Thorn takes care of herself. You did what you had to do to get yourself out of a bad marriage and start over. You supported yourself proofreading toilets and ate Cup O' Noodles like a plucky Little Orphan Annie, and you rose above."

"So inspiring," Sesame whispered.

"I proofed bathroom divider schematics, not toilets," Riley insisted.

"Whatever. My point is you are Riley Fucking Thorn, and you are never going back there again. You're smart, you're brave, you're hardworking, you're loyal, and that shirt makes your boobs and your ass look amazing. Start recognizing that you're a badass and treat yourself."

"And even if this psychic thing doesn't work out for you, you'll find something else," Sesame said.

"It's not really a gig," Riley said.

"Well, I'm sure it could be if you worked at it," Sesame said supportively.

"So what do you say, slugger?" Jasmine asked, throwing her arm around Riley's shoulders. "Are you ready to recognize that you're more than a broke, depressed divorcée who's afraid of how awesome she really is?"

"I hope she says yes," Sesame whispered.

Not seeing a way out of it, Riley pasted a smile on her face. "Yes." Whether they were aware of it or not, Jasmine and Sesame had just shined a light on a problem she'd yet to recognize. One she needed to deal with sooner rather than later.

"Good girl. Now bring it in," Jasmine said.

Sesame squealed. "Are we group hugging? I haven't group hugged in so long!"

Riley groaned as Jasmine yanked her in for a hug. "Fine. Get in here."

"Wilhelm! Take a picture of us!"

———

Riley let herself be talked into a pair of jeans that really did make her butt look like it belonged on the cover of *Nice Butt Magazine*, dress pants that, when paired with heels, made her legs look like they were a million miles long, and not one but two crop tops.

She drew the line at the denim jumpsuit.

"I'm not going to panic about my credit card balance," Riley chanted in the back seat of the limo as she twisted open the ice-cold fancy water Wilhelm had left in the cupholder. Smart man going with a clear liquid this time.

"Lunch is on me, ladies," Sesame announced. "Where should we go?"

While Sesame and Jasmine discussed lunch options, Riley checked her texts.

Nick: How are you feeling? Are you resting?

Riley checked the tracking app on her phone and made sure he wasn't texting her at home just to catch her in the lie.

Riley: Feeling better, thanks.

She paused and bit her lip. Then fired off a second text.

Riley: We should talk tonight.

"There's a sushi place in Mechanicsburg that has the *best* seaweed salad," Jasmine said.

Sesame bounced on her seat and clapped her hands. "Ooooh! I love seaweed! But you know, we can't go for sushi looking like we just left yoga class."

"Fashion show! Fashion show!" Jasmine chanted.

While Wilhelm raised the privacy divider and headed in the direction of sushi, the three women in the back seat pawed through shopping bags and wriggled into new outfits.

None of them noticed the black SUV that followed them.

———

Riley felt like one of the cool kids walking through a high school in slow motion when Wilhelm pulled up in front of the restaurant.

"Your boobs look hot," Jasmine told her.

"Really?" Riley skimmed her hand over her new low-cut sweater and high-waisted jeans. On the way, Jasmine and Sesame had whipped out their purse inventory of dry shampoo and makeup and worked their magic on her. "You're the one who looks like you just got off your own private plane."

Jasmine was wearing leather leggings and a sapphire-blue funnel-neck sweater. Her hair hung in a glossy waterfall from her high ponytail.

Not to be outdone, Sesame was in a new blush-pink business suit with a lacy high-necked bra instead of a shirt.

Kanagawa was a tiny sushi joint in a nondescript storefront on the main street. But inside, a sushi-making genius created works of art on plates.

Every head in the restaurant swiveled in their direction.

"We're so overdressed," Riley whispered in mortification.

"There's no such thing. You dress to suit your mood and personality. If your outfit is better than everyone else's, then that's their problem, not yours."

Riley watched her strut up to the gawking teenage server and point to a corner booth.

"I feel like everything she says is just a tiny bit bullshit mixed with a pinch of bizarre motivational poster," Riley whispered to Jasmine.

"I know. It's awesome," her friend said, linking arms with Riley.

Minutes later, an embarrassing smorgasbord of sushi ordered, Jasmine put down her tea, looked at Sesame, and became a girlfriend interrogator. "So six years pretend-married to a stranger. What was that like? Was it horrible? Did you throw all his shit out on the lawn when you found out what he'd done? Did you drive his car through the garage door?"

"Excuse my friend," Riley said to Sesame. "Jasmine is valued for her loyalty and her vengeance."

"I T-boned Griffin I'm a Real Boy's car after he sued Riley for breaking his face," Jasmine explained.

Sesame looked down at her chopsticks, and Riley wished she could sense what the woman was feeling.

"I didn't do any of those things."

"He kidnapped you and made you think you were his wife for six years, all while your family thought you were dead, and you didn't at least line his underwear with itching powder?"

Riley was torn between wanting the answer herself and not letting Jasmine push Sesame too far. They'd bonded today, sure. But was it enough of a bond to talk about real things?

"Have you ever been in love for real?" Sesame asked suddenly.

"Oh, sure. Dozens of times," Jasmine answered with a wave of her hand.

"Just once for me. I thought he loved me. But when the chips were down and he had to choose, he chose his family over me."

"I'm sorry to hear that," Riley said.

"Want us to make him sorry?" Jasmine offered.

Sesame flashed a sad little smile and shook her head. "Sometimes moving forward is better than wallowing in hurt… or getting revenge," she added quickly.

"Well, If you ever decide you want that guy singing soprano for the rest of his life, you let me and Riley know," Jasmine said.

Sesame gave them a sad smile. "I will."

The sushi arrived on a platter that took up most of the table.

Riley had just popped a picture-perfect piece of salmon avocado roll into her mouth when she spotted *him* through the window. The guy from the antique store. Except this time, his face wasn't obscured by a raffia fan. And this time, she recognized him.

She sucked in a breath and some wasabi and began coughing violently.

"Uh-oh," Sesame said. "Did you choke on your spit again?"

Riley shook her head, tears burning her eyes as the green ball of wasabi seared itself into her lungs. "Goatee," she wheezed.

"Goat? There's no goat in the sushi," Jasmine insisted.

"Here." The server returned with another large glass of water. "It happens all the time."

Still shaking her head, Riley grabbed the water and started chugging. Between racking coughs and wheezy breaths, the burn began to subside.

When she finally managed to look up, the man was gone.

"We need to go. Now," she rasped.

"Oooh, you should record a new voicemail greeting right now. You sound all sexy and hoarse like Mila Kunis," Jasmine observed.

Riley slapped her hand down on the table. "We need to go."

"She sounds upset," Sesame said to Jasmine.

"I'm not leaving without my Hawaii roll," Jasmine insisted.

On a growl, Riley started scraping sushi off the platter into Jasmine's purse.

"Hey! That's new! I'll never get the fish smell out of it," her friend complained.

"I'll buy you a new one," Riley wheezed.

"Well, in that case..." Jasmine shoveled the remaining rolls into her purse and topped everything off with the bowl of seaweed salad.

"Call Wilhelm and have him meet us out back," Riley said, dragging both women from the booth.

"Are you okay, Riley? I know those jeans are a little tighter than what you're used to wearing, but they aren't making you feel dizzy or anything, are they?" Sesame asked.

"Just go!"

With a bag full of sushi and the server chasing them down the alley with Sesame's receipt, they hauled ass toward the limo.

"Why are we running?" Jasmine asked, hugging her purse to her chest.

"Because I recognized someone from earlier today. I think he's following us."

"Really?" Sesame stopped in her tracks. "What did he look like?"

"Dark curly hair, frowny face."

Sesame stopped halfway in and out of the limo. She took Riley's wrist in a death grip. "Did he have a nice butt?"

"No! He had no butt at all," she said, stuffing the woman into the car and climbing in after her. "Punch it, Wilhelm!"

18

M rs. Basil-Thorn, I'm not sure you're understanding the question." Weber looked like he was on hour seven of an interrogation that wasn't going well.

"And I'm pretty sure you're just not understanding my answer," Blossom said, picking up her mug of tea and blowing at the steam.

"I asked you how we can get my sister—I mean, my friend—to open up and tell us what happened to her. And you pulled a card out of a deck and told me I was a fool."

"No, the card is the Fool. And since it was reversed, it tends to symbolize either a bad decision or a new beginning that you'll find worrisome."

Nick smirked at the card on the kitchen table. It was kind of nice not being on the receiving end for once. Of course, his ex-partner hadn't been told that he was going to die or anything like that.

"What does this have to do with my sis—friend?" Weber asked.

"My advice is tailored specifically to the person. If you want me to properly advise you on how to make your cis friend open up, I'd need to do a reading on her since I've never met her."

Roger harrumphed from behind his iPad, where he was researching 1980s TV show trivia. "Jesus, woman! Did you drink too much beet juice? You already met her."

Blossom looked at her husband so fast Nick worried about whiplash. "No. I. Didn't, Roger. And neither did you. *Remember?*"

"Then who was the pink girl with all the hair and the big..." Roger held up his hands in front of his own chest. "At yoga this morning with Riley—"

Nick suddenly no longer found any humor in the situation. "Riley went to yoga today?"

"No. Riley? Ha! No," Blossom said. "She wasn't feeling well today and stayed home. You must be thinking about last week, Roger."

"Huh?"

Blossom gasped dramatically. "Did you hear that?"

"Hear what?"

"Daisy needs you. Her moo sounded so sad," Blossom said. She jumped up and threw open the sliding deck door.

Roger followed her at a run. "What's the matter, Daisy girl? Did that mean old hag next door scare you with her weird hair again?"

Blossom dragged the door closed, and Nick saw her smack Roger in the chest.

"You know, they could be your in-laws someday," Weber said, picking up the tarot card to study it.

Blossom and Roger seemed to be engaged in some kind of argument involving a lot of hand gestures and a confused-looking pet cow.

"Like either one of us can talk when it comes to parents. Your mom is a religious sociopath, and mine—"

"Your mother is a saint to have put up with you and your sister all these years."

"Stop dating my mother. Did you talk to Constance since springing her long-lost daughter on her yesterday?" Nick asked.

"I'm not dating your mother. We just go out for drinks and meals occasionally. And no. Why? Should I?"

136

Santiagos talked. About everything. Usually at excessive volumes and with aggressive hand gestures. He'd always been fascinated by the icy dynamics of Weber's family. If someone had a problem, they didn't blow up at the dinner table and throw a bowl of prawns. As far as he could tell, they never got around to talking about anything other than the weather and church fundraisers.

"It was a pretty big shock. I mean, you almost choked to death on a pork rind when you found out. But your mom didn't so much as blink."

"She's got a poker face. If she didn't think poker was the eighth deadly sin, she'd clean up at Fat Tony's casino," Weber said, tossing the card back onto the table.

The patio door slid open, and a smiling Blossom and a contrite-looking Roger returned.

"Roger has something he wants to say. Don't you, Roger?" she prodded.

The man heaved a sigh. "I'm sorry for getting confused about what day of the week it is. I think it's my cholesterol medicine that Blossom told me I didn't need because I could make more progress with lifestyle changes." He sounded like he was reading off a cue card.

"Uh, apology accepted?" Weber said.

"Good. Now, where were we?"

"You were telling us how we can get Beth—I mean, Sesame—to open up to us," Nick said.

Blossom nodded vigorously. "Right, right, right! I remember."

"Now who's on the statins?" Roger muttered under his breath.

Blossom interlaced her fingers on the table. "Have you tried asking her?"

"Why didn't I think of that?" Weber said dryly.

She giggled. "Oh, you kidder. *How* did you ask her?"

Nick and Weber shrugged at each other. "I don't know. We just told her it was very important that she tell us what happened so we can find these people as soon as possible and prosecute them."

"Or drag them out to the desert and feed their bodies to coyotes," Nick added, hazarding a sip of the murky green tea Blossom had poured for them. It tasted weirdly of licorice and lemon. He didn't quite hate it, but he was probably going to dump it down the sink if she left the room again.

She winced. "I say this with plenty of love and no judgment, but it kinda sounds like you boys were railroading her like her feelings matter less than yours."

"Justice isn't a feeling," Weber snapped, putting his mug down. "If she doesn't tell us what she knows, we may never find these people. They might never pay for what they did."

Blossom held up her palms. "I hear what you're saying, and namaste."

He glared at her. "What?"

"Just *namaste* her back," Nick suggested.

"Namaste," Weber repeated.

She beamed at him. "If you want your sis-spect to tell you what you need to know, you need to meet her where she is."

"She's at my condo. But I couldn't get her to talk there," Weber said.

Blossom picked up the Fool and fanned herself with it. "What I meant was where is she emotionally? Spiritually? If she's scared, you need to find a way to make her trust you."

"Hey, Bloss, why don't you get him that vulnerability tea your cousin made you?" Roger suggested.

Nick smothered a grin when it looked like Weber was about to burst a blood vessel.

"What a great idea, Roger!" Blossom said. She pressed a kiss to the top of his head and skipped to the basement door.

The three men did what three men who didn't know each other well and were stuck in a room together with no wives or televisions did. They sat in silence.

Nick got up and dumped his tea.

"Psst."

Nick and Weber looked up at Roger, who put his elbows on the kitchen table.

"Now listen. I'm gonna tell you how to crack a woman like an egg, but you two are never to use this against my wife or daughters. Got it?"

"Got it," Weber said.

"I can't promise that," Nick said.

"Here's what you do," Roger began. "First you open a bottle of wine, and you pour her a glass all casual-like."

Weber pulled his case notebook out of his jacket pocket and started writing. "Red or white?"

Roger shook his head. "Doesn't matter."

"Is the wine important? Can it be beer or liquor?" Nick asked.

"Wine is best. Liquor can take a gal from buzzed to shit-faced way too quick. Beer makes it seem like it's more about you, plus it's burpy. Wine'll make her feel fancy. It'll look like you're doing something just for her."

"Then what?" Weber prompted.

"Then you give her the wine and tell her you thought she deserved it since she looks a little stressed out. Then, depending on your relationship, you either give her a little foot rub or maybe offer her some kind of snack. Don't try to rub feet that belong to your mom or your boss or really any female relative or coworker. Stick with fancy chocolate for them."

Nick suddenly wished he was writing this down too. "Can I have your notes when you're done?" he asked Weber.

"Shut up and let the man speak, Nicky."

"So you got your wine and your foot rub or your choco-lates. Then you ask her an easy question. Something about whatever she was talking about recently. A movie. A friend. That dumbass in accounting. Something that subtly reminds her that you listen to her."

Weber nodded as he wrote.

Nick fumbled with the recorder app on his phone.

"When she answers, look her in the eye and listen enough

to be able to paraphrase it back to her. *Look at me; I care enough about you to notice your feelings and give you space to talk about them.* I call it ALECTO: *Ask. Listen. Eye contact. Top off.*"

Nick was new to relationships, but this sounded crazy enough to work.

"You top off her wine and do it all over again. Maybe you share something about your day. Something dumb that you don't care about. Like your brother called, and you told him he was being a dumbass. Women love shit like that."

"Shit like sharing?" Weber clarified.

Roger glanced toward the basement door and nodded. "Yeah. Then you keep going. You're building rapport. You wait until she's almost done with the second glass, and then when you top it off again, you lean in close and look concerned." He leaned closer.

Nick and Weber did the same.

Roger's expression shifted to one of concern.

"What's happening right now?" Nick whispered.

"Then what?" Weber demanded, glancing up from his notebook.

"Then you say, 'Hey, you look like something's bothering you. Do you wanna talk about it?'"

"Masterful," Nick whispered.

"What if she still doesn't talk?" Weber asked.

"Then you put your hand on her arm, maintain eye contact, and you say, 'It's okay if you don't feel ready to talk about it. I was just hoping I could finally return the favor.'"

"What favor?" Nick asked.

Roger leaned in until the three men were only inches apart. "'I appreciate how you're always here for me. How you let me talk about my shit all the time. I'd really like to be there for you.'"

"Wow," Weber whispered, his pen falling to the table.

"I feel like I wanna tell you my entire life story and that you'll listen," Nick said.

"That's how you know it's working," Roger said proudly. "One more thing."

"Yes, sensei?" Nick said.

"No matter how obvious the solution is, no matter how easily you could explain how to fix it, no matter how much you want to take care of the problem yourself, don't."

"Don't what?" Weber asked.

"Don't fix it. Don't tell her how to fix it. Don't tell her what you would do if you were in her shoes. Just don't."

Nick frowned. "Hang on. Are you saying we're just supposed to sit there and listen and not do anything about it?"

"That's exactly what I'm saying, kid. I get that it sounds looney tunes. But trust me. It works. If you establish a rapport using ALECTO, you cannot—under any circumstances—swoop in with a solution."

Weber and Nick made eye contact. Not being problem solvers in this case wouldn't be easy seeing as how Weber wanted nothing more than to see the people responsible behind bars and Nick was still leaning toward planting a few bodies in the desert.

"Trust me," Roger said again. "If you play it my way, she'll give you an opening to provide a solution after you do the wine and the listening shit."

Nick shook his head in wonder. "You're a relationship genius, Roger. You should give workshops."

"I do sometimes, down at the farm store in the feed room," Roger said.

"Here it is!" Blossom triumphantly returned to the kitchen with two dusty cardboard boxes.

The three men leaned back, their intimate workshop over.

"Nick, I brought you something to make a poultice for your eye. I can't believe you gave yourself a black eye opening an Amazon package," she tut-tutted before turning to Weber. "Now, Detective, you're going to want to write down these steeping directions. Do you have any organic wildflower honey at home?"

Nick's phone vibrated in his pocket. "Thorn," he said when he answered it.

"Hey, um, so don't get mad."

19

I can explain," Riley said for the third time.

There was a muscle twitching incessantly under Nick's bruised eye. Not a good sign. He held up a hand. "No talking," he snarled before returning to his survey of the window locks in Weber's bland dining room.

Five minutes after Riley and company had locked themselves in Weber's place, the men had arrived with lights blazing. If their sushi stalker had managed to follow them after Wilhelm's aggressive driving, he was long gone now.

Riley hated disappointing people. Especially when those people were Nick. And especially when she was already feeling insecure about their relationship. "Look, I know you said to leave her alone, but—"

Nick whirled on her. "Thorn, one more word spent trying to defend why you disobeyed direct orders and not only left the house but put yourself, your best friend, and the woman I told you to stay away from in danger, and I will…"

He was so mad he'd trailed off in the middle of a threat. That was a very bad sign.

But Riley had been through enough in the past two days to

proceed with caution. "*Direct orders?* What do you think this is, a hierarchy or a relationship?"

Nick moved so he was toe-to-toe with her. "Right now, it's a dictatorship and… Is that a new sweater?"

The power of the boobs.

"Yes, it is, and it's part of what I wanted to talk to you about."

"Was that before or after you lied to my face, left the house, and got followed again?"

"Nicky, calm the hell down," Weber said, joining them.

"I'll calm down when my girlfriend explains why I shouldn't be pissed off about her attracting her second stalker in two days," Nick snapped.

"It's not my fault that people keep following me," Riley argued. It sounded stupid, but sometimes that was exactly what the truth was.

"Hey, who wants some wine?" Weber asked suddenly.

"Aren't these the cutest vegan suede booties you've ever seen?" Sesame pranced into the room in pale purple ankle boots. Unperturbed by their hasty exit due to the stalker, she was going through her new purchases like she was getting ready for a date.

"It's not a great time, Beth…ame," Weber told his sister.

Sesame's eyes went wide when she took in Nick's scowl and Riley's. "Oooh," she said. "Hey, big brother, would you mind clearing out all your stuff from the master closet? I need to organize my wardrobe."

"Uhhh." Weber appeared to be at a loss when it came to women in his home.

"Do you want some wine?" Riley asked him.

"Tell me again what this guy looked like," Nick said to Riley.

Sesame perked up. "Yeah! Tell us again."

Riley blew out a breath. "I told you I didn't get a very good look."

"Tell me what you saw, Thorn. And by *saw*, I mean what

144

you saw, thought, and heard from your damn spirit guides who do not seem to be doing a good job of keeping you out of fucking trouble."

She winced. "He was at the antique store when we went to yoga this morning. At least I think it was him. He was hiding behind some display on the sidewalk when we went in the side door. I didn't get much of a read on him…"

"Then what?" Sesame asked, hanging on her every word.

"And then in yoga, I…" Riley glanced at Sesame and hastily decided to rewrite the truth. "I had another vision and saw him. First he was young and happy. It was just for a split second, but he seemed excited about something. He was waiting for someone. Then he changed, and he was like all sinister with a bad goatee. He was still waiting, but then he grabbed someone and dragged them into his van."

She snuck a peek at Sesame, who hadn't seemed to recognize her own abduction story.

"I've dated guys with goatees, and two out of every four of them are totally sinister," Jasmine said, flipping through the mail on the kitchen counter.

Nick was looking at Riley with a stony expression on his handsome face. He was withholding his dimples from her, and it wasn't fair.

She pressed on. "Then I saw him again, out on the sidewalk when we were in Mechanicsburg having sushi. I recognized the hair from this morning and his face from the vision. Although he didn't have an evil goatee. He looked right in the window at us. It didn't feel like a coincidence, so we ran out the back door, and I called you."

"Is that the guy who took you?" Weber demanded, looking at Sesame. "If he is, you could be in serious danger, and we need to know."

She blinked several times in a row, eyelashes fluttering like butterfly wings. "I…I…think I'm getting a headache. I'm going to go lie down," she said, bringing the back of her hand to her forehead and clomping dramatically out of the room.

Nick wiped a hand over his face and muttered something that sounded like, "We should have made them drink wine."

"Ugh. Who lives like this?" Jasmine demanded, opening cabinets in Weber's kitchen. She pulled out a box of bran flakes. Riley couldn't think of a more on-brand breakfast for the detective.

"Someone who works for a living," Weber called back in annoyance. He winced and rubbed a hand over his ribs.

"I'm an attorney, you insufferable ass. Are you saying I don't work for a living?"

"I'm saying I spent my morning in a dumpster while you bought out half the inventory of retail stores in Dauphin and Cumberland Counties." Weber left them to fight with Jasmine in the kitchen.

"Look, I know you're mad," Riley began.

Nick's hand closed around her wrist and dragged her toward the kitchen. "We're going home, and you're giving Brian a description of this guy so he can put it into facial rendering software." He looked at Weber, who was snatching utensils out of Jasmine's hands as she rearranged them.

"Do you know nothing about feng shui or kitchen organization?" she scoffed.

"You good here?" Nick asked Weber.

Weber grabbed a pair of manly grilling tongs away from Jasmine, then clutched his ribs. "Yeah," he wheezed. "I'm taking personal time for the rest of the weekend. She won't be alone."

"Good. Jasmine, leave the man alone. We'll drop you off on the way home."

And with that, Nick dragged Riley out the door.

———

"There's something not right with the jawline," Riley told Brian as he finessed the computer-generated sketch of the villain.

"Stronger and more pronounced, or weaker and less defined?" he asked, toggling keys to turn the man on screen into a leading man or a secondary character.

"I don't know," she said, scrubbing both hands over her face. She was tired, hungry, and annoyed, and something was tickling at the back of her mind. Something she couldn't bring into focus. Something she couldn't ask her spirit guides to help with because they were gone. She'd locked herself in the bathroom when they got home and tried to drop into Cotton Candy World, but all that she found was a dark, cloudless void.

"Why don't we take a break?" Brian suggested.

"A break sounds good," she admitted. "Where's Josie?"

He opened a sleek mini fridge under the desk and pulled out two beers. "She's interviewing Mrs. Penny's friend again to see if her knickknacks really are disappearing or if she's just really old." He popped the top on one of the beers and handed it over.

"Thanks," Riley said. "How's the gym rat case going?"

He adjusted his glasses and opened his own beer. "Oh, swell. Got banned for life from Muscles Muscles Muscles this morning."

Riley sputtered in her beer. "Seriously?"

"Apparently they have a strict only-selfies-in-the-locker-room. I wasn't even taking pics."

"What were you doing?"

"Using the public Wi-Fi to hack into Brotein's phone."

"Of course you were."

"How's your 'case' going?" he asked.

She shrugged. "I haven't started it yet. Apparently I'm on house arrest."

There was a slam followed by a crunch chased by a loud "fucking hell" from the dining room.

"So Nicky seems like he's in a mood," Brian said.

Riley sighed. "He's mad at me because I didn't follow orders."

The topic of their discussion appeared in the doorway of Brian's office shirtless. His T-shirt was wrapped around his left hand. "Where's our fucking first aid kit?" he demanded.

She jumped to her feet. "It's in the kitchen. I'll get it."

"Do I need to go find a finger?" Brian asked.

Riley grabbed the first aid kit next to the empty Halloween candy bowl in the kitchen. Damn it. She'd forgotten to buy more Halloween candy when she'd been out.

She felt Nick's presence behind her and turned.

A tattooed, shirtless, pissed-off Nick Santiago was not hard on the eyes.

"How bad is it?" she asked, gesturing toward his wrapped hand.

"Everything's still attached," he assured her.

Carefully, she unwound the shirt from his hand. "What were you doing?"

"Fixing a broken window lock."

Was it her imagination, or was he leaning in? She'd missed having him close like this, which she realized was silly given the fact that they'd had sex less than thirty-six hours ago. But a lot had happened in those thirty-six hours.

Riley wrinkled her nose when she found three of his knuckles had nasty wounds.

"Don't get any blood on your sweater," he cautioned. His tone was soft, and she could feel his breath on her hair.

"It's new," she said.

"I noticed."

She hazarded a glance up and saw his gaze was fastened on her cleavage. At least he hadn't suddenly become immune to her boobs.

"This is going to hurt," she warned, soaking a square of gauze in rubbing alcohol.

"I'm not a baby—Jesus Christ! Fucking damn shit!"

Riley felt her lips curve as Nick's vocabulary went nuclear.

"You definitely don't have the vocabulary of a baby," she noted, cleaning the wounds quickly.

"My first word was *shit*. Mom was not amused."

Smirking, she tore open the first bandage and placed it over a knuckle. Being so close to him made her want to get naked, and they had a lot to talk about before getting naked was an option. "I saw your mom at yoga this morning."

"How mean was she to you?"

"She actually didn't get the chance. Sesame convinced her she was your ex-lover, and I rescued you from an on-purpose accidental pregnancy scheme."

Nick closed his eyes. "I'm not sure I want to know why."

"She was trying to make me look good to your mom. You know, show her that I'm not the worst person you could end up with. It was actually really nice of her."

"If my mom thinks you suck, it's because she's a snob. Anyone in their right mind can see you're amazing."

Riley bit her lip and took her time with the last bandage. "Does this mean you're not still mad at me?"

"Oh, I'm still fucking furious," he assured her, but he tipped her chin up to look at him when he said it. There was a lot going on behind those stormy blue-green eyes, and she wished she could read him right now.

"I wasn't trying to put anyone in danger," she said. "I was trying to do the exact opposite."

"From now on, Thorn, leave the keeping-people-safe thing to me."

"Are you sure it's me and not Sesame you're trying to save?"

"Why can't it be both?" Nick asked.

20

12:27 a.m. Sunday, October 27

Nick lay on his back in bed. Riley slept fitfully next to him. She'd rolled over, muttering in her sleep half a dozen times since he'd come upstairs. Burt grumbled in his extra-large dog bed.

He tucked his hands under his head as he stared up at the bedroom ceiling. It was stained from old water damage and needed a fresh coat of paint, which was an item on his to-do list.

When this was behind them, he'd have the time and energy to tackle it. They'd bought this place in the thick of the reignited search for Beth. Every waking moment had been spent looking for her.

Now that she was found, he still needed to see it through. Needed to officially close the book. But he couldn't do that as long as the people responsible were still out there.

Weber's text from earlier rattled around in his brain.

Weber: It took a bottle and a half of wine, but she said she'll be ready to talk in the morning.

Nick wanted to be there when he questioned Sesame. This wasn't just family business. It never had been.

Riley sat bolt upright next to him, scaring the shit out of him. "The window!" she shrieked.

Naked, Nick vaulted out of bed and grabbed his gun from the nightstand. Burt jumped out of his bed with a questioning bark. Together, man and dog hustled across the room to the heavy drapes that covered the windows. With the gun trained in front of him, Nick gave a hard yank. Rather than opening smoothly, the curtain rod ripped off its mounting and fell to the floor.

Finding no one on the other side of the glass, he looked over his shoulder at Riley. Her eyes were wide and unseeing, but her nose was twitching.

"Thorn! What do you see?"

"He came in the window. He's in her room," she squeaked.

Nick dove onto the bed and cupped Riley's face in his hand. "Who?"

Her eyes cleared, and she started blinking until she focused in on him. "The guy from today. I think I saw him climb in Sesame's window at Kellen's. At least I think I did. Maybe it was just a dream?"

"Now, or are you seeing the future?"

She held the covers in a death grip. "I don't know. I can't tell. Everything is still a little jumbled."

Nick swore. He dropped the gun onto the mattress and wrestled his way into jeans commando with one hand while dialing Weber's number with the other.

"I'm coming with you," Riley said stubbornly.

The call went to voicemail.

"Damn it. Fine. But I'm leaving now," he said, stuffing the gun into the back of his jeans.

"I'm ready." She grabbed a pair of those fuzzy boots all women seemed to wear as soon as pumpkin spice hit the coffee shops.

Riley and Burt followed him into the hall, and the three of them took the stairs at a jog. He headed for the tiny useless mudroom off the kitchen, where he snagged his keys and a flashlight off the crooked shelf.

"Who broke the window?" he demanded, then shook his head. "Never mind. Keep trying Weber while I drive," he ordered.

———

"He's still not answering, and neither is Sesame," Riley said. "She gave me her number while we were shopping in case we got separated in the shoe section."

"Goddammit," he muttered.

"Maybe everything is okay? It was probably just a dream. My visions haven't been very…accurate lately."

He didn't answer her. This shouldn't have been happening again. They'd taken precautions. They were being vigilant. Who in their right mind would break into a cop's house? Someone with really bad fucking intentions. That was who.

Nick ignored every traffic law and floored the SUV's accelerator through a red light.

He appreciated that Riley said nothing even as her grip tightened on the oh-shit handle. Burt too seemed to understand this was a serious drive and sat stoically in the center of the back seat.

Weber lived in a personality-less condo building on the other side of the capitol complex. It usually took a good fifteen minutes to get there in light traffic. Nick made it in seven.

He screeched to a halt in front of the building and looked at Riley. "Stay here."

"I should come with you. Maybe I can tell you if he's already in there or not," she insisted, releasing her seat belt.

"Fuck. Fine. But if you get yourself hurt or shot or worse, I'll never fucking forgive you, Thorn."

She jumped out of the SUV before he could change his mind.

Burt whined pathetically from the back seat.

"Burt can wait with me in the hall," Riley volunteered. "He'll keep me safe."

"I'm running a goddamn circus," Nick muttered under his breath.

He didn't give her time to argue before he slammed his door and took off for the front door, where he was met with a keypad. Each resident had their own code, and Nick prayed Weber hadn't changed his—0617. The date Beth had gone missing.

He plugged it in and was relieved when the door lock buzzed. "Let's go."

They made a run for the stairs to the second floor.

Weber's door hadn't been breached, though Riley had said she'd seen the suspect climbing through a window, so it didn't count as good news.

"What's the plan?" Riley whispered.

"I don't know. Let me think." If he knocked or broke down the door, it could make the assailant panic. But they couldn't do nothing.

The door across the hall opened, and a grizzled-faced old man scowled out at them. He was dressed in a checkered bathrobe and had glasses propped on his head. "It's a little late for DoorDash, isn't it?"

"I'm selling Nature Girl cookies for my niece Esmeralda," Nick said.

"Bullshit. You're hovering outside a cop's front door. You ain't selling cookies. And I'm gonna give you to the count of ten to get facedown on the floor before my finger starts twitching."

The man pulled a revolver out of his robe pocket.

Nick moved so he was between Riley and the cowboy and put his hands up. "Look, sir, there's no need to put any holes in anyone. My friend is in trouble behind that door, and I need to get in there."

"Nick," Riley whispered, grabbing him by the back of his shirt.

"It's okay, Thorn," he said. "I've got this under control."

"Thorn? As in Riley Thorn the psychic?" the neighbor took the glasses off his head and put them on.

"Do I know you?" Riley asked, trying to peek around Nick.

"I'm Bob. I go to slam poetry with Fred Bogdanovich. I

follow all your shenanigans on the news. Are you here to catch another bad guy?"

"We're trying to," she said.

"You're not gonna blow up the building, are you?" he asked.

"We're definitely going to try to avoid that," Nick said dryly.

"In that case, you can use my spare key. But be careful. That Kellen's got a pretty lady in there, and he's a damn good shot."

"Thanks for the warning," Nick said.

Bob shuffled back into his apartment and returned with a key. "I'll just wait out here and watch the show if you don't mind."

"Fine by me," Nick muttered as he crossed to Weber's door. "You two stay here," he told Riley and Burt.

"Be careful," Riley urged.

He took a quick deep breath and turned the key in the lock.

Nick went in low and counted his lucky stars that he did because the coffee mug Weber hurled at him flew over his head and hit the wall in the hallway.

"It's me. Don't fucking shoot!" Nick shouted.

"What the hell are you doing breaking in?" Weber yelled back.

The lights came on, and Nick ran past him, taking a split second to note that his friend was wearing nothing but black briefs. "He's in the bedroom! Is that what you sleep in?"

"Who?" Weber demanded, running after him.

"The guy!" Nick snapped as he raced down the hall.

"What guy?"

He heard it then. Sounds of a scuffle.

Nick didn't stop to think. He did what came naturally. He rammed the door with his shoulder and fell with it as it came off the hinges.

It was dark, but he could just make out a shadowy figure standing at the foot of the bed.

"I can explain everything," the man said.

But Nick wasn't in the mood for story time. He went airborne and hit the man in the midsection. He didn't realize until they hit the floor that the intruder was naked.

An ear-piercing scream came from the bed, and Burt howled his response from the hall.

"Ow, that hurt!" wheezed the naked suspect.

"On the floor! Hands behind your head," Weber barked.

"I'm already on the floor, and I can't move my hands. Someone's sitting on me," the man complained.

The lights came on, and Sesame let out another piercing scream.

"Do you need backup, Detective?" Bob yelled from the hallway.

"Don't murder him, Nicky!"

"You have the right to remain silent," Weber barked.

"Get off my husband, Nicky Santiago!"

———

It was the weirdest pajama party Nick had ever crashed.

Riley was in plaid girl boxers and a sweatshirt. Weber had at least had the decency to pull on a pair of sweatpants but was still shirtless. Sesame had added a matching robe over her lingerie. The man she'd claimed was her husband wore a pair of expensive jeans and a buttonless button-down. Apparently Sesame had ripped the buttons off in her excitement.

"Would you at least put on a shirt, man?" Nick asked Weber.

His friend didn't acknowledge his very reasonable request.

"So you two are married," Riley said, accepting the mug of hot chocolate Tommy handed her. The guy had made a batch of homemade hot chocolate for everyone, including Bob.

"It's true! This is my Tommy," Sesame said, plopping herself down into the man's lap and hugging him around the neck.

Tommy clocked in at an inch or two under six feet and gave off rich nerd vibes. He had thick dark hair that curled at the ends and not much fat or muscle to his frame. Nick knew this thanks to getting a little too up close and personal with him.

"I'm sure you all have a lot of questions," Sesame began as if she were addressing a class of second graders.

"I'll start," Nick volunteered. "Did this asshole kidnap you and force you to marry him? Is this that Patty Hearst thing where you think you're in love with your captor but actually you're just brainwashed? Are you legally married or just like cult-leader-polyamory-in-a-bunker married? Does he really have four kids that you thought were yours, and are they waiting in a minivan somewhere down the block? How did he get in here without Weber hearing him? Why is he just now showing up? And where does your brother keep the good liquor?"

Sesame laughed nervously. "Well, that's a lot of questions."

Without a word, Weber got up, walked into the laundry room, and returned with a bottle of scotch.

"Dalmore Twelve. Nice," Tommy said, his head bobbing in approval.

"Shut up," Weber said to him.

Burt snored under the table.

"That's no way to talk to your brother-in-law," Sesame chided.

"Christ." Weber unscrewed the top and drank straight from the bottle.

Riley got up and started opening cabinets until she found Weber's glasses.

"Let me start at the beginning," Sesame said, shifting in Tommy's lap. The man looked besotted, but sociopaths and serial killers could be pretty good actors. "I met Tommy a few months before...well, before I went away," Sesame began. "I knew Mom wouldn't approve, and Tommy had a few teeny-tiny run-ins with the law. So I knew you might not be too happy either, Kelly."

"I was selling fake ADHD meds to drunk college students," Tommy chimed in. "They were actually Canadian Tic Tacs."

"Kelly here ran every guy I ever dated through the system," Sesame explained to Riley when she returned with some glasses.

"So you kept your relationship a secret," Riley guessed as she poured two glasses of scotch. She handed one to Nick and slid the other in front of Weber.

Sesame nodded. "I knew he was the one from the moment he ordered extra dipping sauce for our breadsticks at Olive Garden."

"Oh please," Weber muttered. He ignored the glass Riley put in front of him and picked up the bottle instead.

"Well, if no one's gonna drink this," Tommy said, helping himself to the second glass.

"One night, we were at a party, and there was a little misunderstanding."

"The warehouse," Nick guessed.

Sesame winced. "Yeah. See, the raves were thrown by a couple of low-level drug dealers. It was pretty smart actually. They charged a cover and then exclusively sold their drugs inside. Anyway, someone saw Tommy give a guy seven Tic Tacs in the bathroom and, well, you can imagine our hosts weren't very happy with him."

"You double-crossed a bunch of dealers in downtown Harrisburg," Weber summarized, pinching the bridge of his nose.

"It wasn't a real double cross," Sesame assured him.

"Looking back, I can see it wasn't the smartest move professionally," Tommy admitted.

"Don't talk," Weber said, still refusing to look at him.

"Was one of these dealers named Blight?" Nick asked.

Sesame pursed her lips together and looked up at the ceiling. "Honestly, Nicky, it's been so long, I don't even remember."

She was definitely lying.

"You don't have to be afraid of him. He's in prison. Your brother and I put him there. And if he set the fire, you can help make sure he stays there," Nick said.

Sesame shrugged daintily. "I'm sorry. I just don't remember. Do you, sweetiekins?" she asked Tommy.

Nick couldn't be sure, but it looked as though those pink nails were sinking into Tommy's skin.

"Nope, honeybear," Tommy squeaked without looking away from his wife's eyes.

"Anyway, back to the fire. You see, I was afraid that these scary criminals were going to do something bad."

"They were talking about cutting off my fingers and stuffing them up my own butthole," Tommy said cheerfully.

Weber took six long swigs directly from the bottle.

"Tommy, my eyes are a little dry. Do you mind getting my eye drops from the bathroom? They're in my makeup bag."

"Anything for you, Ses," he said.

She waited for Tommy to leave the room. "Look, the fire was a total accident. Those guys were roughing Tommy up, and they all but threw him into that tiki torch."

"You're saying Tommy burned down the warehouse?" Nick's eye was twitching again.

"It was an accident. And neither of us knew there were propane tanks on the ground floor."

Weber got to his feet so abruptly his chair fell over backward.

"Don't be mad, Kelly," Sesame pleaded.

"Your husband firebombed a ten-thousand-square-foot warehouse!"

"You sound mad. Are you mad?"

"Mad? *Mad?* Why would I be mad?"

"This is exactly why I didn't tell him," Sesame said to Riley.

"What happened next?" Nick asked.

"Well, Tommy was going to turn himself in. But the drug dealers were so mad at him. First they catch him selling Tic Tacs, and then he burns their headquarters down. I did the right thing."

"Which was?" Riley asked.

"I gave a false statement to the police, went home, packed a few necessities, and we left town the next day."

"So there was no abduction? No amnesia?" Weber asked, his voice flat.

"No four kids?" Nick added.

Sesame went to her brother and reached for his hand. "No," she said softly. "I'm sorry, Kelly. I was afraid if you knew the truth, you wouldn't forgive me, and we had to stay away until the statute of limitations expired. I couldn't let Tommy go to jail. None of our dreams would come true with him behind bars."

Weber slowly removed his hand from hers. "Mom is never going to forgive you," he said quietly.

Riley squeezed Nick's knee until he put his hand on top of hers.

Sesame took a deep breath and looked her brother square in the eye. "Kelly, Mom knew."

Weber slammed his palms down on the table. "Knew what?" he shouted.

"Easy there, Weber. This isn't an interrogation room," Nick reminded him.

"Maybe it should be," Weber snapped. "What did Mom know?"

"I told her I was leaving. I told her I was in love and that I didn't want to be without him anymore. I didn't say anything about the fire, but I figured with all the soot on my face and the fact that my hair smelled like that time Dad set the carport on fire grilling, she'd figure it out. She told me I was dead to her. No Weber woman would defile herself by living in sin. I was a disappointment. I was damning myself to hell, blah, blah, blah."

"Get. Out." Weber said the words looking at the table.

"That's exactly what she said!"

"And now I'm saying it. Get out of my house, Beth. And take your criminal husband with you."

21

Thank you again for letting us stay with you," Sesame said to Riley as Nick dumped Sesame's third suitcase and overnight bag in the corner.

"It's no problem," Riley said as she stretched the fitted sheet across the bed.

"Oooh! Look at the glitter on the bedding. Tommy, we need to get glitter bedding!" Sesame opened the door to the creepy, smelly closet and peered inside. Burt pushed past her and went snuffling around.

Riley hoped that the mystery smell was less noticeable now.

"Hmm," Sesame said. "I'm not sure if this is going to be big enough. But don't you worry. I'll make do."

"I'm hitting the shower. Sorry for tackling you while you were naked, Tommy," Nick said, then left the room abruptly.

"Thanks for not killing me," Tommy called after him.

Riley winced. They hadn't had a chance to talk on the way back from Weber's. Not with Sesame and Tommy making out in the back seat.

"Don't mind him. The wallpaper makes him ragey," Riley explained, pointing at the pink roses. That and his girlfriend lying to him. She had no idea how he felt about running in to save Sesame from a bad guy only to find her having sex with the husband she hadn't told them about.

Hell, *Riley* wasn't sure how she felt about it. With no powers to deploy while she was awake, she felt adrift.

"Let me do that," Tommy offered. He snapped the top sheet open and expertly floated it over the mattress.

"Thanks," she said, impressed. "If you guys are hungry, help yourselves to anything in the kitchen."

"What I'm hungry for is right here," Sesame said, eyeing her husband as he did something cool and professional-looking with the corners of the sheets.

Riley didn't need to be psychic to guess what Sesame and Tommy were going to do in that bed instead of sleeping.

"On that note, I'm gonna go," she decided. "Come on, Burt."

The dog let out a low growl from the closet.

"Burt. Come."

Sesame was making bedroom eyes at Tommy as he karate chopped the bed pillows.

Reluctantly, Riley entered the creepy, smelly closet and found Burt on his belly at the back, his nose pushed against the old-fashioned metal grate. His tail was swishing back and forth on the floor, but he was still growling.

She comforted herself with the fact that the smell seemed a little better. More paint fumes and less rotting compost.

"Let's go before our guests get naked," she whispered, hooking her fingers in Burt's collar. She had to physically drag all ninety pounds of him backward but finally managed to get the dog out of the closet. "Good night," Riley called as she tugged Burt into the hall.

"Sweet dreams," Sesame said before shutting the door in Riley's face.

"What's wrong with you?" she asked the dog.

Burt didn't seem inclined to answer and instead trotted happily toward their bedroom on the other side of the second floor. Upon entering, Riley was immediately suspicious.

Nick was in the shower…singing "Girl on Fire" by Alicia Keys.

"Well, that's a first," she observed.

Burt threw himself onto the bed and flopped down on Nick's pillow.

The adrenaline of the night drained out of her, and she was left feeling like an exhausted shell of a human being. She flopped down on her side of the bed and glanced around the room, trying to be objective.

It had potential. The size was ample, the natural light acceptable. And the view of the river was the best in the house. With a fresh coat of paint, new carpet, ducting that did a better job of delivering heat and cold, and maybe some furniture that didn't look like it had come from a great-grandmother's estate sale, it could be great.

But the leap from *potential* to *great* required a leap of faith. Not to mention a serious investment of time, effort, and resources. To further complicate things, there was no guarantee that potential would ever actually turn into *great*. Especially if your partner wasn't willing to go all in.

But the only way to find out was to make the investment.

And that was exactly what scared her.

Burt seemed to sense her rising anxiety and rolled over to plant his gigantic head on her shoulder.

"I can always count on you, buddy."

His tail thumped in appreciation against the mattress.

The water shut off in the adjoining bathroom, and seconds later, a still mostly wet Nick strolled into the room whistling, wearing only a towel.

He spied her waiting for him and gave her a suggestive eyebrow wiggle. "Come here often, beautiful?"

"Are you serious right now?" Riley asked.

"Burt, go away," he ordered.

The dog snorted out a fake snore in her hair.

"Burt, if you don't get off the bed in the next three seconds, I'm switching you to that vegan dog food you hate. Three, two…"

The dog slunk off the people mattress and tiptoed over to his own bed, shooting the mean man an aggrieved look.

Nick took a flying leap and landed next to Riley, head resting on his hand, top leg bent at the knee, showing off the merchandise under the towel. "As I was saying. Come here often?"

"You are *not* trying to have sex with me right now," she said.

"Oh, but I *am*."

"Nick."

"Thorn."

"Don't you need to process what happened tonight?"

He traced his fingers over the bare skin that peeked out above the waistband of her sleep shorts. "Nope."

Riley batted his hand away. "Well, *I* do."

"Come on, baby. Can't you just slide into my head, do some poking around, while I slide my hand into those shorts and do my own poking around?"

"As incredibly romantic as that sounds, no."

He leaned toward her and nibbled at her neck. "What's it going to take to convince you?"

"Nick, the woman you've been obsessed with finding just walked back into your life, lied about where she's been this entire time, and then introduced you to her husband—who, by the way, didn't abduct her and force her into servitude in his family's business. Now you're singing 'Girl on Fire' and trying to get me naked!"

He flopped onto his back. "I guess that means we're talking first."

Riley hit him in the face with a pillow. She was riding a second wave of adrenaline as words she hadn't said for the past several weeks bubbled up. "No. It means we're fighting first."

"As long as sex is still on the list, I'm up for whatever foreplay you want."

She scooted to the side of the bed, but before her feet could hit the floor, Nick hooked her around the waist with a strong, tattooed arm.

"What's gotten into you, Thorn?"

"Me? *Me?*"

"There any other Thorns in this bed?"

"In the past forty-eight hours, I've been followed twice, confronted in the street, passed out and gotten abducted, bought not one but *two* crop tops, watched your ex-partner lose his damn mind over his sister's betrayal, and worry that my boyfriend was going to abandon me for the woman in our guest room."

"Wow."

"Yeah. Wow. Jerk."

"Two crop tops?"

Riley reared back. Her head connected with Nick's face.

"Ow! I already have one black eye. I don't need a second one, Thorn," he said, wrestling her onto her back.

"And another thing! You come home with a battered face and won't even say what happened. How would you like it if I showed up with a black eye and refused to tell you where I got it?"

"Okay. Easy there, killer. I wasn't aware you were a powder keg of anxiety. I didn't mean to light your fuse."

"How dare you be in such a good mood! I've been walking on eggshells for weeks around you."

He frowned. "Why the hell would you do that?"

"Oh my God. Get off me so I can murder you."

"I'm going to deny that request for now until you lose your freakish rage strength. Let's start with the part about why you thought I was going to abandon you for the circus act in our guest room and then circle back to the eggshells."

Riley took a cleansing breath and blew it out slowly.

"That's my girl."

His cajoling tone and the dumb double dimples he flashed her had some of the rage draining from her body. His wet, naked body on top of hers didn't hurt either.

Stupid lust.

"Now, what in the hell would make you think I'd abandon

you for Beth? Or Sesame. I mean, sure, she's got a bigger rack than Beth did, but my God, woman. Were you not in the room when she confessed to lying about everything since birth?"

"You've been obsessed with her since I met you."

Nick shifted his weight so he could look up at the ceiling as if he was the wronged party. "You're kidding me right now, right?"

"Do I look like I'm kidding you?"

"Not really," he admitted. "I've been obsessed with *finding* her. There's a difference."

"Explain it to me," Riley demanded. "And while you're at it, explain to me why Kellen is destroyed over this and you're just-won-the-Super-Bowl happy."

"Because I didn't fuck up."

"I'm pretty certain that's a false statement," she countered.

"No, Thorn. I didn't fuck up and get Beth abducted or 'disappeared' or murdered. Her leaving had nothing to do with me. She met a guy who burned down a warehouse. Tale as old as time."

"Yeah. It's a real meet-cute," she said dryly.

"I didn't miss any signs. I didn't misread a threat. I didn't put her in harm's way. *I* didn't fuck up."

"You're telling me you spent all this time blaming yourself and you thought the only way you could fix it would be to find her. But now that you know the truth, you realize it was never your fault in the first place," she said.

"Bingo."

"Well, *why didn't you say so*, Santiago?" The only part of her body that wasn't pinned down by freshly showered man was her feet, which she kicked enthusiastically against the mattress.

"Why are you mad again? I was all vulnerable and shit just now."

"I'll tell you why," she sputtered.

"I'm all ears, sweetheart."

"Because you made me feel unsafe."

Nick went still on top of her.

"What?"

"I felt unsafe. And not just because I spent the last forty-eight hours worried you were trying to protect Sesame from me but also because you were in love with her and her admittedly magnificent boobs."

He went still and serious. "I'm not the mind reader in this relationship. Explain."

"I lost everything when I divorced Griffin. My job. My home. My car. Everything. And then I fell in love with you, and everything was great while there were murders to solve, but the second you found out Beth wasn't dead, you put it all on hold."

"I had to find out what happened," he said.

"I know that. I get that. But I went all in on you. I work for you. I bought a house with you. We're sharing a life, and you put that life at risk without so much as discussing it with me. Now all I can think about is that I jumped in too fast, and it's all going to come crashing down on me again. And another thing—"

"There's more?"

"Maybe I'm just a little pissed off that all it took was your dumb dimples to make me forget all the lessons I learned from Griffin. No, I'm a lot pissed off about that. And I just realized that I'm not even mad at you. I'm mad at me."

Nick was quiet for a long beat.

"Damn, Thorn. You really know how to hit a guy below the towel."

"I'm not apologizing for my feelings."

"Do you want a glass of wine?"

She opened her mouth to yell at him, then closed it. "Actually, yes. I do want a glass of wine," she said stiffly.

"Come on, baby. I'm pouring."

He pulled on a pair of sweatpants, and they tiptoed into the hallway. They realized caution was unnecessary as the steady thump from the guest room on the opposite end of the floor was punctuated by Sesame's wail. "Oh, Tommy! Yes! Yes!"

"Guess we'll be burning those sheets," Nick said, taking Riley's hand and leading her down the stairs.

In the kitchen, he made her stomach do a mini loop the loop when he picked her up and set her down on the counter. He grabbed a bottle of Sesame's wine and then looked blankly at the cabinets.

"Corkscrew is in the drawer next to the utensils. Wineglasses are in there," Riley said, pointing to the cabinet above the clipboard lists.

Nick followed her directions, producing mismatched glasses and opening the bottle.

"You know where the glasses are." He poured the wine and slid her a glass.

"Duh," she said.

"You know how many outlets are in this room. You're turning this mausoleum into a home with shit that I didn't help you pick out. You bought Halloween candy and crop tops. You mowed the lawn. I assume you're also the reason I've had clean underwear for the past few weeks and that Burt hasn't tried to eat me for dinner."

"What are you getting at?" she asked wearily. The wine was good. Like, really good. Like, rich-person-who-knew-wine good.

"I'm getting at I'm sorry I shoved my head up my own ass and left you to deal with all this by yourself."

Riley looked down at her glass.

"And I'm more than sorry that I made you feel anything like that assclown Gentry did. I never want to do that again. Tell me how I can do better."

She shook her head. "Oh no. I'm not falling for that. I was in the room the last time someone criticized you, and it did *not* go well for any of us. And why are you making so much eye contact with me?"

Nick shrugged and leaned against the counter opposite her, still maintaining a scary visual connection. "This feels like a normal amount of eye contact to me."

"Does it?"

"I'm sorry I made you feel like you had to walk on eggshells. And I'm sorry I didn't say anything when I noticed it."

"You noticed?"

"Thorn, my office looks like an entire fraternity spent spring break in it and someone got murdered. You never once called me out on it."

"I knew finding Sesame was important to you." She stared at her wine.

"Do you know that you're more important to me?" he asked, sounding very serious.

She shrugged. "I mean, I guess?"

"I really put you through the wringer, didn't I?" Nick asked.

"You didn't mean to."

"No, I didn't. But negligence is still a punishable offense, and I'm going to make it up to you so hard."

She smiled into her wineglass. "That's sweet of you."

"Don't think for one second that I don't know how fucking lucky I am to have you, Riley," he said, practically smoldering with intensity.

She couldn't decide whether the warm-and-fuzzy or the turned-on reaction was going to win. "You called me Riley."

"Uh, fair warning. If you tell me that's not your real name and you've been letting everyone call you by the wrong name because you didn't want to be a bother, I'm probably going to flip out."

She tried to stifle a yawn. "You only call me Riley when you're being super serious."

He reached out and tucked her hair behind her ear. "I'm always going to be super serious when it comes to you. Now, is there anything else you want to get off your really sexy chest before we collapse from exhaustion?"

Riley took a deep breath, but instead of just exhaling air, she exhaled the words that had been building up all day.

"I don't think I'm psychic anymore!" she wailed. "Gabe warned me, but I pushed too hard and ended up frying Cotton Candy World. I might have even killed my spirit guides. I mean, if they can be killed. I always assumed they were already dead, but now I'll never get the chance to ask them because they aren't there anymore. And I didn't want to tell anyone because I know I made a big deal about not wanting to be psychic, but I got kind of used to it. Maybe I even started to like it. And now I don't feel like I'm myself. You know?"

She lifted her watery gaze to his face.

Nick was frozen wide-eyed with his hand still behind her ear. "Uhhh, okay. Wow. That's a lot to unpack."

"What am I gonna do if I'm not psychic anymore? My grandmother will disown me. Mom's going to be disappointed. And Gabe. Oh my God. Just picturing his big sad face when I tell him I fried my own circuits after he warned me to be careful makes me want to throw up and cry."

"Those sound like very valid concerns," he said.

She sniffled. "They do?"

"Baby, they're your feelings. Of course they're valid. I mean, this is all fresh. Maybe someone dumber and less awesome would try to say you were overreacting since you were obviously having a vision of Tommy climbing in Sesame's window while you were sleeping."

She frowned. "I was, wasn't I?"

"Unless you believe in really specific coincidences, you definitely did. But if you want to panic about it, I'll hyperventilate with you. If you want to hide it from your family, I'll help you lie to them."

"That's really nice of you," she said, reaching out and rubbing her hand against his stubbled jaw.

"All the things you've done for me? All the ways you put up with me? I owe you, Thorn. We'll figure this out together. And not the version of together where one of us locks themselves away to obsess about something for an extended period of time. I'm here for you. Psychic or not. I love the hell out of you, and I swear on Burt's head that I will never make you feel abandoned like that. I might worry you and I might make you doubt your taste in men on occasion, but I never want to remind you of that spray-tanned puppet."

And just like that, her nerves vanished. "I love the hell out of you too. What are you doing?" she asked when he backed away.

"Topping you off," he said, picking up the bottle.

She gasped. "Nick Santiago!"

"What?"

She pointed at the wine. "You talked to my dad! You're ALECTO-ing me!"

"You know about ALECTO?"

"Of course I know about ALECTO! You think Dad came up with that on his own? Mom said it took her twelve years of positive reinforcement to get him to that level."

"I'm not sure what to do here. Do I start back at the beginning, or do I just keep topping you off? Also, I missed the foot-rub-and-chocolate part. I could start over with that."

Riley bit her lip. "The next step is you take your pants off."

He perked up. "Really?"

"You cared enough to ALECTO me. That's the best kind of foreplay."

22

With Riley's mouth fused to his and her legs wrapped around his waist, Nick decided there was no point in hitting pause just to waste all that time returning to their bedroom.

"We're. Not. Doing. It. In. The. Kitchen," she said between kisses.

He pulled back. "Are you sure you're not psychic right now?"

"Very funny. But we have guests who could come downstairs for a postcoital snack at any second now," she pointed out.

"I hate having guests," he muttered just before sucking her earlobe between his lips.

She shivered against him. "It's a big house. I'm sure we can find a place to get naked without interruption."

"That's the spirit," he said, lifting her off the counter.

She obliged by tightening her legs around his hips. His dick flexed when she moaned low in her throat.

"The noises you make when I'm driving you crazy drive me crazy," he confessed.

"I'm glad we drive each other crazy," she whispered.

They kissed their way out into the dark foyer, and Nick

hustled them into the closest room with a door. His office. He slid the door shut with his foot and proceeded toward the desk, kicking things out of his way as he went while Riley seduced him with her talented tongue. When he got to his desk, he snapped on the light and swept everything else off the surface.

"Okay. That's hot," she breathed as he dropped her on top and dragged her sweatshirt over her head.

"If you think that's hot, imagine me cleaning all this shit up tomorrow," he said, admiring the thin white tank top she wore beneath it.

"Yep. Even hotter," she decided.

His blood was pumping, cock throbbing. His body insistent on the need to take. How had he put this aside? How had he forgotten how much he wanted this? Her?

"Please tell me these sawhorses will hold us," she begged, her eyes a glassy brown that almost made his hands shake with need.

"They'll hold," he promised, yanking the scoop neck of her tank down to bare her breasts. He growled and dove for the first one. Just as his mouth closed over her pretty pink nipple, he felt her fingers slip under the waistband of his pants and close around his hard-on.

Stars exploded before his eyes. It had been too long since they'd been together like this. He couldn't withstand the torture. It was going to be fast and dirty.

"Can't wait. Need you now," he muttered.

"Yes. Please. Oh, shit. Condom?"

Nick froze, then muttered a colorful string of swear words against her soft breast.

"One second," he said, reluctantly removing her hand from his cock.

He pulled open the top file drawer and grabbed the first folder under *C*. Half a dozen condoms went flying.

"You filed our condoms?" Riley laughed as he plucked one off the floor and tore the wrapper open with his teeth.

"I thought you'd like my organizational efficiency." He

expertly rolled the condom on with one hand while yanking her shorts to the side.

"You just keep getting sexier and sexier," she said.

He lined up with her opening and gripped both hips with his hands. His fingers dug into the curves of her ass. "Hang on tight, baby. This is gonna be fast and hard."

"Quit sweet-talking me."

With one swift thrust, he buried himself in her.

Riley let out a scream that rivaled Sesame's.

"That's my girl," he said, slowly withdrawing. He was so fucking hard, and she was so fucking wet. Nick gritted his teeth and tried to think about lawn mower deck heights when he drove back into her. But she was too tight, too welcoming. He couldn't hold anything else in his head.

She dug her heels into his ass, urging him on.

"Baby, I need you to be fifty percent less sexy right now if you want me to last more than a half dozen pumps," he warned.

But she was already quivering around him. "Slow down and I won't show you my boobs for a week," she threatened.

"That's just mean," he said.

She lasted six thrusts. He lasted six and a half. As soon as he felt Riley clamp down on him like a vise, he was a goner. His orgasm ripped through him, and he gave a triumphant shout as the pleasure they shared swelled and shattered.

It had never been this good with anyone else. They shared something amazing together. And not just the orgasms.

She went limp in his arms and dropped back onto her elbows on the desk. "Wow," she panted.

"Yeah. Me too," he agreed as his legs continued to tremble.

She held up a hand. "Go, team."

He high-fived her and then collapsed on top of her. "Hey, Thorn?" he asked, listening to the thump of her heart under his ear.

"Yeah?"

"Since we're being honest and everything. Do you really think my dimples are dumb?"

"No, but I'm accidentally throwing you a surprise party for your birthday."

He lifted his head. "Seriously?"

She grinned and ran a hand through his hair. "It's a long story, but too many people are invested now. I'll make sure they keep it small. You probably won't even know it's happening."

"The things I do for you, Riley Middle Name Unspecified Thorn," he muttered.

"It's really good to have you back," she said, skimming her fingers over his bare shoulders. "So you're definitely cleaning up in here tomorrow, right? I mean, I'm scared you're going to start attracting wildlife with all the moldy pizza crusts in here."

Nick chuckled against her. "Good to have you back too, Thorn."

She was quiet for a few long beats, and just as he was debating between round two or carrying her up to bed, she poked him in the shoulder. "You didn't shut the pocket door all the way, did you?"

"Fuck."

23

Riley finished putting the new wineglasses in the dishwasher and hit the start button.

For a woman who had been disowned by her brother after recently coming back from the dead, Sesame had been in an upbeat mood that morning. She'd regaled them all with her dream of a creepy ghost dog with glowing eyes sneaking out of her closet. Then she'd laughed herself silly while Tommy had recounted coming downstairs to fetch Sesame her morning rejuvenation tea only to find Riley and Nick still locked in the office.

The happy couple—and Wilhelm, who it turned out was from Harrisburg and had a town house ten minutes away—had taken themselves out to brunch to celebrate being reunited. Riley and Nick had celebrated their own reunion by going shopping.

They'd returned home with an SUV full of items off their buy-it list. After a not-so-quick quickie, she'd put the new items away while Nick, with Burt's help, had tackled his toxic-waste dump of an office.

She eyed the last of their haul, which remained on the kitchen counter. Six bags of gummy worms, a candy neither she nor Nick liked, which gave this round of inventory a better shot at surviving until trick-or-treat night.

"Where can I hide you?" she mused, then grinned when inspiration hit.

She carted the candy into her office, where she shoved it into the bottom file drawer behind her desk. None of their elderly neighbors liked bending over to pick things up, so the odds of one of them finding the sugary worms were slim.

Stash secured, she pulled out her chair and sat. Despite the mere four hours of disjointed sleep they'd managed on the couch in Nick's office, she felt good. Happy. Relaxed. A sunny autumn Sunday full of shopping and home organization? What more could a girl want?

Well, besides her psychic powers back.

She grimaced. She'd tried twice that morning to drop into her spirit guide world and both times had found nothing but a shadowy void.

In need of a distraction, she opened her emails and dealt with a few of them. There was a request for a surveillance job from a new client and an armed security gig. She forwarded both on to Nick, who was still making quite the ruckus in his office. That complete, she logged into social media and fiddled with the yoga studio's Facebook and Instagram accounts.

A curious idea hit her. Not one whispered from a spirit guide but one from her own consciousness. She typed *Sesame Hemsworth* into the search and found…nothing.

That felt off. If anyone was built for social media, it was Sesame. She tried a few other name combinations in case Sesame had combined her past life with her current life and still came up dry. There was nothing for Tommy Hemsworth either. Though she didn't know what his pre-Sesame name had been.

Her fingers drummed on the keyboard as something nagged at the back of her mind.

Something Sesame had said last night.

Statute of limitations.

That was it. Riley typed the phrase into the search bar and added the word *arson*.

Hmm. That was interesting.

"What are you doing?"

She jumped and shut her laptop with a snap.

Nick entered and dropped into the chair in front of her desk. "That definitely doesn't make you look guilty, Thorn."

She wrinkled her nose. "Sorry. I'm still used to eggshells."

He wiped his palms on his jeans. "Lay it on me, baby."

Riley opened her laptop again. "I was just thinking about what Sesame said last night."

"The part where she told us she faked her own disappearance or the part where she screamed her husband's name and dented the drywall in the guest room?"

"The part where she said she had to wait for the statute of limitations to expire." Riley turned the screen to face him. "It's five years for arson. But she waited six years and change before coming home."

"If you're thinking she's lying—"

She held up her hands. "I'm not calling her a liar. I just feel like there's more she's not telling us," she said quickly.

"As I was saying. If you think she's lying, odds are she is," Nick told her. "The thing about dead people is the living tend to romanticize them. No one talks about Uncle Ralph being a cheapskate who hated the Irish in his eulogy. Maybe a little bit of that happened with Beth. She disappeared, and so did some of the memories of what a pain in the ass she could be. Now that she's back? It's kinda hard to ignore the fact that the girl is a stone-cold liar."

Riley perked up. "Really?"

"Babe, this is the girl who paid off a fourth grader with pudding to take the blame when she set off the sprinklers in the elementary school to get out of gym class. She's a mastermind at getting away with shit."

"Well, since you're not vigorously defending her or warning me to leave her alone—"

"Come on, Thorn. I was doing that to protect *you*. I didn't want you getting mixed up in any mess she was involved in until I could make sure she wasn't still a target for the bad guys. The bad guys don't exist. Ergo, lay it on me. What's rattling around in that beautiful brain of yours?"

He asked for it. "A lot. Why doesn't Sesame have any social media accounts? Is Hemsworth just another fake name that she gave us so we couldn't find the real fake her? Why didn't Tommy come with her? She came home without him and never mentioned the fact that she was married. Instead she concocts some story based on the plot of *Overboard*."

"I really need to see that movie," he said.

"Then as soon as I said we were being followed by a man, she was all excited, almost like she was hoping to be followed," Riley continued.

"So maybe they had a fight?"

"What kind of a fight would be bad enough to leave your husband and unfake your own death?" she asked.

"It couldn't have been that bad since she opened Weber's window for him."

"Agreed."

"Or maybe it's all part of some grandiose plot to get Bethame some new shiny thing. Trust me, with her, you can never tell."

Riley mulled that over. "I think something else brought her back to town besides making amends with family. I just don't know what."

He rubbed a hand over his sexy, stubbly jaw. "And obviously we can't just ask her, or she'd end up recounting the plot of *Robocop*, which I have seen."

"And every time I did try to poke around in her head, I ended up with psychic vertigo."

"That explains a lot," Nick said.

She winced. "Sorry. I meant to tell you that part last night, but your penis made me forget."

"You're forgiven based entirely on your compliment of my penis."

His dimples had her grinning.

He leaned back and interlaced his fingers behind his head. "Here's another question. What does it matter?"

"You mean to tell me now that you know none of this is your fault, you're not the slightest bit curious about why she came back? Why she changed her appearance? What was she really doing for six years if she wasn't forced into indentured servitude?"

He scratched the back of his head, and Riley couldn't help but admire the way his bicep flexed. "Look, I'm not saying I'm not curious. Or that you shouldn't listen to your instincts, because we both know they've saved our asses a few times. But I *am* saying it's a beautiful day. I've got a sexy girlfriend with new crop tops. There's a couple of steaks in the fridge for dinner and a project or two that involve power tools. Right now, things are pretty fucking great. Let's take the day for ourselves and worry about where Beth Weber was or what Sesame Hemsworth is up to next week."

"And you'll worry with me?" Riley hedged.

"Hell yeah."

"You must have had a whole lot of stress tied up in feeling responsible for her disappearance," she observed.

"Baby, I feel like the weight of the world is off my shoulders. I could run a marathon or bench-press Gabe. I feel so good, I'm not even trying to stop you from throwing me a surprise party."

"Thank God, because Gabe would be crushed."

Nick looked down at his watch. "You know, we've got the house to ourselves right now. We could see how sturdy your desk is."

Galloping dog paws echoed in the foyer, and Burt let out his welcome-to-my-home bark.

"Are you fucking kidding me?" Nick muttered.

"I'm not the one who left the front door unlocked," she pointed out.

"It's just me." Wander strolled in wearing a pair of pink nose plugs and lugging a large plastic storage tote. Burt jogged in after her, carrying his favorite stuffed toy.

Nick slumped in the chair, the anticipation of some afternoon delight evaporating. "A moat, Thorn. We need a moat."

She grinned at him, then turned to her sister. "I take it you can you still smell Larry?"

Wander grimaced. "Like he's decaying in the next room."

"You better give your mom the go-ahead for the cleansing ceremony," Nick advised, getting to his feet.

Riley wasn't certain that the herb smoke and pungent aroma of bad vibes smoke cleanser would be any better than psychic whiffs of dead guy.

"In the meantime, I brought an amazing new pumpkin spice incense," Wander said.

"Is that what's in the tote?" Nick asked.

Wander went stock-still like a rabbit scenting a predator. "Um, yes," she squeaked. "This is my incense collection."

"Well, you ladies have fun sniffing incense. I have power tools to play with," he said, rounding the desk. He gave Riley an NC-17 kiss, tossed Wander a salute, and headed out with Burt on his heels.

"Where are the girls?" Riley asked her sister.

Wander slid the tote onto her desk. "Gabe has them. They're throwing him a garden fairy tea party."

"Uh, that's adorable. I hope you get pictures of him in a tutu and wings."

"I will," Wander promised. "I came to see if you were okay after the Sesame situation under the guise of party planning. I was already nervous about lying to you. Then I panicked when Nick asked what was inside." She patted the tote. The label said *Halloween Decor*.

Wander was humblingly thoughtful. Not only was she raising three daughters mostly on her own, she was also running a successful business, keeping in shape, and dedicating time to enhancing her psychic sniffer powers, but she still managed to carve out time to check in on her hot-mess sister.

A drill squealed to life somewhere in the house.

"You're the best. Want some tea?"

"I'd love some."

———

"So it's all just gone? No pretty clouds? No spirit guides?" Wander asked.

They'd taken their tea to the table on the back patio so her sister wouldn't need to shield her nose from *Eau de Ghost*. Burt was using his gigantic head to push leaves into a pile and then bounding into said pile.

Riley sighed. "Yep. Except for the dream I had last night, it's all gone. I feel like a little kid who's about to get in big trouble. Gabe warned me not to push too hard. Now here I am, powerless. I still don't know why Sesame could send me spiraling like that. What if this is permanent?"

It felt good to get it off her chest. Telling Nick and then her sister had made some of the guilt and shame she felt lessen a little bit.

"You know who would have the answers," Wander said.

Riley groaned. "I know. But she'd just be all snotty and judgmental toward me for being too weak to handle whatever it is on my own."

"That's valid. But Grandmother is judging no matter what. You get to decide whether her judgment affects you."

"It's not that simple," Riley argued, then yawned. She was tired. Weeks of crappy sleep were starting to catch up with her.

"It's simple but not easy," Wander countered. "But I respect your decision, whatever it is. I do think I might have a suggestion on what to do about your powers though."

Riley perked up. "I'm desperate. If you want me to eat a vegan tofu hash and meditate naked under the full moon, I'll do it."

"As tempting as it is to punk you right now, I think the answer might be rest."

"Rest?" Riley repeated.

"You had an extremely stressful summer. You've spent the

past several weeks worried about your life partner. Sesame returning had to have been quite the shock even without the psychic vertigo. And you haven't been sleeping well. It could be like when your body is run-down, you're more susceptible to viruses and infections. I think you gave yourself a case of the psychic flu."

"Do you think my powers could come back?" she asked, trying not to hope for the impossible.

"I think you'd be surprised at what happens if you take care of your body and mind. Be gentle with yourself. Give yourself time to heal. You'll find your way back on track in no time."

Riley bit her lip. "I know this isn't fair of me to ask, but could you not tell Gabe about this? I feel like he should hear it from me."

"Of course. Be vulnerable when you feel safe. Do what you think is best, and I'll support you on your journey," Wander promised.

Riley reached out and squeezed her hand. "Thanks. One more favor?"

Wander smiled indulgently. "Of course."

"Can you invite Marie and Miguel Santiago to Nick's surprise party? Marie is more likely to say yes to you than me."

"I'd be happy to," Wander promised.

"You're a pretty awesome little sister."

"And you're an extraordinary woman. Don't forget it."

They watched Burt dive headfirst into a fresh pile of leaves and then roll onto his back, his gangly legs sticking up in the air. "Speaking of extraordinary, Nick and I are back to having awesome sex."

"How nice for you."

To the untrained observer, the tiny pinch of sarcasm in Wander's tone would have gone unnoticed. Riley's eyes widened. "That's the equivalent of a snide 'It must be nice.'"

Wander squeezed her eyes shut. "I'm sorry. I did not mean to spew venom like that all over you."

"There was no spewing," Riley assured her. "You fixed me. Now it's your time to vent."

Wander stared up at the trees. "Gabe is wonderful. He's kind, generous, compassionate, intelligent, calm, present, peaceful, incredibly good-looking."

"Super handsome," Riley agreed.

"And he hasn't made a move for second base, and I'm so sexually frustrated it's driving me insane."

"What's the holdup? I mean, I can't imagine a man holding out against all this," Riley said, waving her hand in the direction of Wander's rockin' bod. The woman owned an entire wardrobe of crop tops.

"All bodies are beautiful and deserve to be loved," Wander replied.

"Uh, especially yours. You were nine months pregnant and still had an eight-pack. Obviously you're not the problem. If we weren't sisters, I would be attracted to you. Hell, I think Nick's mom is one hot yoga class away from switching teams for you."

"Maybe he's just not interested in moving forward in that direction with me."

"Maybe he's just a big cuddly virgin who needs a sexy older lover to show him the ropes?"

Riley and Wander twisted to find Lily joining them on the patio. Mrs. Penny marched up behind her, armed with a pitcher of what smelled like all the alcohol from the state store. It had a straw sticking out of it.

"You're not sleeping with Gabe, Lily," Riley said.

The older woman pouted and took the empty chair next to Wander. "Party pooper."

"Maybe Gabe's penis is too big to work. I knew this guy in the Marines who passed out every time he got turned on," Mrs. Penny said.

"Just make sure you use two hands when handling it," Lily advised. "Those things can get slippery."

"This is my karma for bringing drama into your home," Wander said with a sigh.

"I'm just here to get drunk and eat candy," Mrs. Penny said.

"There's no candy here," Riley lied.

Mrs. Penny kicked the leg of the table with her orthopedic shoe. "Well, this day just keeps getting better and better."

Wander sniffed the air delicately, then wrinkled her nose. "Is that straight gin?"

"Yeah. I'm too depressed to mix a cocktail. Besides, hard-boiled detectives always have a drinking problem. It's how they do their best work." Mrs. Penny took another long gulp through the straw.

"I take it Burt's poop didn't bust your case wide open?" Riley guessed.

Mrs. Penny wiped her mouth on the sleeve of her crap-brown argyle sweater. "The only lead I got from the lab is that you should be more careful what you feed your dog."

"*Me?*"

The door behind them opened, and everyone turned to look at Tommy, who poked his head outside. "Sorry to bother you, but I'm doing a few loads of laundry. I'm happy to wash yours too. I make my own detergent."

"Is it just me, or is that a huge turn-on?" Lily asked in a loud whisper.

"Definitely a huge turn-on," Riley agreed.

"Is it warm out here, or is it just me?" Wander asked, fanning herself.

Mrs. Penny made a slurping sound with her straw.

24

I 've called you all here today—"

"To fire us?" Brian guessed, interrupting Nick.

"To grovel?" Josie tried. She was unpacking and reorganizing the weapons she carried in her cargo pants.

They were gathered in Nick's office—which actually resembled an office again and not a repository of old case files and moldy fast food—for another staff meeting.

"If it's to tell us that Bethame was never abducted and held hostage in an identity theft ring, Riley already told us," Brian said.

"Was I supposed to keep that a secret?" Riley asked Nick.

She was perched on the corner of his desk. After seven whole hours of sleep, she was feeling perky. And thanks to her new butt-enhancing jeans and the hoodie Tommy had washed that now smelled like lemons, she was also feeling pretty cute.

"Where's the bacon?" Mrs. Penny demanded from the couch. She was wearing a gamer headset around her neck.

Burt perked up at Riley's feet at the word *bacon*.

"What bacon?" Riley asked.

"Someone calls a meeting for nine a.m., I expect bacon and Bloody Marys," the elderly woman said, then shook the Bloody Mary pitcher she'd brought with her.

"Who brings a Bloody Mary to a business meeting?" Nick complained.

"Someone who's expecting bacon. I brought enough for everyone. The least you can do is go fry up a pack of bacon. Some partner you're turning out to be."

Nick thumped his head on his desk. "What did I do in a past life to deserve this?" he moaned.

Riley patted him on the shoulder. "Would a Bloody Mary make you feel better?"

"Maybe."

"That's the spirit. I'll pour!" Mrs. Penny bounded off the couch.

"I gotta side with Stabby McGee on the bacon," Brian said.

"I second the motion," Josie said.

Riley grinned. "Motion passes. I'll start the bacon."

Nick sighed. "Fuck it. What's the point of having your own business if you can't drink and eat bacon first thing in the meeting?"

Riley headed into the foyer, where she found Sesame in a floral dressing gown and Tommy deep in conversation with a stranger holding a camera. She was a bald Black woman wearing a supremely awesome leather jacket and a scarlet scarf that matched her lipstick.

There was a camera on a tripod set up at the foot of the stairs and several pieces of large lighting equipment in various stages of assembly.

A second stranger of indeterminate age hustled into the foyer from the living room. She was dressed in head-to-toe black, including sneakers and a ball cap. "Yo! There's a settee in here that could work and an upholstered ottoman that's so ugly it's actually kind of hot."

"Uh, what's going on?" Riley asked. Everyone turned to look at her.

Sesame trotted over to her on platinum sandals with puffs of fur on the straps. "Riley! Isn't this exciting?"

"I have no idea."

"Well, I hope you don't mind, but we're having a photo shoot for my big comeback announcement. I'll have to do a lot of press once word gets out that I'm back, and I want to control the branding," she said, fluffing her blond hair.

"You're doing a photo shoot here?" Riley didn't have any illusions about her home. Sure, in its heyday, it had probably been a jaw-dropper. But in its current state, it was, well, still a jaw-dropper but for other, less elegant reasons.

"*The* Joplin Jones is doing the shoot. Can you believe it?" Sesame's high-pitched squeal sent Burt slinking into the kitchen.

"I really can't," Riley agreed since she had no idea who Joplin Jones was. "Wait. What comeback?"

"Once the news hits that I'm alive and well, the media storm will be a Category Five. And the public is going to want content. I'll have to launch a brand-new social media presence." Sesame paused her glee long enough to wave over the two strangers in the foyer. "Joplin, Fantasia, this is Riley. She owns the house."

"Nice to meet you," Fantasia said.

Joplin held up the camera and took Riley's picture. The flash temporarily blinded her.

"Yeah. So. Joplin is gonna need an industrial fan. Or maybe a couple of hair dryers," Fantasia said.

"OMG, yes! I *love* that," Sesame said, clasping her hands under her chin.

"Uh, Nick? Can you come out here?" Riley called.

Nick appeared in his office doorway with two Bloody Marys and stopped short. "What the hell is going on?"

Riley crossed to him, blinking back stars. "Sesame is having a comeback photo shoot and needs a wind machine." She took one of the Bloody Marys from him.

"For my hair," Sesame said.

"I've got a leaf blower in the garage."

Twenty minutes later, all employees of Santiago Investigations had Bloody Marys, bacon, and toast. And Sesame had her leaf blower.

Nick, unfortunately, had to keep the office door open so they didn't get locked in. "As I was saying, I called you all here today to inform you that despite the fact that I was completely right about everything and therefore don't owe you an apology, as of today, Santiago Investigations is looking for paid work again. I've got an armed security gig for Josie this afternoon, a surveillance for Brian tonight, and I just accepted a shit ton of serves," he shouted.

The leaf blower stopped.

Josie cocked her head. "So we're officially back in business?"

"Yes. Not that we were ever officially out of business," he added quickly. "But we will be resuming normal gigs immediately."

Riley noticed a lot of long looks being exchanged in the room, and no one looked very happy.

"This is bullshit!" Mrs. Penny yelled.

"That was not the reaction I was expecting," Nick said, looking at Riley.

She shrugged. "Beats me."

The leaf blower started again, and so did the flashes from the foyer.

"I'm closing in on the Dog Doody Bandit! I just had two hundred of these freaking posters made." Mrs. Penny held up a hot-pink flyer.

"'If you see doody, say doody,'" Riley read out loud. The Santiago Investigations phone number was at the bottom. "Oh boy."

"Okay, fine. You stay on the Dog Doody Bandit. Everyone else can get back to your regularly scheduled gigs, and I'll work on getting our phone number changed," Nick shouted.

Josie and Brian shared another look. "Uh, actually, boss, I think we'd like to follow through on our cases too," Josie said at full volume.

"You're fucking with me as payback, aren't you?" Nick asked.

The leaf blower cut off again.

"Not this time," Brian insisted. "I finally hacked into Gym Rat's dating app account. Turns out he's a naughty bank vice president who's been sending unsolicited dick pics to his female matches. And as someone who's actually seen him in the shower at the gym, that's not his dick."

"False advertising!" Mrs. Penny shouted into her glass. "Automatic jail time."

"Do you have any idea how the justice system works?" Nick asked blandly.

"*Anyway,*" Brian continued, "I'm working on a pretty badass takedown involving his LinkedIn account and his work email."

"Me and Esther have a sting planned for her stupid grandson tonight," Josie said. "We're gonna bust him with a clown down his pants. She said I can scare the hell out of him. And you know how much I love scaring people."

"It's one of the five whole things you like in this world," Nick said.

"Exactly. If you can handle the armed security, I can focus on nailing Junior to the wall and scaring him straight."

He looked incredulous. "You're seriously turning down a paying gig that requires you to carry guns so you can save an old lady's clown collection?"

"I'd just like to clarify that you're not actually nailing anyone to a literal wall, right?" Riley asked.

"Yes."

Riley waved her hands. "Yes, you're seriously turning down a paying gig, or yes, you're literally nailing someone to a wall?"

"Now I know you're fucking with me," Nick said.

Riley noticed his bruised eye was starting to twitch again.

"I know you gave us these cases as a 'fuck you,'" Brian said. "But I gotta admit, I'm having fun playing hacker vigilante."

Nick scrubbed a hand over his face. "Fine. Whatever

the fuck you want. How long do you guys need to wrap up your"—he glanced in Mrs. Penny's direction—"*primo* cases?"

"I need twenty-four hours to set everything in motion," Brian said.

Josie nodded. "I can have Junior pissing his pants in twelve hours."

"And I'm closing in on the Double D Bandit."

Nick threw his pen on the desk. "How are we going to make any money if you pains in my ass are all working pro bono cases?"

"You literally just said the business was fine and that you were right about everything," Brian pointed out.

"Fuck me. Fine. Whatever." Nick's desk phone rang, and he answered it. "Santiago Investigations." He frowned. Then frowned some more before holding the receiver out to Mrs. Penny. "It's for you," he growled.

Mrs. Penny sprang off the couch. Half a strip of bacon fell from her lap and was inhaled by Burt before it hit the floor.

"This is Penny, PI."

"You're not a licensed PI. You can't say that!" Nick hissed, pressing his palm to the twitch under his eye.

Mrs. Penny ignored him and hefted herself onto the opposite corner of his desk. "You got doody? You found it in your front yard? I'll be right there." She threw the receiver in Nick's direction. "Gotta go! I've got doody!"

She slid off the desk, landed with a fart, and jogged for the door. Burt trailed after her, snarfing up the bacon crumbs she shed.

Josie hooked her thumb in the direction of the door. "I'm also gonna roll. I have a clown costume to rent."

"Yeah, Nicky. I've gotta go too. Gym Rat's about to match with an assistant district attorney who's on Hook Up under her cousin's name."

"I'm running a damn circus," Nick complained as his team left the room.

"I believe this is what's called karma," Riley said innocently.

"No one likes a smug girlfriend, Thorn."

She hopped off his desk and grabbed the zipper of her hoodie. "How about a smug girlfriend in a crop top?"

Nick had her in his lap before she unzipped all the way. "I'd like to revise my previous statement."

"I thought you might."

"Yoo-hoo!"

Riley turned to see Sesame standing in the open doorway. She wore a dress that was short in the front and tapered off into a long, sequined train in the back.

"Since you two aren't busy, can I borrow one of you? I need someone to stand behind me off camera and fluff my train."

"Gee, sorry, Sesame. But I have to go to school to see about a bully," Riley said.

"Don't do this to me, Thorn," Nick pleaded.

"Sorry, babe," she said, kissing him on the nose. "I can't get in the way of karma."

25

Sheepford Junior/Senior High School was a squat brick building that looked like it could have used a facelift twenty years ago. It was sandwiched between Route 15 and an industrial complex, which meant traffic snarls at all times of the day.

Riley swung her Jeep into the pickup line behind a minivan with several children already hanging out the open windows and doors.

"That looks legal," Jasmine observed dryly from the back seat.

"That's nothing. I once saw a car drive away with an eighth grader hanging on to the luggage rack," said Riley's other passenger.

Roz Cooper was a spunky, sweaty brunette in her early sixties wearing knee socks and guzzling a protein shake in the passenger seat. At her request, Riley had picked her up at the gym. "I appreciate you driving, dear. I usually have to wait an hour or two after leg day before I regain the use of my legs enough to drive home."

"No problem," Riley said.

According to Mrs. Penny's questionable intel, Roz was great-aunt to Kory Cooper, victim of Lance the Bully. Roz and

Kory were related to Mrs. Penny in some complicated way that sounded more like a family shrub than a family tree.

After the fun everyone else seemed to be having on their cases, Riley had decided she might as well save a nice kid from a bully. But it was weird being in her vehicle without hearing Uncle Jimmy's chatter in her head. It made her sad.

"So, Roz, tell me about your great-niece," she said. "What kind of trouble is she having with this Lance kid?"

"Kory is a super nerd, and I say that with love," Roz explained. "She's in seventh grade. Smart. Small for her age. This Lance prick moved here at the beginning of the school year and was forcing her to do his homework for a couple of months before she got sick of it and got him a failing grade on an English essay. He's been making her life a living hell ever since."

"Have you tried talking to the school?" Riley asked.

"Her parents have. I have. Lance is the entitled son of the vice principal and the pain-in-the-ass band director, who act like they're some kind of 'super couple' who rule the district with an iron fist. We're at our wits' end. This Lance is dangerous, and I'm willing to do whatever it takes to get him out of this school."

"Understood. How are you and Mrs. Penny related again?" Riley asked.

"Her daughter-in-law's niece is my cousin. Oh! There she is, my little Kory!" Roz waved out the window to a small girl making her way across the grass toward them.

Kory was shorter than pretty much every other student pouring out of the building in search of freedom. She had brown skin, thick dark hair pulled up in a high pouf, and purple glasses. She was wearing the standard student uniform of a baggy hooded sweatshirt and leggings. She raised a hand to wave back, then hefted her overfilled backpack higher on her little shoulders.

"She's so cute. Who would pick on her?" Jasmine wondered.

"Lance is an only child and has never heard the word *no*.

Last month, he stuffed a freshman in the ice maker in the cafeteria, and everyone was too scared to tell on him. Poor kid was blue and shaking so hard he lost two fillings before the custodian found him. He was the one who got detention for a month while Lance's parents named him Student of the Month."

"He sounds like a peach," Jasmine said dryly.

"We'll talk to Kory and get a little background information. After that, we'll get into why he's lashing out, figure out what his weaknesses are, dig up any dirt on him. Then we'll try reasoning with him," Riley explained, trying to sound like a professional who intimidated teenagers often.

"And if that doesn't work?" Roz asked uneasily.

"Then we snap him like a wishbone," Jasmine said. "Trust me. Reducing teenage boys to tears was my superpower from ages eight to eighteen. I mostly practice on men over thirty now, but it's always good to return to your roots."

"I can't thank you two enough," Roz said. "This really means the world to my entire family."

It was right about then that Kory took a header and went sprawling into the grass over someone's foot.

"Did that teacher just trip her?" Riley asked in disbelief.

"That's Lance. The mustache and 'roid rage make him look older," Roz growled. "If I could walk right now, I'd go over there and kick him right in the crotch."

"We'll take care of this," Jasmine said, jumping out of the back seat.

Riley followed her. "We can't assault a teenager, Jas. At least not on school grounds with all these witnesses."

"When I'm done with this punk, he's going to beg to be homeschooled," Jasmine said, storming toward the overgrown teen who was standing over Kory and laughing. "Jesus! How many grades did you fail? All of them?" Jasmine demanded, stomping right into Lance's face as Riley helped Kory to her feet.

He gave them both a smirking once-over. "Who the hell are you? Somebody's grandmas?"

It was official. Lance the Dick was a dead man.

Riley gripped Jasmine's shoulder. "Not on school grounds. Remember?" she whispered.

"Yeah, not on school grounds," Lance's friend, Pale Skinny Guy with Body Odor, said in a high falsetto.

"I forgot how much I hated school," Riley said.

"Did they even have school back in the dinosaur ages?"

"Don't mind him," Kory said to Riley. "This idiot doesn't know that dinosaurs were extinct long before humans evolved."

"Speaking of evolution, this one missed a few steps," Jasmine hissed, looking at Lance like he was gum on a pair of Ferragamos.

"What's your problem, old lady? Did you lose at bingo?" Lance taunted. He pulled out a vape pen and blew a cloud into Jasmine's face.

Riley tightened her hold on her friend.

"Yeah, Lance! You tell her," crowed the second crony. This one was well over six feet tall and had a face not even a mother could love.

"Is this what growth hormones in meat and dairy do?" Riley muttered.

"I have a theory that he was dropped on his head repeatedly," Kory said.

"Old bitch says what?" Lance said, bouncing back and forth on the balls of his feet, his hands balled into fists.

Riley flinched as he threw a few shadowbox punches at her face. "Back off," she said more calmly than she felt.

"Granny wants us to back off," Tall Idiot said.

Lance threw a few more punches in her direction that came close enough for her to feel the breeze.

Jasmine jumped between them and stabbed her finger in Lance's chest. "I'm going to kick you in the dick with my pointiest shoes so hard your bloodline ends with you."

Lance frowned. "Huh?"

"He still thinks babies come from storks," Kory said from behind Riley.

"You wanna say that to my face, you little bitch?" Lance howled. "How about I tape your mouth shut and lock you in the janitor's closet again for the day?"

"You think you're a man because you've got six hairs on your upper lip?" Jasmine snarled. "You're nothing but a teeny-tiny little boy who deep down knows that he's nothing but a loser."

"A loser? A *loser*?" Body Odor squealed. "Bitch, my boy Lance here gets laid on the regular by college girls."

"Yeah, yeah," Tall Idiot said, bobbing his head. "Lance got scouted by the NBA, and he's not even on the high school basketball team."

"They're all idiots," Kory explained wearily. "Why can't you just leave me alone, Lance?"

Lance glared at her over Jasmine's and Riley's shoulders. "Because you tried to take me down. Now you're gonna pay." He stuffed the vape pen into his pocket and then pulled out a pocket knife. "Maybe I'll have my friends here hold you down and cut your hair."

"And maybe I'll call the cops 'cause that sounds like you're about to assault my friend here," Riley said.

"Who's gonna believe you over me? Huh, skank?" He waved the dull blade in her face.

"Why don't you call the cops, Ry, and I'll sue him for being a dickless moron?" Jasmine suggested.

"You got a death wish, Granny?" Lance snarled.

"Mr. Rhinehard, unless you're looking to be nominated for in-school suspension and student counseling, I suggest you go the hell home." This came from a haggard-looking man dressed in wrinkled Dockers and a darker beige sweater.

Lance sneered. "What are you gonna do about it? My dad can make your tenure go away like that." He tried to snap his fingers but failed, so Body Odor stepped up to do it for him.

"Uh-oh. Mr. Volch has crazy eyes again," Kory observed. "We should probably go."

Mr. Volch waved his arms to encompass the school. "Do

I look like I care about keeping this job? Do you think it's my dream to try to cram information into tiny little pea brains like yours while smelling BO all damn day? Put on some goddamn deodorant for once, Troy," the teacher shouted, shoving his hands into his already unruly hair and pulling on the ends until it stood straight up.

"Let's get out of here," Riley said, pulling Kory and Jasmine toward the Jeep.

"Who are you guys anyway?" Kory asked.

"We're friends of your...er... How are you related to Mrs. Penny?" Riley asked.

"Who?"

"Never mind."

"Just think of us as the not-at-all-old ladies who are going to kick Lance's ass for you," Jasmine vowed through gritted teeth.

26

Riley had just dropped off Roz and Kory at home and was discussing the options for a late afternoon snack with Jasmine when Nick called.

"What's up? And keep it clean. You're on speakerphone."

"I've got a problem. I could use your help," he said.

"It doesn't involve Sesame's photo shoot, does it?"

"That's over, thank God. But it does involve the Weber family. I just got a call from Dockside Willies. Weber's shit-faced, and they want someone to come pick him up, but I'm at this armed security gig. Can you pick him up? Maybe babysit him and make sure he's not gonna do something stupid?"

Jasmine grabbed Riley's arm and bounced in her seat. "Oh my God! Yes! I bet you twenty bucks I can get him to give me permission to draw a mustache on him with a Sharpie."

"I'm not betting against you," Riley told her friend. Then she asked Nick, "Since when does Kellen get drunk and do stupid things?"

"Only when his personal life goes to shit. He went on a weeklong bender after his divorce and ended up with the worst tattoo in the world."

"What is it? Where is it?" Jasmine demanded.

"If you pick him up, I bet it wouldn't take much to get him to show it to you," Nick said.

"We'll go get him," Riley promised.

"I owe you one, Thorn."

"Don't shoot anyone if you can help it," she said and then disconnected the call.

Jasmine rubbed her palms together. "I can't wait to see Detective Smug Shit drunk off his ass. I bet he's a crier."

"Be nice. He's dealing with a lot."

"Maybe if he didn't have such a huge stick shoved up his ass, his family would feel comfortable being honest with him."

"I've never seen you dislike someone so cute before."

"You think he's *cute*? He's a pigheaded, judgmental, always right, suit-wearing monster."

"Honestly, he sounds perfect for you," Riley teased.

———

Detective Kellen Weber was indeed shit-faced.

They found him shoveling peanuts into his face under the watchful eye of the bartender at Dockside Willies. It was decked out for Halloween with skeletons and pumpkins everywhere. Despite the bar being busy, the stools on either side of the detective were empty.

"And another thing," he slurred to the bar in general. "When she accidentally dropped Mom's soap Jesus in the bathtub, who was the one who took the blame? Me. I was grounded for the entire summer I got my driver's license because I protected her."

"He belong to you two?" the bartender asked hopefully.

"Ew. Gross," Jasmine said, covering her mouth to dry heave.

Riley sighed. "Yeah. He's ours. Do you know who he's talking about?" she asked, trying to sound casual. Even if Sesame wasn't in danger anymore, she probably wouldn't appreciate spoilers before her big reveal.

"It's always a woman," the bartender said wearily.

"On behalf of my fairer sex, I apologize. Did he close out his tab?" Riley asked.

"I don't wanna close out my tab. I wanna drink until I don't feel stuff," Weber announced.

"Feeling stuff is overrated," Riley agreed. "How about we go drink our feelings away someplace else?"

He looked at her with one eye open and one eye closed. "You're not just tricking me, are you?"

"That depends," she said, helping him off his stool. His suit jacket was missing, and his tie was loosened to reveal two open shirt buttons. It was as disheveled as the detective got.

"Depends on what?" he asked.

"Jasmine and I wanted tacos. Can you switch to margaritas or beer for a bit?"

"Jasmine?" Weber snorted, then hiccupped. "She's so mean."

"That's because you're an uptight asshole," Jasmine pointed out.

"See?" Weber turned to Riley and nearly went down. "Mean."

"A little help here," Riley begged Jasmine as she supported his weight.

"Ugh. Fine. But you owe me," her friend said, sliding an arm around the man's waist.

"Grab his wallet," Riley insisted.

"I'm not going through his pockets. That's penis territory," Jasmine hissed.

"Since when are you afraid of penis territory?"

"Riley Middle Name Thorn!"

"Sorry, Jas. I didn't mean it. You know how I get after being accosted by a teenage sociopath and then crushed under the weight of a drunk homicide detective."

"Apology accepted," Jasmine said, taking more of Weber's weight. "Listen, Detective Assface. I need to put my hand in your pocket and find your wallet. But before I do it, I'd feel better if I had your consent because I don't know what I might accidentally grab in there. Got it?"

"You're trying to get into my pants," Weber snickered.

"You're the worst."

"Everyone says that. I promise to be consensual," Weber said.

Jasmine squeezed her eyes closed and reached into his front pocket. "Ugh. I really don't want to do this."

"Look at it this way. The sooner you find it, the sooner we can get out of here and you can draw that mustache," Riley suggested.

"I found it! Oh. Whoops. No. That is *definitely* not his wallet. Well, that's a pleasant surprise."

Weber made some kind of noise that skirted close to giggle territory. "That tickles!"

"Moving my hand immediately," Jasmine said, narrating her movements. "And nope. That's still definitely not wallet. Wow, you really don't have much room in here, do you?"

A man shorter than Riley strutted up to them. He sported a *Federal Bikini Inspector* T-shirt. "Either of you ladies wanna find my wallet for me?" he cackled and grabbed his crotch through his jean shorts.

"Men are pigs," Weber said.

"Amen, brother," the bartender agreed.

"Listen, Short Stop. If you don't get your nonexistent ass out of my way in two seconds, I'll make sure you never stand up straight again," Jasmine said.

"I don't suppose you could use your legs to hold some of your weight, could you, Kellen?" Riley asked through gritted teeth as the tiny man slunk away.

"Hey! Whaddaya know? My legs work," Weber said, standing upright.

"It's a miracle." Riley wheezed a sigh of relief.

"Aha!" Jasmine held up the wallet in triumph. She handed it to Riley, who snatched the tab off the bar and threw down some cash.

"Hey, guys. Let's take a smelfie," Weber suggested as they started for the door. "We can send it to Bethame and show her that I'm super fun and awesome, and she should feel like a jerk for everything."

"That's a great idea. I just need to make you look extra fun first," Jasmine said as they helped him toward the door.

"You're not gonna make me wear a Hawaiian shirt, are you?"

"No. I'm just going to draw a handlebar mustache on your face with permanent marker."

"Okay."

———

Tres Hermanos was an authentic Mexican restaurant on Cameron Street with the best tacos al pastor on the East Shore. The hostess didn't bat an eyelash at Weber's new mustache, which arched gracefully down on the left but slashed up on a diagonal toward his ear on the right due to a poorly timed sneeze.

"Wanna see me blow bubbles in my margarita?" Weber asked, trying to find the straw with his mouth.

Jasmine slapped it out of his drink.

"Hey! I was gonna use that," he complained.

"How about you eat one or ten of these tacos to soak up the gallon of scotch you drank?" Riley suggested, pushing his plate closer.

He picked up a taco and then put it down again. "And another thing. Not only did my own sister fake her own disappearance and make me think she was dead somewhere, but my own mother knew she left town with her dumb boyfriend-husband and let me think she was dead somewhere. You know why?"

Riley shook her head but didn't speak because she had a mouthful of tacos.

"Why?" Jasmine asked, egging him on.

"Because she's an intolerant, coldhearted, frowny-faced jerk who cares more about soap-carved Jesuses than her own family."

Riley swallowed. "Kellen, I'm sorry you're dealing with all this right now, but you don't want to be dealing with this *and* a hangover tomorrow. Please eat a taco."

"I never get hungover because I never drink too much because I'm a responsible adult."

"A responsible adult with a lustrous mustache," Jasmine said.

"Neither one of them told me the truth. Once again, Beth didn't want to face the consequences of her stupid, dumb actions. And Mom didn't want to be embarrassed in the eyes of Soap Jesus. So they both let me think my sister was dead!"

Weber ended his last sentence at several decibels higher than necessary.

Everyone in the restaurant swiveled to look at them.

"He's telling us about his soap opera," Riley explained.

"*Lies of the Mother* or *A Family Betrayed*?" one of the customers at the table next to them asked.

"No. That sounds like the last season of *El Corazón*," a man in the back corner booth said.

The rest of the diners chimed in with their favorite telenovelas and soap operas.

"I thought I got my sister killed," Weber said sadly. "And they let me believe it. That's not right. That's the opposite of right. That's…left."

"That's pretty awful, even for someone as annoying as you," Jasmine admitted.

With a sigh, Weber hunched over his margarita and blew into his straw. It erupted over the lip of the glass and splattered everywhere.

"How did you get your straw back?" Riley asked, then realized hers was missing.

"You should confront her," Jasmine said.

Weber frowned. "Confront who?"

"Your mom."

"Oh, her. She sucks."

"Jas, I know you don't like him, but getting him to blow up his life like this isn't funny," Riley warned.

"No, it's not funny. Look at his face." Jasmine reached across the table and grabbed his face in her hand.

"Owie," he said through squished cheeks.

"He's hurting," Jasmine insisted.

"Because you're smashing his face."

"No, because his mom and his sister didn't trust him with the truth. That's fucked up. Isn't it, Detective Stick Up His Ass?" Jasmine asked, releasing his face.

Weber nodded. "You're so mean and pretty. It's confusing."

"Want me to help you be mean to your mom?" she offered.

"You would do that?"

"Only if you eat your damn tacos so you don't puke in Riley's car."

He immediately scooped up a taco and shoved most of it into his mouth. The rest landed on his shirt.

"Good boy," Jasmine said.

"You're scary when you use your powers for good," Riley observed.

"Speaking of powers, I need you to dig into Lance's peanut-size brain and figure out a way to get him to stop torturing Kory and the rest of that school," Jasmine said. "He's got to be afraid of something."

"There's just one problem," Riley began.

"Don't give me any of your psychic ethics bullshit," Jasmine warned.

Riley shook her head. "It's not that. I kind of lost my powers."

"You're no longer psychic?" Jasmine shouted.

"They're definitely talking about *El Corazón*," the lady at the register said.

"It's a long story. I'll explain later," Riley said.

Weber startled Riley with a loud snore.

"Aww, look at him."

Jasmine studied their sound-asleep charge. "Yeah, they're cute when they're asleep. Too bad he's such a dick when he's awake and sober."

"I'm just gonna take a quick picture," Riley decided, holding up her phone.

She snapped a picture and sent it to Nick.

Nick: Jesus. Did you shoot him already?
Riley: Not yet. That's just salsa, taco, and strawberry margarita. Question: How awful is Mrs. Weber?
Nick: She makes your grandmother look like a kindergarten teacher who doesn't hate children.
Riley: Oh good. So if we drive over there so Drunk Kellen can confront her, we won't be ruining his life?
Nick: You'd be doing him a favor.

Weber's snore jolted him awake. "And another thing," he said, slamming his palm into a bowl of salsa.

"Oh boy. We're gonna need to leave a really big tip," Riley said.

"Speaking of. When I was feeling around for this guy's wallet—"

"I don't want to hear it," Riley said, plugging her fingers in her ears.

———

Riley pulled up in front of Mrs. Weber's house and looked at Weber in the rearview mirror. "Are you sure you want to do this?"

"I am one thousand percent sure," he insisted.

"You might want to fix your tie," Riley suggested.

He attacked his tie with more enthusiasm than dexterity. "Stupid tie!" He yanked it over his head and threw it out the window of the Jeep.

"I think it's go time," Jasmine announced, slipping off her seat belt and opening the door.

"Let's do this," he said, his nostrils flaring aggressively.

"Your mom doesn't own any weapons, does she?" Riley asked uneasily as they headed for the front door.

"Just her perpetual disdain."

"Okay then."

Weber got to the door first and pounded on it. "Open up, Mother!"

"Ten bucks says he keels over like a tree on her when she opens the door," Jasmine whispered.

"I'll take that action," Riley said.

A pinched-faced woman yanked the door open. "What is the meaning of this, Kellen?"

"You knew about Beth. You knew she was alive, and you let me spend six years thinking she was dead. That it was my fault."

Mrs. Weber clutched at her cross necklace like it was a string of pearls. "How dare you come to my home smelling like a vat of sacramental wine!"

"How dare *I*? How dare *you*, Mother."

"You have no right to come to my home and speak to me this way. I am a good Christian woman!"

Weber's scoff nearly folded him in half. "No! You're not! You're mean and selfish, and you hate everyone!"

"This display is undignified."

"What's undignified is letting me believe my sister had been murdered, Mother. You knew. You knew all this time."

"Elizabeth was as good as dead to me," she snarled, her face twisting in an ugly mask.

"Why?" Weber's question was a broken plea that hurt Riley's heart.

"She humiliated me! Just like you're doing now! Neither one of you was ever good enough. Neither was your father. I'm the only one who lives this life the way we're supposed to. I follow the rules. I do the right thing. You lived in sin with that woman and then got a divorce! You shouldn't get an escape from marriage! Not when I had to wait patiently for all that processed meat to catch up to your father. And Elizabeth?" Mrs. Weber laughed bitterly. "Your sister came to me dressed like a whore and told me she was running away with the love of her life."

She spat out the word *love* like it was poison.

"And neither of you thought to tell me." Weber shoved his hands into his short hair, making it stand up.

"It was better that you thought she was dead," Mrs. Weber said stubbornly.

He turned abruptly to face Riley and Jasmine. "I'm not hallucinating this, am I? She really is a horrible person, right?"

"Yeah, she's awful," Riley agreed.

"The worst. I'm impressed you're not more fucked up," Jasmine said, crossing her arms and staring down Weber's mother.

"You'll watch your tongue, young lady," Mrs. Weber hissed before turning on her son. "How dare you bring your trollops to my home. The neighbors can see."

"Trollops?" Riley repeated.

"You want this trollop to watch her tongue?" Jasmine said. "Watch this!"

Constance and Riley watched as Jasmine grabbed Weber by the shirt and dragged him in for a hard kiss.

"Disgusting! You're not welcome here ever again." Mrs. Weber slammed the door so hard it blew Jasmine's hair back like she was standing in front of Sesame's wind machine.

Jasmine ended the kiss and began reapplying her lipstick.

Weber blinked several times before turning to pound his fist on the door. "Just remember, Mother. You won't be able to tell everyone I'm dead. They'll all know the truth. That you lost both of your children because you're a *shitty human being*!"

"Well, that went well," Riley said dryly as they returned to the Jeep and climbed in.

"I feel like I need to shower for at least an hour to get rid of that negativity," Jasmine said.

"I have no family. I'm an orphan. Like that redhead who sings all the time," Weber said morosely from the back seat.

Riley looked at him in the rearview mirror. "Just because your mom is terrible doesn't mean Sesame didn't have her reasons for not telling you."

"Sentence too long." He crossed his arms like a petulant three-year-old.

"Great. You melted his brain with that kiss," Riley told Jasmine.

"Wouldn't be the first time."

"You kissed him before this?"

"Ew! No. I meant other men, not Little Orphan Annie back there."

Riley tried again with Weber. "Maybe your sister had an important reason for not telling you."

"Or maybe she sucks too," he said.

"Hey, who wants a drink?" Riley asked.

"Me!" they all said.

27

Nick scanned the block in front of him. The town house he was watching sat in the middle of one of those neighborhoods that was designed like a small city. Usually it wasn't easy to lurk in a vehicle in a place like this. Too much foot traffic. Too many nosy neighbors. But good fortune was on his side, planting him across the street in the parking lot of the neighborhood's brewery.

The windows were cracked so he could enjoy the crisp autumn air...and so his SUV wouldn't smell like the crappy burger and fries he'd snagged on his way from the security gig hours ago.

He was on his third episode of a murder podcast, and his legs were dying for a good stretch.

Surveillance was boring as hell. A lot of the job was boring as hell. The paperwork. The waiting. The watching.

But the parts like tracking down a corpse in an abandoned house or getting into a gunfight with a murderous politician standing in knee-deep water provided the sort of balance that he liked. He'd take the boring in exchange for a few adventures as long as he came out alive in the end and the bad guy got what he deserved.

Though now he was a little less enthusiastic about the gunfights and rescuing hostages from bomb-wielding serial killers than he once would have been.

He blamed Riley for that.

It was one thing for him to put himself in the line of fire. But with Riley involved in every dangerous caper, he found himself being more cautious.

His phone buzzed in the cupholder, and he picked it up.

Brian: Gym Rat just sealed his own fate and DMed Lady Assistant District Attorney a dick pic. I'm a goddamn hero.

Nick: I'll get you a cape. Does this mean you can start on those background checks that came in this afternoon?

Brian: And give up this vigilante justice?

Nick: You can wear your cape while you do them.

Brian: Deal.

Josie: Keep it down. I'm lying in wait.

Nick jolted in his seat when he saw the selfie attached to Josie's text. He must have also yelped because the rottweiler sitting in the passenger seat of the car next to him shot him a suspicious look.

"Boof," the dog said from its cracked window.

"Sorry, buddy. My cousin's wife is dressed like a murder clown."

The dog cocked his huge head.

"Didn't your mother teach you not to talk to strangers?"

Nick blinked at the dog whose mouth hadn't moved. "Uhhhh."

The passenger door opened, and a grinning Riley climbed in. "Did you think you were hallucinating, or did you really think he was talking to you?"

"I knew it was you all along," he lied.

"Liar." She leaned across the console and gave him a kiss.

"This is a nice surprise. What are you doing here?" he

asked, checking her out. She was beyond cute in a ball cap, leggings, and the other girlie staple of the season—a puffy vest.

She held up a large paper bag with handles. "Thought you could use some dinner, and since all the sushi ended up smashed in Jasmine's purse, I figured I'd try a do-over."

"You're a goddess." There was something that seriously didn't suck about being in love with a woman who remembered all your favorite sushi rolls. "That settles it. I definitely love you," he said, reaching for a pair of chopsticks.

"My mom always used to say that the way to a man's heart is through a giant glob of wasabi."

"What's the occasion?" he asked, splitting the chopsticks apart and pouncing on the rainbow roll.

She shrugged and popped a piece of sashimi into her mouth. "We haven't had much time to ourselves. Figured we could make a date of surveillance. Who are we surveilling anyway?"

Nick pointed through the windshield at the brick town house. "We're looking for a midforties white guy with blond hair."

"Well, that narrows it down. What did Blond White Guy do?"

"Custody agreement violation. According to the agreement, his son and daughter are supposed to spend the night here in Dad's place when he has custody every other weekend. My client heard through the kids that Dad is dating and he's been stashing the kids at Grandma's place so he can spend time with his nineteen-year-old hand-model girlfriend."

"Gross."

"How did it go with Drunk Weber?" he asked.

She sighed. "It was…funny and sad and weird."

"That sounds about right."

She filled him in on Weber's drunk funk and his confrontation with his mother.

"How did ol' Constance handle that?" he asked when she told him about Jasmine kissing Weber on the front steps.

"Not well. There was some two-sided disowning after Constance told him it was better for the family image if everyone thought Beth was dead rather than living in sin on the West Coast."

Nick shook his head. "That's fucking cold. I knew her Frosty the Snow Witch routine was a little off even for her when Bethame came back."

"Always listen to your gut," Riley said. "I ended up leaving Kellen with Lily and Fred for happy hour because he insisted he wasn't drunk enough yet. He'll be hungover as hell tomorrow. How was your day?"

"The security gig was fine. Some vice president of whatever who thinks he's a bigger deal than he is likes to show up to business meetings with armed security to make a statement."

"Aww! You were a trophy bodyguard," she teased.

"Josie should have been the trophy," Nick grumbled.

"I think it's sweet that she's so invested in an old lady and her clown collection."

"Except *sweet* means I have to do all the work," he complained, showing Riley Josie's selfie.

"I can't decide if that's hilarious or horrifying." She aimed those big brown eyes at him. "It's nice of you to let them finish their cases."

"Yeah. Yeah. I'm a nice guy with employees working *pro bono* cases."

"I believe the word we all agreed on was *primo*. And I'm going to choose not to point out whose fault that is."

"I blame Penny. That woman is a hazard to my mental health."

"Speaking of Mrs. Penny. I saw her taking pictures of her 'evidence' in the parking lot because Lily wouldn't let her catalog it inside the house."

"What kind of evidence?"

"Two dozen bags of poop."

Nick snorted.

"I didn't have the heart to tell her that the neighbors are

using her as a free dog waste cleanup service. She's too excited about it."

"Just what Santiago Investigations needs to be associated with: shit."

"Yeah. You might need to change your name after this," she agreed, carefully cutting a piece of tuna sushi in half. "I took a swing at my own primo case today."

"You really don't have to do that, Thorn."

She shrugged. "Well, everyone else was having so much fun with theirs. And we learned exactly what bullying can lead to, thanks to the Channel 50 hostage situation. So Jasmine and I went to see what we were dealing with this afternoon."

"I'm not gonna like this, am I?"

Riley filled him in on her run-in with Lance the Shithead.

"Is he old enough for me to punch in the face?" Nick demanded when she was done.

She shook her head. "Unfortunately no. He looks like he's thirty, acts like a spoiled four-year-old, but he's only seventeen."

"Hmm, that could push me into first-degree misdemeanor."

"After meeting Kory and seeing this Lance kid in action, I'm invested. He's terrorizing the entire school. Unfortunately I don't think dressing up like a clown and hiding in a closet is going to be enough to force him into developing empathy. Got any ideas?"

"Sounds like you need to get to know your enemy," he said. "The more you know about him, the more weapons you'll find to use against him."

"Yeah, but without my powers, I'd have to do it the old-fashioned way. How much trouble can I get into spying on a teenage psychopath?" Riley asked.

"A medium amount."

"Hmm. It might be worth it," she mused. "Your influence is definitely rubbing off on me."

He grinned. "Does that bother you?"

"It should, but right now, I'm too enraged to care."

"After Josie's done scaring the piss out of this kid, talk to her. This is her area of expertise," Nick advised. "Vengeance is her middle name."

"I'll do that. Thanks."

"Speaking of middle names…"

"No. Eat your sushi."

They ate in silence for a few minutes before Riley spoke up again. "In brighter news, we still have a Halloween stash. None of our neighbors or roommates have found the gummy worms yet."

"Where'd you hide them?"

"Filing cabinet in my office."

"Nice." He straightened in his seat as a red sedan eased up to the curb in front of the town house. There were two people in the front seat. "Showtime," Nick murmured, picking up the pair of binoculars. "Yep. That's our guy. Wanna do the honors?"

"Gimme," she said.

He handed her the digital camera and then set his phone to video.

"This is so exciting!" she hissed.

"Yeah, Thorn. Thirty seconds of excitement after three hours of ass-numbing boredom."

"All in moderation," she said, snapping away as the man got out of the car with a significantly younger girl. "Huh. She does have nice hands."

The couple engaged in a heavy make-out session on the front steps before the guy finally got the door open and they disappeared inside.

"Lights on," Nick murmured, noting the time in his log.

"This guy really needs to invest in curtains," Riley observed as clothing went flying in the large front window.

A teenager walking a small dog in a sweater stopped on the sidewalk and gawked at the scene unfolding inside.

The nearly naked couple hit the stairs. The lights on the first floor went out, and the ones on the second floor lit up.

Nine minutes later, the town house went dark.

"And lights out." Nick snorted as he noted the time. "Amateur."

"Not everyone is as gifted in the libido as you are," Riley reminded him.

"You're damn right they're not." He checked the time. "Wanna go watch a kid piss his pants?"

She grinned at him in the dark. "You sure know how to show a girl a good time."

28

Even after the late night of celebration at the diner with Josie and Brian, Riley woke early thanks to a creepy dream about a finger that kept pointing at her and a creature with glowing eyes. Nick was snoring softly, curled around her in a hot, hard, naked ball of sexiness.

She lay there for a few moments, enjoying the quiet before her brain demanded caffeine.

Knowing it was futile to go back to sleep, she slipped out of bed and dressed quietly.

"Wanna go out?" she whispered to the dog, who yawned at her from his king-size dog bed. Burt stood up, but instead of following her to the door, he slunk to the side of the bed she'd vacated and climbed in.

"Fine. You two sleep in. I need coffee."

Thankfully there were no signs of life—or sex—coming from Sesame and Tommy's room.

She padded into the kitchen, noting that the stove top now gleamed and all the fingerprints had been erased from the cabinets. There was already a fresh pot of coffee waiting for her. Tommy Hemsworth was proving himself to be an excellent guest. No wonder Sesame was enamored with the man. He was the perfect househusband.

Riley yawned and grabbed a mug out of the cabinet. She was just pouring the first glorious cup when she heard a polite knock on the mudroom door.

It was barely 7:00 a.m. There were only a handful of people who thought that was an appropriate time for a visit. And only one of those people was polite enough to knock.

"Morning, Gabe," Riley said when she opened the door and found her friend standing on the stoop outside. He was dressed in what she thought of as his fall uniform: black sweatpants and a clingy long-sleeve top—also black.

She felt instantly guilty, knowing he was about to be very disappointed in her. But she needed to own up to her mistakes and hope that Gabe would not only forgive her but help her get her powers back.

"Good morning, Riley. I am very sorry," he said.

She frowned. "You? No. I'm sorry. What are you sorry for?"

"For this," he said and held up his phone.

Elanora Basil, Riley's crabby psychic medium grandmother, scowled back at her from the screen.

"Well, isn't this a…surprise?" Riley said. Forget the guilt. Now she was just bracing for her punishment.

"It has been brought to my attention that you are failing in your duties," Elanora huffed.

Behind the phone, safely out of frame, Gabe shook his head to let her know that those were Elanora's words and not his own.

On a sigh, Riley took the phone from him and returned to the kitchen.

"It's nice to see you too, Grandma."

"You may dispense with the pleasantries," Elanora snipped. "Gabriel tells me you are unable to read a subject."

Either Gabe hadn't realized that she'd fried her own powers or he was protecting her from the wrath of Elanora.

"A person," Riley interjected. "I was having trouble reading someone and was worried they could be in trouble."

Elanora lifted a glass mug filled with steamy gray liquid and sipped. "You will tell me everything."

Briefly, Riley filled her in on the psychic flu and Sesame's situation.

When she finished, Elanora tut-tutted. "Given your location, I'm shocked you haven't vomited your way around the city." Her grandmother never missed an opportunity to make jibes at any number of people, places, and things.

"Yeah, yeah. You don't like Harrisburg. Why should I be vomiting everywhere?"

"Urban areas by definition contain larger populations. Larger populations mean more crime, more garbage, and more nefarious motives."

Riley was going to need a second cup of coffee if she was expected to translate that.

"This woman you describe is a liar."

"Well, obviously."

Elanora shook her head, sending the black feathers in her hair fluttering. "No, not just someone who is untruthful about their age or tells outlandish stories to improve their standing. She is a gifted liar who is able to believe her own lies. She's rewriting reality to better suit her. You are reacting to the rewrite."

Riley blinked and thought about Happy Tommy morphing into Villain Tommy. It made a bizarre kind of sense. "But she's so nice. Genuinely nice."

"Oh, grow up, Granddaughter. Everyone lies. Some for nefarious reasons, others for selfish reasons. Controlling one's own mind is the highest enlightenment a nongifted human can aspire to. With a controlled, focused mind, anything is possible. Of course, you'll have to take my word for that, seeing as how you have no control over your own."

"So how do I hang on through the merry-go-round of lies to get a read on her?" Riley asked, ignoring the insult.

"Try harder."

"Care to be more specific? I dragged in psychic backup in the form of Gabe, Mom, and Wander and still couldn't break through the lies."

Her grandmother's gaze shifted off-screen. She gave an imperious nod and returned her attention to Riley. "Then find someone or something who can't rewrite the answers you seek."

"That's actually…very helpful," Riley mused. Or it would be if she had spirit guides and psychic powers.

"Of course it is."

"Hey, if you're not doing anything for Halloween, I'm throwing Nick a surprise birthday party. Fred's been asking about you," Riley said, changing the subject.

"Birthday parties are a waste of time. And I made it clear to Fred that I wasn't looking for a relationship."

"I guess once you get a taste of fine wine, there's no going back to boxed," Riley teased.

"I must go. I am very busy and important, and this conversation has become trivial."

"Love you too, Grandma," Riley said. "Thank you for your help."

Her grandmother paused and stared hard from the screen. "I believe you are old enough to dispense with such a ridiculous title. You may call me Elanora." With that, she disconnected the call.

Riley handed the phone back to Gabe. "Well, *that* was a fun way to start the day."

"I am very sorry," Gabe said again. "I only thought to seek Elanora's counsel as to why we could not see inside Sesame's mind clearly. She demanded to speak with you immediately."

"It's okay, Gabe. At least we can rule out Sesame being some kind of powerful, evil psychic. And Grand—I mean, Elanora gave me an idea to try."

"I am relieved you are not angry with me."

"Well, hang on to that feeling for a minute because it's my turn to apologize to you."

"You are forgiven," he said immediately.

"I'd rather you wait to hear what I did before forgiving me. I don't think you're going to like it."

He nodded. "I will try to temporarily withhold my forgiveness."

Riley took a deep breath. "I didn't listen to you and pushed too hard with Sesame. I thought finding out what we needed to know was more important than my psychic health, and I was wrong. Now my spirit guides are gone and so is Cotton Candy World. The only time I get any kind of messages or visions is when I'm asleep. And that was only once, unless someone is going to show up today and start pointing fingers at me."

She ran out of steam with her confession and stared at her feet, waiting for Gabe's disapproval.

"You are forgiven," he said again.

She peeked up at him. He didn't look like he was going to cry, which took some of the tension out of her shoulders. "Are you sure? I didn't listen to your warnings and now I'm not psychic anymore."

"I am your friend. As such, I am here to support you, not judge you."

Gabe and Wander were a match made in do-the-right-thing heaven.

She let out a breath. "I really am sorry for not listening to you. I thought I could handle it and I was wrong. Now I'm paying the price, and I don't know if I'll ever get my powers back."

Gabe patted her on the head with one gigantic hand. "I believe in you, Riley Thorn. We will get through this together."

"Do you think I can be psychic again?" she asked in a small pathetic voice.

"I believe with the right path, you can do anything you wish," he said.

"I'd really love a yes or a no right now. I'm feeling too vulnerable for philosophy."

"Then yes. If you wish to become psychic again, you shall. And I will help you."

She threw herself against his cinder block chest and hugged him. "Thanks, Gabe. You're a good friend."

He returned the hug, cracking Riley's back like bubble wrap. "I am honored to be your friend."

"Want some breakfast?" she offered.

He set her back on her feet. "I am humbled by your invitation, but I must regretfully decline. I am taking Lily to the grocery store before all the good cupcake icing is gone."

"You're a good man, Gabe. Hey, what is your last name anyway?"

He cocked his head. "I have no last name."

"Like Cher?"

"I am unfamiliar with Cher."

"Oh, my friend. You are missing out." Riley took his phone back and opened his music app. "Here. Now you have a whole Cher playlist for your trip to the grocery store."

He beamed at her, his smile brighter than the morning sun. "Thank you, Riley."

"Thank you, Gabe."

She waved him off from the mudroom, watching him expertly pick his way through Burt's land mines. A velour tracksuit–wearing Lily was waiting for him in the parking lot next to her vehicle.

Sesame's limo was missing from its spot in front of the garage. Riley frowned. Where would she have gone so early in the morning? And should she even be concerned? If Sesame wasn't in any real danger, did Riley actually have to care that she was lying? Maybe it was time to take a break from the drama and focus on resting her broken brain.

She headed back to the kitchen for more coffee.

"Good morning!"

The chipper greeting had Riley almost upending the contents of her mug. "Jeez, Tommy! You scared me."

He was putting what looked like a casserole into the refrigerator. "Sorry. Sesame always says she's going to put a cat collar on me."

"Where is your wife this morning?" Riley asked. "I saw the limo is gone."

"She's taking a Sesame Day," he said as if that explained anything.

She handed him a mug. "What's a Sesame Day?"

"Whenever she's been working too hard, she takes a day and treats herself. Today she's shopping," he explained, pouring coffee.

Riley leaned against the counter. "Don't you like to shop with her?" she asked, recalling one of her earlier visions.

Tommy grinned and started shoveling sugar into the mug. "I sure do. But when she says she needs alone time, I respect that."

He was the human equivalent of a golden retriever, and if she hadn't destroyed her powers, she could have taken her grandmother's advice and jumped straight into the man's head for all the answers she sought.

"Where is she shopping?" she asked. It was too early for retail stores to be open.

"She's spending the day at the Hershey outlets," he said, stirring his coffee with enthusiasm.

The outlets didn't open until 10:00 a.m. Maybe Sesame was going to breakfast first, Riley rationalized. There was probably a perfectly reasonable explanation. She should definitely let it drop.

Her phone rang in her pocket. Nothing good came from phone calls between the hours of 10:00 p.m. and 8:00 a.m. Especially not when the caller was Mrs. Penny.

"Hello?"

"I've got a code sesame chicken," Mrs. Penny squawked.

"Are you placing a lunch order? It's not even eight a.m."

"No! Although I wouldn't say no to a big plate of hotcakes right now. Following people makes me hungry."

Feeling uneasy, Riley smiled at Tommy and backed out of the room. "Who are you following?" she whispered.

"Your big-boobed friend and her limo driver. And now I've got a code sesame chicken."

"I'm going to need more information," Riley hissed as she headed for the dining room.

"For Pete's sake! All that studying investigative crap, and

I still need to spoon-feed you. She's my prime suspect," Mrs. Penny snapped.

"Prime suspect for what?" Riley demanded.

"The Dog Doody Bandit. Keep up! This Sesame just so happens to show up while someone's been stealing snacks and pumpkins and leaving poop on porches? That's not a coincidence in my book."

Riley slapped a hand to her forehead and prayed for patience. "Uh-huh. You think Sesame is the kind of person who steals snacks and has no problem handling feces, so you followed her shopping?"

Mrs. Penny snorted. "Clean the gunk out of your ears! She didn't go shopping. Unless you count buying a train ticket and leaving the state as shopping."

Riley stopped pacing. "She got on a train?"

"You don't think she's moving her game to the city, do you? If she starts pooping on porches in New York, that's outside my jurisdiction."

Ignoring the fact that Mrs. Penny didn't actually have a jurisdiction because she wasn't a licensed PI or a law enforcement officer, Riley concentrated on the important part. "You're sure she got on a train?"

"Am I sure?" Mrs. Penny scoffed. "Of course I'm sure. I double-parked right out front, snuck in behind them like a ninja, waited until she and that buff limo driver headed down to the tracks, and then I paid the gate agent a ten-spot to tell me where she was going. By the way, you owe me a hundred sixty bucks."

"Oh God. You didn't actually follow her onto the train, did you?"

"No! I would have, but someone got their panties in a bunch over me double-parking while on official PI business, and I got a parking ticket."

Riley looked over her shoulder to make sure Tiptoeing Tommy hadn't followed her into the room. "So where did she go?"

"Who?"

"Sesame. Where did Sesame go?" she asked in exasperation.

"Oh. Right. Penn Station."

"Crap," Riley muttered.

"That's in New York City, you know."

"I know, Mrs. Penny."

"You want me to catch the next train and track her down? I think I've got my spare zip ties in my bag."

A sleepy-looking Nick strolled into the room and crossed his arms.

"No! It's not necessary for you to make a completely illegal citizen's arrest."

"Mrs. Penny?" he asked.

Riley nodded.

He rolled his eyes and swiped her coffee.

"Look, Mrs. Penny, you did good. Why don't you see if you can get the ticket guy to tell you when Sesame is coming back?" she suggested.

"She's following Sesame?" Nick demanded.

"Yes, but somehow it turned out to be a good thing," Riley whispered.

"That might be a problem," Mrs. Penny told her.

"Why?"

"Well, I kinda got thrown out of the station after I hit a security guard with my cane."

"Gimme the phone," Nick insisted, crooking his fingers.

Riley shook her head. "You know what, Mrs. Penny? Why don't you just come home? Immediately. And don't hit anyone else with your cane. You can write up a report about your findings for Nick."

"He'll have it on his desk by noon," Mrs. Penny said with enthusiasm. "I need a second breakfast. I always work up an appetite trailing a suspect."

Nick reached for the phone, but Riley danced out of the way.

"Okay. I'll see you at noon—"

"Of course, I'll also need a lunch break. Breakfast always makes me hungry for lunch. And then I like to take a nap after lunch so I can start the afternoon fresh. I'll get the report to him by tomorrow morning."

"Great. Bye!" Riley said, disconnecting the call before Nick could take the phone from her.

"What the hell, Thorn? You know I like to yell at employees first thing in the morning."

"We don't have time for you to yell at Mrs. Penny. Sesame told Tommy she was going shopping in Hershey today, and Mrs. Penny tailed her to the train station, where she and Wilhelm just got on a train to Manhattan."

"Maybe she's having an affair with Wilhelm," he suggested.

"I don't think so." There was something genuine about the affection between Sesame and Tommy.

Nick perked up and looked hopeful for a second. "Maybe she's looking for an apartment in the city so they can move out of our house."

"Or maybe she's still lying to everyone," she pointed out.

Nick grumbled under his breath. "Fine. I'll talk to Tommy, but if she is getting it on with her limo driver, you're the one who has to mop up his tears."

29

N ick's plans for talking Riley back into bed for some lazy morning sex had evaporated.

He blamed Mrs. Penny. And Sesame. And Tommy, who was probably too stupid to know that his own wife was screwing the limo driver.

"You know," he said, slinging his arm around Riley's shoulders as they headed back to the kitchen. "Sooner or later, everyone is going to move out, and we'll have the house to ourselves."

She gave him a pitying look. "Sure we will," she said, patting him on the arm.

"I'm serious, Thorn. When these two are out of here, I'm putting in a moat and a security system that will electrocute anyone who tries to ring the doorbell before eleven a.m." He was thinking about moats and piranhas and if piranhas could survive Pennsylvania winters when the doorbell rang. "See? Whoever that is would be toast right now."

Riley rolled her eyes and started for the front door.

"I'll get it," Tommy announced from the kitchen.

He appeared in the foyer with Burt on his heels.

"I'll get it. Nick wants to talk to you," she said and gave him a helpful shove toward Tommy.

"Oh, sure," Tommy said eagerly. "Do you want some eggs Benedict? I just whipped up a fresh batch of hollandaise."

Nick did like eggs Benedict. But he came to a halt when Riley answered the door to the beefy suit on the front porch.

"I'm lookin' for Sesame and Tommy Hemsworth," the stranger announced.

The guy was at least six feet six inches tall, and his shoulders filled out the suit jacket like he was wearing the protective padding of a defensive end. He had a shaved head and a scar that went through his upper lip.

Tommy's knees were knocking together loud enough that it sounded like a drummer keeping time.

Nick shoved him backward through the swinging kitchen door before their hulky visitor could spot him.

"Uh, Nick?" Riley called, sounding nervous.

He and Burt headed for the front door and planted themselves between Riley and the stranger.

"Who are you?" Nick demanded.

"I have some important papers for Sesame and Tommy Hemsworth."

"You a process server?" Nick asked.

The guy smirked. "Something like that."

Burt growled low.

"They're not here," Nick lied and snatched the thick manila envelope from the man's gigantic paw. Under other less vaguely threatening circumstances, it would have been entertaining to stand him next to Gabe. "I'll see that they get this."

"You do that," the stranger said. He managed to make three little words sound menacing.

"Need me to sign a receipt?" Nick asked.

The man smirked again. "Not necessary. I'll tell my employer the message was delivered."

Nick slammed the door in the man's face and studied the large envelope in his hands. "Tommy? Forget the hollandaise and get your ass out here now!"

"What the hell was that?" Riley asked. "He was handing out villain vibes like candy from a parade float."

"Let's find out," Nick said.

Tommy poked his head out of the kitchen, looking fifty shades of pants-shitting nervous. He held a pair of tongs like a weapon.

"You got a delivery, Tommy."

"I'll, uh, open it later."

"I don't think so. You'll open it now," Nick informed him.

Tommy took a few tentative steps toward them, then stopped again. "I can't let the hollandaise separate. It'll ruin breakfast."

"Fine. I'll open it," Nick decided.

"No! Don't!" Tommy shrieked as Nick tore open the envelope.

He dumped the contents onto the table Sesame had dragged into the foyer for her photo shoot. A fat sheaf of papers hit the table, followed by a long thin object.

Riley gasped. "Oh my God. Is that a…"

"Give me those tongs," Nick said, snapping his fingers at Tommy.

The man had lost all color in his cheeks. He stumbled forward and handed over the tongs.

Nick picked up the item in question and held it up. "Yeah, that's definitely a finger."

Riley let out a strangled cry.

Burt, convinced the finger was a hot dog that was terrifying his mom, began to bark.

"I think I'm gonna be—" Tommy finished his sentence by ralphing into the antique urn also from Sesame's photo shoot.

"Who would send you a fucking finger, Tommy? What the hell are you mixed up in?" Nick demanded, ignoring the vomiting.

"I don't know," Tommy wailed.

Nick strode back to the front door to get a look at the guy's vehicle. But when he flung the door open, he found someone else standing on the porch.

The photographer from Sesame's photo shoot had an envelope in her hand.

Nick tossed the tongs and finger over his shoulder, ignoring the sounds of Burt's toenails scrabbling on the floor as Riley tried to keep him from chasing what he thought was a hot dog. Tommy yelped and ran face-first into the kitchen door.

"Everything all right in there?" the photographer asked. "It sounded like someone was in distress."

"Tommy separated his hollandaise, and he's real upset about it," Nick said. "Isn't that right, Tommy?"

Behind him, Tommy gulped in a breath of air, then bobbed his head. "Yes. Separated. Uh-huh."

"Uh, Joplin? Right?" Riley said, still wrestling with Burt. "What can we do for you?"

"Sesame asked for a sneak peek, so I thought I'd hand-deliver them," Joplin said, holding up the envelope. Her gaze slid around the foyer like she was looking for something or someone.

"Sesame isn't here right now. She had an emergency shopping trip come up," Riley said, dragging Burt forward. "But we'll be happy to make sure she gets the shots as soon as she comes home."

"I don't mind waiting," Joplin said.

Nick gave Tommy a hard glare. "She said she'd be gone all day. Didn't she, Tommy?"

He let out a strangled cough. "Uh. Yes. All day. She's going shopping all day," he parroted.

"You sure everyone's okay?" Joplin asked, clearly not buying a word of their explanation.

"Everyone but the hollandaise," Nick said glibly, ushering her out the door.

"Thanks for checking though," Riley said.

"Have Sesame call me when she gets back," Joplin said from the doorstep.

"Yep," Nick said before slamming the door in her face.

"Oh my God! Where's the finger?" Riley hissed.

Burt was quivering. Tommy was shivering. "Neither one of you fucking move," Nick told them. He gave the marble floor a quick once-over. Unfortunately, it appeared that a gray severed finger blended in well with the silver veining.

"Did you see where it landed?" Riley asked Tommy.

With a shaky finger, he pointed in the direction of the staircase.

"Thorn, you take the north side. I'll take the south."

"I never should have gotten out of bed today," she muttered.

"You better get ready to talk, Tommy, 'cause your ass isn't leaving here without telling me why a human giant just delivered a finger to you in my fucking house," Nick warned as he crawled on his hands and knees.

"I—I think I'm going to be sick again," the man moaned.

"Go barf and then get back here," Nick told him.

Tommy ran in the direction of the powder room.

"Aha! Found it," Riley said. "Gimme the tongs."

He found her on her hands and knees, her face pressed to the floor, peering under a console table Jasmine had gifted them when they'd moved in.

"Do *not* tell Jasmine we got severed finger on her house-warming present," Riley said when Nick handed over the tongs and positioned himself behind her.

"My lips are sealed," he promised.

The front door swung open, and their neighbor Fred walked in. He was rocking a blond toupee this morning and holding a tape measure. "Oh, hey there! Didn't think anyone would be awake yet. Whatcha doin'? Never mind. You're obviously having s—"

"Not now, Fred!" Riley said as she reached under the table.

"Get out!" Nick bellowed.

"Jeez! I'm going. I'm going." Fred left, muttering about morning grumps.

"Got it!" Riley triumphantly held up the tongs and the finger.

"You're a hell of a girl, Thorn. You sure that's the right one?" Nick quipped.

Her jaw dropped. "There's more than one?"

"Kidding," he promised, taking the tongs and digit from her. "Can you grab me a freezer bag and a pair of gloves?"

"Isn't it a little late to be worried about contaminating evidence now?" she asked dryly.

"Funny," he called after her.

Burt tentatively wandered over and eyed the finger.

"Don't even think about it, bud," Nick warned.

Riley returned with several different-sized bags and two pairs of gloves. "We might have a problem," she said, pulling on one of the pairs of gloves.

"Yeah. Someone sent a fucking finger to our house."

"In addition to that. Tommy's gone. He went out the window in the bathroom."

Nick swore under his breath and bagged the finger.

Then he went to check the bathroom. Someone had tiled the whole room from floor to ceiling in Cookie Monster–blue tiles. That same someone had decided a pea soup–green sink and toilet were just what the room needed. The window above the toilet was indeed open.

"Damn it," he muttered before closing and locking the window.

He returned to the foyer and found Riley reading the paperwork that had accompanied the finger. "He's definitely gone. What's that?"

"It looks like some kind of NDA," she said. "There's a copy signed by Sesame and one signed by Tommy."

"Great. So someone wanted to send the message that snitches don't get stitches; they get their fingers cut off."

Riley shuddered. "And now they know where we live. You wanna lock all the doors and windows while I call the cops?"

Nick shook his head. "We can't call the cops."

"Nick, there's a *finger* in a *freezer bag.*"

"Yeah, a finger addressed to the woman who's supposed to be dead."

"I think we've given Sesame enough time to plan her big coming-out party. Finger trumps party."

"What about Weber's career? His missing sister came back to life, appears to be involved in some dangerous shit, and he didn't bother telling anyone at work. That could get him suspended. Or worse."

Riley ran a hand over Burt's head and down his long spine. "Crap. He's already so mad at her. If he gets fired because of Sesame, Kellen will never forgive her."

"Bingo, baby. Besides, if he gets fired, I'm the one who's going to have to hire his tight ass. He'll drive me insane, and eventually I'll have to take him out and bury him at your mom's relatives' commune."

"Nice catastrophizing," she said, sounding impressed.

"Thank you."

"So what do we do?"

"We call Weber and let him decide."

Riley winced. "Yeah. I picked up the finger. You get to call hungover Kellen."

30

Y ou were right," Nick said, hanging up his desk phone. "Weber sounds like a hungover bear that some drunk camper woke early from hibernation."

"And when will our drunken bear friend be here?" Riley asked as she disconnected her own call.

"As soon as he finishes puking." Nick tucked his gun into the waistband of his jeans. "Did you get a hold of Brian?"

"Your cousin was not happy about me waking him up this early, but he's digging into the corporation from the nondisclosure agreements as we speak," she reported. "What do we do until Kellen gets here?"

They'd secured all doors and windows on the first floor and given Burt a hot dog snack so he would stop pouting. The dog was now snoring like a four-legged lumberjack somewhere on the first floor.

"We find out if we should freeze the finger or put it in the fridge," Nick said, frowning at his laptop. "Huh. Vegetable crisper. Who knew?"

"Our life is so weird," she said.

"But never boring. Come on." He got to his feet and held out a hand.

"Where are we going?"

"Upstairs," he said, towing her toward the door.

"We're *not* having sex again until after the finger is out of this house and we've both showered at least twice."

"Relax, Thorn. We're searching Sesame's room."

"Oh. Okay. This makes me a little nostalgic for when we searched Dickie's apartment after…"

"After he got himself murdered and you tackled me down the stairs, thinking I was the murderer?"

"Yeah. Good times. Hey, what do you think couples who don't find dead bodies everywhere talk about?" she wondered as they hit the second floor and peeled off toward Sesame and Tommy's room.

"I have no idea."

"Holy crap! What the hell happened in here?" Riley said when Nick opened the door.

The guest room had been what Riley would have termed "habitable" before Sesame and her husband had moved in mere days ago. It'd had a bed—on the small and lumpy side. The faded pink carpet had been worn but not too hideous, and the walls had been papered in a dizzying flower petal pattern that had inexplicably made Nick ragey.

The wallpaper was still there. But the rest of the room was unrecognizable.

"When did she get a king-size bed? Is this rug real fur?" she asked as she sank ankle-deep into the thick tangerine-colored area rug.

"It looks like she skinned a Muppet," Nick grumbled.

There were tall silver lamps on mirrored nightstands that matched the new dresser.

One entire wall had been turned into an open wardrobe with a snazzy closet system that was full of Sesame's clothes. Tommy's suitcase was tucked next to the Hollywood-style makeup vanity in the corner.

"How did she do this in two days? It takes me three days just to put a load of laundry away," Riley noted in wonder.

"Focus, Thorn. We're looking for anything linked to the finger," he snapped.

"You mean like a hand?"

Nick was too busy scowling at the wallpaper to be impressed with her wit.

"Stop staring at the walls," she told him.

"I just hate them so much."

"Okay. You focus on the floor and the furniture. I'll start with the wardrobe to the stars," Riley suggested, only partially because she wanted to try on some of Sesame's shoes.

They worked methodically. The woman clearly liked to shop and had enough money to buy designers with names Riley couldn't even pronounce. Fortunately, so far she hadn't found any other severed body parts in the pockets.

"Got something," Nick called from the makeup table.

"Please tell me it's not another body part."

"Not a body part," he promised. He was sitting on the tufted bench, studying the contents of a sparkly binder.

Riley peered over his shoulder. Inside was a series of photos all of a blond woman with a deep tan who looked to be in her midfifties. The kind of midfifties where people would say she didn't look a day over forty. In one shot, she wore big sunglasses and a designer bag with a tiny dog inside. In another, she was on the phone as she left some kind of gym in clothes way too expensive to sweat in. The next pictured her on a yacht with a mimosa in one hand and several pounds of gemstones on the fingers of her other hand.

"That's Valencia Van den Verk," Riley said.

"Who?"

"You know. From that reality show *Real Bosses: The Women Behind the Mob*. She has her own lines of athletic clothes, nonalcoholic mixers, and makeup. She also owns one quarter of a UK football team."

"Van den Verk as in Franco Van den Verk?" he asked.

"Yeah. That's her ex-husband. He's in prison for—"

"Corruption, racketeering, and tax evasion."

"Why would Sesame have photos of a mob boss's ex-wife?" she wondered.

"It's not just photos." Nick turned the page. "It's interviews, real estate listings, product launches. Jesus. Who pays that much for shit to smear on your lips?"

"She's a mogul. Worth more than when her husband was laundering millions through nail salons and casinos," Riley explained, relieved that her guilty pleasure viewing habits were actually paying off.

"And Sesame just happens to have a complete dossier on the woman. Not loving the mob ties," he admitted, still studying the pages.

A severed finger, a disappearing act, and the ex-wife of a mob boss. Riley didn't know what it all added up to, but she knew it wasn't good.

"Are your spidey senses picking up anything?" he asked her.

"They're still on the fritz."

"It's probably this stupid fucking wallpaper that makes me want to punch it."

She patted him on the shoulder. "Hey, look. There's an espresso maker in here. And a mini fridge," she noted.

Nick eyed the retro off-white fridge. "Those things cost, like, a grand."

"So do those cashmere throw pillows," she told him as she waded across the carpet to the appliance. Riley opened it and found a small selection of sparkling water, some expensive-looking cheese, and four small unmarked vials. "What do you suppose these are?" she asked.

Nick joined her and plucked one of the tubes from its plastic stand. "Unmarked clear liquid in lab vials. Fun." He held it up to the light.

"Maybe it's some kind of weird cosmetic or, like, one of those expensive face-peeling solutions."

"Or maybe it's something worth losing a finger over," he guessed.

The doorbell rang.

Riley gathered the rest of the vials, and together they marched down the stairs.

Nick pulled the gun out of the back of his jeans. "Go into the kitchen and put those vials in the drawer that doesn't have the finger," he ordered, advancing on the door.

"Aren't you going to tell Kellen about these?" she hissed.

"The finger is priority. We'll play the vials by ear."

She didn't argue. Instead, she took the vials and added them to the cheese drawer, burying them under a bag of shredded cheddar.

A minute later, Nick, Weber, and Burt strolled into the kitchen. Weber looked like hell.

"Where's your car?" Nick asked him.

"Wherever I left it last night."

"How did you get here?"

Weber closed his eyes. "I walked."

"From where?" Riley asked.

"Apparently from next door."

"You didn't go home last night after happy hour next door? Oh God. You didn't sleep in Lily's room, did you? She gets handsy."

"I woke up on a couch in a room with Gabe doing three thousand push-ups. This better be good," he rasped.

Riley handed him a glass of water and a bottle of aspirin.

"We've got a situation with your sister," Nick began.

"Whatever it is, I don't care."

"She disappeared again," Riley began.

Weber thumbed off the cap of the aspirin and shook the tablets directly into his mouth. "This is me still not caring."

"Yeah? How about now?" Nick began, heading toward the fridge. "Sesame disappeared early this morning after telling her husband she was going shopping. But she didn't go shopping. She hopped a train to Penn Station."

"Good for her," Weber said, gingerly taking a seat and putting his head in his hands.

"Shortly after she left, some bruiser in a suit showed up with a delivery for Sesame and Tommy," Nick continued.

Riley pushed the legal papers toward Weber.

"Look, I'm still seeing double. I have no idea if this is a takeout menu or a signed confession to being the worst sister in the world."

"You recognize this?" Nick tossed the bagged finger on top of the paperwork.

"What the…" Weber made the mistake of picking up the baggie. "Christ. Did you just throw a finger at me? Oh God. You did. Trash can."

Her boyfriend managed to kick the trash can under Weber's face in the nick of time.

"There's a lot of barfing happening in this house this morning," Riley observed as Weber hurled what was probably straight alcohol into the trash.

"Ow," the detective moaned, holding his ribs.

"Ha! You puked over a finger. It wasn't even a whole body!" Nick crowed, recording the moment on his phone.

"Nick, seriously?" Riley wet a dishcloth and handed it to the pasty, sweaty Weber.

"What? I puked one time over a corpse, and he never let me live it down. Paybacks are hell."

"Do you feel better?" Riley asked Weber.

"I feel slightly less like death," he admitted.

"Well, hurry up with the reincarnation because our friendly delivery guy brought some NDAs and a severed finger for your sister. And after your brother-in-law got done hurling his guts out, he climbed out the bathroom window in his pajamas."

"I have no sister. I have no brother-in-law. I have no family. These people are strangers to me."

"Then you don't care if we call the cops and tell them everything? Including the part where your long-lost ex-sister and key witness to an unsolved crime came home not dead and you didn't take her straight into interrogation. Now she's being threatened with severed body parts, not answering her phone, and she's got a dossier on some mob boss's wife in her room," Nick prompted.

Weber put his head on the counter. "I hate everyone."

"How about we put the finger back in the crisper, and I make you some breakfast?" Riley suggested. The hollandaise on the stove was a lost cause, but she could at least make some toast.

"What's the point of eating? I have to choose between the career I've dedicated myself to for over a decade and the sister who faked her own kidnapping and/or death without telling me."

"I didn't say it was a good choice," Nick pointed out.

Riley slid a mug of coffee into Weber's line of sight.

Nick came up behind her and wrapped his arms around her.

"Did I really break up with my mother yesterday?" Weber asked.

"You did," she said with sympathy. "Do you remember anything else?"

"I remember one old lady trying to sit in my lap at the piano to play show tunes. The other one kept asking to see my gun."

His eyes opened wide in evident panic as he patted his pockets before relaxing.

"Do you remember kissing someone?"

Nick tensed against her. "Did this asshole kiss you?"

"He didn't kiss me," Riley said.

"Oh God. I kissed an elderly woman, didn't I?"

"It's possible," Riley said. "I left after you and Lily did that duet of 'Moon River.'"

"Who else would I have kissed if it wasn't an octogenarian or you?" Weber asked.

Riley watched as the realization dawned slowly.

"Oh no. That's not good," he groaned.

"Who did he kiss? His mom?" Nick demanded.

"Worse," Weber moaned.

31

While Riley took Burt for his morning constitutional, Nick and Weber faced off alone in the kitchen.

"What are you doing?" Nick asked as Weber pulled out his phone.

"What does it look like I'm doing? I'm calling this in."

Nick snatched the phone from his friend. "You're not calling it in."

"You said it was my choice."

"Yeah, but I didn't think you'd pick the blow-up-your-career option."

Weber's bloodshot eyes blazed. "You're holding a freezer-bagged finger that was hand-delivered to your house, Santiago. We're calling it in."

Nick felt a familiar frustration building. He and Weber had always butted heads. There were reasons why Weber was still a cop straitjacketed with regulations and procedures while Nick had left to make his own rules. "Look. I know this is a shitty situation. But give me twenty-four hours, and I'll get this straightened out."

"What are you going to do in twenty-four hours, Nicky? Find Beth or Sesame or whoever the hell she is and march her into an interrogation room? We looked for six years. If she's in the wind again, we're not going to fucking find her." Weber covered his face with his hands. "I have such a headache right now."

"We'll find her," Nick insisted. "Or Tommy. Or the muscle with the finger. Give me twenty-four hours. If I don't have one of them by then, I'll drive your ass downtown myself so you can do your penance or whatever the hell your rule-abiding ass calls it."

"You and your I-know-better-than-everyone attitude," Weber snapped, his voice rising.

"I do know better," Nick argued. "Not everything is black and white. Most of life is a whole lot of gray. You can't live by some generic rule book that doesn't take the gray into account."

"What am I not taking into account, Nicky?" Weber demanded. "I let myself be manipulated. I didn't tell my bosses that Beth was back. I didn't drag her down to the station and force her to give a statement. Hell, I didn't even push her for answers. The only way to clean this up is to call it in and deal with the consequences."

"This is probably why she didn't trust you in the first place," Nick said. It was a cheap shot, and he knew it, but he couldn't stop himself from taking it.

"Maybe," Weber said with a shrug. "But guess what? She didn't trust you either. So you can cut the vigilante hero bullshit."

"Look, we don't know what really went down—"

Weber slammed his hands on the counter. "That's the point. We're never going to know what went down. She didn't trust either one of us enough to tell us then, and she sure as hell isn't being honest now. You know what gets me? Even after she left, she knew everyone thought she was missing, and she still didn't reach out and let us know she was at least alive and safe. She made her choice. She was done with me then, so now it's only fair that I'm done with her."

"She came back, man," Nick pointed out. "So maybe she

hasn't gotten around to being honest, but when she got into trouble, when the chips were down, she came home to you."

Weber's jaw clenched. "And that's why I need to do this the right way. I need to do the right thing. I fucked up. I should have insisted on taking her in, getting her statement the second she showed up in town. It was my mistake, and I'll pay for it."

Nick was already shaking his head. "You're willing to put your career on the line because of some bullshit rule book. Everything you worked for, you're just going to kiss it goodbye because you didn't follow procedure?"

"Rules exist for a reason. And not just so you have something to break for fun," Weber said wearily.

Nick rubbed the back of his neck in frustration. It was the same damn argument they'd had six long years ago. Nick hadn't wanted Beth to be a witness in the arson case, not with its connection to the Harrisburg drug trade. He hadn't seen the point in opening her up to the danger when it had been completely unnecessary. Weber had been just as emphatic that she should have "done the right thing" and testified. And while they'd stubbornly dug in on opposite sides, Beth had vanished.

He'd lost a job and a partner over it.

Not that Nick would ever admit it to anyone, but he'd missed Weber. Missed their friendship, their ribbing, their patented opposition to each other. Just when they were starting to get along again, the same old shit headed for the same old fan.

The question was—had either of them learned from it?

"Fine," Nick said quietly.

"Fine, what?"

"Fine, call in the fucking badges and do what you need to do."

Weber stared at him for a long beat, then nodded. "Thanks, Nicky."

"Yeah, well, don't expect me to be happy about it. And don't expect me to stay the fuck out of it either. Some hulk in a bad suit threatened people I care about on my own doorstep.

I'm not gonna sit back and take up knitting while the cops fuck everything up. I'm working this thing with or without you."

"I wouldn't expect anything less," Weber said, scrolling through his contacts.

"Don't get in my way, Weber," Nick warned him.

Weber's bleary gaze landed on him. "Same team, Santiago."

––––––

Detective Teddy Wu was a large man in jeans, cowboy boots, and a rumpled corduroy blazer. He hadn't been on the force during Nick's tenure, which was probably a good thing.

Riley insisted on inviting him into the living room, probably in hopes of keeping things friendly, but she was the only one who sat. The men remained standing in some sort of face-off.

"Why did you call Detective Weber instead of 911?" Wu asked Nick in a slow southern drawl as a uniformed officer bagged the finger and nondisclosure agreements.

"I'm not a fan of the Harrisburg PD after a couple of your dirty boys in blue tried to kill my girlfriend and then burned down my business," Nick said, crossing his arms over his chest.

"So let me get this straight." Wu flipped back a page in his notebook and glanced at Weber. "Your sister disappeared without a trace six years ago. She reappears without warning, claiming she had amnesia and was abducted. You think she hasn't been honest about what she's been doing all this time. Then you," he said, pointing at Riley, "got 'the psychic flu' trying to read her mind."

"That's correct," Riley said like she was under a spotlight in an interrogation room.

Nick stepped closer to Riley's chair. "You got a problem with psychics, Detective?"

Wu ignored him and flipped another page in his notebook. "And then you, a former cop turned private investigator, gave Detective Weber's sister and her husband a place to stay after finding them in bed together and discovering that she not only wasn't abducted, she'd left willingly."

"Yeah, so?" Nick snapped.

Riley cleared her throat pointedly.

"This morning, you discovered the sister had disappeared again. You answered the door to a man in a 'bad suit' who handed you an envelope that contained two signed copies of a nondisclosure agreement and one severed finger."

"That's correct," Weber answered.

Wu closed his notebook and fixed Weber with a stare. "So what I'm wondering is why in tarnation you, a homicide detective in the Harrisburg PD, didn't feel your captain needed to be informed of the situation until now."

"Christ. Either you boys are working for megalomaniac villains or you've got the rule book shoved so far up your ass it tickles when you cough. Where's the fucking middle ground?" Nick growled.

Weber held up a hand. "Shut up, Nicky. Detective, I let my personal feelings get in the way. I thought my sister was dead. But that's no excuse for ignoring my duty as an officer of the law."

"So what is your sister involved with that involves delivering a finger and legal documents?" Wu asked, not looking particularly moved by Weber's admission that he had human feelings.

"We don't know. She hasn't been forthcoming," Weber said.

Wu turned his attention back to Nick and gave him a long assessing look. "How'd you get the shiner?"

"I smacked my face on a not-relevant-to-this-case," he told the detective.

Wu tucked his notebook into a pocket in his jacket. "Since we're here and all, you mind if we take a look at this Sesame's room?"

"Not without a warrant," Nick said.

"Seriously, Nicky?" Weber said under his breath.

"You can take the finger with you. But if you boys wanna do this by the book, then get a damn warrant."

He purposely hadn't mentioned the vials they'd found in

Sesame's room to Weber or Wu and wasn't about to open up his home to a legal search until he knew exactly what was in them.

"I need to make some calls," Wu announced.

"Well, do it someplace else," Nick said.

"You can use my office," Riley offered. She ushered Wu toward the door and shot Nick a pointed look. *Behave*, she mouthed at him.

"I need coffee," Weber said and slunk off in the direction of the kitchen.

Nick yanked out his phone and dialed.

"You got Penny, PI," Mrs. Penny said with a full mouth.

"I need your lab contact," Nick said.

"Well, hello to you too, partner. My investigation is coming along just fine. Thanks for asking. I'm staked out in front of a duplex with a basket of six different kinds of potato chips on the porch."

Nick pinched the bridge of his nose. "And I'm in my house with a severed finger and a bunch of cops."

"The cops cut off your finger?"

"No, damn it! It was someone else's finger."

"The five-oh cut off some poor sap's finger and brought it to you?" she asked.

Nick's eye twitched. "Listen to me, Penny. I need your contact at the lab. Now."

"Well, okay. But I don't know what you want her to do with a finger."

"I don't want her to dissect a finger. I need her to identify a liquid for me."

"Does the Dog Doody Bandit have diarrhea?" Mrs. Penny demanded. "Try scooping it up into a Tupperware container, and I'll be right over."

"There's no diarrhea," Nick snarled into the phone. "Just text me her contact info."

"You can count on me. As soon as I'm done with this bag of chips. My fingers are too greasy to work the screen."

He hung up just as Wu clomped back into the room. "We

put out a BOLO on the unidentified suspect's car. If you can get me a recent photo of the Hemsworths, we can start the search for them."

"I don't have a picture of Tommy, but I'll text you one of my sister," Weber said, returning from his quest for coffee.

Wu bobbed his head. "Appreciate that. One more thing. Captain said you're on leave until this investigation is completed."

Weber's face remained impassive, but Nick noticed the tightening in his friend's shoulders.

"Understood," Weber said.

Wu nodded. "If any of you sees Beth, her husband, or the enforcer again, I want you to call me immediately."

"We'll do that," Weber promised like the natural-born kiss-ass he was.

Wu glanced at Nick. "This city has had enough vigilantism. Leave the police business to us."

"Yeah, yeah. Save your speeches for the bad guys."

"I'd encourage all of you to stay out of trouble," Wu said and then headed for the door.

32

"S o then, I jumped out of the closet, and I was all like, 'Rawr! Give me back my clown baby,'" Josie said, cackling.

Nick, Weber, and Brian were holed up in Nick's office, poring over public and not so public records from Lucore Labs and putting the word out on the streets to be on the lookout for a pajama-clad doofus and his cleavagely gifted wife.

Josie and Riley had been tasked with getting one of the vials to Mrs. Penny's lab contact. They'd met Delilah, a forensic science undergrad, by the recycling bins behind Harrisburg University's lab building and handed over the vial, two hundred dollars, and a number one with a Diet Coke from McDonald's.

Handoff complete, they'd decided to drive around the city looking for Tommy.

After a few fruitless hours, they grabbed ice cream and parked the Jeep at the train station in hopes of catching Sesame's return. Of course, nothing said Sesame had to return. Maybe she was moving to the city indefinitely.

Which meant Sesame's shoes could become Riley's shoes.

While Josie relived last night's clown-terror glory, Riley had spent a lot of time thinking that this wasn't necessarily such a bad outcome.

The knock at her window startled them both.

"Jeez, Jas! You scared the hell out of us," Riley said, rolling down her window.

"Speak for yourself." Josie pocketed the tiny but deadly blade she'd pulled.

Jasmine looked like a sexy femme fatale dressed in head-to-toe black. She also looked smug. "Lemme in."

"Did you bring snacks?" Josie demanded.

"Of course I brought snacks," Jasmine said, sliding into the back seat when Riley unlocked the door. "I also brought Lance Rhinehard's home address."

"Who's Lance Rhinehard, and what kind of snacks?" Josie asked.

Jasmine tossed a bag of goodies into Josie's lap.

"Lance is the deranged bully torturing the entire Sheepford Junior/Senior High School, including our primo client, Mrs. Penny's great-aunt's bridge partner or something like that," Riley explained.

Josie ripped open a pack of Jelly Krimpets.

"I say we drive over there and do some reconnaissance. You know, get in the stupid twerp's evil little brain. See if we can find a way to bring him down," Jasmine said.

"He called us old," Riley explained to Josie.

"What size body bag do we need? I'm fresh out of larges," Josie responded around a mouthful of Krimpet.

"We're not plotting to murder a teenage boy. No matter how horrible of a person he is," Riley insisted in her best voice-of-reason tone.

"Relax, Ry. We'll just go on over there, spy on the little turd, and brainstorm ways to get him out of Kory's life."

"I vote yes," Josie said. "It beats sitting around waiting for Mega Rack to come back."

"Fine. But we're *not* doing anything illegal," Riley insisted. "I've been personally warned by the police today against getting into trouble."

"That was the Harrisburg cops. We're in Camp Hill," Josie pointed out.

Lance's house was a large white house on a fenced-in corner lot in Floribunda Heights. It was close enough to Nick's parents' house that Riley worried she'd break out in hives.

"I have it on good authority that Lance's parents are at some faculty fundraiser to get all the teachers therapy or something," Jasmine said.

"How do you get your information?" Josie asked, sounding impressed.

"I bribed one of the school's admin assistants. He was into feet, so I let him take pictures of mine in exchange for Lance's student record, his parents' pay stubs, and all the hot gossip in the district," Jasmine explained.

"I worry about you sometimes," Riley told her friend.

"I'm impressed," Josie said.

"I have a bad feeling about tonight," Riley muttered to no one.

They circled the block twice before parking in front of a brick bungalow across the street.

"Gee, I think I know which room is his," Jasmine observed dryly.

Instead of curtains, the window in the front right corner of the second floor was covered with a bedsheet with the words *Suck My* painted above an amateurish rendering of a cartoon penis.

"Are we sure about the body bag?" Josie asked.

Riley turned off the engine. "We should be able to see any comings and goings from h—Jasmine! Where are you going?"

Her friend was already on the sidewalk, feeding her ponytail through the back of a ball cap.

Josie got out too.

"You guys, we can't wander around this neighborhood. They call the cops on all suspicious activity," Riley whisper-shouted out the window at them.

Jasmine gasped. "Wait. *This* is where you and Nick got busted doing the dirty?"

"I can see his parents' house from here," Josie noted.

"They have neighborhood security, and I do not want to end up on the front page of the newsletter again," Riley complained. "We can't just trespass on private property," she called after them, but they were both already crossing the street.

Riley thumped her head against the seat twice. Then on a groan, she exited the vehicle and marched across the street after her friends.

"You can come back online anytime, spirit guides," she muttered.

She was halfway up the driveway when an arm reached out of a bush and grabbed her. Riley yelped.

"Shh!" Jasmine hissed. "Are you trying to get us busted?"

"Are you trying to get us arrested?"

"Nobody's getting arrested," Josie assured her from her squat under a Japanese maple. "I never get caught. But if you're too much of a good girl to get a little dirty to help little Cookie—"

"Kory," Riley corrected her.

"Whatever. I'm just saying, if you don't have the stomach to do what it takes to rid law-abiding society of this pubescent asshole, then maybe you should wait in the car."

"I don't have the stomach for jail…or fire."

"Who said anything about fire?" Jasmine asked.

Wide-eyed, Riley pointed toward the backyard, where a blast of flames lit up the darkness. It was accompanied by eerie laughter.

"He sounds like an evil villain," Josie observed.

"That's our guy," Jasmine said.

Together they crawled through the shrubbery to the backyard.

"Huh. Definitely a villain in training," Josie said, peering through the leaves of a large rhododendron.

In the middle of the backyard, Lance was juking and jiving with a plastic tank strapped to his back and a hose in his hands.

"He looks like a deranged Ghostbuster," Josie whispered.

"I said back the fuck off, Luke Skywalker!" he snarled at some invisible enemy. Another huge flame exploded out of the hose, turning the leaves on the closest tree brown. The yard was already full of charbroiled spots and dead or dying plants.

"Who in the hell gave this kid a flamethrower?" Jasmine whispered.

"Who fantasizes about killing Luke Skywalker?" Josie asked.

"That's a magnolia tree! They're so hard to grow here," Riley groaned.

Lance paused his yard assault and took a beer off his tactical belt. He chugged it, burped, then hurled the half-empty can into the air and turned the hose on.

"Eat hellfire, Betty White!" Lance roared, aiming the flames at the can, which landed close enough that Riley felt the heat.

"Betty White? That woman was a national fucking treasure! This guy is going down," Josie said, starting to get to her feet.

"Uh, guys. He's drunk. I think we should retreat while we still have eyebrows," Riley whispered, grabbing Josie's wrist and yanking her back down. A twig snapped under her combat boot, and they froze.

"Who's there?" Lance slurred, stalking crookedly toward them, his flamethrower hose at the ready.

Riley slapped a hand over Josie's mouth and dragged her to the ground.

Together the three of them lay in the dark in the mulch and held their breaths.

She really missed her spirit guides. They would have at least warned her to wear flame-retardant clothing.

"You better run, because if I find you, I'll torch you," Lance said in a creepy singsong voice usually reserved for terrifying movie murderers. He burped again.

Josie let out a low growl. Riley pinched her.

Lance stomped into the flower bed, crushing plants. "Come out and pla—aaaaaaaaaagh!"

His high-pitched squeal and frantic thrashing had Riley jumping into action. She grabbed her friends and started crawling along the fence toward the street.

"What the hell was that?" Jasmine asked.

"I fucking hate spiders!" Lance howled at the top of his lungs. Flames exploded behind them as the kid fired his flamethrower at the landscaping.

"I believe our friendly neighborhood bully just walked into a spiderweb," Riley said as they got to their feet and jogged the rest of the way down the driveway.

"We're not just gonna go, are we?" Jasmine said, stopping Riley with a hand on her arm when they got to the sidewalk.

"We almost turned into well-done lady steaks back there," Riley reminded her.

"That kid is a menace to society. We can't just let him flame broil his way through life," Josie insisted.

Riley pointed toward the backyard, where Lance was still howling and setting things on fire. "What do you want us to do? He's off his rocker."

"I have an idea," Josie said.

Riley was already shaking her head. "Unless it involves calling the cops and going home, I don't want to hear it."

"Psst!"

All three of them jumped. Riley slapped a hand over her heart, then noticed that Josie had a knife in one hand and a can of pepper spray in the other. Jasmine was inexplicably holding a shoe in an attack position.

"Over here," the disembodied voice called from the neighboring yard.

Josie led the way, weapons at the ready.

Illuminated by solar landscaping lights, they found a large bearded man clutching a trembling Yorkie in a pink sweater. Spying the knife, pepper spray, and shoe, he hugged the dog tighter. "Please don't kill me and Princess."

"We were just out for a walk," Riley lied. "Nobody is killing anybody. Put the knife down, Josie."

"What's your name, address, and business here?" Josie snapped at the man.

"I—I'm Jim. I live here. I'm out so Princess can do her business. She won't go in the backyard anymore since that flamethrowing future serial killer moved in next door."

"Forget you ever saw us, Jim and Princess," Jasmine advised, putting her shoe back on.

Lance let out a maniacal laugh that echoed eerily in the night air.

Jim's shoulders slumped. "I was really hoping you guys were SWAT or murder ninjas or something."

"Sorry, we're just regular people out for a regular night walk," Riley said, trying to tow Jasmine and Josie backward.

"This guy been giving you problems?" Josie asked, crossing her arms and gluing her feet to the sidewalk.

"He's a nightmare. When he first moved in, he drilled holes into the fence and aimed fireworks at my poor sweet dogs. He blasts Russian death metal from speakers at three a.m. He stole the Santiagos' lawnmower a few weeks ago and used it to mow down the rose bushes Priscilla's late husband had planted. He threw full cans of beer at the UPS lady, then threatened to sue her when she almost ran over him with her truck. And two weeks ago, he hit our security guard with a potato gun. The poor guy's been off work with a concussion ever since."

"How does he get away with all this?" Riley asked.

Jim shrugged. "I blame the parents. Plus, his mom's first cousin is the chief of police. If one more person says, 'Boys will be boys,' Princess is going to lose her damn mind. She's already lost fifty percent of her fur due to stress. I'd do anything to get him out of this neighborhood."

"Anything?" Josie asked.

Jim nodded. "Anything." He turned to Riley. "Hey, you look familiar."

She sighed. "I may have made the newsletter a few weeks ago."

"Ohhhhh. Now I remember. I didn't recognize you with your clothes on."

"Let's go have a talk, Jim," Jasmine said.

———

One hour later, Riley had a full-blown headache and a mug of green tea in Jim's living room. Princess and her sister, Highness, were settled on matching mini dog sofas next to personalized toy bins.

Jasmine and Josie were leading a briefing that was guaranteed to result in prison for everyone.

"We've got house access here, here, or here," Jasmine said, pointing at the whiteboard they'd liberated from Jim's basement gym. Now instead of a weekly powerlifting schedule, they were looking at a crudely drawn illustration of Lance's house next door based on the old real estate listing photos. "Josie will act as the distraction by ringing the doorbell and pretending to be a lost pizza delivery driver."

"Once I distract Lance, Jasmine will gain access to the house via the open garage door and take the stairs to the second floor," Josie said, pointing at the floor plan with a stick of beef jerky.

"I'll plant a couple of the fake spiders on the way up, then leave the bulk of them in his bed, and exit the way I came in," Jasmine said.

"In the meantime, I'll maintain surveillance from the perimeter and be ready to extract Jasmine if things start to go south," Josie continued. "Riley, you've abstained from tonight's festivities, so you can wait in the car."

Riley raised her hand.

"Question?" Jasmine said, acknowledging her.

"Yeah, just one or seventeen. Um, how are we all not going to jail for breaking and entering? Don't they have a security system? Why aren't we calling the cops?"

"It's not breaking and entering if the garage door is already open," Jasmine insisted.

"Also, there is no security system because Lance's parents don't want any of his behavior recorded," Jim chimed in from the kitchen as he sautéed ground turkey for dinner. Riley wasn't sure if it was his dinner or the dogs'.

"And we *are* calling the cops. Just not yet," Josie said. "We just need to wait for Lance to start wrecking his room as soon as he finds his bed full of spiders. Then concerned neighbor Jim who just happens to be out for a walk with his dogs calls 911."

"I'm pretty sure this is still highly illegal. And honestly, it doesn't sound like a good plan at all. What if he doesn't trash the house? What if he quietly stomps the spiders?" Riley argued.

"I've got this," Jasmine said to Josie. "Riley. Ry-Ry. Rye Bread. You're a good girl. A goody-two-shoes. Josie and I are the kind of girls who spent our teenage years crafting elaborate schemes to get away with all kinds of shit. You know I love you, but you wouldn't know a good revenge plan if..."

"If it dressed up like a murder clown and hid in your closet," Josie chimed in.

Jasmine snapped her fingers. "Yes. That."

"I don't have to have been a discipline problem throughout my teens to know this is a bad plan," Riley argued. "Jasmine, I expect terrible plans from you. It's part of your charm. But, Josie, you're usually diabolical. Fake spiders? You're better than that."

Jasmine reached out and pinched Riley's lips together with her fingers. "Zip it. We're doing society a favor by catching Lance in the middle of an illegal act that no law enforcement officer could ignore. And we're totally fine that you want to keep sitting on the sidelines and let other people play hero."

Riley wiggled away from Jasmine's pinchy fingers. "Hey, I saved your ass from the murdery mayor *and* rescued the hostages at Channel 50. I wouldn't call that sitting on the sidelines."

Jim appeared in the doorway wielding a wooden spoon. "You're the psychic from the news? That's so cool! Hey, is my nana doing okay? She died a few years ago, and she was kind of a meanie in her later years, so I was worried she wouldn't have any friends in the afterlife."

"My psychic powers are kind of on the fritz," Riley explained to him. Jim looked disappointed, and she felt guilty. "But as soon as I get them back online, I'll ask about your nana," she promised.

"Thanks. I'd appreciate that. That's who I inherited the girls from."

"Back to the plan," Josie prompted.

"I'm not taking part in something that is definitely going to end up with us in jail," Riley said firmly.

"There's no way this could possibly go wrong," Jasmine insisted.

33

It took less than five minutes for the whole plan to go to hell.

Sure, it started off fine. Riley and Jim stayed in Jim's yard, peering through a fireworks hole in the fence, while Josie and Jasmine went next door.

Josie rang the doorbell.

Jasmine tiptoed into the garage with her spare bag of fake spiders.

Unfortunately, none of them had anticipated Lance answering the door with his flamethrower.

Josie hadn't even gotten the word *hi* out of her mouth before she dove sideways into a holly bush to avoid the cloud of fire the inebriated teen shot at her.

"Oh my God," Riley breathed.

"Is she…?" Jim was squatting down at the next fireworks hole, holding both dogs like footballs under his arms.

Lance burped into the night, then slammed the door.

Josie's head popped up out of the shrubbery.

"Oh, thank goodness," Jim sighed.

But Riley was shaking her head as the petite but deadly woman climbed back onto the porch. "Josie's going to kill him."

"Look! Jasmine's in his bedroom," Jim said.

Sure enough, Riley caught a glimpse of Jasmine tossing fake spiders into the air like confetti through the corner window over the garage.

Riley groaned. "Lance isn't distracted. He could be heading upstairs right—shit."

They watched in horror as Jasmine stopped her spidering and disappeared from the window a moment before Lance stepped into their view.

"I feel like Jimmy Stewart in *Rear Window*," Jim confessed.

"Does he still have his flamethrower?" Riley asked, panic making her voice two octaves higher.

Highness gave a nervous yip under Jim's arm.

It was right about then that Josie kicked in the front door. But Lance didn't notice because he was too busy torching his bed.

Riley jumped to her feet. She might've been a good girl, but she was no Jimmy Stewart. She was Grace Freaking Kelly, and she was going to go to jail with her friends.

"If you see me in handcuffs, call Santiago Investigations," she told Jim as she hoisted herself over the fence.

———

"I had no idea bedsheets were that flammable," Jasmine said. Her ponytail was sagging, and she had bits of ash all over her.

"I think the fake spiders acted like a super accelerant," Josie mused. Her cheeks and chin were smeared black with soot.

"You think?" Riley snapped. She was dressed in a borrowed sweatshirt from Jim that came down to her knees, and she held one of the man's Yorkies. They shared the sidewalk with most of the rest of the neighborhood.

"I can't believe you dragged him out of the house by his hair," Jim said to Riley.

"He couldn't walk very well after Josie punched him in the face and he fell down the stairs."

None of the spectators looked overly upset as a handcuffed and flailing Lance howled about spiders while two officers half carried, half dragged him to a waiting patrol car. Behind him, flames shot out of the second floor of his house.

"It's just so beautiful," Jim whispered, pausing to wipe a tear on Highness's fur.

Josie nodded toward the fire and rolled back on her heels. "Shouldn't you be documenting this for your client?" she asked Riley.

She shook her head vehemently. "Nobody is documenting anything. We were never here. Let's go before someone sees us and starts asking questions."

"Riley Thorn, what are you doing here?"

"Oh shit," Riley said, trying to burrow farther into Jim's hoodie as Sergeant Mabel Jones approached from the other side of the caution tape.

"We were just out for a walk," Jasmine said, sliding an arm through Riley's.

"Yeah," Josie agreed. "Our friend Jim here has a nice neighborhood for night walks."

Jim waved with a dog in his hand. "This is Highness."

"Walk," Riley croaked. "We like to walk." She grunted as Jasmine and Josie both elbowed her from opposite sides. Even Princess looked at her like she was an idiot. Yorkies could be so judgmental. "What are you doing here? Isn't this the wrong side of the river for you?"

"It's a two-alarm blaze, so they called in extra units," Mabel explained. "Plus I was spending the night at my boyfriend's." She nodded toward a tall studly firefighter who looked like he'd just stepped off a calendar with puppies. He blew her a kiss before dragging a hose up the Rhinehards' driveway.

"Wow," Jasmine said. "Nicely done."

"Thanks. You got a minute?" Mabel asked Riley.

"Er, uh, sure." Riley handed the dog to Josie and followed the curvy cop farther down the crime scene tape, wondering what lawyer she should call from the police station since she was about to be arrested with the only attorney she knew.

"Okay. You didn't hear this from me," Mabel began.

"Hear what?"

"The thing I didn't tell you yet."

"Oh, right." Riley bobbed her head and willed herself to not act like an arson-causing idiot.

"That unattached digit that showed up at your house today? They ran the print. It belonged to an FDA data auditor named Wilson Trots."

Riley frowned. "FDA as in Food and Drug Administration?"

Mabel nodded, scanning the crowd. "Figured Santiago and Weber might be interested in that information."

"Thanks, Mabel. I mean, Sergeant," Riley said. "I'll make sure they get the message."

"Maybe don't tell Weber it was me who told you. He gets a stick up his ass about right and wrong," Mabel suggested.

"Along those lines, maybe don't mention that you saw me and my friends here," Riley said.

Mabel's eyebrows shot up her forehead. "You are *not* telling me you had anything to do with this mess."

Riley shook her head violently. "Nope. No. Definitely not. It's just I don't want Kellen to think we had anything to do with this. You know how suspicious he is."

The sergeant gave her the scary eyes, then sighed. "All right. But if there's anything I need to know about this particular fire that looks like it was caused by a lone, intoxicated, hormonal lunatic, I'd appreciate a courtesy call."

On cue, Lance started howling about spiders from the back seat of a nearby police cruiser.

"Absolutely," Riley said. Her eyes were so wide she was afraid they were going to pop out of her head.

"You all better get out of here before anyone gets the wrong idea," Mabel said.

Riley glanced over her shoulder, where her Jeep was blocked in by two fire trucks and an ambulance.

Dammit.

She started back toward her friends, then stopped and pulled out her phone.

Riley: Finger belongs to Wilson Trots, FDA auditor.

Nick: Damn, Thorn! Did your woo-woo come back online?

Riley: I wish. Ran into Mabel Jones at a fire in Camp Hill. Don't ask.

Her phone rang instantaneously, and Nick's dimples flashed across the screen.

"Uh, hi," she answered.

"By *fire*, you better mean you're at some bonfire with a bunch of drunk college kids and not an actual fire," Nick said.

"I told you not to ask," she reminded him.

"I'm definitely locking you in the creepy, smelly closet when you get home."

"Well, that might be a while. I'm parked in by half of the rescue vehicles in Cumberland County."

"You want a ride? I can take a break here and be there in ten."

"No. You keep working on your end. We'll get a ride. Oh, and don't mention to Weber that Mabel was the finger source. Or that we're at a fire. You know how suspicious he gets."

Nick's sigh sounded like a Category Three hurricane. "Fine."

"Are you guys making any progress digging into Lucore?"

"It's slow going with Weber being a dick about Brian hacking into their corporate servers. Doing things by the book is stupid and annoying."

"Poor baby," Riley teased.

"Keep an eye out for a big guy with extra fingers. I don't want my girl getting herself into any more dangerous situations."

A window shattered on the second floor, raining glass down onto the driveway. "No problem. I better go. I love you."

"Love you too, Thorn," he said with affection. "But I'm totally locking you in the closet when you get home."

She disconnected and returned to her friends. Jasmine was flirting with a firefighter, and Jim was still staring at the fire in glassy-eyed delight.

"What was that about?" Josie demanded.

"Nothing," Riley said, nodding in Jim's direction. She held up her index finger and wiggled it. Josie got the hint and gave her a cool nod.

"This time, he's gone too far," barked a familiar voice.

"Oh shit," Riley whispered, ducking behind Jim as Miguel Santiago, Nick's father, stormed down the street in a plaid bathrobe and house slippers.

"Miguel, you're making a spectacle of yourself." Nick's mother, Marie, dressed in silky black pajamas and a matching robe, followed her husband.

"Huh?" Miguel was hard of hearing and refused to admit it.

"A spectacle!"

"Who's a spectacle?"

"You are!" Marie shouted.

"Jeez, woman. Stop screaming in the middle of the street. People are looking," Miguel told her.

Jim shifted to the right, and Riley glued herself to his back. "Don't move," she ordered.

"Jimmy, you know what's going on here?" Miguel demanded.

"Looks like a house fire, Mr. Santiago," Jim said, stating the obvious.

"I can see that," Miguel groused. "Who burned it down? It was that punk kid with no manners, wasn't it?"

"Miguel," Marie hissed.

"What? You're the one who said he was a hoodlum destined for an orange jumpsuit," Miguel said.

"Josie! What are you doing here?" Marie asked, sounding surprised.

Riley went into full cringe mode.

"Hey, Marie. Hey, Miguel. We were hanging out with our friend Jim," Josie said.

"We who? Is my nephew here?"

"No, Brian's working tonight. I'm here with Jasmine and—Riley, what are you doing?"

Damn it.

With great reluctance, Riley unglued herself from Jim's back.

"Oh. It's you," Marie said with the same amount of enthusiasm she might have had for a colonoscopy.

"You and Nicky gotta stop by the restaurant and try my new risotto," Miguel said in lieu of a greeting.

"Uh, sure. That would be great," Riley said, wishing the house would explode and distract everyone.

"What are you doing with Jim?" Marie demanded, eyes narrowing in suspicion.

"You know the Santiagos?" Jim asked.

"They're my boyfriend's parents," Riley explained.

To her credit, Marie almost managed to hold back her shudder at the word *boyfriend*.

"Holy cow! You're the girl who got Nick Santiago to settle down? I heard rumors after the newsletter, but I didn't believe it," Jim said. "Good for you."

"Thanks," Riley said.

Marie sniffed indignantly. "Yes, well, we'll see if they last."

"On that note, I think it's time for us to be going," Riley said. "I'll see you guys at Nick's surprise party."

"Yes. Please tell Wander we're grateful for the invitation and we're looking forward to seeing her," Marie said.

"Who's Wander?" Miguel asked.

"Tell Brian we said hello, dear," Marie told Josie.

"I think that went well," Jasmine said as they walked down the middle of the street.

34

Put some pants on, man."

A foot nudged Nick in the ribs. "Ugh. I don't wanna go to school, Mom," he grumbled.

"I'm not your mother, and I sure as hell don't want to see your junk."

Nick cracked open one eye and found himself staring up at a weary-looking Weber and the ceiling of his office. The rug was rough and scratchy against his ass.

His cousin wheeled into view with a yawn. Brian's glasses were crooked, and his chin was covered in blond stubble. "Still doing that sleep-stripping thing? Classic Nicky."

"What time is it?" Nick asked, performing a full-body stretch on the floor.

"Seriously, man?" Weber groaned and turned his back.

"Almost dawn. We fell asleep digging through Lucore's financials," Brian said.

Nick got to his feet and gave Burt a good morning thump on the chest. "Hey, buddy."

"Santiago, if you don't put some damn pants on, I'm going to start punching you in the face," Weber said.

Burt let out a short sharp bark and sprinted out of the room.

"I'm very comfortable with my body. I can't believe the girls didn't wake us when they came home," Nick said, looking around for his phone.

"That's because they didn't come home," Brian said, looking at his phone.

"What?" Nick barked.

Just then, Riley, Josie, and Jasmine strolled into the room with Burt happily trailing them. They were a disaster, Nick noted as he covered himself with one of the reports they'd spent the night poring over.

All three of them were covered in dirt, their faces streaked with soot. Riley was wearing a sweatshirt that was four times too big for her. It said *Big Al's Gym* on the front, framed in a pair of bulging biceps.

"Sleep stripping again, Nicky? Or did we just walk in on an orgy?" Josie asked. She pressed a kiss to Brian's cheek and flopped down into his lap.

"You smell like pancakes and house fire," Brian noted.

She ruffled her husband's hair. "Did you guys know you're under surveillance?"

"Seriously?" Nick snapped.

"There's an unmarked car parked next door with a pair of heads with binoculars," Josie explained.

"What did you expect, Nicky?" Weber asked. "They're looking for Sesame, Tommy, and the finger guy, and they don't trust either one of us."

On a yawn, Riley fished Nick's jeans out from under his desk and handed them to him. He stepped into them, then used the shirt he found hanging from an open file drawer to wipe the smudges off her face.

"Aww, sweet," she said on another yawn.

"Where the hell have you been? I've been worried sick in the ten seconds since I woke up and Brian said you guys didn't come home last night."

"After the fire, we ran into your parents, and then I needed comfort food, so we called a Lyft and took our new friend Jim out to a diner. I ate six pancakes. Are those candy wrappers?" she asked, scanning the office.

"What fire?" Weber asked.

"My mother has that effect on people," Nick said. He kicked one of the empty candy bags in the direction of the trash can.

Riley put her hands on her hips. "Did you eat all our Halloween candy? Trick or treat is tonight!"

"We had to keep our brains fueled," he said.

"By the way, in case anyone is wondering, if you eat an entire bag of glitter gummy worms, you get a blinding headache," Brian cut in.

"What fire?" Weber demanded. His hair was sticking out in tufts all over his head. After a second mostly sleepless night, his eyes were so red he could have passed for a vampire.

"You look like shit," Jasmine observed. "Don't you ever shower?"

Riley shook her head at Nick. "I can't believe I have to go out and buy more candy. You couldn't have…I don't know, made everyone sandwiches or something?"

"Okay. Everyone is tired and grumpy, so here's what we're gonna do," Nick announced. "We're taking five minutes to get everyone up to speed. Then we're all going to our separate homes to shower and sleep. We'll reconvene back here at five and figure out what to do next. Deal?"

"Deal," everyone echoed wearily.

"Great. I'll start," Nick insisted. He plucked a printout off the floor and held it up. "Wilson Trots was a Food and Drug Administration auditor in Arizona who reviewed data from clinical drug trials. I say *was* because it was his finger Igor the Henchman delivered yesterday. Trots was reported missing yesterday when he didn't show at work. Local authorities found his place trashed. Odds are he's punching the big time clock in the sky. Take it away, Brian."

His cousin stretched his arms overhead and gave a loud yawn. "We dug into Lucore Laboratories. What we could glean legally"—he paused and shot a pointed look at Weber—"was that they're a brand-new company in the pharmaceutical sector. Founded in Arizona. They don't seem to have any kind of online presence. But I did find a list of corporate officers. Lurlene and Royce Lionworth and Sesame and Tommy Hemsworth."

"Do you think Lucore is linked to the vials?" Nick asked.

"What vials? What fire?" Weber demanded. He turned and stared at Jasmine for a beat. "Did we kiss?"

"Did we kiss? *Did we kiss?*" Jasmine repeated. "I gave you the best kiss of your sad life to piss off your mother, and you ask if we kissed."

"I was drunk! What vials? What fire?"

"Speaking of the vials," Riley said, pulling her phone out of her sweatshirt pocket.

"Whose shirt is that?" Nick asked, not liking the fact that she was definitely wearing another man's clothes.

"Jim's," Josie said as if that explained anything.

"Mrs. Penny's lab tech turned out to be not only easily bribed but also great at her job," Riley continued. "She worked overnight and isolated the compounds from the vial I gave her. She said it's an organic herbal formula with exotic plant extracts. It's not something that exists on the market. But it's also not liquid cocaine."

"Who's Jim?" Nick demanded.

"Your parents' neighbor," Riley said. "We met him and definitely did not set anything on fire."

"I'm going to ask one more time about the vials and the fire, and if someone doesn't answer me, I'm going to start arresting people," Weber announced.

"You're suspended. You can't arrest anyone," Nick said without looking at him. "Big buff Jim from the gym? Never eats carbs? Carries two tiny dogs around like they're teddy bears?"

"That's the guy. He says hi, by the way. I had to borrow a sweatshirt because Lance threw up on me after I dragged him out of his house fire. But now your mom thinks I'm having an affair."

"She's definitely not though," Jasmine cut in. "You're not, right?"

"I have the kind of headache that's never going to go away," Weber said and sank down on the couch, putting his head in his hands.

"Want to split a bottle of ibuprofen?" Riley offered, joining him.

"There isn't enough ibuprofen in the world to make me feel better about my life right now," Weber lamented.

"Okay, now that we're all caught up except Weber, who is on need to know until he can prove he's not a narc, everyone go home and get some shut-eye," Nick announced.

"What's the point of sleep? I'm just going to wake up to a life that's still shit," Weber complained as he stood up to go.

"If you're not gonna sleep, then at least take a shower. You smell like a nightclub floor after a Saturday night," Jasmine suggested helpfully.

"Let's go get some sleep and have some sex," Josie said to Brian.

Brian practically burned rubber wheeling them toward the door. "Later, losers!"

"I'm not going back to my place. I don't want to miss out on any of the fun," Jasmine announced.

"You can sleep in Sesame's room since everyone using it went missing," Riley offered.

Nick crossed to her and tugged her off the couch. "Good work, Thorn. You bribed a lab tech, defeated a bully, saved someone from a fire, and survived running into my parents all in one night. I'm impressed."

"Under these circumstances, I'm not sure if that's a compliment," Riley admitted.

The front door burst open, and Lily galloped inside. She had curlers in her hair and a fussy pink housecoat flapping in the breeze. She took one look at Nick and stomped her foot. "Double darn it!"

"What are you doing here so early?" Riley asked. "Is everything okay?"

"Josie texted me a code man fanny," Lily said, brandishing her phone.

"Where's the fanny?" Mrs. Penny huffed into sight, leaning hard on her cane. She was wearing men's boxer shorts and a sweater that said *Grammy Hugs Are the Best Hugs*.

"We're too late," Lily said sadly.

"I gotta work on my cardio," Mrs. Penny lamented.

35

4:32 p.m. Wednesday, October 30

Riley woke with a start from a dream about the creature with glowing eyes again and glanced at the clock. She groaned. "Nick?"

"Mmm?" he mumbled, his face buried in her hair.

"We should get up. Everyone's going to be here in half an hour."

"Mmm. Don't care. Let's sleep for another fifteen hours and then have sex until we can't feel our sex parts."

She yawned. "As great as that sounds, imagine how many windows they'll break if we don't let them in."

He groaned. "I thought moving in here was going to give us privacy. We were supposed to have Naked Tuesdays and kitchen sex."

"I blame your dimples. They draw people in," she said, extricating herself from his grasp. "Come on. Let's go solve this mystery and go buy more stupid candy." She gave him a slap on his very firm, very naked butt. And then giggled.

"Are you laughing at my ass?" His voice was now muffled by the pillow he'd pulled over his head.

"I didn't know you had dimples back there too," she teased. He clenched his butt cheeks, making the twin dimples deeper, making her laugh again. "You've practiced that in the mirror, haven't you?"

Nick rolled onto an elbow, looking sleepy and sexy. "After your time-out in the smelly closet, we're going to the beach and not telling anyone where we are."

Burt let out a happy yawn as he stretched his massive body.

She grinned. "Count me and Burt in."

Not knowing what the rest of the day would hold for them, Riley dressed all in black just in case. She made a mental note to look into flame-retardant clothing.

Nick joined her in the closet and yanked a pair of clean, neatly folded jeans off the shelf. "I gotta say, I miss Tommy more than Sesame. The clean laundry, the home-cooked meals. He even fixed the wobbly leg on my poker table."

"He was a really good househusband," Riley admitted. She slid her arms around Nick from behind and gave him a squeeze. "Look on the bright side. Once this mess is over and we go back to getting paid to solve cases, maybe we can hire our own househusband."

"That sounds—"

He was cut off by a shrill scream.

"That's Jasmine," Riley said, running for the door.

Nick grabbed her by the waistband and hauled her back. "Stay behind me, Thorn," he ordered, pulling his gun from its holster.

"The number of times you've had to draw a gun in the house is ridiculous," Riley said as they jogged around the stairs to the opposite wing.

The door to Sesame's room burst open just as they reached it, and Jasmine came flying out. She was wearing clothes she'd borrowed from Riley, and an eye mask sat askew on her forehead.

"What's wrong?" Riley demanded.

"I–I don't know. I woke up, and something was *looking* at me!"

"What do you mean 'something'?" Riley asked.

Nick stepped around the semihysterical Jasmine and headed inside to sweep the room.

Jasmine brought her hands to her face and slowly shook her head. "I don't know. One second, I was sound asleep, dreaming about hot firefighters. The next, I felt something on the bed with me. I took my eye mask off, but the curtains were drawn so it was dark, and the eye mask is a little tight, so everything was blurry—"

"Jasmine, what did you see?" Riley prompted.

"I don't know. Some big whitish blob...I think."

"Is it possible you were still dreaming?" Riley asked, drawing her friend away from the room. She could hear Nick searching the room.

"Damn, it still stinks," he said when he opened the closet.

"Maybe? I guess?" Jasmine admitted.

Nick returned to them and shook his head. Riley didn't know whether to be relieved that he hadn't found a white blob hiding in the room or concerned about Jasmine's mental well-being.

"Let's get some coffee and a snack in you. You'll feel better about the white blob with something in your stomach," she suggested.

"Can I have some tequila?" Jasmine whimpered.

Riley patted her friend's hand. "Sure."

They headed downstairs, where they found a fresh pot of coffee in the kitchen. They also found Lily and Fred arguing over four trays of cupcakes. There was frosting everywhere.

Now Riley *really* missed Tommy.

"I told you the orange was too orange," Fred complained.

"It's supposed to look like a pumpkin," Lily insisted.

Mr. Willicott was sitting at the table, braiding orange-and-black streamers. He wore a suit with a black bowler hat, and there was a tiny mustache glued to his upper lip.

"Don't you guys have your own house to destroy?" Nick asked.

"Oh, Nick, such a funny man with a perky fanny," Lily said

before turning to Riley. "Here. Try this." She stuffed a cupcake into Riley's mouth.

"Mmm. Good," Riley said, handing the other half to Jasmine.

"The house is too drafty, what with the whole not-having-a-roof thing," Fred explained. His toupee, this one a dark brown with a center part, had green frosting in it.

"I heard ghostly noises all night last night. Thumping and swearing," Lily said. "I think we might have a poltergeist. Isn't that exciting?"

"Very exciting," Riley said, handing Nick and Jasmine extra large mugs of coffee before pouring one for herself.

"I thought you were getting the roof fixed," Nick prompted. "I gave you the names of three reputable contractors."

"Well, the first one quit because the crew didn't like being ogled," Fred told them.

"Ogled?" Riley asked, knowing she was going to regret the question.

"Yeah. Lily and Mrs. Penny sat out in the parking lot in lawn chairs and ranked the workers with numbered signs."

"Lily, remind me to explain sexual harassment to you again," Riley said on a yawn.

"The second contractor was trying to scam us out of money," Lily said, squirting black frosting onto a cupcake and the stove top. "She pretended like the whole roof, including the trusses, needed to be rebuilt and replaced. Can you believe that nonsense?"

"It does and they do," Nick argued.

"That roof held up for three generations. I don't see why now all of a sudden, it needs to be replaced," Lily insisted.

"Seventy years is *not* all of a sudden."

"Don't worry. Willicott and I took a look, and those trusses are fit as a fiddle," Fred said.

Nick rolled his eyes. "If you don't get it fixed, the whole roof is going to collapse, and you'll all end up as walking pancakes."

Lily patted him on the cheek. "You're such a good boy to be concerned about us."

"I'll get a contractor over here tomorrow, and you will *not* scare them off. Got it?"

"Just make sure they're cute and not running a scam," Lily insisted.

"What are the cupcakes for anyway?" Nick asked.

Lily giggled nervously.

"Well, they're definitely *not* for a surprise party," Fred said. He gave Riley an exaggerated wink.

As if on cue, Mr. Willicott put down his streamers and held up a sign that said, *Surprise.*

Riley snapped her fingers. "Charlie Chaplin!"

Mr. Willicott twitched his nose. The fake mustache moved back and forth on his upper lip.

"Ooooooh," Nick said. "I thought he was civilian Hitler."

Mr. Willicott gave him the middle finger, causing Riley to sputter into her coffee.

The doorbell rang, and Nick and Riley shared a glance.

"I hope it's not another body part," she whispered.

Nick put down his coffee and unholstered his gun again. "Only one way to find out."

Their elderly audience didn't bat an eyelash.

Thankfully, it wasn't a body part delivery. They found Gabe, Wander, and Riley's nieces on the front porch. Nick shoved the gun back into his waistband.

"Trick or treat," the girls sang in unison. River and Rain were both dressed as Wonder Woman. Janet wore a long skirt, glasses, and a bun. Gabe and Wander were dressed as a gender-bending Sonny and Cher.

Riley groaned. "Crap! I forgot the candy. I wonder if I can get some delivered in time?"

"Hey, guys. Who wants some nice canned goods?" Nick offered.

"Me!" Janet said, scampering past him into the house.

"Who is she supposed to be?" Riley asked, hooking her thumb in Janet's direction.

"Marie Curie, the scientist who discovered radium,"

Gabe answered. He tossed his long black Cher hair over his shoulder.

"Raphael is picking up the girls to take them trick-or-treating, so we thought we'd help you two with trick-or-treat night," Wander said, stepping inside and pressing a kiss to Riley's cheek. Her fake mustache tickled, and it smelled like eucalyptus. She was wearing a paisley shirt under a suede vest plus bell bottoms.

"Nice mustache," Riley said.

Wander grinned. "Thanks. I soaked it in essential oils so I didn't have to wear nose plugs."

"This is really nice of you guys, but we're kind of in the middle of something," Riley said.

"Then we'll handle the trick-or-treaters, and you can focus on whatever you need to do," her sister said.

"Thank you. And good luck finding food to give out. Someone ate all the gummy worms," Riley said, pointing at Nick.

The gummy-worm thief closed the door only to have it open itself.

A freshly showered Weber strolled inside in jeans and a sweater. Riley couldn't remember ever seeing him in casual clothes before.

"They're still watching the house from next door," he reported. "I couldn't get a good look at who it is."

"Look at you, dressing up as a real boy," Jasmine said.

"I see a few hours of sleep didn't make you any less of a pain in my ass," Weber observed.

Brian and Josie entered from Brian's office.

Nick shut the door again. "Guess it's time to get to work."

"You're feeding us, right?" Josie demanded.

"I'll order pizza," Riley promised.

"Green peppers and black olives," her friend said.

"Meat lovers," Nick and Weber said together.

"Mushroom and spinach for us, please," Wander said.

Lily poked her head out of the kitchen door. "Extra sausage on mine. Make it a sausage fest!"

Mr. Willicott's head appeared above Lily's. He held up a sign that said, *Pepperoni*.

"Did he just make that sign, or did he actually come over here with a pepperoni sign on the off chance someone was buying pizza?" Nick asked.

Riley sighed. "We'll probably never know."

"I'll get the briefing set up in the dining room. There's more places to sit, and it's farther away from whatever the hell your weirdos are doing in the kitchen."

"I think you mean *our* weirdos, babe," Riley said, sliding her arm around Nick's waist. "At least with trick-or-treat night, the cops won't be able to keep track of who's coming and going."

"Neither will we, Thorn," Nick said.

"Oh." The gravity of it hit her. They were expected to open the door to strangers in costumes all evening. It would be too easy for a bad guy to blend in with the rest of the population of Harrisburg. "That's really not good."

"Exactly."

She called in the pizza order, filled a couple pitchers of water, and then joined everyone else in the dining room.

Nick shut the door.

They all took seats around the table. Someone, most likely Tommy, had cleaned up the broken pieces of the chandelier and plaster that had fallen a few days earlier.

She looked around the table at their friends. They were an army of concerned citizens fighting fatigue and searching for answers.

Nick and Weber started speaking at the same time, then stopped to glare at each other.

"After you," Nick said.

"Right. Fine. My sources in the department claim that Sesame, Tommy, and the unidentified suspect are still at large," Weber said. "But the limo is no longer parked at the train station."

"So either it got towed or someone came back to retrieve it," Nick said.

"Seeing as how Wu added Wilhelm and the limo to the BOLO, I'm guessing it's the latter," Weber explained.

"We need to get to one of them first," Nick said. "Tommy still has family in this area. Josie, you and Weber are going to go shake them down for information. Odds are that's where he would have gone when he ran."

"I'm not shaking down an innocent civilian," Weber snapped.

"Think of it as playing good bad guy and bad bad guy," Josie suggested. "I'll let you be the good bad guy."

Nick turned to his cousin. "Brian, I need you to nail down the whereabouts of the Lionworths. Make sure they didn't come to town with No Neck."

Brian nodded and opened his laptop. "On it."

"Riley, you and Jasmine watch the train station. I don't think Sesame is officially in the wind. Not with her husband and her wardrobe still in town."

Jasmine clapped her hands. "Yay! I get a job!"

Riley was less impressed with the assignment. The odds of Sesame coming back into town the way she left were slim. Especially if Tommy had been able to warn her about the finger.

"This time, don't burn anything down," Nick said sternly.

"We didn't start the fire," Jasmine said haughtily.

"Fine. Don't incite anyone to arson," Nick conceded.

"What fire?" Weber demanded.

"Unrelated. There's no way that situation is related to the one we're dealing with, so quit worrying about it," Nick told him.

"And what are you gonna do, Santiago?" Weber asked.

"Since it's unlikely anyone connected with the case is going to wander back into this house and explain what's going on, I'm going to start rattling cages. Someone in this city knows what the hell is going on. I'm going to find them and make them talk."

Jasmine raised her hand. "Am I hallucinating again, or is Dolly Parton delivering pizza to the backyard?" she asked.

Sure enough, in the waning afternoon light, a Dolly Parton look-alike traipsed into view carrying two pizza boxes.

"You didn't seriously order only two pizzas, did you?" Josie asked Riley.

"No. And I didn't order them from Dolly either."

Nick and Weber both drew their weapons.

"Everyone get down and stay out of sight," Nick hissed, moving soundlessly toward the patio door.

They did their best, but there weren't exactly a lot of places to hide in a room full of windows with one table in the middle. Brian wheeled into the corner, where he was partially concealed by one of the heavy drapes, and produced a gun. Josie crawled under the table with everyone else and readied her stun gun.

Nick gestured at Weber, who nodded and skirted around to the other side. He held up three fingers as Weber reached for the doorknob.

Riley's heart pounded. She was kicking herself for being absolutely useless in this situation. They had no psychic advantage. No way to know who the intruder was or what they wanted.

Three. Two. One.

Weber threw the door open just as Dolly stepped up to peer in through the glass.

Nick jumped in front of her and leveled his gun. "Freeze!"

Dolly gave a little squeal and dropped the pizza boxes.

"Nooo!" Josie yelled.

Dolly recovered quickly and put her hands on her hips. "Nicky, that was not nice! I almost got grease all over my costume."

"Sesame?" Nick growled.

Burt appeared out of nowhere and pounced on the first box.

"*No!*" Riley shouted. "Not the extra sausage!"

Weber grabbed his sister by the arm and yanked her inside. "You have five seconds to explain what the hell is going on, or I'm calling the police, and you can explain everything in an interrogation room."

"He will too, because he's a narc," Nick said, adding weight to the threat.

"Explain what?" Sesame asked innocently. "I was shopping and decided to spend the night at the Hershey Hotel. Didn't Tommy tell you?"

Weber looked as if he were about to explode.

"We've all had enough of your bullshit. You have three seconds. Start with why you lied about where you were going and how shortly after you disappeared *again*, a thug delivered a warning addressed to you. Then you can move on to where the hell your husband ran off to after he got spooked. And how about we wrap it all up with an explanation of Lucore Laboratories and why your name is listed as a corporate officer."

Sesame gasped. "Tommy ran off?"

"Somewhere in the timeline of him finding out you lied about going shopping and being threatened with a signed NDA and a finger," Riley explained.

The woman pawed through her bag and produced her phone. She plugged in a number and impatiently held it to her ear.

"Won't work," Nick said. "He left his phone here when he jumped out the window in his pajamas."

"Is that why he wasn't answering my calls or texts?" Sesame looked frantic now. "Oh, my poor Tommy!"

There was a loud thump and a muffled curse that sounded as if it was coming from inside the dining room wall.

"You've got to be fucking kidding me," Nick groaned.

Riley frowned. "Wait a second. That's coming from the secret staircase."

"I thought it was boarded up after the whole guy getting murdered in there?" Jasmine said.

"I didn't get to that page of the to-do list yet, okay?" Nick snapped.

Brian rolled over and knocked on the wall. "Tommy? Are you in there?"

There was a beat of silence and then a faint, "No."

Sesame stepped up to the wall. "Tommy Hemsworth, you get your handsome behind out here right now!"

"Sesame? Is that you?" Tommy called back.

"Of *course* it's me! What are you doing hiding in the walls?"

Nick opened the dining room door just as the hutch in the hallway swung open. Tommy emerged, still wearing his pajamas from the previous day. He had a sloppy homemade bandage made out of some kind of silky white material with what looked like little skulls wrapped around his forehead.

"I knew it wasn't a ghost!" Jasmine said. She slapped Weber in the chest, and he doubled over on a groan. "Oh, right. I keep forgetting about your ribs."

"I didn't know where else to go. Nick and Riley said you didn't go shopping, and then Gunther showed up here with a finger."

Sesame gasped. "Gunther was here?"

Josie sidled up next to Riley. "I'm assuming Gunther is the goon?"

"I panicked and climbed out the bathroom window," Tommy continued, taking his wife's hands. "I wanted to call you, but my phone was here, and I didn't have your number memorized. So I hid next door on the third floor, but it was so cold. Plus, I got hit in the head with a couple of roof tiles, so I ended up sneaking back over here to hide."

"Is that ladies' underwear on your head?" Josie asked.

"I thought it looked familiar. Mrs. Penny has a pair just like that," Riley said.

"I needed a bandage, and it was the only thing I could find that would stay put," Tommy explained.

"Was that you crawling on my bed while I slept?" Jasmine demanded.

"No, I swear! I stayed in the secret passageway the whole time. Except for when I needed to go to the bathroom or make a snack."

"I really need to install that security system," Nick muttered.

"You poor thing," Sesame crooned to her husband. Then

her shoulders went tense. "Did you say Gunther brought a *finger*?"

Tommy nodded vigorously. "I think it was Wilson's."

"Oh no! What's he going to do with only nine fingers?"

"Nothing, seeing as he's dead," Weber snapped.

Sesame's face drained of color. "W-what do you mean dead?"

"I saw it. Aunt Lurlene and Uncle Royce. They shot him. I didn't want to tell you," Tommy admitted. "I didn't want you to be an accessory after the fact."

"That's when you followed me here?" she asked.

He nodded vigorously. "I was already going to tell them that I was going after you. But when I walked in and saw what they'd done, I realized you were right. I was an idiot. I should have listened to you."

"No, *I* was the idiot. I didn't trust them after I told them about the initial results from the trial. I should have made you come with me," Sesame said.

"Not to break up this touching moment," Weber said, his voice dripping with sarcasm, "but you both knew the murder victim *and* you know the man who delivered part of his body to threaten you?"

They nodded.

"Fuck this. I'm done. I'm out. I don't even want to know why someone would fly across the country to threaten you with a dead man's digit. I'm calling Wu," he said, starting for the door.

"Wait! Kelly!" Sesame ran after him and threw herself in front of the door. "Let me explain."

"Explain what? That you never trusted me with the truth? That you never will?"

"I was trying to protect you," she said, her lower lip trembling. Her gaze slid to Tommy. "And you. All I ever wanted to do was keep you both safe."

"That's not all you ever wanted. What you wanted was to be rich and famous. Now I'm suspended from my job, the only thing I have left to be proud of. And you led a murderer here, so now everyone under this roof is in jeopardy thanks to you and your lies," Weber snapped.

The truth of his words hit Sesame like a cartoon anvil.

"He's right, kid," Nick said quietly. "Whatever you're up to, you brought it into my home and put Riley and me and our friends at risk. Now we've got cops watching our every move, and if they catch you and Tommy here, we're all up shit creek. I hope it was worth it."

Sesame's eyes welled with tears, and she shook her head. "It's not. I thought it would be, but I never meant for anyone to get hurt."

And then she started to cry real tears.

36

Nick took no pleasure in watching Dolly Parton cry into her husband's shoulder.

"It's okay, Ses. We'll be all right. We just need to figure out a way out of this mess," Tommy said, stroking her back.

Everyone else—except for Weber—was eating the pizza Wander had brought back to them. Weber was too mad and probably still too hungover to eat.

Sesame straightened her shoulders and took a deep breath that challenged the zipper on her glittery Dolly Parton jumpsuit. "I'm ready now."

"Start at the beginning," Nick said. "You and Tommy left town after the warehouse fire so he wouldn't be charged with arson."

"Why would I be charged with arson?" Tommy asked.

Sesame took his hand in hers and squeezed. "That's correct."

"But you didn't go work for his family's small-town pharmacy, did you?" Nick continued.

"No, you're right," she admitted. "We did work for the family business, but it wasn't a pharmacy."

"My aunt and uncle were grifters. At the time, they mostly dabbled in identity theft," Tommy explained.

"Christ," Weber muttered under his breath.

"That's how we got our new identities. But Sesame didn't like the work."

"I thought it was too skeezy. I mean, who wants to be associated with people who insert skimming devices on ATMs and gas pumps? There's no finesse to it," she chimed in. "And the profit margins were too low."

"When Sesame sees something that needs to change, she finds a way to change it," Tommy said with a soft smile for his wife.

"I watched this news special on prescription drugs and how pharmaceutical companies were inflating the prices, forcing many patients to choose between medicine or other necessities. And I decided to stop it."

"Okay. How?" Nick asked, shooting a glance at Weber, who was pretending not to listen.

"I started importing prescription drugs from Mexico, Canada, and Europe and put Tommy's family in charge of distribution."

"It was really impressive," Tommy said, squeezing his wife's hand.

Sesame beamed. "Thanks, babe. Within a year, we had a network of distributors that covered eleven states selling direct to consumers. Within two years, we were up to twenty states that had significant elderly populations and had international pharmaceutical companies courting us to bring their products to market."

"So what you're saying is you were an international drug dealer?" Weber said, unable to feign disinterest anymore.

"Well, I mean, if you want to ignore all the subtleties," Sesame said.

Her brother got to his feet. "I don't want to hear another word."

"This is why I didn't tell you, Kelly. You're such a stickler for the law you can't even see that we were doing something good."

"You were importing illegal prescription drugs!"

"No, we were illegally importing prescription drugs," she countered.

"It's an important distinction," Tommy agreed.

"Sit down, Weber," Nick said. "Hear them out."

Sesame smiled at him. "Thank you, Nicky. Things were going great. We had millions of elderly Americans who could now afford their medicine. The companies who couldn't legally distribute their drugs in the U.S. now had a channel to do so. And, of course, our income also increased."

Weber scoffed. "Yeah, to private planes and limo drivers. How charitable of you."

"Shut up and eat some pizza," Nick ordered.

"No, he's right," Sesame admitted. "I've never lied about my desire for wealth, and this was the first time in my life that I was actually climbing that ladder. It felt good to be able to afford whatever I wanted. Being able to splurge on a new pair of shoes or boobs made me feel so...powerful. So secure. And Tommy's aunt and uncle liked their newfound financial security too."

"Uncle Royce gave up collecting golf balls and bought himself two golf courses," Tommy said. "Aunt Lurlene went from scrubbing toilets at a country club so she could steal wallets to being a board member."

"How did it start to go wrong?" Riley asked Sesame.

She looked down at the table. "I saw the potential for another move. A big one. We'd been importing prescription drugs that had been approved in other countries for a few years when one of our South American representatives brought us a brand-new drug that they were excited about."

"This is ridiculous," Weber muttered. "My sister faked her own death to run a cartel."

"This particular company wanted our help getting their new drug approved. It was all-natural, worked better than other existing medications, and, best of all, there was a huge market for it. I'll admit, I was blinded by dollar signs," Sesame said.

Tommy squeezed her hand. "We all were."

"I convinced Tommy's aunt and uncle to form a pharmaceutical company, and thanks to our previous criminal resources, we were able to identify a Food and Drug official who was, shall we say, comfortable being influenced to help us fast-track our clinical trials."

Weber covered his ears. "I shouldn't be listening to this. We should be calling the authorities."

"What was the drug for?" Jasmine asked.

Tommy cleared his throat. "It was a...um...male enhancement drug."

"But there are already medications for that," Brian said. "Not that I'm familiar with them or ever took one once in college."

"That was a fun night," Josie said fondly.

"So you found a new little blue pill. What was the problem besides bribing government officials and running a domestic prescription drug cartel?" Weber asked.

"In addition to the product branding and launch, I was also in charge of monitoring the trials," Sesame explained. "It soon became clear that there was one problem."

"Tell me you didn't accidentally kill a bunch of patients," Weber said.

"No! I swear. No one was harmed. But you know those drug commercials where there's a list of side effects?"

"Like anal leakage and sudden death?" Josie asked. "Tell me your sex drug caused anal leakage."

"I wish," Tommy said, shifting in his seat.

Sesame started braiding the ends of her Dolly wig. "This formula is unique because, in addition to raising testosterone, it also amplifies the effect of any estrogen in the body. So not only does the subject experience sexual arousal, they also experience uncontrolled giggling."

"Something about the dilation of the blood vessels apparently loosens the vocal cords," Tommy added.

"Giggling?" Riley repeated.

"Not just a chuckle or a guffaw," Sesame said. "Fits of hysterical giggling."

"That doesn't sound too bad," Brian said.

"It's not dangerous at all," Sesame assured them. "The trial proved that the drug did what it was supposed to. But it also showed that the patients' partners were too annoyed to actually want to have sex."

"Which makes it a disastrous side effect," Riley guessed.

"Exactly."

"So it works great to turn men on and their partners off," Josie surmised.

Sesame nodded, still braiding her wig. "I realized that even if we managed to get FDA approval, the lawsuits would lead an investigation straight to our doorstep. I told Tommy's aunt and uncle that we had to shut it down or we would run the risk of losing everything we'd already built. They refused to listen. The valuation in the billion-dollar range convinced them that it was worth the risk."

"My aunt really likes her mink eyelashes," Tommy said.

"*Billion* with a *b*," Riley asked, wide-eyed.

Sesame nodded. "They made it clear that they were moving forward with the trial and the launch. I told Tommy we had to get out while we could. Sesame and Tommy Hemsworth had to disappear. They gave me no choice. We were on a sinking ship, and I knew if it went down, they wouldn't hesitate to pin it all on Tommy and me. That's when I knew it was time to come home."

"That's why you wanted us to leave?" Tommy asked.

Sesame nodded. "Your aunt and uncle were furious that I wanted out. I didn't trust them to do the right thing. And when you balked at leaving, I decided to come home to my brother and work out a plan to get you out of the business whether you wanted it or not."

"Aunt Lurlene convinced me that you left because you didn't like having to split the profits four ways. She said you would never settle for a millionaire when there were billionaires out there to marry."

"Oh, Tommy." Sesame sighed.

"So when exactly did you decide to follow her out here?" Nick asked Tommy.

"You weren't answering my calls, and I was missing you so much. I decided I was going to fly out here and make a grand gesture to win you back. You were right—we didn't owe my family more than what we'd already given them. You built them an empire, and they were careless with it. I stopped by their house on my way to the airport to tell them I was leaving. I let myself in, and that's when I heard the gunshot. I didn't think, I just ran inside, and that's when I saw them." Tommy's face was stark white. He shook his head as if to get the image out of his mind. "Gunther was standing over Wilson's body holding a gun. There was this pool of blood on the tile floor. I was shocked. When I looked up, Uncle Royce said he was just tying up loose ends to keep our investment safe."

"Now I'm calling the cops. They can sort this shit out," Weber said, reaching for his phone.

Sesame put her hand on his arm. "You can't call the police."

"Give me one good reason why," he demanded. "One honest truth that will convince me not to report all this to my superiors."

She nodded solemnly. "Okay. I didn't actually go shopping."

"No shit," Josie said, working on her fourth piece of pizza.

"I went to Manhattan to meet with a lawyer and"—she paused dramatically—"the FBI."

Tommy's pizza slice fell out of his hand to the floor.

Burt pounced on it and gobbled it up.

"The FBI?" Tommy repeated.

"We couldn't start the next chapter of our lives if we were tied up in all this illegal activity. And the Lionworths were a sinking ship."

"Lionworth is definitely a made-up name, right?" Jasmine guessed.

"Oh, totally," Sesame said. "Their real name is Klump."

"Can't say I blame them for the change," Josie mused.

"Anyway, I found a lawyer and set up a meeting to make a deal. I'd give up everything on Lucore and HardMax and our prescription business in exchange for immunity for me and Tommy. The FBI agreed. I gave them enough evidence, including a sample of HardMax, for them to get arrest warrants for your aunt and uncle. They're making their move on them tomorrow. In a couple of hours, we won't ever have to worry about them again," Sesame promised.

Tommy stared at Sesame in awe.

Nick had to admit even he was impressed. Sesame was still the same diabolical genius she always had been, just on a grander scale.

"I am under strict orders from the FBI not to get into any trouble before they arrest your aunt and uncle. Any sign of us talking to the police could tip everyone off. That's why I had to get creative about getting inside to explain everything."

"So you didn't even come back to reconnect with me. You came back because you were tired of running your cartel empire and thought you could once again avoid paying the price for any of your actions," Weber said flatly.

"I'm gonna need you to hold off on the brotherly outrage for a bit," Nick said. "Because right now, they're in more danger than they've ever been. If Gunther the Goon and Tommy's relatives catch a whiff of this deal Sesame made, there's nothing stopping them from snipping all the loose ends."

Weber heaved a sigh and scrubbed his hands over his face. "You're right. Fine. Get your lawyer on the phone now," he said to Sesame. "I'll update him or her about the FDA guy's homicide and tell them we need an FBI security detail to protect you until Aunt and Uncle Whoever are in custody."

Sesame's eyes went damp again. "I always knew I could count on you, Kelly. Even when you're mad at me, you still do your best to protect me."

Weber didn't look like he was pleased with the compliment, but he didn't pitch a fit either when she handed him her phone.

"Brian," Nick said, snapping his fingers at his cousin.

"Bring up photos of all the bad guys so everyone can take a good look and memorize their faces."

"On it." Brian pulled out his laptop.

Nick turned to Riley. "Thorn, you and Jasmine are going to have to kick everyone out. They're gonna be safer in their own homes than here. No trick-or-treaters. No elderly visitors."

Riley nodded and Jasmine threw him a mock salute. "You can count on us."

"We've already got law enforcement eyeballs on us, so we might as well just lie low here for the night," Nick said. "Jos, you're with me. We'll turn this place into Fort Knox on lockdown."

Josie flashed him a thumbs-up before reaching for her fifth slice of pizza.

"Here's our gallery of baddies," Brian said, turning his laptop around to show everyone the photos.

Next to Gunther's creepy, scarred face was a photo of a couple standing in front of a *look-at-how-rich-we-are* mansion. The woman was a medium-height unnatural redhead with pale blue eyes and a large mole on one cheek. The man looked to be close to six feet tall. He had broad shoulders, a square face, and a neck tattoo of a spider. Both looked like they wouldn't have a problem throwing down and starting shit.

"Uncle Royce has two more spiders on his neck and more hair now," Tommy said.

"Yeah, he got a hair transplant through one of our South American suppliers," Sesame explained.

"Memorize these faces," Nick said. "None of these people are getting inside this house."

Weber hung up Sesame's phone and nodded at Nick. He joined him next to the door.

"What's up?"

"I talked to Sesame's attorney, and she's making contact with the FBI about security. They could be here in a few hours."

Nick nodded. "Okay. We can hold down the fort until then."

"There's something else," Weber said, pulling out his phone. "Christian Blight was released from prison yesterday."

"Are you fucking kidding me? As if dealing with some prescription cartel hit man isn't enough, now we've got to deal with Blight?"

"Look, the guy's been locked up for six years. Let's just hope he decides to spend his first few hours of freedom with his family, not looking for revenge."

Nick was kicking himself for not getting around to installing that damn security system.

"So what do we do?" he asked grimly.

Weber looked surprised that he was asking for advice. "We have each other's backs. That's what we do."

Nick nodded. "Thanks, man."

"Now, let's get this shit done so I can suffer through day two of my hangover in peace tomorrow," Weber said.

"Okay, people," Nick said, clapping his hands. "Everyone has their assignments. Let's get to work. Remember, no one gets access to this house!"

"Is anyone else excited?" Jasmine asked. "This is even better than the fire and the spiders."

Nick opened the door and froze.

"*Surprise!*"

"Fuck me."

37

R iley felt her mouth drop open.

"How long were we in there?" Jasmine wondered out loud as they stared at the spectacle before them.

There was a Halloween party in full swing in their house. Music thumped to life, and a rainbow of LED lights showered the foyer, courtesy of a live DJ. Food and drinks were everywhere. Skeletons danced with mermaids. Pirates partied with sharks.

"What the hell, Thorn? You didn't think to give us a heads-up?" Weber demanded.

"I—I didn't know," she admitted.

"Don't be mean to Riley. She's being the best psychic she's capable of being," Sesame said, patting her brother's arm.

"She thinks I'm a bad psychic," Riley explained to Nick, who still appeared to be in shock.

"Happy birthday, Nick," Blossom said, pushing her way to them through the crowd. She was dressed in a long, rumpled black robe and wore a stringy gray wig.

"Thanks?" Nick said, regaining the power of speech.

"I like your witch costume," Sesame told Riley's mom.

"Oh, honey. I'm a crone, not a witch," Blossom said. "Come on. I'll tell you all about crones over some party punch."

"Happy birthday!" Wander Sonny approached with Gabe Cher's huge arm around her.

"I hope you are very surprised," Gabe said solicitously.

"I'm fucking flabbergasted," Nick admitted.

"Let's get this party started," Blossom shouted from somewhere in the crowd. "Who wants some spiked-kombucha party punch?"

Riley's dad waved to them from across the foyer. He was dressed as a farmer, in overalls and a straw hat. Riley took a peek around just to make sure he hadn't decided to bring Daisy the spite cow as a plus one.

"I swear, this wasn't supposed to happen until Halloween," she told Nick.

The doorbell rang, and a chorus of "Come in!" rang out over the music.

Weber appeared on Nick's right. "This is a fucking disaster. How are we supposed to keep an eye out for the bad guys when everyone's in costume and no one's watching the door?"

"Look at it this way. Everyone we care about is in one place. So much easier to keep an eye on them," Riley said, trying to put a silver lining on it.

"Happy birthday, Nicky!" Miguel Santiago, in a bullfighter costume, bellowed as he waded through the crowd.

Riley tensed, knowing that Mean Marie wouldn't be far behind.

"Thanks, Dad," Nick said, still scanning the crowd.

A pouty Marie Santiago, wearing some kind of athletic uniform with a Canadian maple leaf on it, arrived at her husband's side. Riley tried to fade into the crowd, but Nick caught her around the waist and anchored her to his side.

"Where's your costume? If she doesn't have to dress up, then neither should I. It's undignified," Marie said, looking at Riley's outfit.

"Who are you supposed to be, Mom?" Nick asked.

"I'm Jocelyn Tremblay, captain of the Canadian women's curling team."

Lily pushed her way forward in a Little Bo-Peep costume. "There you are! There's a food table in the living room, two snack-and-booze tables in the foyer, a bar in Riley's office, and Fred set up a photo booth in the mudroom."

"This wasn't supposed to happen until Nick's actual birthday. What happened, Lily?" Riley asked, accepting the plastic goblet of punch from a tray-carrying Zorro.

"Ask Cleopatra," Lily said, pointing her staff in the direction of the dance floor.

Riley blinked several times, not trusting what she saw. Mrs. Penny was lounging on a daybed and eating grapes, wearing a gauzy white nightgown that was a few sizes too small.

"Yoo-hoo! Mrs. Penny," Lily called.

The woman snapped her fingers, and four shirtless men in masks appeared. They each lifted a corner of the bed and carried her toward Riley and Lily.

"Mrs. Penny?" Riley said, still not believing what she was seeing. The masked, oiled-up men dropped the bed at her feet, and the elderly Cleopatra squirmed into a seated position. Riley thought she heard the tearing of fabric.

"Well, whaddaya think?" Mrs. Penny asked, grunting as she gained her feet.

"How…why…what?"

"Penny, what the fuck are all these people doing in our house? Also, what are you wearing?"

"I'm Cleopatra, you dingbat! Gabe was worried that some yahoo had ruined the surprise, so I rescheduled the party. Surprise. Have a drink. The party punch is pretty good."

Zorro magically appeared and handed Nick a plastic goblet.

"I don't want a drink. I want to find the asshole who delivered the dead guy's finger."

Zorro loomed in front of Nick expectantly.

"It's my birthday. Don't piss me off, Zorro," Nick advised.

"I think he wants you to drink," Mrs. Penny guessed.

Nick glared at the masked man.

"Hey, maybe don't start a fight this early in your birthday party?" Riley suggested.

Nick rolled his eyes. "Fine. Happy fucking birthday to me." He guzzled the drink and put the empty cup back on the tray.

"Who are all these people?" Riley demanded. A person wearing a Guy Fawkes mask was handing out shot glasses to an eager line of partygoers from behind one of the snack-and-booze tables. "I had twenty people on the guest list."

Mrs. Penny snorted. "Your guest list was a snooze fest. I invited a few friends, then spread the word with the doody flyers. Every client who called about suspicious doody got an invite."

Riley heard the distinct sound of Nick slapping his own forehead.

"Great," she sighed. "We've got a house full of masked strangers and a greedy prescription drug cartel on the loose."

Mrs. Penny adjusted her unwieldy boobs in her nightgown. "Eh, loosen up. I've got the security covered."

"Oh really?" Nick didn't sound confident.

"I got a trap all set for the Dog Doody Bandit, and those greased-up whippersnappers carrying me around? They all belong to a mixed martial arts gym. I hired them for the night and paid them out of petty cash. By the way, between the posters and the hot security, we're out of petty cash."

"Oh, there's definitely going to be a murder tonight." Nick took a threatening step toward Mrs. Penny.

But she merely brought her fingers to her mouth and whistled.

Her personal security appeared immediately and formed a shield in front of their temporary employer.

"You don't think I'd punch my way through four MMA fighters, Penny?" Nick said, peering over the wall of muscle.

"Oh, I think you'd try. But I don't think you'd make it through the third one." With that, Mrs. Penny flopped back down onto her bed. She pointed at Riley. "Your costume's upstairs. Better get changed. Take me to the cupcakes, boys."

Riley and Nick watched as Mrs. Penny and her minions disappeared into the living room past the cupcake tower.

"Do you still want me to kick everyone out?" Riley asked Nick.

He shook his head. "I need to think. Maybe this can work to our advantage. But I'd actually feel better if you were in disguise. That way, no one can kidnap you for once."

"Well, it's your birthday party," she joked. "Besides, maybe no one will try anything since we have a house full of witnesses."

"Yeah. Maybe. Go change. I'll get Weber and Josie, and we'll start ripping masks off."

She started for the stairs.

"Hey, Thorn?"

She turned back to Nick.

"Wear something sexy."

She grinned at him. Even midcrisis, Nick Santiago had sex on the brain.

"What do you think, Riley?" Tommy was coming down the stairs decked out in a suit of armor. He held a sword in one hand and a shiny helmet in the other.

"Wow, Tommy. You're a literal knight in shining armor."

"Think Sesame will like it?" he asked hopefully.

"She'll love it," she predicted.

He beamed at her, pulled on the helmet, then rattled his way back to the party.

Riley continued on up, giving a side-eye to the amorous unicorn and soccer player she found making out at the top of the stairs. She headed into the bedroom and stopped short when she spotted the costume on the bed.

"Seriously?"

———

Twenty minutes later, Riley headed back downstairs in costume. The wig was heavy and a little itchy, and the denim jumpsuit was a tight squeeze. She had no idea what she was going to do when she had to pee. But she didn't mind having a guitar to carry. It could be used as a weapon if necessary.

While she'd been gone, someone had turned the lights down low. Between the sexy music and the shadowy dance floor, the foyer had been transformed into a nightclub. Everywhere she looked, couples were grinding on each other and making out.

Someone grabbed her from behind, and she'd just raised the guitar to hit them when Nick nuzzled her neck.

"Oh boy. Do you have a Dolly Parton fetish or a cowgirl fetish?" Riley asked breathlessly.

"Yes," he said, dragging his teeth over her exposed flesh.

"Wait. Why aren't you being overly protective grumpy guy right now and kicking people out of the house?"

"Because then I couldn't be here telling you how I want to bite my way over every inch of your perfect body."

Someone tapped Riley on the shoulder. It was Sesame as Glitter Dolly. "Sorry to interrupt, but we have a problem."

"I didn't pick my costume," Riley said, trying to pry Nick's lips off her neck.

"Not that. *This!*" Sesame pointed at the scene in front of them.

"Hold that thought," Riley said to Nick and stepped out of his grasp.

"As if I could think about anything but you and unzipping that jumpsuit," he said wolfishly.

His eyes looked a little glassy.

"Did my mom bring edibles to this party?" Riley wondered out loud.

"It wasn't your mom, and it's not edibles," Sesame said.

Jasmine danced over to them in a vinyl catsuit.

"Where did you get the costume?" Riley asked.

"I keep a spare in my purse." A guy dressed as a jack-o'-lantern danced up on her. Jasmine put her palm to his oversize pumpkin head and shoved him back. "Not now, Pumpkin Boy."

The pumpkin stumbled backward into the snack table.

"Guys, I don't know what's going on, but there are boners everywhere," Jasmine said.

"What do you mean everywhere?" Riley scoffed, shoving

the synthetic blond curls out of her eyes. "Oh. *Oh.* No, no, no, no."

Her friend was right. It looked like a high school make-out party after everyone had shared a bottle of Mad Dog.

A ghost with a haunted erection under its sheet was whispering sweet nothings into the ear of Velma from *Scooby-Doo*. Little Red Riding Hood and the Big Bad Wolf were dirty dancing with a pair of skeletons and a vampire. Darth Vader had no need for a light saber considering what was standing up in his pants. Riley's parents were making out like about-to-be-grounded teenagers on the cupcake table.

Riley spied Josie on Brian's lap. They were attached at the mouth when they disappeared toward the back of the house.

Gabe was on bended knee in the middle of the foyer, kissing his way up Wander's arm as she blushed. Riley refused to look below her spiritual guide's belt.

"That's what I was trying to tell you. I think we've been HardMaxed," Sesame said.

"Attention, everyone!"

Riley turned with the rest of the crowd at Nick's voice coming from the DJ's speakers.

"Ohhhhh noooooo," she moaned.

"I just want everyone to know that Riley Thorn is the sexiest woman in the world," he said, breathing heavily into the microphone. "You turn me on every day in every way."

"Oh God," she groaned.

"Aww, how poetic," Sesame said.

"I'm going to need another drink," Marie said.

"Get one for me too," Miguel yelled. "And shake that moneymaker when you walk away."

"What has gotten into you?" Marie tsked. Miguel slapped her on the butt as she walked away from him. Riley couldn't tell if she was imagining the exaggerated sway in Nick's mom's hips or if the woman really was flirting with her husband.

"Oh. My. God." Jasmine enunciated each word.

"What?" Riley spun around and then wished she hadn't.

Weber was standing behind them, hands on hips, looking pissed off. But what caught the eye was the impressive action happening below the belt. "Wow."

"No offense, Kelly, but you're my brother, and I can't look at you like that," Sesame said, looking up at the ceiling and gesturing in the direction of his crotch.

"I might have to start calling you Detective Dick instead of Detective Assface," Jasmine said appreciatively.

Her cheeks flaming, Riley unhooked her pink-fringed belt and pushed it at Weber. "Here."

He snatched it out of her hand and secured it over his hips. "Did you do this?" he demanded of his sister.

Sesame shook her head rapidly from side to side until her Dolly wig quivered. "No! I swear, Kelly!"

"I'd like to dedicate this song to the woman I can't wait to get naked tonight," Nick said into the microphone. "Hit it, DJ."

Christina Aguilera's "Dirrty" drew an appreciative cheer from the oversexed crowd.

"Maybe it was an accident?" Riley suggested hopefully over the music. "Nick hid the rest of the vials in the refrigerator next door. Lily could have put the drug in the cupcakes."

"No. To affect this many people, it had to be a much bigger supply," Sesame insisted.

Tommy clanked over to them in his suit of armor. "Is there a fair maiden in need of servicing?" His hips gyrated lewdly in Sesame's direction, and Riley said a prayer of gratitude for codpieces.

"Stop staring at my groin, Patel," Weber said through gritted teeth to Jasmine.

"Your groin is staring at *me*, Detective," Jasmine shot back.

"That means Lurlene and Royce or at least their henchman is here," Riley guessed.

Sesame cuddled into her husband's chest. "Tommy, I think we're in real trouble."

"I don't understand. Why would they drug an entire party?" he asked, sniffing his wife's hair.

"It's a distraction," Riley said grimly. "No one is going to fight back when their libido is in overdrive."

"And high dosages of HardMax can result in an overwhelming sense of well-being," Sesame added.

"Did someone say *libido*?" Nick appeared at Riley's side. His hand settled on the curve of her butt and squeezed.

She yelped. "Nick, focus! The Lionworths are here, and they slipped the drug into the punch."

"I can focus all night long, baby. I can focus so hard. You're gonna love how big my focus is," he promised.

She could barely keep up with Regular Libido Nick. Turbocharged Nick could kill her.

Lily burst through the swinging kitchen door. "Code man fanny," she shrieked before running back into the room.

Mrs. Penny grabbed her cane and her plate of cupcakes and hurried after her. Several other partygoers, mostly of the female persuasion, followed.

Finding the Cleopatra bed empty, Fred launched himself onto it and landed suggestively on one elbow, his leg bent at the knee, showing way too much downstairs action beneath his kilt. He patted the mattress and made eyes at an older woman in scrubs. "You with the stethoscope. Wanna check my pulse?"

Tommy leaned an armor-clad hand against the wall above Sesame's head. "Why don't we go talk about this naked and lying down? I'll spell out my top one hundred favorite things about you *with my tongue*."

"Everywhere I look, it's an orgy about to happen," Riley whispered.

"Let's take this birthday celebration upstairs, and I'll give you a full-body massage followed by shower sex, staircase sex, dining-room sex, and then I'll play with your hair until we're ready for front-porch sex," Nick suggested.

His hands were roaming her shoulders, thumbs digging into the tense muscles.

"What do we do?" Sesame asked, batting Tommy away.

Brian and Josie reappeared with messy hair and satisfied

smirks on their faces. She hopped off his lap and gave him a parting kiss before he headed into Nick's office.

Riley waved her over.

"Great party," Josie said smugly.

Riley turned to face Nick and squished his face between her hands. "We need to get Sesame and Tommy somewhere safe now."

"I hear you, Thorn. Loud and clear. But all I want to do is go down on y—"

She clamped a hand over his mouth and turned to Sesame. "We need to take care of this. Now."

"By my calculations, the side effect should be kicking in any minute now," Sesame warned. "And when it does, all hell will break loose."

"Damn it," Riley muttered under her breath as she scanned the room. Her gaze landed on Nick's office door, and she grinned. "I have an idea. Huddle up, ladies."

Riley, Sesame, Josie, and Jasmine formed a circle.

"The guys are of no use to us until they get some blood back in their heads, right?" Josie began.

Sesame nodded. "Right. And that will take between thirty and forty-five more minutes."

"So we have no choice but to lock them up, hide Sesame and Tommy, arm ourselves with some weapons, and find these assholes ourselves."

"It shouldn't be hard to pick the bad guys out of the crowd," Jasmine said. "They'll be the only ones not dry humping someone else."

"Excellent observation," Riley said.

"I'm done hiding," Sesame said fiercely. "They came after *my* husband. They're ruining the respectable cartel that I built from scratch. I'm not going to run away and hide again while you guys are stuck cleaning up my mess."

"Sesame, that Gunther guy looked like he was seven feet tall," Riley pointed out. "Defending yourself against an attack is a lot different from negotiating a business deal."

"I have a second-degree red belt in tae kwon do," she said. "And my screams have been known to puncture eardrums."

Josie nodded. "Respect. Good enough for me."

"I'm wearing my stabbiest boots," Jasmine said.

Josie looked at Riley. "You in?"

"They ruined my boyfriend's surprise party and made me pick up a severed finger," Riley said. "They're going down."

"Looks like these sons of bitches messed with the wrong Dolly Partons," Josie observed.

38

Riley looped her arms around Nick's neck and cuddled her hips against his erection. She fluttered her eyelashes rapidly. "Meet me in your office, and I'll make all your birthday wishes come true."

"Now?" he asked, his voice as rough as gravel.

"I'm just going to grab a tray of ice cubes and that jockey's riding crop, and I'll meet you in there."

Nick's smolder was so intense she was surprised she hadn't caught fire yet. "I'm so turned on and happy right now I don't even remember what it feels like to be grumpy," he confessed.

"Hurry," she said, pushing him in the direction of his office.

Nick sprinted into the crowd and pumped his fists in the air. "Best birthday ever!"

Everyone who wasn't actively making out on the dance floor cheered.

Sesame rose on tiptoe and whispered something in Tommy's helmet-covered ear.

He raised his visor. "Did you say you wanted my clock or my—"

"The second one," Sesame said, biting her lower lip seductively.

"Yippy!"

She pointed toward Nick's office, and they watched as Tommy sprinted through the crowd.

"Your turn, Jas," Riley said, nodding at Weber.

He was taking deep breaths and muttering to himself. "Ten-fifty-six: intoxicated pedestrian. Ten-sixty-eight: livestock in roadway."

"Hey there, Detective," Jasmine purred. She sauntered up to him, swinging her cat tail like a whip. "Wanna play with my tail?"

Weber gave up reciting response codes and took a threatening step toward her. "Stop talking. Stop looking at me. Stop breathing. And stop smelling so good."

"You can't tell me what to do," Jasmine snapped, her eyes flashing fire as she closed the distance between them.

They were standing toe-to-toe until Weber moved forward, backing her against the wall. "I. Just. Did."

"I want to slap you so hard your face spins around to the back of your head," she hissed.

"I detest you," he responded.

"Back at you, Detective Dick," Jasmine said, sharpening the emphasis on the word *dick*.

Weber's nostrils flared, and Riley decided to look at the ceiling on the off chance that she ever wanted to make eye contact with the man again.

"Okay, I'm into some kinky shit, but this is weird even to me," Josie observed.

"We need a fire hose," Riley agreed.

Without warning, Jasmine pushed away from the wall and started to walk away.

"Where are you going?" Weber demanded.

"I'm going to go into Nick's office to open his mail," she said, tossing her long dark hair over her shoulder.

"That's an obstruction of correspondence," Weber said. His face suddenly contorted, and he let out a giggle.

"Did he just *tee-hee-hee*?" Josie asked.

"Oh, that's really bad," Riley said.

"Yeah. So bad," Sesame agreed sadly.

Jasmine was unfazed. "What are you gonna do about it, cop?" She blew him a kiss that ended with a middle finger and disappeared into the crowd. Weber waited all of half a second before chasing after her. They could hear him giggling as he went.

Riley, Josie, and Sesame climbed the first few steps to get a better vantage point of the action. The rear end of the zebra at the foot of the stairs began to titter.

"Oh, she's very good," Sesame said, watching Jasmine yank Weber by the tie into Nick's office.

"If this were an Olympic sport, we'd be holding perfect tens," Josie agreed as Jasmine spun them around so she was the one in the doorway. She gave the detective a shove into the room and yanked the door shut in his face.

"Are you sure that will hold them?" Sesame asked.

"It held Nick and me. Plus the windows are painted shut. And if they're as turned on and warm and fuzzy as everyone else, it won't even occur to them to break the door down," Riley pointed out.

Jasmine held up her arms in a V, then snatched a shot glass out of Buzz Lightyear's gloved hand and downed it.

Riley shook her head. "Every time I see her in action, I feel like I'm in the presence of greatness."

Jasmine finished her victory lap and joined them on the stairs as they applauded for her. "Thank you. Thank you," she said, taking a bow.

Someone on the dance floor was hiccupping at full volume.

"Okay, here's the plan. Sesame, you and Jasmine go next door and lure the cops in the SUV here for backup. Stay together, and don't trust anyone in a mask," Riley instructed. "Josie and I will search the guests for the Lionworths."

"Hang on," Josie said, patting her pockets. "Here. Take your pick." She produced two knives, one tactical pen, a small stun gun, three cartridges of pepper spray, and half a dozen zip ties.

"Oooh! I love accessorizing." Sesame chose the stun gun.

Jasmine went with the tactical pen and pepper spray.

"I don't have any pockets," Riley said, patting her denim jumpsuit.

"That's why God gave Dolly cleavage." Sesame pointed at her breasts.

"You could hide an automatic weapon in there," Riley complained. "I've only got room for travel-size pepper spray."

"Hands in, ladies. Let's bring these assholes down." Josie put her hand out.

"'Kick ass' on three," Jasmine said, adding her hand to Josie's.

Sesame and Riley put their hands in.

"One. Two. Three. Kick ass!"

They parted ways, with Jasmine and Sesame headed into the crowded foyer and Riley following Josie toward the back of the house. It was dark and crowded. Everywhere men were giggling and snort-laughing.

"It sounds like the front row of a Jonas Brothers concert," Josie complained.

"We should probably stick together," Riley said, hefting the guitar onto her shoulder so it would be ready to swing. "In the movies, everyone always gets murdered by splitting up."

"Good point. Don't get lost," Josie suggested over her shoulder as she walked up to the Grim Reaper and yanked his hood off.

"Hey!" the guy said. "I rented that, and if you mess it up, I won't get my deposit back. Tee-hee!"

"Not our guy," Josie said unnecessarily.

Riley noticed the door to the small closet under the staircase was ajar and moved closer to get a better look. Inside was a couple wrapped around each other like ivy.

"Oh, Miguel," the woman said on a breathy sigh.

"What did you say, Marie?" the man hollered.

Blanching, Riley turned her back on Nick's parents before she could see any more of them.

A cacophony of hysterical laughter rang out from the kitchen.

"What's gotten into you, Albert?" asked a zombie bride of her undead groom.

Albert tittered out a giggle as he tried to tickle her under the corset.

A tingle ran up Riley's spine, but just as she reached for her pepper spray, something black and silky swirled in front of her, wrapping over her head and around her torso.

"Hey!" She tried elbowing her attacker, but her arms were pinned to her sides. She fought to free herself but was unceremoniously lifted into the air and thrown over what she assumed was a very hard shoulder. The landing knocked the wind out of her, rendering her speechless when she heard Josie's faraway voice calling her name.

Well, crap. Nick was never going to let her live this down.

39

6:44 p.m. Wednesday, October 30

Riley was dumped unceremoniously onto the floor and immediately began fighting her way free. They'd taken her upstairs. The music and giggling were much fainter.

Someone whipped the material off her head, and she fought to get a full breath into her lungs.

It was dark, so it was the smell that hit her first, and she knew exactly where they'd taken her. The creepy, smelly closet.

She had to keep her wits about her, Riley reminded herself. Any second now, Sesame and Jasmine would arrive with the cops and the drugs would wear off. Nick would break out of his office and find her in no time. And if she kept the bad guys occupied up here with her, everyone would be safe.

The overhead light snapped on.

"You *idiot*."

Riley blinked, trying to bring the woman into focus. She had a faint southern accent. Not the bless-your-heart genteel kind but the wrestle-gators-in-the-swamp kind.

"Here we go again," said the man who'd carried her upstairs. "You told me to bring you Dolly. I brought you Dolly. Nothing I ever do is good enough for you."

The woman gestured angrily at Riley with the gun she

held. "Does she look like the right Dolly Parton to you? I swear, I should have divorced your dumb ass years ago."

The man sneered. "Well, good news for you because my cousin Otis never got ordained, so we ain't never been married." It was Zorro. The guest who had been handing out cups of punch.

The woman peeled off her Guy Fawkes mask and glared at Zorro.

"Lurlene and Royce, I presume?" Riley said. She scooched up against the back wall of the closet. She could have sworn she heard a hissing noise coming from the grate.

"Great." Lurlene threw up her hands. "Second Dolly knows our names. That means that tramp already opened her big mouth."

"What's the big deal?" Royce dragged off his Zorro hat.

Lurlene threw up her hands in exasperation. "The *big deal* is now we have to kill them all."

"Uh, can I interject here?" Riley asked, raising a hand. "I'm sure we can work something out so no one needs to die."

Lurlene beaned her with a roll of painter's tape. "Shut her up, and then tape her hands and feet together," she ordered Royce.

"She ain't goin' nowhere," he argued.

"Well, I don't want her screaming or trying to run away when we kill her."

"Have you always been this bloodthirsty?" he wondered.

"Yes! You just haven't paid any attention to me for thirty years!"

"It sounds like you two are under a lot of stress," Riley said, frantically searching for a way to connect with her captors. That was what her favorite show, *Made It Out Alive*, always said. Well, that and *don't ever let yourself be taken to a second location*, which she'd already screwed up. "Running your own business isn't easy."

"Oh, for Pete's sake. Shut your damn trap, whoever the hell you are," Lurlene snarled, pointing the gun in Riley's face. "Tape her up good, Royce."

"Don't get your panties in a twist."

"If you think for *one second* I'm going back to scrubbing country club toilets or worse, you got a rock in your head where God shoulda put a brain. We have a billion dollars on the line here. I'm not walkin' away from yacht money."

"All right. All right. No need to lose your dang mind again. If you want Dolly dead, she's dead," Royce muttered. He grabbed Riley's hands roughly and wrapped the tape around her wrists several times.

"Wait," Riley said. But the next piece of tape covered her mouth. Which was a stupid, amateur mistake to make seeing as how she could just reach up with her bound hands and remove the tape. But she decided to keep that information to herself until she could use it to her advantage.

There was a very distinct hiss behind the grate.

Royce made quick work of taping her ankles together. "Happy now?" he demanded, tossing the tape. It bounced off the floor and hit the grate, knocking it askew.

"Not yet." Lurlene crossed her arms and tapped her foot.

Royce made a big show of being annoyed when he pulled a knife out of his belt and opened the blade in Riley's face. She flinched and flattened herself against the wall.

She was *not* going to die in a stinky closet during Nick's birthday party.

"Wait," Lurlene said suddenly.

Riley sagged against the plaster wall behind her as a trickle of sweat slid down her back.

"Don't kill her yet. I'll get that bitch Sesame, bring her up here, and then we'll torture Second Dolly to make Sesame tell us who knows what. She's too do-gooder-y to hold up to that."

"So you don't want me to kill Second Dolly yet?" Royce confirmed.

"Why God saddled me with a moron, I'll never know," Lurlene said to no one in particular. "No. Don't kill her yet. Wait for me to get back with Sesame."

"You want me to look for Tommy in the meantime?" he asked, closing his knife and putting it back on his belt.

Riley breathed a sigh of relief through her nose.

"I don't trust you to pick up the dry cleaning. You can't even kidnap the right Dolly." Lurlene was working herself back up into a state. "Stay here and make sure she doesn't move a muscle. I'll be back with Sesame, and then we'll kill 'em both."

"Yes, ma'am."

"And try not to draw any attention to yourself," Lurlene ordered.

She left, turning off the light and shutting the closet door.

They were plunged into darkness.

"'Try not to draw any attention to yourself,'" Royce muttered in a falsetto. "That woman is the worst. I can't wait until this deal goes through and the brakes on her Ferrari 'accidentally' fail.'"

Riley assumed he wasn't expecting an answer, so she kept quiet.

She heard a muffled vibration, and then Royce was shifting around. The interior of the closet was lit with the blue screen light from his phone.

"Yello," he said.

She used the distraction to reach up and start to peel the corner of the tape free.

"No, I do not want to extend my car warranty, ya dang robot. I drive a brand-new Range Rover. Now quit callin' me!"

He disconnected, and Riley dropped her hands.

"Dunno what this world is comin' to," he complained. "I got robots callin' me all hours of the day. Do they think they're foolin' me? I worked my ass off as an identity thief for twenty years, and they think they're gonna trick me? Ha! I'm untrickable."

He looked at her like he was expecting a response, so she nodded solemnly.

Royce glanced back down at his phone and started playing a game. "Sorry 'bout all this murder business, by the way. It ain't nothin' personal. But we got a lotta money ridin' on this here deal. You understand, don't ya?"

She shook her head vehemently back and forth. No, she very much did not understand why she had to get murdered so he could be a billionaire.

A new sound caught her attention. The tip-tap of dog toenails outside the door.

Riley perked up. There was only one tip-tapping dog in this house—at least as far as she knew. Burt was coming to the rescue. Not that he had opposable thumbs or a weapon, but he could bark and get someone's attention. Someone like Josie, who had weapons and the means to take down Zorro.

The light under the door got dimmer, and she heard a loud snuffle as Burt sniffed under the door.

"What in God's name is that?" Royce demanded.

He put down his phone and got to his feet, pulling out his knife again.

Riley yanked off the tape. "No! Burt, run!" she shouted. At the same time, she scooted forward on her butt, bent both knees, and kicked Royce right in the ass.

He wasn't expecting it and slammed into the wall. Burt barked on the other side of the door.

"Run, Burt!" she said again.

Royce regained his feet and advanced on her. "Now you've gone and done it. You disrespected me, and I don't care what Lurlene says, you ain't long for this world."

The phone screen dimmed, and she scooted to the back wall.

"You can't run, Dolly. You might as well just hold still and get this over with."

"Nick! Josie!" Riley shouted. "Help!"

He was looming over her now. She realized not even her psychic powers would have helped in this situation. She was going to have to do this the old-fashioned way.

She found the zipper on her jumpsuit with her taped hands.

"Now, have some decency, Dolly. You don't need to be goin' to meet your maker with your cleavage out like that."

Her sweaty fingers finally made contact with the pepper spray, and she yanked it free.

She heard the hiss next to her, and something hit the grate from the inside.

"Sweet baby Jesus! What is that godforsaken thing?" Royce screeched just as the closet was plunged into darkness.

Riley thought she caught a glimpse of glowing yellow eyes, then decided she had bigger fish to fry.

She aimed the canister in Royce's direction and depressed the trigger.

The howling told her she'd hit her mark. But her proximity to the spray meant she didn't get to escape unscathed. Her eyes were burning, as was her nose.

"You bitch!" he screamed. She felt the breeze and realized he was wildly stabbing the air.

She lashed out with her legs, catching him in the knees.

Burt's incessant bark was growing frantic.

Between the pepper spray and the dark, it was impossible to make out anything...until the closet door opened.

But it wasn't Burt who had grown opposable thumbs in the moment. It was a blurry stranger holding a guitar.

"Didn't anyone tell you it's not nice to kidnap Dolly Parton?" the man said before bringing the guitar down on Royce's head.

The stranger used the neck of the guitar to reel Royce in and punch him in the face.

Royce went down like a felled redwood, and Burt bounded into the closet. He joyfully licked Riley's face and then immediately began to sneeze.

"You must be Riley," the man said, tossing the guitar aside. He entered the closet and nudged Burt off her. "Let her breathe, buddy."

Burt sneezed again.

"Pepper spray," Riley rasped.

The stranger nodded. He picked her up, carried her over Royce's prone form and out of the closet, then set her gently on the edge of the bed.

She blinked through the burning tears.

The man was wearing a Batman costume with the mask shoved up on top of his head. Medium height with an I-work-out-seven-days-a-week build. He had a shaved head and tattoos everywhere.

"Thank you—"

The rest of the words died on her lips when he whipped out a switchblade.

She yelped and threw her arms up to block him.

"Relax," he said, gently pulling her arms toward him. He ran the tip of the knife through the tape binding her wrists, then moved to her ankles. "Now we're even," he said with a nod.

"Even?" Riley repeated.

"You saved me significant jail time for a parole violation," he said with a crooked grin.

"I did?"

"I just got out of prison yesterday. Time off for good behavior," he said with a wink, returning to the closet. "And after I kissed my grandma hello and sat down with the whole family for a chicken-pot-pie dinner, there was one thing I needed to do."

Riley coughed. "What was that?"

He grabbed Royce by the ankles and dragged him into the back of the closet, threw the remains of the guitar on top of him, and then shut the door.

"I needed to take care of a problem. But you beat me to it. You did it with more finesse too."

"I think you're going to have to be more specific," Riley suggested. Burt hopped up onto the bed next to her and leaned into her.

Batman spied Sesame's fridge and opened it. He grabbed one of the fancy waters and opened it before handing it to her. Eagerly she accepted it and drank greedily. "I was there. I watched you and your friends sneak inside. I watched the flames blow out the second-story windows. And I watched you drag that stupid motherfucker out of his own house and turn him over to the cops."

Riley squeezed her eyes shut. "Lance."

"Splash some of the water on your face. You'll feel better," Batman instructed.

She did as she was told and immediately felt less burn-y.

Batman helped himself to a water. "That waste of DNA has been torturing my cousin for months, and I couldn't do a damn thing about it. I knew that as soon as I got out, I'd be going right back in. But I'd be solving that problem permanently for little Kory."

A shiver went up her spine at the word *permanently*.

"See, no one messes with my family. You understand?"

"I do." Riley nodded and leaned into Burt.

"Good. Because now that family has extended to you. Think of me as a guardian angel. You ever need anything, you come find me."

She'd gone from almost being murdered to being inducted into a parolee's family. Things were definitely heading in the right direction.

"Well, thank you for saving my life," she said weakly as she got to her feet.

"Thanks for saving my little cousin and keeping me out of prison."

"Uh, anytime?"

"Tell Santiago that Christian Blight says hi. And you can let him know that the only connection I ever had to Beth was when I caught her boyfriend selling drugs at my party and she burned down the whole damn place because she thought I was actually going to make good with the threats."

"The fingers and the butthole?" Riley recalled.

He grinned. "I was just trying to scare the little shit."

"Wait. So *Beth* started the fire?"

"She said if I told the cops what she'd done, she'd do the same to my grandmother's house. I love my grandmother. And let me tell you, Beth was crazy enough to do exactly what she said. Guess she's pretty loyal to her family too."

"I guess so," Riley said, shaking her head.

"Well, I've got shit to do. Nice meeting you, Thorn. Thanks for fucking up Lance for me."

"You're welcome. Thanks for knocking out Zorro for me."

He threw a little salute in her direction and exited... through the second-story window.

Riley looked at Burt. "Okay. Let's go find Lurlene and take down a cartel."

Burt barked and then sneezed.

40

Nick was going to find Riley, have sex with her for at least twelve hours, and then lock her ass in the creepy, smelly closet for locking him in his office.

He tried her phone again, then Josie's. Both went to voicemail again. No one at the party was answering their phones, and therefore no one was coming to let them out.

"I think it's starting to wear off," he said. "Feels like I'm getting slightly more blood flow to the brain."

"My rage is starting to come back," Weber agreed.

Nick was a straight dude, and as a straight dude, he made it a habit to never look at another dude's crotch. But he was also a trained observer, and even a nearsighted granny with cataracts wouldn't have missed the circus tent in Weber's pants.

"Tommy hasn't laughed like a hyena in almost five whole minutes," Brian observed.

"Why didn't the girls come back?" Tommy asked, kicking a metal boot against the couch.

"Because they're evil," Nick said.

"Or because we turned into useless horndogs at the worst possible moment?" Brian suggested.

"Stop looking so satisfied," Weber snapped.

Brian grinned. "Can't help it. Sex is awesome."

Nick's own hard-on throbbed painfully in his jeans.

"Make it stop," Weber said to Nick.

"Look. We need to get mad enough to stop thinking with our dicks and start smashing our way out of here," he decided.

Every time one of them had tried to take a run at the locked door, they came to a screeching halt inches from it. It was as if their biological drive to bang had taken control of everything, including any natural aggression.

"There's a couple of goddamn psychopaths out there with our women. We're not gonna wait around for someone to rescue us," Nick said, pointing toward the door.

Tommy held up an armored hand. "Question: What if we break out of here and then the girls come back for us? They won't know where to find us, and I won't be able to immediately have sex with Sesame."

Nick doubled over and willed his penis to listen to reason. "Forget *s-e-x*," he said through clenched teeth.

"Impossible," Brian grinned.

"I hate your cousin," Weber growled.

Nick stood back up. "We are men. Men with women who are in danger right now on the other side of that door. Are we going to lie around in here being useless and horny, waiting for them to come along and have sex with us? Or are we going to smash through that door and save them?"

"I don't have a woman," Weber pointed out.

Nick rolled his eyes heavenward. "We'll find you one."

"Fine," Weber agreed. "But she needs to be over thirty and single and has to have read an entire book in the last month."

"We will discuss your standards on the other side of this door," Nick promised through gritted teeth.

"I'm still leaning toward the wait-here-and-then-have-sex option," Tommy admitted.

"Tommy, you're dressed like a knight in shining fucking armor. This is your chance to save your fair maiden. You get to be the hero tonight. Are you with me?"

Tommy was taking too long to think about it.

"Heroes get laid," Nick said.

"I'm in," Tommy said, lowering his visor.

"Let's get this over with. No one lead with your dick. That's how you sprain things," Weber reminded them.

"Shoulders, not dicks," Nick said. "On the count of three."

He, Weber, and Tommy lined up a few paces from the door.

"I'll, uh, just hang out back here." Brian waved from his wheelchair, holding his phone up. "And record."

Nick glared at the door, willing his anger to push aside his libido. There was one obstacle that dared stand between him and Riley's satisfaction...er...safety. Yeah. Definitely safety. And he was going to destroy it. "One...two...three!"

"Shoulders, not dicks," Weber and Tommy said.

Nick put his head down and charged. There wasn't time to register that the door slid open on its own. Or that a gigantic body was filling the open doorway. What *did* register was the fact that Weber and Tommy both pulled up short as Nick plowed directly into the man in the doorway.

At least he thought it was a man as the momentum carried them into the foyer. The long black hair and spidery fake eyelashes threw him. But when he landed on top of them, he got a definitive confirmation on the anatomy of his rescuer.

The party was still going around them. Music still thumped. Lights still flashed. Though it looked as if there was less dirty dancing happening on the dance floor. Fewer giggles too.

"Gabe?" Nick said.

"Yes, Nick?"

"Please tell me you have an umbrella shoved down your Cher pants."

"I am afraid I do not. Are you in need of an umbrella?"

"No," Nick whimpered.

"I'm just gonna take a picture or ten," Brian said, wheeling closer.

Every muscle in Nick's body contracted, and he all but levitated off the man. "I'm sorry for tackling you and for all body parts that made contact afterward. It would make me very happy if we never spoke of this again," he said, looking everywhere but at Gabe Cher.

"I too am sorry. First for being distracted by Wander's unmatched beauty," Gabe said as Nick pulled him to his humongous feet.

"Let's skip past the part where you tell me about having sex with my girlfriend's sister."

"A gentleman never procreates and discusses," Gabe said. "I will skip ahead in my apologies. I am also sorry that contact with my genitalia made you uncomfortable. Every human body is a miracle. Especially Wander's."

"Yep. Fast-forwarding through all that." Nick made a circular motion with his hands, encouraging the man to talk faster.

"Then I will tell you the reason I opened the door is because I feel that Riley is in danger."

"Should have led with that," Nick said.

"I am sorry. I am having difficulty thinking straight."

"Those Thorn women will do that to a guy," Nick said. "Now, where the hell is Riley?"

"Nick!"

He turned and found her on the stairs. Relief and arousal warred as he pushed his way toward her. Her wig and guitar were missing, but she was in one piece, and she still looked damn good in that jumpsuit.

He was ten feet away from her when all hell broke loose.

The kitchen door flew open, making Nick doubt his own sanity. Josie was clinging to the shoulders of a gigantic octopus that seemed determined to dislodge her. The mask came free, and she shouted triumphantly as Gunther's face was revealed. "Got him!"

Before Nick even managed a step in their direction, Gunther got a good grip on her and dragged Josie over his shoulder, tossing her forward like a volleyball. Josie rolled into a ball, somersaulted twice, and came up on her feet next to Brian's wheelchair.

"That's my wife, you son of a bitch!" Brian said, producing a Taser and firing it with impressive accuracy at the henchman.

The attachments hit the man in the face and chest, and one press of the button brought him to his knees.

"My hero," Josie said, giving Brian a kiss before walking over to kick Gunther in the junk.

He toppled over and crashed to the floor.

"Nick!"

He turned and caught Riley as she threw herself into his arms. His engorged cock cheered at the friction even as he told it to shut the hell up and focus on the danger.

"Royce is unconscious in a closet upstairs. Lurlene is here somewhere looking for Sesame. She's going to kill...well, everyone."

"Did they hurt you?" he growled.

She shook her head. "They didn't have enough time."

There was a loud crash followed by a shrill scream that sounded like it came from the front porch. Mrs. Penny vaulted off her Cleopatra bed and pointed her cane at the front door. "Get 'em, boys!"

Her greased-up security detail giggled and snickered their way to the door.

"I want my money back," Nick snapped. He wanted to put Riley someplace safe, but there wasn't time. "You stay with me. Do not let anyone kidnap you or knock you unconscious or infect you with the psychic flu."

She gave him a watery grin. "I'll do my best. But first..." She turned and cupped her hands to her mouth. "We've got a code man fanny in the dining room! I repeat! A code man fanny!"

Lily led the charge toward the back of the house.

"Keep them away from the front of the house," Riley yelled to Josie and Brian.

"On it," Josie said.

"Good work, Thorn. Let's go." Nick gripped her wrist and pulled her toward the front door as he unholstered his gun.

Neither one of them was prepared for what they found on the front porch.

A woman dressed like the guy from *V for Vendetta* was fighting her way out of a comically large net near the gigantic trick-or-treat bowl, using swear words even Nick had never heard before. Mrs. Penny's security guards were pissing in the hedgerow along the driveway, oblivious to the chaos on the porch.

It would have been funny had the ensnared woman not been pointing a gun at Sesame and Jasmine.

"So that's Lurlene," Riley said as she clung to Nick's back.

"Yeah. Thanks for clearing that up, Thorn," he said.

"I'm not letting you ruin this deal," Lurlene howled with a distinct twang.

Sesame stomped her sparkly high heel on the porch. "News flash, Lurlene. It's already ruined. Nobody wants a man with an erection and a hyena laugh!"

"Psst! Jas! Did you do that thing I asked you to do?" Riley hissed.

"We tried, but the car was empty," Jasmine said, still holding up her hands and glaring daggers at Lurlene. "Then this crazy bitch pulled a gun on us."

"She and Sesame tried to lure the cops over here," Riley whispered to Nick.

"Let's hope they're already here, and it wasn't just a decoy car to piss me off."

"A decoy car?" she croaked.

Lurlene took offense to Jasmine's assessment. "I am *not* crazy! I am a future billionaire, thank you very much. And what the hell are *you* doing here?" She turned to aim her gun at Riley. "You're supposed to be in the closet, taped up."

"There was a situation with a parolee," Riley explained.

"What?" Nick snapped.

"We'll talk later," she promised, patting his arm.

She was right. He had all the time in the world to yell at Riley while they had sex after he neutralized the twangy wannabe billionaire.

"Listen, lady. You better move that gun real fast because this is my birthday party, and if you try to shoot *my* woman or any of her friends, I'm going to put so many holes in you, the coroner won't know your front from your back," Nick snarled.

"Burn!" Sesame cheered.

"And *that's* how you drop a badass line," Jasmine said, applauding with her hands over her head.

Out of the corner of his eye, Nick saw Weber inching closer to the porch through the yard.

Lurlene finally freed herself from the net and kicked it out of her way.

"Hey, yo. Trick or treat or whatever," said a teenager wearing a tiger-striped onesie and holding a liquor-store bag full of candy.

Lurlene swung her gun around and spotted Weber in the shadows. "Trying to sneak up on me? You'll never get the drop on me! I shot my first gator when I was four."

"Whoa! Crazy costume. You got any full-size candy bars?" the kid asked.

Nick picked up a can of cranberry sauce from the trick-or-treat bowl and winged it at him for ruining the element of surprise. "Get the fuck off my lawn!"

Weber collared the kid and dragged him away from the porch.

"Where's the doody?" Mrs. Penny yelled, appearing in the door and trying to push past Nick.

Riley grabbed hold of the straps of the woman's nightgown. "Not now, Mrs. Penny! She's got a gun!"

"Who? Me?" Mrs. Penny said, reaching down and drawing her own gun from what Nick could only assume was a thigh holster. "Of course I've got a gun."

"Everybody, get down!" Nick yelled.

Everyone but Lurlene hit the deck. Unfortunately, when Riley dropped to the porch, Mrs. Penny's borrowed nightgown came with her.

"Whoa," the kid said.

Weber shoved him headfirst into a bush. "Get the fuck out of here before I shoot you myself."

"Excellent body positivity, Mrs. Penny," Sesame said, giving her a thumbs-up from the porch floorboards.

"You know what?" Lurlene said to herself. Nick held her steady in his sights. "It doesn't matter who I start with. I'm just going to kill every single one of you, and then I'm going to fly back to my desert mansion and wait for my FDA approval."

"Not gonna happen, Lurlene," Sesame said, returning to her feet. "It's too late. I already talked to the FBI, and they're really interested in having a chat with you."

"You did what?"

Sesame smirked. "It's true. There are warrants out for your arrest already."

Lurlene gave an enraged roar and leveled her gun at Sesame. "I'm gonna kill you!"

Nick put his knee in Riley's back to make sure she stayed down, and took aim. But he didn't have to pull the trigger. Because Weber vaulted onto the porch.

Lurlene swung around, pointing the gun at him.

"You leave my brother alone!" Sesame screamed and hurled herself onto Lurlene's back just as she pulled the trigger. The bullet went high, and the two women went down.

At that exact moment, Zorro charged out onto the porch. "What in tarnation is going on?" he demanded. He still had part of Riley's guitar around his neck.

"That's Royce," Riley said.

"Got that too, baby," Nick said.

Sesame was straddling Lurlene and slapping her in the face. "Don't. Ever. Try. To. Shoot. My. Brother."

Weber raced to her side and pulled Sesame off the woman.

"You!" Zorro snarled, spotting Riley still pinned under Nick. Nostrils flaring, he drew his sword.

"Bring it, bozo," Nick snarled. He took aim.

But before Royce could take a step toward him, there was another crash.

Tommy, still in his knight armor, fell out of the living room window onto the porch. It sounded like a canned soup display collapsing in a supermarket.

It took Tommy almost ten whole seconds to get to his feet, but when he did, he charged his uncle, sword drawn.

The clang of metal echoed off the porch ceiling as Zorro and the white knight swung awkwardly at each other. "I wasn't really gonna kill you, Tommy. Sure, probably your wife and all your friends here. But we're family. That's gotta mean something," Royce said.

"I would have killed you. I never liked you. Even when you were a baby, you sucked," Lurlene said from under Weber, who was zip-tying her hands behind her back.

"You're wrong, Aunt Lurlene. You two suck! You're the worst aunt and uncle in the world. You should be grateful for Sesame. She gave you everything, but you just wanted more!"

"Aww! Thanks for appreciating me, babe," Sesame chirped.

Sesame's praise seemed to give Tommy extra strength. With a roar, he sent his uncle's sword flying into the yard.

"Ow," said the moron in the onesie.

"I told you to get out of here," Weber yelled over his shoulder.

Two gunshots rang out, and everyone froze as a hunk of the porch ceiling crashed down.

"Now that I have your attention, I'm going to ask one more time! Where's the doody?" Mrs. Penny shouted.

"Oh, fuck this," Royce said, pulling a gun from the sash around his waist and pointing it at the mostly naked woman.

"Nick!" Riley shrieked.

On an oath, Nick took one for the team and tackled his nearly naked partner to the ground just as Zorro fired.

"Everybody on the ground now!" barked the voice of authority. A half-dozen flashlights winked to life in the front yard as a familiar-looking woman in a flak vest stepped onto the porch.

"Joplin Jones?" Sesame said, squinting at the woman's shiny badge.

"DEA! Everybody calm the hell down," Joplin shouted.

There was the sound of screeching tires, and two black SUVs jumped the curb from Front Street and drove into the yard. The doors flew open, and people in suits jumped out, guns drawn.

"FBI!"

"Ugh! What is this? Is this poop? Did you assault me with feces?" Lurlene screeched. "You'll be hearing from my lawyer!"

41

R iley woke to blissful silence and the bright autumn sun. Nick was on his back, and she was sprawled over him with her head resting on his chest. Blindly she reached behind her for her phone and squinted at the clock on the screen. It was after one in the afternoon.

After all the arrests had been made, the party guests sent home, and a vigorous round of early birthday sex, they'd managed a solid ten hours of sleep.

She couldn't believe Burt hadn't tried to wake them up. She sat up and found Burt's dog bed empty.

She was sore from her kidnapping, escape, being tackled to the porch floor, and the awesome sex. There was a massive mess downstairs to clean up. And probably some personal relationships in need of repairing. But right this second, she felt good. Damn good.

So good, she didn't even notice herself slipping into Cotton Candy World until she was surrounded by puffy clouds in vibrant shades of pink and blue. She had to fight back tears of joy as she felt an overwhelming sense of welcome.

"Well, look who's back," she said to the clouds.

They pulsed brighter, seeming to almost sparkle with energy in response.

"Yeah, yeah. I finally got that rest we needed. I'll be more careful in the future." The clouds pulsed again, and she said her goodbyes. "I'll be back soon. We have a lot of work to do. A lot of work and a lot of rest."

Feeling nine million times better, Riley let herself slip back into her body and the present. It was time to put things right… and have lunch.

Nick's hand snaked out and grabbed her when she tried to slip out of bed. "Too early," he grumbled into the pillow.

"It's after one in the afternoon," she pointed out, ruffling his hair fondly.

"'s my birthday," he said, rolling to his side in all his naked glory and staring at her with a sleepy smile.

She was a lucky, lucky girl.

"For someone who doesn't care for birthdays, you sure are hanging on to that with both hands," she observed.

"This is my first birthday with you. It's already the best."

"Violent criminals broke into our house, drugged your entire birthday party, and tried to kill us both last night. I think you set the bar too low," Riley teased.

"Still the best," he insisted.

"Come on," she said, pressing a noisy kiss to his cheek. "I'll make you a birthday pot of coffee, and you can watch me shovel garbage out the front door."

"Oh no, you don't, Thorn. You've earned some time off. I had a lot of time to think when I was locked in my office last night," Nick said as he got out of bed and dragged on a pair of sweatpants.

"What did you think about?" she asked, reaching for the closest sweatshirt. It was Jim's, which she had yet to return. Nick snatched it out of her grasp and handed her one of his Santiago Investigations hoodies. She hid her smile as she pulled it over her head.

"I thought about how if I had just fixed the pocket door

and scraped the paint off the windowsills like I said I would, you wouldn't have been able to lock me in there."

"Ahh. Good old consequences," she said when they started for the stairs.

"I'm done obsessing." He slung an arm over her shoulders. "It's time to focus on making this place our home. On growing our business."

"On finding our missing dog," she suggested.

"On spending some alone time with you," he said as they hit the staircase.

"On figuring out what demon is living in the creepy, smelly closet."

Nick yawned. "Speaking of closets, last night you mentioned something about a parolee."

"Yeah," she said, drawing out the word. "I forgot to tell you. Christian Blight says hi."

Nick stopped so abruptly on the stairs that she almost lost her footing.

"What?"

"Shaved head? Neck tattoos? He made it sound like you knew him."

"I do know him. How do *you* know him?" he demanded.

"Uncle Royce was trying to slice me to ribbons, but Christian knocked him out cold with a guitar and cut the tape off me."

"Christian Blight? Fresh out of prison? Hideously ugly and born to piss me off?"

"I don't think he was hideously ugly. But maybe that's because I have a thing for Batman," Riley teased, tugging Nick into motion.

"Filing that away for future reference," he said. "Why in the hell would he save you? He hates me."

"Apparently I'm family." Nick froze again, and she laughed. "Not literally. He just considers me family since I got his cousin's bully arrested for arson. Technically there's a possibility he's related to Mrs. Penny."

"You've got to be shitting me."

"Surprise!"

They both froze on the next to last step to find Riley's parents, Wander and Gabe, and Josie and Brian all lounging around eating cake in the sparkling-clean foyer. Burt was sprawled out on Mrs. Penny's Cleopatra bed, which had been pushed up against the wall outside the living room.

"What's going on?" Riley asked, looking everywhere for signs of last night's debauchery.

Blossom nudged an ashtray with smoking herbs out of her way and got out of her chair. "Happy birthday, Nick." She gave him a hug and a kiss.

"Thanks, Blossom."

Wander handed him a piece of cake. "We didn't think you should have to do cleanup on your birthday."

"And we thought you would enjoy a quiet celebration with cake," Gabe said.

Nick avoided looking directly at the man and seemed extremely uncomfortable. "Ah, yeah. Thanks, man."

"Is something wrong?" Riley asked him.

"He is embarrassed about our genitalia touching last evening," Gabe explained.

"We said we were never going to speak of it again," Nick reminded him.

"I am sorry. I am not used to feeling shame toward my body."

The man was so happy he was practically glowing. Riley noticed her sister was even more radiant than usual too. They kept sharing shy, smiley glances. It looked like things were finally progressing with the happy couple.

"What's with all the candy?"

"Mrs. Penny stole all the neighborhood candy to set the trap for the Dog Doody Bandit," Josie explained.

The front door flew open, and Mrs. Penny bounded inside. "I did it! I solved the case!"

"Speak of the devil," Riley said.

"You caught the Dog Doody Bandit?" Nick asked.

"Dog Doody Bandit?" Mrs. Penny scoffed. "You sound like an idiot. There's no such thing as the Dog Doody Bandit."

"Two hundred flyers printed with my business phone number beg to differ," Nick said.

"I got dashcam footage from one of the guests last night right up until someone shot out their windshield."

"Someone? *Someone* shot out their windshield?" Nick prompted.

"Well, the footage stopped recording when the bullet hit the camera. Guess we'll never know who did it," Mrs. Penny said innocently.

"But you did find the person responsible for the poop?" Riley asked.

"Person? Don't you know anything about digestion?" Mrs. Penny harumphed.

"Are you saying the Dog Doody Bandit wasn't human?"

"Not human and not even a dog. Take a look at this." She tossed her cell phone at Nick and took his cake.

Riley peered over his shoulder and watched the footage of the front of their house. "There's a couple of trick-or-treaters," she said.

"Keep watching," Mrs. Penny said, shoveling cake into her face.

While the party raged on inside, Riley watched a furry white blob appear on the porch roof, shimmy down one of the columns, and paw through the overflowing candy bowl. Satisfied with its haul, it waddled toward the steps, paused in a squat, and then climbed back up to the second floor, where it disappeared.

"The Dog Doody Bandit is a possum," Nick said.

"Oh my God. Nick, that possum is our roommate," Riley said. "It's been living in the ducting behind the creepy, smelly closet. Something with glowing eyes hissed at Royce last night and scared him enough to distract him."

Nick's eye started to twitch again. "I can't believe a possum and a prisoner saved your life while I was locked in my office with a hard-on. I'm ripping that fucking door out today."

"Uh, after you set a humane trap and catch our friend, right?" Riley said.

"I got one of those Havahart traps you can borrow," Roger told Nick. "Consider it a birthday present."

"Thanks, Roger."

"Case closed," Mrs. Penny said with satisfaction. "Six more of those, and I'll have paying clients banging on your door."

There was a loud knock at their door.

She smirked. "See?"

Burt raced to the door, getting there just behind Nick.

Weber strolled inside in a fresh suit. His badge and service weapon were clipped to his belt.

"If the cops are invited to this party, I'm outie," Mrs. Penny announced. She grabbed another slice of cake and headed for the kitchen.

"Looks like someone's back on the job," Riley said.

"Reinstated this morning," Weber said.

"Knock knock!" Sesame called from the open front door. "Oh good! You're all here!"

She pranced into the foyer wearing a surprisingly subdued business suit and silver sparkly stilettos. Tommy was just behind her, also wearing a suit.

"You two clean up nice," Josie observed.

"We just came from a meeting with the FBI and DEA. We're officially immune from all prosecution. Yay!"

"Oh gosh. Okay," Riley said as Sesame wrapped her in a perfumed hug. "Congratulations."

"Thank you, Riley. See? If you keep working at the whole psychic thing, eventually you can make things happen for yourself."

Riley took a breath and held eye contact with Sesame. "When you were seven, you wanted to get Weber a birthday present, but your mom told you birthday gifts were the work of Satan, so you went to the library, stole a book about becoming a police officer, removed the barcode, and wrapped it up in Sunday comics for him."

Sesame released her. "Whoa."

"Yeah. I do okay," Riley told her. "Now, you might as well tell everyone your other news."

Nick pulled her in front of him and wrapped his arms around her. "You're so sexy when you show off, Thorn."

Sesame turned to face her audience. "Riley's right. I have another announcement. It's time for Tommy and me to take the next step in our relationship!"

It looked like the announcement was news to Tommy. He looked confused, then perked up. "Are we starting a family?"

"No, silly! Well, maybe. Depending on the ratings. We're moving to New York and getting our own reality show!"

"I thought you went to New York to talk to a lawyer?" Weber said.

"I did. An *entertainment* lawyer. I've been working on this deal ever since I knew HardMax wasn't going to go the distance. But the network and production company both had pretty strong feelings about illegal ventures. I had to clean up any snafus with the law, past and present. The working title is *Beth Is Back*. It'll be all about how I'm a reformed criminal mastermind and readjusting to law-abiding life."

Only Sesame…er, Beth could make the truth sound like fiction.

"I already have an endorsement deal with a juice company." She flapped her hands like an excited bird and squealed. "Can you believe it?"

Weber rubbed his forehead. "No. No, I can't."

"So you're moving out? That's great news! When? Today?" Nick asked.

Riley elbowed him in the stomach.

"We are. Wilhelm has been in New York getting our new apartment ready for us. He's very excited for some camera time on *Beth Is Back*."

"That explains all the push-ups," Josie said.

"I'll help you pack!" Nick said and sprinted up the stairs.

Weber shook his head. "I can't believe you're just leaving again."

"Aww, Kelly," Beth said, straightening his already straight tie. "You know I always wanted more than what Harrisburg had to offer. But this time, it'll all be different. You won't think I'm dead. You'll have my address. And New York is just a train ride away."

"You always manage to land on your feet, don't you?" he said ruefully.

"Maybe that's because my big brother is always there to soften the fall. Special Agent Joplin told me you called her."

He cleared his throat. "Well, someone has to look out for you. Except, I guess, last night you looked out for me."

"No one messes with my brother," she said, digging through her purse. "I got you something that you should have been given a long time ago." She handed him a plain white envelope.

"What's this?"

"It's the letter I wrote you before I left," Sesame said. "I broke into Mom's house while she was at the Halloween protest and stole it. I also rearranged all her crucifixes just for fun."

Weber looked down at the envelope in his hands.

"You deserved the truth from me then and now. I might mess up again. But one thing's for sure, you're never going to go another day without hearing from me. Go ahead and read it."

Reluctantly, he opened the envelope and unfolded the notebook paper inside.

Riley watched his Adam's apple work as his eyes scanned the page.

When he finished, he made a manly effort to hide his emotions. "I'll miss you. Even if you do drive me nuts," he rasped.

"I'm only a train ride away. And we have a guest room stocked with your favorite scotch," Sesame said, pressing a kiss to his cheek.

Nick jogged down the stairs with four suitcases under

his arms. Articles of clothing were hanging out of unzipped sections. "I packed a couple of things for you," he said, huffing his way to the front door. "Here you go. You should probably hit the road and avoid traffic." He shoved the bags into Tommy's arms and propelled the couple toward the front door.

"Nick! You're ridiculous," Riley said.

"It's my birthday, Thorn."

"Oh, Nicky. You're one in a million." Sesame gave him a noisy peck on the cheek.

"Damn right I am."

"But your girl is one in a billion. Don't forget that."

"I promise," he said.

Riley joined Nick and Weber on the porch as Sesame and Tommy got into the black SUV that idled out front. Riley waved as the car backed down the driveway and turned onto Front Street. Burt trotted outside and down the porch steps to the yard. He made a beeline for the hedge.

"No candy, Burt," Riley called after him. The dog shot her a morose look over his shoulder and then slunk back into the house.

"You okay, man?" Nick asked Weber after the vehicle disappeared.

"I don't know. Maybe," he said. "Here."

He handed Nick the letter, and he read it out loud.

Dear Kelly,

I'm finally doing it. I'm taking your advice and leaving town. That totally accidental fire last night made me realize that life is too short to spend it doing things I don't want to do, which includes working and living with people I don't like (Mom, not you).

I met someone and he's really special. Making me happy is what makes him happy, and I think he could be the one.

I'm going to tell Mom face-to-face, and I'll give her

this letter to give to you. I'd tell you not to worry, but we both know you will no matter what.

You might not hear from me for a while, and I can't tell you where I'm going. I have my reasons, and they're as much to protect you as me. I promise I'll explain later. I want you to know that I love you and I'm so glad you're my big brother.

Please, go have some fun. If you're not careful, you're going to end up living for your job. Take Nicky along for the ride. He always makes you loosen up a bit.

Oh, and confession time: I'm glad you and Bridezilla divorced. I never liked her. She reminded me too much of Mom. Find someone who drives you crazy in a good way.

Love,
Beth

Nick cleared his throat and handed the letter back to Weber. "Guess she wanted you to know all along."

"I guess so," Weber said.

"Are you going to visit her?" Riley asked.

"Maybe. But I'm sure as hell not going to be on camera." He shook his head ruefully. "A reality TV show. My mother is going to hate that." The corners of his mouth turned up. "Think I'll go back inside and get some cake."

They watched him go back inside. Well, Riley watched him. Nick inspected the hole in the porch roof from one of Mrs. Penny's bullets.

"That explains the dossier on the mob boss's ex-wife," she said. "It was like a vision board for Sesame."

Nick slung an arm around her shoulders. "I guess we're supposed to call her Beth again now."

"She's going to make a great celebrity," Riley mused. "I wonder what storyline she'll go with about the warehouse fire."

"What do you mean?"

Riley glanced at the open front door to make sure Weber

wasn't within earshot. "Christian told me how he and Beth are connected."

Nick slapped a hand on the porch railing. "I *knew* he knew something! I can't believe that fucker never cracked."

"Beth was the one who started the fire. It seems she got mad when he threatened Tommy, so she burned down his headquarters and told him if he went to the cops, she'd burn down his grandma's house."

"That guy loves his grandma," Nick said.

"Hey! We found a stash of champagne in the fridge," Blossom said, poking her head out the front door. She was holding two bottles. "You want some?"

"It's my birthday," Nick said. "I want champagne and cake for breakfast."

They followed Blossom inside.

"Who else wants champagne with their cake?" Wander asked, lining up cups.

Hands went up everywhere.

"Looks like everyone," Roger said.

"None for me," Josie said. Her expression was unreadable, but Riley got a little nudge from the beyond. The smirk on Brian's face confirmed it.

"No!" Riley said, then clamped her hand over her mouth.

"No, what?" Nick asked.

Josie shrugged, pretending to be blasé. "Yeah. Looks like I won't be drinking for a while."

"Why? You on some weird diet?" Nick asked.

"If eating for two is some weird diet, then yes," Brian said.

"Eating for—no shit? Really? Congratulations!" Nick pounded his cousin on the back and then picked Josie up off her feet. "I'm gonna be an uncle…or whatever a cousin is to a cousin's kids."

"First cousin once removed," Roger chimed in.

"Removed from what?" Brian asked.

Riley hugged the parents-to-be. "This explains why you came up with that horrible fake spider plan," she said to Josie. "You have baby brain already."

"I'll admit it wasn't my finest tactical operation. But in the end, it did get the job done."

"You sound like Nick."

"Speaking of Nick," Blossom said, handing her a glass of champagne.

Riley raised the glass. "To Nick Santiago, who is never wrong and always has our back. Happy birthday."

He flashed both dimples at her, and Riley felt her stomach swoop.

"Happy birthday," the others echoed.

But before anyone could clink glasses, a loud rumble shook the walls.

"Oh my gosh! Was that an earthquake?" Blossom asked.

"I don't think so," Riley said. They all ran out onto the porch and stared in horror at the cloud of dust rising off the now missing third floor of the Bogdanovich mansion.

"Holy shit," Nick said.

"Oh my God," Riley said, stepping off the porch.

"I see movement," Blossom reported.

Out they came through the back door, one by one like dusty little ants, carrying their precious possessions.

Nick groaned. "They're headed this way. Quick, get everyone back inside and lock the doors."

"Poor baby. And on your birthday too," Riley said, rubbing his back.

Mrs. Penny huffed and puffed her way up the porch steps, a duffel bag slung over her shoulder. She punched Nick in the arm. "Looks like my commute to work just got cut in half! Dibs on the master bedroom!"

Lily skipped onto the porch behind her. She was carrying a casserole balanced on top of a record player. "Look at us. Roomies! Just like old times."

"Noooooo! Why?" Nick moaned.

Fred gave Nick double finger pistols as he strutted inside wearing four toupees. He had his yoga mat in a sling over one shoulder.

"Look on the bright side," Riley said as Mr. Willicott wandered past with a laundry basket of bread and four encyclopedias. "At least this time we didn't have to deal with Griffin."

Just then, a sleek sports car flew into their driveway, tires squealing. The driver didn't stop soon enough, and the car smashed into the gate.

"Not my gate!" Nick wailed.

The driver hit the accelerator and forced the car through the opening, scraping gouges down both sides.

Griffin Gentry jumped out from behind the wheel. "You have to help me! They're going to cut me into teeny-tiny pieces and murder me!" He collapsed at Riley's feet and hugged her around the legs.

"Nice to see you again, Griffin," Blossom said.

"Man, I hate that guy," Roger muttered.

"Why would you tempt the universe like that on my birthday, Thorn?"

"I don't know what I was thinking."

Author's Note

Dear Reader,

Confession time! When I started writing Riley Thorn 1, I thought that I had a nice neat trilogy on my hands. Nick and Riley would fall in love in Book 1, get engaged in Book 2, and then get married in Book 3. As you can see, that hasn't happened.

I have a notebook with over a dozen cases for Nick and Riley to solve. I drew a floor plan of the first floor of their house. I still haven't revealed Riley's truly awful middle name. What I'm trying to say is, I really hope you loved this book so I can write more Riley Thorn!

If you did enjoy *Blast from the Past*, please feel free to leave a review and insist that all your book-loving friends start the series. Now if you'll excuse me, I'm off to take an overdue shower!

Xoxo,
Lucy

What to Read Next?

Will there be more Riley Thorn? Lucy sure hopes so! She'd really like to torture Griffin Gentry for an entire book. In the meantime, she recommends you dive into the small-town, laugh-a-minute Blue Moon series.

Sincerely,
Mr. Lucy

Acknowledgments
and Confessions

- Tim for your big heart and your hot tub water management skills.
- Joyce, Tammy, Dan, and the rest of Team Lucy for all your enthusiastic support.
- The editorial eyeballs of Mandi, Jessica, Heather, and Dawn.
- My ARC and street teams for the best cheerleading an author could ask for.
- My delightful readers for making all my dreams come true.
- The talented Kari March Designs for another stellar cover.
- ELOE and Tiki author pals for providing both writing distractions and motivation.
- Tres Hermanos is a real Mexican restaurant in Harrisburg, but it does not serve alcohol.
- I made up my own calendar. Books 1 and 2 were based on 2020 dates. While writing this, I needed certain things to happen on certain days of the week, and the calendar wasn't lining up. So I have officially gone rogue and created my own timeline. I LOVE WRITING FICTION!
- I wrote this back matter with a terrible case of allergies…or a head cold (I can't tell the difference). I think the lack of oxygen caused by my stuffed-up nose made me less funny than usual.

About the Author

Lucy Score is a #1 *New York Times*, *USA Today*, and *Wall Street Journal* bestselling author. She grew up in a literary family who insisted that the dinner table was for reading and earned a degree in journalism. She writes full-time from the Pennsylvania home she and Mr. Lucy share with their obnoxious cat, Cleo. When not spending hours crafting heartbreaker heroes and kick-ass heroines, Lucy can be found on the couch, in the kitchen, or at the gym. She hopes to someday write from a sailboat, ocean-front condo, or tropical island with reliable Wi-Fi.

Sign up for her newsletter by scanning the QR code below and stay up on all the latest Lucy book news. You can also follow her here:

Website: lucyscore.net
Facebook: lucyscorewrites
Instagram: scorelucy
TikTok: @lucyferscore
Binge Books: bingebooks.com/author/lucy_score
Readers Group: facebook.com/groups/BingeReaders Anonymous
Newsletter signup: